THE EG
APPRENTICE

Maurice Leitch was born in County Antrim and
educated in Belfast. His first novel, *The Liberty Lad*,
was published in 1965, followed by *Poor Lazarus*,
winner of the 1969 *Guardian* Fiction Prize. *Silver's
City* won the Whitbread Prize for Fiction in 1981.
The Smoke King was published to critical acclaim in
1998. He has also written radio plays, short stories,
television screenplays and documentaries. He lives in
North London with his family.

ALSO BY MAURICE LEITCH

Maurice Leitch

THE EGGMAN'S APPRENTICE

VINTAGE

Published by Vintage 2001

2 4 6 8 10 9 7 5 3 1

Copyright © Maurice Leitch 2001

Maurice Leitch has asserted his right under the Copyright,
Designs and Patents Act, 1988 to be identified as the author of
this work

First published in Great Britain by
Secker & Warburg 2001

Vintage
Random House, 20 Vauxhall Bridge Road,
London SW1V 2SA

Random House Australia (Pty) Limited
20 Alfred Street, Milsons Point, Sydney
New South Wales 2061, Australia

Random House New Zealand Limited
18 Poland Road, Glenfield, Auckland 10,
New Zealand

Random House (Pty) Limited
Endulini, 5A Jubilee Road, Parktown 2193,
South Africa

The Random House Group Limited Reg. No. 954009
www.randomhouse.co.uk

A CIP catalogue record for this book
is available from the British Library

ISBN 0 09 942225 5

Papers used by Random House are natural, recyclable
products made from wood grown in sustainable forests.
The manufacturing processes conform to the environ-
mental regulations of the country of origin

Printed and bound in Great Britain by
Bookmarque Ltd, Croydon, Surrey

A dwarf knows more about everything than his master
                              – Pär Lagerkvist, *The Dwarf*

Five foot two, eyes of blue,
Cootchie, cootchie, cootchie-coo . . .

BOOK ONE

ONE

My earliest recollections are by far the sweetest, for then it was I felt perfectly at one with the world which enfolded me lovingly like my own dear little nursery quilt. Pink, patchwork bunny rabbits crouched ready to run the instant I closed my eyes. Sucking on a favourite wetted corner, each morning I would awaken to a fresh tableau of Nature newly fashioned while I slept.

The colour scheme in my bedroom was also rose, as I recall, a deeper band of colour encircling its dimensions where a picture-rail might be. There was a white painted chest of drawers, a trunk to house my many books and toys and, of course, the cot itself with bars that could be raised and lowered on one side like a portcullis. And, yes, a dainty little night-light with mushroom-shaped shade to ward off the bad fairy. Not that anything in that airy upper bower could ever have induced a nightmare. Thinking back on some of the places I've slept in since – including the present chamber of horrors – I can but only lament the loss of my beautiful room and that pampered early life I had of it in the very heart of the heart of the countryside.

Beyond the window which I could make an unsteady run

to, having reached the toddling stage, lay an overgrown garden and beyond that again fields alive with proper rabbits which hopped and hid and scampered. There were blue copses like ink-stained triangles, hills, then more fields and, finally, unimaginably far off, the distant Irish Sea, someone else having planted an image of it there, azure, warm, crystal clear.

Now as anyone will know our coastal waters are anything but like that, yet that is how I visualised them because that is the way Sinbad Scully described the invisible ocean to us as he sat in our kitchen darting a hand like a cormorant's neb into my mother's biscuit tin with the butterflies across the lid. While we watched he gorged himself as though reliving those terrible days and nights adrift with his five shipmates, and we were in that open boat along with him sharing his hunger and thirst, the baking days, the interminable, freezing nights. I know I was and feel certain my aged timid parents were as well.

Such a snug and sheltered life the three of us had of it in our russet villa at the end of its winding gravel drive. Above the front door, which I remember was protected from the sun by a bleached awning of deckchair linen falling straight down like a stiff, striped, cream and maroon flag, for our Antrim summers were much fiercer then, or certainly seemed that way to me, was the word Endeavour chiselled into the brickwork. That was the name of our house. Endeavour. It could well have been the name of a steam locomotive of the time, or a racehorse, say, even a ship like the one that foundered under Sinbad and those two hundred and forty-three other poor unfortunates. Such exactitude, which we swallowed guilelessly, for who were we to question it, having little experience of the outside world, for I saw my parents as almost if not quite as innocent as I was, venturing out rarely, or if ever we did, catching no other glimpse of a living soul save the breadman, or the fishman

4

with his trays of herring and mackerel on a Friday, although we certainly weren't Catholic.

But unlike those other tradesmen Sinbad had no reason to come whistling up our avenue. He had nothing to sell, apart from his stories. One evening he was sitting in our kitchen clasping a beakerful of tea in his paw while expertly rifling the butterfly tin with the other and then he seemed to have become a regular visitor. Normally he would arrive prior to my bedtime on a Friday night, but never, ever, with the smell of drink on him, I have to say that for him, even though that was when men got paid and in their coarse way celebrated afterwards in Lyle's public house.

Sinbad would take in a great gulp of tea to wash down the bolus of chewed gingersnap in his mouth and begin, 'Did I ever tell you . . .' for the tale blossomed in his head – ours, too – like some exotic bloom constantly putting forth fresh shoots until the narrative stem would almost disappear under the luxuriance of his invention. Much later in life I came to discover this invariably was the hallmark of the professional liar and here I have to confess I may have gone in for something of the same myself, but more to deflect the anticipated blow or minor cruelty my proportions attract than to impress the gullible. And certainly we were that all right, sitting mesmerised across from our visitor in his buttoned-up raincoat, never taking our eyes off his lips. Under the ferocity of his chewing, moist crumbs would rain down on the oilcloth-covered table, and in the corners of his mouth a dullish paste would accumulate, lodging there, it seemed, until refreshed with more of my poor mother's store of biscuits. But then perhaps it was a small price to pay, a tin full of McVitie's Braemar Assorted, for what he left us in return. In my case a tale that has stayed with me ever since. Even more bizarrely, seems to have become my very own.

Not that I would ever wish to tell it to anyone, for that would only serve to diminish its potency. Instead, as I do

5

now, I run it through my head yet again while watching the light fade beyond my small reinforced window, waiting for the hellish din of day to die down to some sort of bearable level. And it's then I travel back to that kitchen of ours with its Cardinal red tiled floor and purring Modern Mistress range, while overhead the wooden clothes raft slung with my airing baby things imperceptibly sways. No child, I have to tell you, none, ever enjoyed so many changes of clothes or bedding. With that single exception, of course, my baby quilt. If ever it did come in contact with soap and water, then, heaven help us, I would wail and roar and beat with my tiny fists until the whole house quailed.

Once old Sinbad witnessed such a tantrum. Stretching forward, he patted me on the head. 'Poor wee Hugo,' he crooned and I was treated to the sight of his open mouth clogged with a horrible mash of crumbs and strong tea and saw he had barely a tooth remaining in his head. Dentures, then, of course, were still very much a luxury item among the country people and even if they happened to possess a set never stayed inside their mouths for long. My own parents stored theirs in matching mugs beside the bed like a pair of sinister anatomy specimens, bubble-encrusted and ever so slightly agape as if removed in mid-bite.

When I stared deep into Sinbad's mouth that time how his breath assailed me. It had the taint of damp plaster and old houses about it, very much I imagined like the one in which he lived deep among the fields, someone's forsaken out-farm with half the roof missing. And sometimes when I saw that thread of smoke rising high above his circle of beech trees I would convince myself he must be in there, hands out-stretched to the fire, rehearsing the latest twist in that never-ending saga of shipwreck and delirium.

For a long time his palm remained on my hot, baby scalp and, young as I was, I felt something disturbing in the touch. He was forever stroking, caressing and toying with my hair for some reason. For my part, I could well understand such an attraction for I was immensely taken with those same golden curls myself and never tired of admiring their reflection in the long, oval mirror on our hallstand, the illustrations in my story-books all convincing me I looked the perfect image of some fairytale prince. And so I would race my toy charger on its cotton reel castors the length of our worn old Turkey runner, waving my wooden sword in the air, imaginary foes breaking before my roaring advance.

'Wee Hugo. Wee Hugo.' I can hear the sound of my name on Sinbad's lips to this day. And whether I liked it or not, that particular combination was to become what people called me from then on, and soon there came a time when I loathed the echo and implication of my pet name, especially the diminutive, accurate though it was to turn out to be. Later when I went to school there were infinitely crueller pairings, which came as a tremendous shock for, up to then, certainly, I had realised I was different, but not in that way.

There also came a time when I began to tire of Sinbad and his Friday night performances. It may well have been that constant, greedy cramming of his craw with our biscuits that turned me against him, or perhaps that smell of damp old houses and rotting plaster. Or it may really have been because I'd grown weary of hearing about men's ravings in the bottom of an open boat, for surely that must have come to an end at some stage or other, for the living proof was sitting there three feet away pebble-dashing us with damp crumbs. And, yes, he did fill his pockets from the butterfly tin, for I caught him at it once when my parents were momentarily distracted by something on the range. He saw me watching him, yet merely smiled across at me in my high-chair as if there was as much likelihood of me denouncing him as our old cat Fluff.

But, no, looking back, it had to be the relentlessly unravelling tale itself. You see, I had long since exhausted that particular epic in my young imagination, was sated with all those details of the great hospital-ship before, during, and especially after, being holed and going down in ninety fathoms in something called the Aegean, and then those endlessly drawn out days and nights adrift with their dramas of drinking water and meagre rations and what course to steer by, and then one man, Able Seaman Dusty Miller from Tottenham, going mad and having to be lashed to the tiller, whatever that might be.

Only one tiny nugget lodged with me, shining out from all that dross, and that was the part about the collar-stud. According to Sinbad it had belonged to him, but I've since had my doubts, not merely about the ownership, but whether the episode ever took place at all. In a curious way I should prefer to believe he made all of it up, maybe even heard it from some other source, for then that makes it easier for me to lay claim to that little bleached bone and metal gewgaw for my very own.

And unlike some of the other expressions that kept bobbing up in the story like torpedo, sextant, Pole Star, I knew exactly what it was, for wasn't there a cache of them in a round leather box on top of the chest of drawers in the big, front bedroom upstairs? Often I'd amuse myself by shaking them out on a tin tray to make snowflake patterns. And when that sequence concerning the collar-stud tightened its hold on me, didn't I also secretly take one of those same little dumb-bell shaped counters to bed with me, keeping it safe, yet convenient, under the base of the night-light so that I could cup it in my tiny hand every so often then place it on my tongue just like Sinbad was supposed to have done when the thirst pangs became too much for him. Even though it had no taste he sucked on it like a lozenge, he told us, and it was that which saved him from going mad with the drouth. The one they'd had to tie up for his own good, Able Seaman Miller, had drunk seawater.

'Never, ever swallow salt water,' Sinbad cautioned us, 'for if you do you'll surely go out of your mind,' and for a long time afterwards I was terrified of bathing in the sea because of his words.

But for me there was one final and powerful twist to the episode of the collar-stud, for one hot, airless day, the sea flatter than any millpond, alas, didn't it slip from Sinbad's mouth, plopping overboard, then going straight down. In despair he watched it sink in the clear water, drifting down for an eternity, spinning ever so slightly, its pale outline shrinking to a dot, then nothingness. And that was the part that haunted me so. Ever since, if I close my eyes, I can conjure up the image of that tiny, twinkling, jointed circle of metal and bone sliding to oblivion, down, down in slow motion into the terrible deep. Who knows, it may be falling still. And in my own life I've often felt a little like that too, spiralling lost and helpless in the downward pull of other people's desires. But in those early infant years I still ruled the roost and so the time arrived when poor Sinbad came to be banished from our kitchen along with his thousand and one variations.

Ears cocked for his Friday night whistle, I would sit in my high-chair, elbows resting on its little half-moon table. There would arrive the first, but still distant, crunch of boots on gravel, for he preferred not to walk on the grassy middle for some reason, and at that point I would beat my puny clenched fists on the stencilled wooden shelf before me and if there happened to be a bowl or mug in the way it would end up on the polished tiles below, never breaking, however, because my own little set of dishes was made of some early plastic material imprinted with bunny rabbits like the ones on my quilt. I would make myself swell and go red, gasping for breath, and at that point my anguished parents would race to the front of the house drawing down the blinds as if a sudden death had taken place in the family, little knowing just how soon such a sad bereavement would strike for real.

The two of them sat straining and listening in the darkened kitchen. Me, too, like some pocket-sized general on my high-chair. The bell set into the brickwork beside the front door rang out in the musty stillness of the hallway and the sound was startling for it had become hesitant through lack of use. More a broken, rusty croak than a proper peal. Seven times in all, our visitor – our no longer welcome visitor – stubbed his thumb on that little pearly dome before giving up. We heard his footsteps die away on the gravel. They seemed dragging, leaden, and I noticed my parents look at one another as if already regretting their actions. And seeing them sitting across from me, conscience-stricken in the near-dark in that way, and more than a little frightened, too, with only the glassed-in opening in the face of the range casting any light, a fiery square no bigger than a matchbox, tiny window on Hell, I was filled with sudden contempt for them and their timid ways.

The following Friday Sinbad Scully came again as usual and the same ritual re-enacted itself. At least we three sat dumb and frozen in the dark, for the roller blinds shrouding the windows on either side of the front door had stayed as they were all week. They hung straight down, permanently drawn from then on, right up until that terrible day when we had the traditional excuse for keeping them that way.

It felt unsettling entering those sombre, twin drawing-rooms, for I had the run of the house then, padding tirelessly about in my little fleece-lined slippers with their pale pom-poms like bunny down. The light had a curious underwater quality to it, filtered through taut linen the colour of milky tea. The furniture looked different, the glass in the matching china cabinets and the mirrors and picture frames opaque and unfamiliar. Even the designs on the carpets seemed to have sunk without trace into the pile, the original colour darkening from a cheerful cherry red to a featureless grey.

As I mooned through the gloom alone, for my parents rarely left the kitchen, all was muffled as if fallen into a deep sleep. It made me uneasy, recalling, as it did, the sequence in one of my story-books about the spell cast on everyone in that ancient fairytale castle down to the very kitchen mouse and cricket on the hearth. Sinbad was certainly no Prince Valiant, but after a week, then two passed, I began to think he might be the only one to free us from that shadowy prison we had made for ourselves. Rather, *I* had. Part of me longed to bring the light flooding back in again – a tug on that little polished wooden acorn on the end of its plaited cord was all it would take – but even then I was obdurate, unyielding as stone.

So we endured and waited. For what we had no idea, unless it was for our nocturnal visitor to give up, and indeed it seemed that way, for on the third Friday, a wet and blustery October evening, we heard no footsteps on the gravel, no ring at the bell. We sat there listening to the halting clock far beyond my bedtime. The sound of the rain faded, then died, and still we stayed up. I must have fallen asleep where I sat for I remember I had to be carried upstairs.

Some time in the small hours the first real nightmare of my young life awakened me. I lay there in terror, for while I had slept my room seemed to have undergone a transformation similar to that which had taken place downstairs. The night-light still glowed but seemed to pulse now to the flutter of my heart. The mushroom knobs on the chest of drawers had become eight round, bulbous, staring eyes. Most mysterious of all, the bars of my cot would appear to have receded while separating in some terrifying way, leaving me without protection against whatever might be about to happen next. Down at the further end my beloved quilt had rolled itself up into a hard, tight ball, yet I lay curled where I was, too petrified to reach for it. Some other child might have cried out and kept on bawling until one or more parents came rushing up to soothe and reassure, yet I did not. Instead, fighting my fear, I stretched my hand out towards the collar-stud cupped in the hollow of the night-light and, finding it, slipped it into my mouth like a comforter. Closing my eyes I felt the saliva flow and with it my terrors gradually subside.

I can really offer no explanation for why I did what I did next, instinct being such a mysterious and delicate thing, but that night under its urging I slipped the catch on the side of my cot. It was something I had taught myself to do with ease, taking care my innocent parents never discovered my secret, which was only one of many I enjoyed. Yet something always seemed to hold me back from climbing out through that open, white, painted wall of my cage. But on that October night, with the room returned to its familiar, comforting self, and while my parents slept dreamlessly across the hall, I lowered myself over the edge of the mattress until my feet found the floor.

I remember I was wearing a one-piece, fleecy garment buttoned top to toe and sprigged all over with these tiny blue flowers. Rabbits must not have been an option, obviously. That particular outfit, it strikes me now, had to have been well in advance of its time. Something similar called a Baby-Gro is, they tell me, standard nursery issue today, but at the beginning of the fifties it could only have come from America. But, then, despite being what you might call a couple of back numbers, my parents were tireless when it came to providing their beloved with only the best that money could buy. To this day I can still recall the smell and texture of that sleeping-suit, just as I do my unwashed quilt, and if I close my eyes, concentrating on both those senses, I'm back once more in that bedroom at the top of our old house on a night in Autumn about to go forward to the window drawn there by something I cannot explain.

Like a diminutive sleepwalker I advance until my out-stretched palms meet the curve of the sill. In front of me the blind is pulled down against the night but the fabric glows as though lit from outside, the power of the night-light almost eclipsed. Collar-stud still in my mouth, I reach out towards that other tiny, comforting talisman on the end of its cord and pull on it until it will go no further. One final gentle tug and the blind rolls itself into a furled cylinder at the top of the glass.

Over the distant rim of trees, as if invisibly tethered there, hangs a full moon shining directly in at me like a great dimpled silver balloon. Even though I've never seen one in reality before I know what it is for my picture books are full of the things, invariably furnished with eyes, a nose and wide, smiling mouth, and even though such features are only hinted at in the big, dented dial floating motionless out there the resemblance still comes as a shock. In my dreams, somehow, I've managed to stray into one of my own nursery rhymes. Misting the glass, I stand looking down on a landscape I thought I knew well, turned now to extremes of black and white where nothing moves. Imagination can be a terrible curse and I seem to have retained much of that childish capacity to project demons and that night one stepped out from behind a tree and looked straight up at me framed there in the light of that high window.

We stared at one another across the breadth of a brightly lit field. I recognised the overcoat and the face above it instantly, but Sinbad looked strangely different, which is why I thought of the bad fairy. He was grinning – or grimacing – it was hard to make a distinction at that distance, and the old familiar raincoat hung down as though drenched, utterly bedraggled, even though the rain had long since passed over.

He had been standing in that spot a long, long time,

something told me, again I can't say why, and the thought of those eyes fixed all that while on my window pane while I slept made me shiver and long for the protection of my quilt. Yet still I stood there, unable to move, pinned through and through by the force of his upward gaze. At one point I fancied I even saw his lips move and, even more singularly, convinced myself of the words '*Wee Hugo*' read across all that expanse of metallic-looking grass.

I cannot say how long I stood there or, indeed, how long my night visitor continued to keep vigil. I've often tried to review it through his eyes, from his vantage point, down there on the ground among the firs, that pale oblong of light the only sign of life in a household that had pretended to be dead before its time. But just what was it that drove him to keep coming back at night like that to us? Sentiment might well lead one to suggest he was a genuinely lonely soul and we had been the first real listeners ever to take his wartime memories seriously. It would be hard to give up an audience such as that, even if it was only a doting couple and one spoilt brat in a high-chair. Deep down, of course, having no truck with sentiment, I believed it was because of me he was there, knowing in some instinctive way who was really responsible for his banishment. He meant me harm, that had to be the only reasonable explanation, directing his silent spite up at me as I slept like some disinherited and vengeful creature of the night. And as things were to turn out he hadn't long to wait to enjoy his satisfaction.

A month later, with the windows still blinded, back as well as front, first my mother passed away, and then my father followed her, sliding rapidly under like a drowning sailor giving up his grip on the life raft that had kept him afloat for so long. Like Sinbad Scully's collar-stud he went down without trace, and I was left abandoned to drift orphaned through the next years of my young life in a place and with

14

people as different from what I was used to as one could
possibly imagine.

TWO

My mother's funeral affected me deeply but not in the manner expected of me. For when I clapped my hands and squealed with delight at the sight of so many shiny motor cars bumping up our neglected driveway I couldn't help noticing how the mourners already in the house shook their heads, murmuring, 'Poor wee Hugo,' as if I were more to be pitied than congratulated on my innocent high spirits. Yet some short time later when food and drink were being consumed I noted how their mood seemed to have changed utterly. Relatives, even total strangers, kept manhandling and kissing me, passing me from one to the other like some small human parcel. I heard laughter, strangest of all, someone sing a verse or two, and smelt tobacco smoke in rooms which had never been tainted with anything stronger than Lavendo furniture wax.

It was all desperately confusing this adult world and for the first, yet certainly not the last time, I felt like a pygmy set down amongst a race of giants. They had florid, sweating faces these grown-ups and at their further extremity great, shiny, shod feet that crushed the pile of our carpets or detonated on the burgundy-red tiles in our kitchen. Moving amongst the thicket of legs I sucked in sensations avidly. I remember I was greatly smitten by the scent of the women, many of whom wore fur coats, for my mother's side were well-off and worldly, and I would bury my cheeks in the fragrant folds of those beautiful swishing garments till my head swam with their dense aroma. I decided I liked my relatives from the big city enormously, with their beautiful motor cars – a spanking new model every Spring, as they kept on reminding one another – and their wives, my aunties, the seven beautiful Cathcart sisters in their chinchillas and mink. Why hadn't I been introduced to this glamorous branch of the family tree before? And why, oh, why, when it did come about, did it have to take place at a time such as this?

The answer, of course, was sitting there in the form of my poor old father, bless him, staring straight ahead at a break in the legs while all around his rich relatives by marriage gossiped and laughed and caught up with one another's business triumphs. At one stage I toddled across to him and laid my tiny paw on his thigh. He was wearing an ancient suit of clothes I had never seen before in rusty, greenish black and smelling fiercely of mothballs amidst all that haze of feminine allure. It hung on him like a sack, his mourner's tie had somehow got itself twisted over to one side and the morning razor had missed the greater part of his dear old turkey neck.

I uttered the word, 'Da-da', for I wasn't entirely heartless – not yet, anyhow – and one of my aunts standing nearby with a sherry glass in her hand caught the expression and, dropping down beside the pair of us, planted a wet cupid's bow kiss on my forehead going, 'Aaaah.' But Da-da went on staring into the dead grate. And even though I continued to gaze beseechingly up into his face I realised I might as well have been invisible.

The lady on her knees – it was Aunt Lottie – murmured

17

'Alec, Alec' in gentle chiding tones, but I knew then he had no time for me, perhaps never had, and felt the onset of that lifelong resentment that was to blame him for everything that was happening to me and would go on happening to disrupt my beloved, bunny rabbit paradise. Incidentally, the way things were to turn out, my comfort quilt was about the only memento I was allowed to salvage when the time came for me to leave my adored Endeavour forever.

Aunt Lottie continued hugging me. She had very large, conically shaped bosoms, soft, yet oddly firm to the touch – it would be some time before I would be properly introduced to the abiding mysteries of the brassière – but it was the lower parts of her which excited me in a troubling, yet intensely pleasurable way. All the while she had been pressing me tightly to her I kept catching glimpses of bare, powdered thigh above the demarcation of garter biting into tan, silk stocking top, then, higher up, an even more alluring glimpse of something sheer and silken, palest peach in colour. Looking back, I suppose I must have become over-stimulated by it all, running from one hot, scented embrace to the next. In moments of distraction from their talk of money-making and horsepower the men would observe me with knowing little smiles which never lingered very long, I noticed, so I concentrated all my charms on their wives instead.

One of the aunts, I remember, seemed unable to keep her hands off me for an instant and this created a dilemma, for I yearned desperately to share myself equally among all. I would pull away from her, offering myself up to yet another damp shower of lipsticked kisses from some new quarter – my face was soon as streaked as a pippin – but she always managed to draw me back. Her name was Beryl, and if this sounds a cliché, I apologise, but she was the plainest of the lot by far. Not only was her touch not quite so delightfully cloying as her sisters, she had rings that scratched and tore, and her coat was plain velour, respectable enough, but not fur. At one point she became tearful. 'Oh, I could eat you,' she moaned, clasping me to her meagre frontage.

'Couldn't you just eat him, Trevor?' This to her husband standing solitary and grim-faced nearby. For some reason he seemed to have been left out of much of the other uncles' conversation and banter. His only response was to tap his wristwatch. Indeed, they were the first to leave after a final barrage of scalding kisses. They drove off in a beige-coloured Ford Popular, the most ordinary little car imaginable. Already, you see, I was pitying them.

Some little time later when my father dutifully followed my mother's example, just as he had always done in life, a suggestion was floated that they should adopt me. I don't know where it came from but, naturally, I was affronted at the very notion, when I could have exchanged my well-nigh perfect existence for an even more pampered one with some other aunt and uncle. Alas, as it turned out, none of them seemed to want me. Looking back, it might not have been such a bad idea ending up with Trevor and Beryl in Orlock in their modest seaside bungalow with that old jam-jar of theirs slowly rusting away in the salt spray outside. My life could well have turned out very differently, without so many wrong turns to it. I tell myself that now, but *might have been* are the three most pointless words in the language, as I've discovered. *Grin and bear it*, as a credo, seems to be a much more practical alternative.

After the mourners had all left, the house seemed as though it was no longer our own. The odour of pipe and cigarette smoke lingered for a long time, mixed with a heady *mélange* of female aromas. My sailor-suit retained traces of the last for days, while my skin continued to burn as though deliciously and indelibly branded by all those red, smacking lips. The debris of plates and glasses remained untouched, for my

19

father had almost given up the ghost by now. Left to wander at will from room to room, I sniffed ashtrays – now where on earth had they come from? – or sampled the red and orange dregs in glasses. For the first time in my young life I had only myself to rely on, for that stranger sitting in the parlour, hunched and catatonic, neither saw, heard nor experienced anything around him. He might as well have been encased in glass, a fossil, already, and when I came to touch him it was, indeed, like tapping on a shell.

Peering up at him I felt no real pity for, let no one tell you differently, a young child is as yet incapable of such an emotion. Compassion arrives later, something inculcated, like learning to wash one's face unaided, or cut up one's food, after watching the way grown-ups manage it.

And so I foraged for myself, living on squares of Battenberg and fruitcake, slivers of ham smeared with piccalilli, a thrilling change from the rusks and milk I was used to. I drank flat lemonade from the half-empty bottles I discovered hidden in the shadow of sofas or behind curtains. One afternoon an almost full glass of something purple and syrupy tempted me. Putting it to my lips I felt its heavy, sugar-laced potency invade my senses and soon after a delicious languor enveloped me, much nicer by far than anything my old rabbit quilt could ever induce. My legs turned to jelly, I began to stagger, falling down a few times, yet pain seemed non-existent. Convincing myself I was invincible, I flailed at the parlour upholstery with the flat of my toy sword, raising a dust storm, while all the while that ancient man I once called Da-da sat on in the hardest chair staring at his hands, oblivious. A silvery growth now frosted his cheeks, while the front and legs of his trousers were soaked and stained with something not too dissimilar to the contents of my own.

A short while later I toppled from my wooden horse, sleeping on the carpet where I lay until the world outside changed from dark back to light again. How many times that transition occurred I have no recollection, which is curious, because I have a superb memory for the detail and chronology of events, but not that one. My first brush with alcohol may have had a fair bit to do with it because I do still have some faint recall of searching out more glasses to drain, the stickier and darker their dregs the better.

For all I know I might well have been stocious drunk by the time Aunt Dolly arrived to rescue the pair of us. Anyone less like those fur-coated glamour-pusses I had fallen in love with earlier it would be difficult to imagine, a Dinsmore through and through, and despite the playfulness of that pet name of hers, anything but soft or girlish. A gaunt creature who wore a hat indoors all year round, and the same pattern of print apron cinched tight as a tourniquet, she ignored me completely. Gathering my father up out of his chair she half carried him to the stairs, seeming to make light work of it, but then he was by now the merest rickle of bones held loosely in place by that ancient, rust green, Sunday suit of his.

I followed them up to the big bedroom across the hall from my own little room and watched as she laid him on the stripped mattress ticking. Naturally I had never seen either of my parents naked before and I clung to the doorpost anxious not to miss such an important part of my education, but just as she was about to peel off his long, sodden drawers in what turned out to be his final disrobing she caught sight of me peering in and slammed the door with a detonation that set all of the pictures a-tremble. I shrank back against the wall outside, suddenly seeing all those familiar scenes of Irish country life shimmer and shake in their frames, just as though an earth tremor was passing through our little locality, and Aunt Dolly continued to make everything around her quake. For someone so paper-thin she affected the whole house with the ferocity of her tread. Glass and china rang, windows rattled, cupboard doors shook, even that little postage stamp of red in the kitchen range seemed to falter and change hue as if the wind of her passing had somehow managed to penetrate the thickened glass.

She kept racing up and downstairs with steaming pots and kettles while I waited below for my turn to come, because by now I knew there was no hope of my getting around her. Even so, I made one final effort at charm when the tin bath was lifted down from its nail on the scullery wall and filled with water, hot and cold. Not near enough of the latter, I decided nervously. Or was it the other way round? Whatever it was, those proportions were not correctly balanced, I could have told her so. But she didn't seem to care, not even bothering to use her bared elbow as a thermometer the way my mother had always done. I stood there shivering in my pelt, my little instrument of pleasure jutting out so delightfully, but she took no notice. Even when it came to attention, directing a jet of liquid gold to strike and ring on the metal of the bath, a party-piece which had never failed to entertain hitherto, her face didn't change.

Now at this point I should have learned a valuable lesson in life but, of course, didn't, for like most men I continued to believe misguidedly that women must be as fascinated by the male member as we all are. Hey presto and a roll on the drums each time wonder-wand is unveiled. And here I must confess I've been as guilty as the next man, even more so, because despite the rest of my other bodily proportions I've been more than compensated when it comes to that particular part of the anatomy.

But to return to that terrible day when my life went from bliss to despair and I convinced myself there could be no possibility of it ever going back again. Forgetting all self-control, I started bawling for my little rubber plaything which was kept on a convenient shelf for bath time.

'Daffy Duck, indeed!' snorted my terrifying relative.

22

'Them days are finished for ever, Master Hugo Dinsmore.' And Lord, was she right.

Sleeves rolled up high over chalk-white, sinewy forearms, she subjected me to a chill baptism which smote me like a plunge into our water barrel. She began soaping me, not with our customary gentle Palmolive, but a hard block of something carbolic, red and stinging. Later I found out Aunt Dolly was what people called an 'old maid' who had worked on farms most of her life. People and animals, consequently, she treated in the same robust fashion, making little or no distinction between the two. And so this poor, little, human piggy was scrubbed and towelled mercilessly. Standing me pink and naked on an old cast-off shirt of my father's, she looked me up and down as she might survey a side of bacon or a plucked pullet.

'What age are you, anyway?'

Proudly I told her, supplying months as well as years, for I was immensely pleased with my mastery of the calendar and figuring in general. She continued to eye me.

'You're very wee for your age, I must say. You don't take after the Dinsmores. But, then, how could you, you poor wee cratur?'

And those were the first and last soft words I was to receive from her lips. Perhaps because of what she'd said and the way she'd said it, I began to blubber again.

'Dear, dearie me,' was her caustic reply and I stared back at her through tear-clogged lashes.

Starting to hate her I noticed how the hairs sprouting from the corners of her mouth looked like fine wires. In that moment I wished her ill, concentrating all my budding powers of spite on her. And when later she did have a mishap with one of her many boiling kettles I felt torn between jubilation and fear that I might have been responsible in some way. Or, rather, that I might get found out, which is a lot closer to the truth. Later on in my life I would feel no

23

qualms whatsoever when it came to my enemies' undoing, enjoying their discomfiture to the full. Sometimes I think I might have turned out a far nicer person if it hadn't been for Aunt Dolly and people like her. Then, again, I've seen far too many people in this place degrading themselves with the aid of so-called 'counsellors' eager to fill folders with reams of self-deception without any additional contribution of mine.

'What's that you have in your mouth?' demanded my tormentor, visiting on me an infinitely greater terror.

'Nothing,' I lied.

'We'll soon see about that.' And aiming a crooked finger at me she leant closer.

'Nothing,' I told her a second time, promptly swallowing my little collar-stud which I had placed there for solace. It went down as easily as a chocolate drop and in my imagination I followed its smooth descent with something akin to what Sinbad Scully must have felt when his own tiny talisman slipped from his mouth. My stomach. His Aegean. Gone for ever. Although, in my case, for a long time afterwards, I did persist in the belief it must still be inside me there like a kidney stone or the lurking pip in an appendix. And who knows, stranger things have happened, even though the most rudimentary knowledge of the digestive process must surely rule it out. Yet to think of it turning up some day in an X-ray, confounding the medics while thrilling yours truly, would be something. Later I was to see it as heroic, the sort of thing a foreign agent might get up to with a secret code mashed to a pellet just before the Gestapo come breaking down the door. And then my very own lady storm-trooper forced me to further swallow a draught, dark brown and vile, concocted, as I understand it, from senna pods. To keep my bowels open, I was told.

For bed she dressed me in a garment I had never worn or even seen before, some form of ancient shift affair folded to the outlines of the drawer it had lain in since God knows when, reeking of mothballs and rough as sandpaper. But by now I was too tired to protest, simply stood there allowing myself to be bent and twisted to its constraints like a pipe-cleaner manikin.

Curled up in my cot a little while later, I wondered whether Aunt Dolly had pinned a nappy on my father as well, stretched out, rigid as a plank and about as lifeless, in the next room. But where would she lay hands on one big enough? Such were the kind of innocent notions coursing through my head in the dark, for she had taken my night-light away, leaving me to stare at the drawn blind, which was the other thing she had done, after tying up the side of the cot so it couldn't be moved from the high position. But at least, I reassured myself, she hadn't taken my quilt away, and I still had the collar-stud in a place where no one would ever be able to find it.

That night the sky was black as pitch, the blind only fractionally paler than the wall itself and, feeling betrayed and friendless, I would even have welcomed the thought of old Sinbad standing guard out there in our field, moon or no moon. It was curious but I missed him, a lost link with happier times, gladly forgiving him all those raids on our biscuit tin. And I had a story now to match his, I told myself. Fantasising freely, I fell asleep, believing that he might even be someone, perhaps the only one left, to turn to if things became even more unbearable than they already seemed to be. At this point I should make it clear not everything I set down here is purely the result of first-hand experience. By far the greater part is, but certain sections of my history still remain where I've had to trust to instinct, unable to retrieve what actually happened from other sources. So when I say my father passed peacefully away in his sleep a few days later, I'm relying on a mixture of the two.

The day of his funeral I did overhear someone remark that

that, indeed, was the manner in which he left us and my own memories, green as they are, certainly seem to support such a theory for I witnessed no sudden alarms, no dashing up of stairs, no last gasp sounds of any kind coming from the room across the hall from mine. In undertaker's parlance, he simply loosened his hold on the tiller. And, actually, I did hear one of those same professional men in black utter those exact words as he stood with cup and saucer in hand close to the still open coffin.

After he'd finished his tea and ham sandwich he produced a mysterious little gadget from an inside pocket, using it to screw down all four corners of the casket lid. I tried my best to get a closer look at this fascinating tool but he managed to palm it as if jealous of an outsider, even one as young as myself, picking up trade secrets. Observing him pat the side of his jacket after he'd put it safely away, it struck me he must love it in much the same way as I did my collar-stud. He was an exceptionally tall, thin individual with a bluish complexion and raw knuckles, the result, I imagine, of spending so much time bareheaded and gloveless on freezing hillsides. The previous undertaker who had handled my mother's interment had been very different, plump, cheery, more like one of the mourners themselves than someone in the dying business. And he smelt, too, of something heady and verbena-scented. Of course it was cologne. I remember he chucked me under the chin, popping a boiled sweet into my mouth.

At the time it puzzled me why there should be two undertakers making separate arrangements for one family, especially in a community as small as ours. Much later things became clearer as the full extent of the family feud dividing the Cathcart side from the Dinsmores revealed itself. Even in death they resented each other, the match between my father and mother, if one could call it such, always a contentious one. And, of course, being the self-obsessed little wretch I was, I resented my own involvement in that schism, taking it personally, as if those two poor, dead darlings might at least have considered me when they took up with each other in the first place.

As I think I've made clear, I enjoyed myself enormously at my mother's funeral and was naturally looking forward to a repeat performance, two holidays arriving back to back, as it were. So when the time came round for our house to fill with visitors once again, there I was, eager, ready and waiting in my little sailor-suit with its starched shoulder-flaps like one of Sinbad Scully's navy ensigns. Kneeling on our old, high-backed settee under the front parlour window, I lifted up a corner of the blind to catch a first, triangular glimpse of all those shiny Humber Hawks and Snipes bobbing like fairground mounts up our embarrassingly potholed avenue. For, yes, I burned to dissociate myself from everything that was dowdy and neglected, conveniently forgetting how happy those earlier times had been, now that I had been introduced to the glamorous world of limousines with leather upholstery and their own cigarette lighters and the men and women who rode inside smoking and laughing in a haze of really tremendous scents as if going to a wedding and not some poor, backwoods, country burial.

Well, I have to say, I was in for the most awful shock and disappointment. No cars, just bicycles, accompanied by the slow, measured crunch of heavy, reinforced boots on gravel. The bicycles ended up in one almighty tangle against our gable-wall, while the mourners, all men, congregated in a silent arc fanning out from the front door. I watched in disbelief. Such faces, such great, heavy limbs, such enormous hams of hands hanging straight down from the sleeves of overcoats heavy and stiff as harness leather. Who were these people? Where had they come from?

And then I saw Sinbad Scully. At first I thought I must be

27

mistaken, as he blended in so well with all those stern-faced rustics. He was wearing an outsized, belted overcoat, mossy-looking about the shoulders, and his face bore the same expression of serious intent as the others. Not a hint of its usual crooked grin. In my confused state it seemed to me he had come to settle old scores and I let go the blind, terrified he might catch a glimpse of my face between the stiff, cream linen and the windowsill. And as I did so, Aunt Dolly materialised at my back, lifting me down from my lookout post.

'I want you to behave yourself today,' she cautioned me sternly.

It was the first indication I had done anything wrong, and I looked at her in hurt surprise.

'I don't want you making a holy show of yourself like last time, like some wee heathen. Do you understand?'

But I didn't, although for days afterwards I hoarded the sound of that phrase 'wee heathen', some vague image of me dancing bare-skinned and filthy, with a ring in my nose, through an empty house, running in tandem. Having a collar-stud lodged somewhere in my innards, like a three-penny bit in a Christmas pudding, naturally only embroidered the fantasy.

At some stage the house began to fill with the Dinsmore clan and various neighbours come to pay their respects. They seemed almost to arrive by stealth, hugging the darkest corners where they stood staring silently at the pictures and furniture as if they'd never seen the like before. I may not have mentioned this, but we did have a piano, an ancient Bechstein, kept permanently locked, with two brass candle-holders jutting out from its fretworked face like hinged horns and I took up my stance directly in front of it. And there I waited, confident in the belief that sooner or later I must become the centre of attention just as before. But those great cow eyes kept roving past and through me, ignoring, as I saw it, the two most fascinating objects in the room, namely me, and that old oxblood, burnished upright.

Eventually Sinbad sidled in. I noticed he was chewing. After a leisurely look around, finally he fastened his gaze on me and that familiar, lopsided grin of his broke through. As a bonus he gave me an enormous wink, just like all those other times before in our kitchen, and quite suddenly I had this urge to run to him, clasping his legs the way someone my age might be expected to behave. But something held me back. Instead, we continued observing one another across a room criss-crossed by restless eyes, none of which ever seemed to alight on either one of us. And so, preposterous as it may sound, there we were, a grown man and a small child duelling silently for supremacy. I just wouldn't give in to Sinbad Scully, wouldn't please him, no, no, no, and I convinced myself that he knew it. And so, after a time, he gave one long, slow, final wink, but not in defeat, more like calling a truce, adjourning our tiny tussle of wills to some other more convenient time.

A little while later I was taken into the other parlour to see my dead father laid out in his coffin. A clergyman was in attendance, as was the undertaker already described. They looked like blood relatives, for one was as raw-boned as the other. The room smelt strongly of lilies, although I could see no sign of flowers anywhere. In keeping with her hard and masculine ways Aunt Dolly had rid the entire house of every vase, pot and hanging basket and what grew inside. All three watched me closely as I was led right up to the edge of that gleaming, mahogany ark.

'Allow me, little man,' murmured the clergyman irritatingly, and before I knew what was happening he had hoisted me up so that I was able to look directly down on my father's blanched face. An almost meaty, floral scent rose from the open coffin making my head swim. Someone, most probably the undertaker, had placed a small posy in his folded hands, so that he looked, for all the world, like some country swain dreaming of his intended. And it was the image, as well as the idea, of that nosegay, and my poor old father dressed up to the nines about to go courting, that unsettled me more than the appearance of the rest of him did. Years later it came to me just what it was he truly reminded me of. A ventriloquist's dummy. For, yes, whoever it was had prepared him for his final appearance had also managed to get things wrong in that subtle, yet disturbing way that always renders such figures so unnerving. His snowy white hair had a parting now, something which it never possessed before, with an over-all, wet and curiously varnished look, and what could only have been rouge had been applied to both cheeks. Whoever had given him his last shave on earth had also left his upper lip untouched as if there might still be time for him to cultivate a moustache. To impress the new lady love with, no doubt.

One of the great platitudes you hear at funerals is – 'he looks very like himself' – but in my father's case nothing could have been farther from the truth. I think it was the shock at the sight of that painted stranger in his wooden case waiting for his cue to come upright and perform for us that made me react as I did. Or, rather, didn't. The instant I was set down on the carpet again the other three people in the room watched me almost hungrily, and so rapt was their scrutiny I felt I could scarcely breathe. I knew I was being tested. But for what? I scanned the faces for a clue, a glance, but it was as if they were determined to make me suffer in my ignorance. Of course I know now I should have put on a show of grief, even bawled a bit. It wouldn't have been beyond my capabilities, and wouldn't have taken much in the way of tears to make them feel secure in that tight, wee world of theirs where even little children behave according to rules which they haven't yet learned or had drummed into them. But all I knew at that time was that I'd failed their test and would have given anything, anything, to be given another chance.

And then the Reverend Gillespie, for that was the gentleman's name, murmured, 'Poor wee Hugo,' and I regarded him with the purest hatred. But then I've always found hate to be such a healthy, cleansing emotion, and began to feel much, much better. So I stood there in that twilit room listening to my heart, surrounded by enemies, and looking at them I made a vow never to grow up, never, not if it killed me, never, ever to grow up to be like them. And, curious as it may seem, I do believe I may have managed to achieve that.

THREE

And so I entered this next stage in my young life, days –
weeks, even – drifting past leaving no trace in their wake.
Aunt Dolly and I, we went about our solitary concerns, me
above with my crayons and picture books, she in the kitchen
with her skewered balls of wool. As it turned out she was one
of those prodigious knitters and a great, striped snake of a
thing like the sleeve of some gigantic Joseph coat coiled
about her ankles while the needles flashed red in the glow
from that little bloodshot eye in the hinged door of the
range. As I watched, the soft, fat ribbon seemed to inch
across the tiles towards me for, yes, I did peep in at her
clicking away in my father's chair, her poker back turned to
the doorway.

'What is it?' I asked.

But she kept on knitting as if nothing mattered in the wide
world save the creation piling up at her feet. What made me
do it I cannot tell but, reaching out, I laid hold of the tail-end
of that old snake of hers and somehow she must have sensed
movement in the flat and nerveless thing – I swear it had to
be twelve feet at least by this stage, a foot, maybe more,
growing daily – for the click of the needles ceased.

'What is it?' I repeated in my best baby voice, for I was afraid now, afraid of her and, let it be known, the snake, too, for it threatened to rear up in nightmares later like one of those Indian cobras swaying out of its basket.

She turned in her chair and for the first time I saw she was wearing a pair of my father's old spectacles, recognising them by the strip of soiled Elastoplast that held one leg in place.

'How should *I* know?' she snapped. 'Sure, it isn't finished yet.' And that was the only exchange the two of us were ever to have on the subject.

But the whole business continued to plague me. Who was it for, I kept asking myself? What was it for? Never would it have occurred to me, you see, not then, anyhow, that anyone, even someone as flintily secure in herself as Aunt Dolly, might derive ease from mindlessly feeding her frustrations, inch by inch, into a never-ending rope of many colours. And such colours – have I mentioned them? For instance, a lemon yellow the like of which I never could have imagined, and an azure like Sinbad Scully's Aegean, and an emerald, sharper, more acid green than young apples. And, of course, all the fiery tints as well, bleeding from pillar-box red right through to an almost black aubergine, all spilling out from those stabbing needles like a rainbow with the stripes running against the grain.

Only later did I discover, like so much of what I put down here, that in her inventory Aunt Dolly had come across an entire drawer upstairs crammed with all these odd balls of wool. What they'd been saved for over the years must be anyone's guess, as was my aunt's determination to transform them into a giant muffler.

But, come to think of it, we have a man here on this very wing who has been labouring over a matchstick replica of the tower of Pisa for five years or more. His name is Winston McGarry and he tells us it helps slow the thinking processes down something wonderful. Oh, far, far more effective than any little, deadening, two-toned capsule ever could. He works from picture postcards, for he has never been to Italy – by the looks of things never will – and the famous tilt is something he has decided to ignore up to now. Like the original architect, I guess. In a way he and my Aunt Dolly have much in common. He has never travelled farther than Groomsport, and she certainly had never set eyes on one of those trailing, hippie scarves, a fashion accessory some considerable way off in the future.

But then one morning when I awoke I detected something different in the air. The clicking had ceased. The needles had finally been sheathed. Rushing downstairs eager to view the completed masterwork I found, instead, the kitchen bare and the old Windsor chair with its needlework cushion empty also. A smell of burning drifted in through the open back door. Following my nose I crept forward until I could look out on the sunny world beyond, the first time in fact since my poor father had been borne away by four strangers shoulder-high. Smoke was rising from a heap of what looked like old clothes and beside it was my aunt feeding the flames from another pile nearby. Her face was brick coloured and beaded with sweat, which may well have been to do with the heat from the bonfire, but then her hair had also escaped from that tightly clenched, wire-wool bun of hers, which certainly was something else entirely. In short she looked as excited as any young girl, and seeing her that way infected me with some of the same fervour.

Eager to take part in whatever was being celebrated, for that was how I viewed what was happening, I, too, started adding my own contribution to the blaze. Soon the pair of us were silently hurling on more and more armfuls of stuff, not just bedding, coats, hats, underwear, even, but books and pictures too, which so far had lain hidden at the bottom of the pile. The glass in the frames spat and crackled and pages curled lazily like brittle, brown tongues. At one point as our old photograph album caught hold I suddenly saw the faces of relatives darken and disintegrate before my eyes, an entire family tree, as it were, swallowed up by smoke and flame. I suppose it's fanciful to say this, and the recollection most probably is tainted with hindsight, like so many things here, but when I caught sight of that record disappearing for ever I experienced an odd feeling of elation. My aunt with her hot face and damp hair looked as though she was in the grip of something similar but in her case it turned out to be closer to spite and revenge than my own innocent excitement at making a clean start.

When the fire was at its fiercest and we were hurling on shoeboxfuls of letters, bills, old Christmas cards and, of course, ancient newspapers, for every drawer in the house was lined with those, we kept retreating further and further from the blaze. The grass had started to steam and the leaves on the apple tree were shrivelling and turning the colour of tobacco. My aunt leant up against its ancient trunk for a moment. She was panting.

Then, 'They won't have them, I tell you! No, no, I'll not please them!' I heard her cry out and she tore back into the house again, re-emerging with the curtains from the front parlour. The brass rings were still attached and chimed as she flung the lot in one great, red, dusty ball on the flames. Then she disappeared yet again to carry out another selective raid on my father's possessions, although why a set of old velvet curtains should have the Dinsmore name associated with them, and not my mother's, must always remain a mystery. When the pyre was as high as herself she dragged out his kitchen chair and, sinking its legs deep in the grass, climbed up on to it so she could place more items on the very top. She was burning his carpentry tools now, not just the plane and mitre-box, and the folding yellow beechwood rule he

35

always kept in a dungaree side pocket, but files, hammers, saws and chisels, as if even iron would combust.

And at that point I began to cry for I feared she might burn the house itself down, so terrible was her anger, and that I would be blamed for it. Now, whether she took pity on me standing there with cheeks like a little piccaninny I do not know, but something made her hesitate. Raising a sooty hand to her face she seemed to sway, then, recovering, climbed down to drop heavily into the chair again, the pair of us regarding one another oddly all the while as if seeing a reflection across that width of seared grass. Pale smoke rose curling up, and at the very heart of the roaring heap these muffled, small explosions kept breaking out as household items I would never, ever see again were consumed and turned to ash. And then it was my turn to go into the house and my aunt made no move to hinder me, just kept on sitting there looking down at her hands as if lost without her needles and yarn. And when I came out again, clutching my quilt and as many of my colouring books as I could manage to carry, she was still there invisibly knitting away inside her head.

Some time after that the pair of us set off down the drive together with not a word or backward glance, she with a bulging meal-bag, and me with my own little bundle of private treasures. Strange to say I didn't feel all that terrible about turning my back on my old life. I didn't, and can't really explain it. Something about burning boats and bridges comes to mind, but then isn't there always some slippery adage to cover most things that happen to one in life? One last thing I do remember, however, as I walked away, was a fearful smell of burning wool, for I may have omitted to mention Aunt Dolly's final flourish before she went off with me in my little, belted overcoat with its velveteen collar, cream-coloured pull-ups and, yes, the sweet little pixie hood which was to cause me so much mortification later on. A proper little Fauntleroy figure and no mistake, despite the blackened, minstrel face. That farewell gesture was to feed the knitted snake to the flames and when the last vestiges had curled and melted into a blackened mess, as wool does, whilst giving off that awful, acrid stink, she took me by the hand and marched me off. As I've said, not one syllable was uttered, not a look passed between us. It was as if, conspiring together, we had completed something to our deep and mutual satisfaction and had the sooty hands and faces to prove it.

After being shut up for so long in the house I recall the joy of walking on that soft, grassy stripe running down the middle of our avenue while my aunt held resolutely to the gravel alongside. Soon my buttoned shoes were soaked through but somehow that only seemed to enhance the adventure. I heard birds sing, cows moo, the bleat of sheep. All that was missing were for a few of my beloved bunny rabbits to appear. Real life seemed to be almost as heady as the imaginary one I used to pore over in the picture books bundled in my quilt.

About halfway along our route to the county road we heard the sound of a motor vehicle labouring towards us, up our very own drive, would you believe. At first we couldn't, didn't, and stopped dead in the middle of the track, straining with our heads angled in the direction of the sound. Presently there hove into view a great, greenish lorry with a radiator pierced with a million perforations, surmounted with the word Leyland set in a glass orb like a seaside paperweight. The reason I paid such particular attention to the front was because it came right up to us, shuddering and steaming as if it would devour us whole. A couple of headlights as big as baking bowls sat on either mudguard and the number plate was on a level with my chin. Closing my eyes I clasped my aunt's hand more tightly in mine, for it was obvious she wasn't going to budge. There we would stand holding our ground until the great juddering giant rolled right over us leaving the imprint of its honeycombed radiator on every square inch of skin. I wondered what it would feel like to be stamped so extensively in so many places.

Then I heard a voice call out, 'This the Dinsmore place, missus?'

It came from high overhead and opening my eyes I saw a red, grinning face looking down on us, while a tattooed, swollen forearm hung over the side of the lorry like a side of bacon.

'What if it is?' retorted my aunt tartly.

But the man only laughed. 'Any chance of a cuppa Rosie Lee? Bob and me here, we're fair parched, missus.'

And then another head came poking out of the far side of the cab like the twin handle on a jug and wearing a cap just like the driver's. 'Aye, how's about it, missus?'

It was the repeated use of that word 'missus' that stiffened my aunt's entire body, for I felt the surge of resentment like electricity in the hand holding mine. Oh, the cheap and easy familiarity of the city person, for it was obvious where they came from, that and that townee whine which sounds so ugly to a countryman's ear. Cocksure, condescending, caustic, oh, how we hate them, just as they despise us in turn for our slow, sly, rural ways.

'Come,' Aunt Dolly ordered, jerking my hand. 'We'll be away out of here,' and she pulled me back from that great throbbing brute of a thing and its hot, holed radiator.

Both men laughed down on us from their exalted position and the one nearest, he with his arm wreathed blue in snakes and daggers called out, 'Not to worry, missus, me and Bob'll find it. Sure, we're the right coupla bloodhounds when it comes to sniffin' out a new place. Aren't we, Bobby, oul' han'?'

The moment the words left his lips the most awful thing occurred. Oh, the sheer shame and degradation of it, for there came, clear as clear, above the rumble of the engine, the sound of a clock chiming, our old parlour clock, to be precise, with its twin winding holes in the face like eyes, and the maker's name, Jos. Prentice, Banbridge, curving below like a lettered grin. I saw it as in a vivid flash of light even though it nested in the hidden depths of the meal-bag my aunt gripped by the neck. For an instant we stayed there immobile while the clock performed its allotted carillon, ten peals in all, slow and unhurried as always. The contents of the bag hardly seemed to muffle the sound at all, or perhaps my ears were so finely attuned because of the shame I felt for the pair of us.

When the last note came and went, the lorry driver thanked us most kindly for reminding him it was time for him and his mate to have their tea-break and, laughing, did something to make the engine give an almighty jerk and roar. Stepping back to the grass verge we watched as the dark green monster rolled slowly past.

'The key's in the door!' my aunt called after them as if having a change of heart, but as soon as the tail-end had disappeared around a bend in the avenue I heard her mutter to herself, 'Let them have their oul' piano if it's so precious to them. There'll be little need for a fancy item like that where *you're* going, wee man.'

And in that moment I believed I detected a softening in her tone towards me and took some comfort in it, even though the thing about the piano was worrying. Feeling my eyes water I gripped her hand even more tightly and she seemed to return the pressure. She had very hard hands, as I recall, ridged and calloused as a man's. Like being cupped by a seashell, only hot and dry.

As we walked in the open together I was intensely conscious of her presence, her touch, her breathing, the swish of her skirt, the sound her boots made on the gravel. But, above all, her scent. I suppose one's sense of smell is never so acute as at that early age. Young animals are, after all, governed by what their nostrils tell them and at that time in my life the notion that I might be all that different from the snuffling rabbits and, yes, foxes, too, I saw from my bedroom window, would have been unthinkable. Accordingly, I wallowed secretly in the smell of her, while glorying in the notion she had no inkling of what I was about.

Let me try to recapture that blend of odours that was the essence of my Aunt Dolly Dinsmore. Well, there was carbolic and methylated spirits — how I adored that amazing blue in its square bottle — and, yes, liniment and embrocation, and, of course, the harsh taint of naphthalene, for mothballs careered around in the corners of everyone's drawers in those days. These were all the chemical tones. There was also the merest whiff of old-fashioned lavender water, but very, very faint, for anything that even hinted at vanity would have been anathema. Greedy little truffle-hound that I was, I kept straining for ever deeper, more secret smells that betrayed her sex, even though she toiled and sweated like a man. And so, bathed in the swirl of her scent, I trotted along, happy to be led by the hand towards whatever future fate held in store for me . . .

Our avenue seemed endless, for the previous limits of my exploration had only been as far as the copper beech hedge and the solitary monkey-puzzle tree at the foot of the garden. Soon I began to tire but my aunt appeared not to notice the dragging weight by her side. Grim-faced, she stared straight ahead as if towards some invisible goal, certainly invisible to me, that is, as I trailed my bundle alongside in the grass. The morning dew had already started to seep through it, my shoes, as well, turning both to pulp. Under the wool of my pull-ups I could feel that clamminess climb my legs like sap

40

up a stalk but, stubborn to the end, I held firm to the path I'd chosen.

It would be hard not to feel sorry for that poor little mite struggling so manfully not to cry, and looking back down all those years I see him there as if at the distant end of some telescope, foreshortened and removed as a mote on its lens. It's me, of course, the me I once was before I gave up striving to rise to others' expectations. Not that I've ever had much hope of measuring up, given the circumstances. Forgive the joke, but as someone once said, it would all be laughable if it weren't quite so tragic. And certainly it seemed very much that way to me as the road leading me away from my dear little red home in the west kept unrolling in front of me like some endless ribbon. Distances, of course, all seemed enormous then, legendary, even, like the ones in the storybooks lapped in my knotted quilt. I was on a quest, I told myself. Yes, that was it. Like one of my counterparts in the *Golden Treasury of Fairy Tales* and, for a moment, at least, I forgot my damp, tired legs and smoke-grimed face, becoming, instead, Prince Hugo the Valiant, rescuer of damsels and slayer of dragons, for, yes, I had brought with me my toy sword as well as the picture books. I have to confess that word *damsel* did puzzle me somewhat. What exactly were they, I asked myself? More to the point, would I recognise one when I met up with it?

Eventually we reached the end of what was once our avenue, or its beginning, I suppose, and I was astonished to see we had a gate as well, a sturdy, weathered, wooden affair with the name of our house on it, just like the inscription over the front door. It was wide open, those two townee removal men being far too lazy to bother to close it after them. Without hesitation my aunt marched straight through and out on to the road running past.

After the homely track we'd stepped from it looked bare

and forbidding, very like the terrible Road to Back of Beyond I'd often read about, and her nailed boots rang out on its dark, metalled surface. Basalt is its correct geological name, and when there's rain, as there often is, it takes on a glistening, jet-like appearance as if there are exposed coal seams snaking through the damp, green entrails of the countryside.

I truly believed I could travel no further over this cruel surface for I could feel its stony teeth bite through the ruined leather of my shoes. But a little way along this forsaken country road we came to a platform built into the side of the ditch on four wooden supports. A gleaming milk churn sat squarely on its flat top and my aunt lifted me up and placed me alongside its chill, cylindrical bulk, my legs dangling a good two feet from the ground. So I sat there feeling the perspiring metal work its slow way through the thickness of my coat and wondering what was to become of me.

Gazing about, I felt buffeted by so many new sensations. The great wide world beyond my little pocket paradise was certainly a raw and intimidating place. Like a released prisoner drunk on fresh air after being cooped up so long breathing the stale atmosphere of darkened rooms I was dazed by it all, the unrelenting bird song, the tremendous, breeze-borne stink of freshly dunged fields, the heat of the sun on my face, when another lorry appeared in the distance labouring up the incline towards us. Suddenly I felt even more frightened, two such monsters arriving together in this way and both bearing down on us.

My aunt, meanwhile, stood four square on the grass verge, arms folded over her chest, glaring at the approaching vehicle as if defying it to do its worst, and my panic became infused with a sort of outrage. *How dare she involve me in this way!* I was still only a very small child, I wanted to protest, far too young to be made to confront such terrors. I prayed the lorry would drive straight past leaving us in peace, but it did not, drawing up directly alongside, all the while clattering like a million tea-trays, for I saw it carried a load of closely packed milk churns like the one I was leaning against.

'Come,' said my aunt, 'up with you,' lifting me down, not up, for a door had swung out towards us and for the first time I saw what the inside of a real lorry looked like, greasy knobs, levers and switches and blinking dials, while a hot, oily wave of something poured out like the breath from some mechanical beast's lair. I could also see two great dungaree-covered knees far above me and, presently, I was hoisted up then lowered into place alongside this giant, my aunt squeezing in on my near side.

'So this is the wee orphan, is it?' a voice said, and the word passed over me as though in a foreign tongue. Like *damsel* it was to become a puzzling irritant, only much, much more so, for a part of me even then detected that faint taint of disgrace whenever it was mentioned, which was to be quite frequently over the months ahead.

The driver of the creamery lorry turned out to be my new Uncle Harry, regarded by the rest of the Dinsmores with considerable respect, for it transpired he was the only one of the connection ever to have a regular job. He was also the tallest and stoutest of a family of very large men and one woman. When I saw them assembled together for the first time like a thicket of oaks, the notion of being a changeling, which I took to be a near cousin of that other word *orphan*, seized hold of me in earnest and, once rooted, was to dominate my life from that point on and I began to feel as if I were different and that my relatives were as alien to me as night is to day.

But all of that was ahead of me. The here and now of it lay in that cramped, oily cockpit far above the ground, hemmed in between my enormous uncle and his equally tall, raw-boned sister. My entire body vibrated to whatever it was that ground away beneath me. I imagined something with teeth

43

straining to tear through the greasy leather, barely kept in check by the spreading bulk of my uncle bearing down on it. Not for the first time has it struck me how drivers of heavy loads all seem to possess that same amazingly rooted quality as if concentrating all their powers of gravity inside the glazed seat of their pants, and my Uncle Harry was the archetypical driver of a ten-tonner, and gradually I grew to envy him, for at that particular time every small boy in our part of the world had their hearts set on a Leyland or a Foden Four in preference any day to that foreign *Flying Scot*.

That first day of my new life as an orphan I was taken on a tour of what was to become my new world from then on, no bigger than a parish or a smallish townland, but to me the size of some newly discovered continent. The creamery lorry with its jingling load would draw alongside all these solitary milk churns sprouting out of ditches like metal milestones, although some had been sunk in runlets to keep them cool, and Uncle Harry would lower himself ponderously, hefting each chill and dented container up on to the back of his lorry as if it was filled with air and not packed to the brim with that immense liquid, white weight. And even though the churns were stoppered tight as sweet-jars his hands and dungarees stank of milk gone sour. That and the reek of diesel oil and grease. All my uncles carried it about with them, on their clothes, hands, even hair, like it was their natural scent, which in a way I suppose it was, for their entire world, as I was soon to discover, seemed centred on engines or machinery and their component parts.

From my throbbing cockpit I observed the world through glass on three sides. There was another window directly behind about the size of a shoebox lid. They had propped me up between them, my two relatives, on a spare leather cushion so I might have an uninterrupted view of what would be my home terrain from then on. Did I also imagine it, but weren't they also secretly observing me for my reactions? It seems odd, these two silent giants – they barely communicated except in grunts – taking any real interest in little me and my feelings, but I don't think I was wrong, somehow, so I determined not to betray the slightest emotion about what lay on the far side of the smeared glass. I kept my gaze fixed in a gravely, unconcerned expression, remembering too well the day of my poor mother's funeral and how my innocent reactions then were so woefully misinterpreted. Being the quick learner, ever since I've cultivated that same look of serious intent. People often remark on it, but I have to say it suits me just fine to be regarded as a sobersides. As I was to discover, there's an expectation that someone of my proportions will look introverted, anyway, if not out and out melancholy, most of the time, as though weighed down by the thought of their physical shortcomings. But on that day, at least, I was on a level with the best of them, higher, even, for I rode aloft like a little charioteer on my twin cushions.

Looking back, I don't suppose I could have been given a better or more exhaustive introduction to the locality and what served to make it unique. For, oh, yes, the population of my new neck of the woods liked to flatter themselves they were vastly different from those who happened to live only a mile or so away beyond the next hill, or where a road or river marked that invisible twist of parish boundary. It was like that then, parochial rivalries as intense, and as bloody, too, sometimes, as any ancient faction fight. Uncle Harry, of course, kept crossing and re-crossing those same boundaries because his job and route took him there. After all, milk was milk, no matter whose cow it came from, although more churns seemed to be left out for collection in areas where the grass appeared greener and the shorthorns more velvety, compared to our own barren bit of whin and bog and scrubby planting.

If there was a Presence up there looking out for me, then, I have to say, He had a funny way of showing it, for the place I had been taken from lay at the very heart of one of those same sappy havens and couldn't have been more different to the Fews, as it was known.

Squashed tight as a bug between my aunt and uncle I took in everything that lay anchored out there as we floated by. I saw the famous Lyle's public house for the first time with its peppered sign displaying a foaming bottle of stout, and nearby the First Unified Presbyterian Church and the school alongside with its sympathetic, high, ecclesiastically pointed windows. Rolling past, we heard the children inside singing about a Lass from Richmond Hill and a little further on, at the Cross, the lorry silently coasting now, for Uncle Harry liked to shut the engine off on the down gradients, I saw a figure I felt sure I recognised. As we approached he turned to face us as if expecting our appearance, silent running or no.

To my great dismay I recognised Sinbad Scully and that fear intensified as the lorry slowed to roll to a halt beside him. Crouching as low as I could, I shrank from that remembered grin, but to no avail, for he had picked me out as surely as if I had been perched on the radiator cap like a mascot, instead of being protected, as I believed, behind bleary glass.

My aunt pushed the door open on her side and he promptly stepped on to the running-board.

'I see you've got the wee man with you,' he said with his face level with ours and then, to my horror, addressing me directly, 'How about a wee hullo for an old friend? Don't be shy now.' And reaching across he flicked me lightly on the cheek with a nicotine-stained talon.

Instinctively I drew back, but he only laughed. 'We'll be seeing a lot of each other from now on, wee man. We will, won't we, Harry?' and my uncle smiled.

It was the first time I had seen his face behave in that

fashion. It was just like a flower opening, a great, fleshy chrysanth, and suddenly I wanted him to smile at me in that very same way. Indeed it became my goal from that point on, me working shamelessly for his approval.

My aunt coughed and said, 'We're going as far as McGivern's shop. There's room, if you want a lift.'

Sinbad looked in at the three of us. 'Well, if you're sure it won't be too much of a squeeze,' he replied, aiming a wink in my direction as if he and I were back in our cosy kitchen the way we were before he'd been banished, all forgiven and forgotten.

And so for the rest of our journey to my new home I sat on my aunt's bony knees. She kept them tight and prim as scissor blades and although her scent had never been headier I could take no real relish in it because of who was wedged in alongside me. Being the right wee mollycoddle, I was wearing the dinkiest little pair of mittens, joined, as I recall, by a knitted cord threaded up inside my coat sleeves. Palms down, they lay on my lap, and presently I saw another hand, a grimy, grey, mottled paw reach across and cover one. Staring straight ahead I bore the heat and weight of it for the rest of the journey.

Please don't ask me where it might have come from, this gift, if it can be called such, feigning unconcern even when the most awful things were happening to me, oh, infinitely worse, believe me, than Sinbad Scully's sly pawing. Blood-lines offer no real help in the light of what I was to discover, or not, about my origins later, so I can only assume little stone-face here created it unaided all by himself from within, the way a spider spins his web from his insides, or a snake creates its own venom, or the mountain hare changes his summer coat for a winter one in tune with the seasons. As you can see I believed passionately I was an animal still, different, distinct, and very much having to look out for number one.

Each time we drew up by the roadside for another full churn the shock of it landing on the lorry travelled straight through me and I wondered if Sinbad could sense it in the hand clasping mine. I kept thinking it must be like cupping a bird, say, or one of my little furry friends, and concentrated all my powers on not allowing that tiny pulse contained there to race too fast. Still, there came a moment when all my efforts failed me. We were travelling at the time through a part of the route where there seemed to be few farms and fewer milk churns and Uncle Harry drove faster perhaps because of it. The land appeared neglected hereabouts and the fields full of thistles. We passed short runs of labourers' cottages lining the roadside with small children and dogs tumbling about their doors.

But then as we ground up a steep incline past some old mill buildings with starred windows and weeds sprouting from every chimney, a fierce rain of stones descended on us, rattling down on the curved roof over our heads. They made a noise like hail on the painted skin of the lorry and its bare, metal load, pinging and bouncing and, my terror getting the better of me, I cried out and clutched my aunt. It was like hugging a hatstand for all the heed she took, yet, to my shame, I howled and wept, dousing the front of her stiff pinny with my blubberings.

Not once did Uncle Harry slacken pace throughout, which to me seemed incredible, outrageous, even. Indeed, he appeared to have the semblance of a smile playing on his face throughout; Sinbad, as well, as if sharing some joke all their own. My aunt, meanwhile, stared straight ahead.

Presently, with a chuckle, Sinbad remarked, 'Them Cogry lads. Them's the bold, bad boys, sure enough,' and my uncle nodded as if in amused concurrence.

'Too true,' he grunted, changing gear, while I still clung close to my aunt's unresponsive chest. 'One of these days they'll put somebody's eye out,' and they both laughed heartily together as if at something even more hilarious.

All the while Sinbad had my hand in his. Squeezing gently, he brought his face up close until I could feel the bristles against my cheek. My father's beard had felt that very same way in those last days. His breath had smelt bad, too, although Sinbad's retained its own distinctive tang, a mixture of old clothes, mildewed rooms and decay.

'You'll be attendin' school with that same crowd of young savages. Them's the boys'll put the grand notions out of your head, so they will.'

Then, as I buried my head for a second time in my aunt's lavender-scented bosom, 'Don't fret now,' he murmured. 'Sinbad'll be lookin' out for you. You'll come to no mischief while he's around.' Finally coming out with the truly nauseating, 'You really like old Sinbad. You do, don't you, wee man?'

It was that, I believe, that hardened me, although I took care not to let him be aware of it, for he was sly as a fox, I realised, when it came to reading me and my reactions. So I continued to snivel. It really was surprisingly easy to keep up the act while feeling dry as a pebble inside. Something which has stood me in good stead ever since.

Naturally I kept my hand where it lay and in this fashion we travelled on until we arrived at Mrs McGivern's wee shop. The lorry pulled up opposite the Player's cigarette sign, a melancholy jack tar staring directly out at us from the weathered tin of his hoarding. For some reason I thought of the collar-stud still inside me, the story of its adventures infinitely more plausible coming from those bearded lips than Sinbad Scully's lying ones. We exchanged glances, the nice sailor and me, while I imagined the barest hint of a wink, the pair of us sharing our little secret. I have to say it cheered me up no end. The small private fantasies usually do. But Sinbad broke the spell.

49

'Let me get the wee man a sweetie,' he said as nice as ninepence, climbing down and going into the shop.

We heard the bell ping and minutes later, inside, laughter breaking out. I persuaded myself it must be connected with myself, Sinbad telling more of his lies about me and what had been my family.

He came out with a tremendous grin on his face, his stained raincoat swinging jauntily from a single loose button at the throat and my hatred for him hardened into something more implacable. I could feel it there inside keeping company with the collar-stud, inseparable now, connected, as they were, with my tormentor climbing up alongside and holding out a small paper bag. I looked at it, then down at my mittened hands, then up at him, and he laughed. As all three of us watched he drew out an aniseed ball with almost feminine delicacy and before I could lock my jaws he had pressed it between my lips. And even though I sucked vigorously on that hard, round, striped sweet I convinced myself I could still taste his vile fingers in my mouth, eclipsing even the dark foreign flavour of the gobstopper, a great favourite of mine, incidentally, up until then. But not any more.

'What do you say?'

I stared at my aunt in astonishment.

'Where's your manners?' she persisted.

So I murmured 'Thank you' under my breath, seeing nothing else for it.

Thereupon Sinbad said, 'If it's all right with you two, I'd like to see the wee man safely settled into his new home. His dear mother, God rest her soul, made me promise to look out for him. I'd only feel bad if I didn't keep my word. If you don't mind.' But, of course, how could they 'mind', those two great gulls swallowing every lying breath someone like that cared to blow in their direction?

And so I found myself transferred across to his knee like

the helpless package I had become. That was me at my lowest ebb. But out of it there came one important resolution: that one day Sinbad Scully would pay for the lies he was peddling about me and mine, right down to that first concoction of his concerning a collar-stud. For, yes, if he could lie about me and my family, why not about something as slight and ordinary as that? Only it wasn't slight and ordinary. Not to me, it wasn't. Like every small child before or since, I promised myself when I grew up – *oh, those magic words, that blessed state* – I would be a force to be reckoned with, never dreaming that the first part of that fulfilment might not be mine.

So we drove on, the sweet in my mouth dwindling to a tiny crumb, then to nothing but a taste of aniseed on my tongue. Sinbad sang a song, something about a mermaid and a sailor. Another of his tall tales, I reckoned, while my free hand reassured me my precious quilt was still where I had placed it for safe keeping at the back of me. And thinking of its remembered touch and smell in that way, I wondered where and in what sort of a place I would get to sleep that night.

FOUR

'Welcome to Larkhill.'

After what seemed like the longest, most wearisome day of my young life, Uncle Harry's lorry had swung in finally through an arched gateway, bumping to a halt in the middle of a cobbled farmyard. Staring straight ahead, he switched off the engine, and the four of us sat on in silence inside our hot, ticking, oily cave.

Once more Sinbad said, 'Welcome to Larkhill.' Same proprietorial tone as well, as if it had been his idea all along and no one else's to bring me to this outlandish place. I looked about me. By now it was getting dark, the outlines of the encircling outhouses beginning to blend then disappear into a blue-black sky.

'Wait till you see it in the daylight,' whispered Sinbad, squeezing my hand. But already I had the feeling there would be no delighted cries on my part, no racing around making excited discoveries in the early morn. Which was how it turned out, Larkhill's setting, for the most part, being low-lying, bog-ridden and barren. As for the first syllable of its name, alas, not ever in all my time there did I catch a glimpse of that near-invisible, palpitating dot in the heavens, accompanied by that tremulous cry that the poets so love to write about. But I had my quilt and my collar-stud. Not forgetting, of course, that high opinion of myself which has never really deserted me, not even at the very worst of times.

God forgive me for the two-faced little conniver I was fast becoming, but I heard myself enquire sweetly, 'Are we home?' and the response was immediate, Sinbad positively cooing, Uncle Harry smiling his great chrysanthemum smile, even Aunt Dolly thawing out sufficiently to pinch me awkwardly on one cheek. Clutching my tiny bundle, I let myself be swung out, then down on to hard cobblestones. A powerful stench hung in the air. It seemed to come from a colossal midden close to one of the outhouses, a wheelbarrow lying flat against the sloping side of it. All this my nose and eyes registered instantly, but I could still hear nothing save the slow tick of the lorry's cooling engine. Whereupon Uncle Harry pumped the horn and a light came on in the buildings in front of us, followed by a din of dogs barking and, mystery of mysteries, children yelling. A door opened, throwing a yellow stripe across the stones to where I stood caught in the glare.

Sinbad shouted something – it sounded like a private language – and along the carpet of lamplight there streamed a raucous tribe of animals, boys and one girl straight towards us. The moment they reached me the dogs started sniffing and licking my face. Indeed, one great black and white brute with lolling tongue and foul breath placed its front paws on my shoulders like some long-lost, rowdy relative and just as I was about to go down under the weight of him, Sinbad, stepping into the yapping scrum, plucked me up and carried me off head-high. Borne away, I looked back over his shoulder. One of the children – well, he was almost a man, or certainly seemed that to me – was puffing on a cigarette. He had a close, almost metallic, gingery crop, all the rest having blond hair just like mine, or variations of the same, and he grinned at me, his freckled face splitting open like a great red raw pippin. This was Junior Dinsmore and someone who was to have a profound and, at times, painful effect on my life.

However, at that precise moment I was confident that if I could so easily charm the likes of my aunt and uncle, as well as Sinbad Scully, I could do much as I liked with this rough lot, dogs included. And so, feeling almost all-conquering already, I allowed myself to be carried across the bumpy yard like a royal baby towards the lighted doorway that was to lead to my new home.

But that first night I was in no fit state to absorb or appreciate the finer points of Larkhill or its layout. All I could take in was a hurried impression, a rapid plunge from dark to light and back again, as one passageway, then room, opened on to the next. And there seemed so many of them, too, with no rhyme or reasoned connection as in a proper house like the one I'd been used to. Actually the impression was of several joined on to one another haphazardly, like a run of dominoes.

As I was borne through these same rooms, each lit by the glow of a fire in a grate or a solitary oil lamp – a hurricane, in one case, as in a byre – I encountered strangers surprised there. They regarded me oddly as if they hadn't been told about me or my coming. Some women were amongst them, mostly young, not dried up, stringy creatures like Aunt Dolly. They stared at me in Sinbad's arms as though comparing me with their own little whippersnappers, and I stared back, mittened hands clutching him about the neck. Close up, he smelt of tobacco and aniseed, that other pervasive reek of running walls and mildewed plaster melting into retreat before all the newer scents which assailed my animal nose.

That night Sinbad Scully put me to bed. I watched him make

ready the cot, the face on him so serious, the careful laying out, then tucking in of the bedding, daintily, almost, which he sniffed as if only the very best must be good enough for the little lordly one. When everything was to his satisfaction he proceeded to undress me, starting with my buttoned shoes. I stared down at him kneeling at my feet. The crown of his head had this bare, livid spot as if an egg was trying to break free through the thin covering of its nest. It seemed genuinely fascinating, even then it did, that part of the male anatomy which rarely is visible to its owner. Who knows, I may well have a little tonsured something of my own lurking shyly back there . . .

When I had been stripped to my vest and pants he lowered me into the cot, which is not strictly true, for it was nothing near as grand as that. Let's be accurate, it was an empty wardrobe drawer, a temporary measure, I assumed, until a proper bed could be found for me.

However, as things turned out, I never really moved out of my narrow, shallow box on the floor. To this day I can only sleep on my back because of it, hands folded prettily across my chest like some pocket-sized Crusader on his tomb. Still I would hate to give the impression I was forced to lie like a kipper in a tray for all of those years. I wasn't. On quite a few occasions the choice to share a proper bed with three, even four of the Dinsmore siblings was offered me, but always I made it clear that having made my bed, so to speak, I preferred to continue to lie in it.

Despite the restrictions of my new sleeping arrangements, that first night I felt pampered as if nothing had really changed. The bedding smelt fresh and clean and I had my quilt on top as always. Fondly Sinbad looked down one last time, then left me there by the light of a single candle stub stuck to the base of a saucer. Not as ideal as my own little night-light, certainly, but a reasonable replacement, I felt. It didn't quite reach into the darkest, most remote corners, but it would keep the bad fairy at bay which was all that mattered. And so, drifting off, I lay there with the favoured corner of the quilt in my mouth as usual making the saliva flow.

Over where my clothes had been neatly folded lay my invisible sword. Having it closer to hand, as Prince Hugo the Valiant, would have been ideal, but I could always imagine it.

Now whether I rode out in dreamland that night or not I cannot be sure. I may well have been slaying dragons and rescuing damsels – as I say, the two always connected for some unfathomable reason – but when I awoke in the dark, not knowing where I was, any remnants of that other familiar, fantasy world vanished without trace or memory. I could see nothing, blackness pressing down on me like a heavy weight, constricted, yet not knowing why or how. For a terrible moment I believed I must be in my coffin, having had so much personal experience in that area recently. Lying there, quaking, I convinced myself another person was in the room with me for the shadows seemed to bunch, then separate in one far corner.

'Sinbad,' I whispered, 'is that you?' and someone giggled.

Then a light came on, blinding me, a shaft of searing brightness beamed directly at my face.

'Just look at it, would you?' a voice said softly. 'Look at the wee fucker in his box,' and pulling myself up, I cried out, 'Who is it?'

'Who is it?' the first voice echoed. 'Ain't nobody here but us chickens,' going *cluck-cluck-cluck*, and the giggling resumed, but as a more concerted effort this time.

Then, finally, out of the darkness came the children I had seen earlier. The biggest, the eldest, was holding a torch in his fist still trained on my face, but beyond the dazzling rim I could make out grinning faces, the girl's as well.

Shading my eyes, while propped up in my drawer, I said,

'My name's Hugo,' for I felt some form of introduction should be offered. These were relatives, after all, Dinsmores like myself, although I wished they would stop shining that cruel light in my face. But then the idea took hold of me they had come out of simple, innocent curiosity. So, let them look their fill, I told myself. Why shouldn't they? Admire, also, if so inclined, for I have to confess momentarily I felt just that tiny bit like the little Lord Jesus Himself surrounded in his crib by the Wise Men. At least six or seven in this case.

Then the one who had done the talking and the clucking, their leader, despite being called Junior, as I was shortly to find out, said again, 'Look at the wee fucker.'

I have to admit the word was one I had never come across before, although I thought it might well be some form of endearment, even homage, for the tone in which it had been delivered on both occasions had been friendly, pleasant in the extreme.

'What's this?' demanded the big boy, grabbing my quilt and holding it up in the light of his torch. 'Rabbits? You like rabbits, wee fucker?'

And to my shame I heard myself tell him, 'They were on it when I got it.'

He tossed the quilt from him and the others caught it in mid-air, twisting and pulling on it like a tug-of-war rope. By this time I had realised a terrible mistake had been made, all of it on my part, apparently, and pure terror taking over, I whispered, 'I'll tell Matt Scully.'

The big boy only laughed. '*Him?* Sure he's only an oul' cunt.' But even though the expression was as unfamiliar as the previous one something told me this wasn't a nice word. Far from it.

At this point the torch went out and I thought my tormentors had tired of me, but I was mistaken, for in the dark a match was struck and the candle re-lit. I saw the red-headed boy bring his great raw, glossy face close to it. In the

57

glow it looked like a mask, all bumps and shadowy planes. Put on specially to terrify small children just like me, although Hallowe'en had come and gone. In his mouth he had an inch of cigarette butt which he proceeded to light from the flame, pinching up his lips and tightly closing his eyes as though in pain.

Then, as if at a signal, the rest of the children surged forward in a pushing, whispering pack and, surrounding me, started to prod and fondle me where I lay at their mercy. I looked up at them as they bent over me and although I still was frightened I could sense they meant me no real harm. They seemed genuinely curious as if nothing like me had ever entered their lives before. The girl, in particular, stroked and played with my hair, then switched her attentions to the fine cut and materials of my vest and little matching pants. I supposed she was only following her natural feminine bent.

I won't say her touch was unpleasant, for that would be untrue. Indeed, I felt a strange, warm tremor as if I wanted to pee, as her fingers probed beneath the elastic. So unexpected was the sensation it distracted me from what the others were up to outside the candle's reach, for by this time they had discovered my colouring books and losing interest in the quilt two of them were having a silent pulling match with my toy sword.

'Where's his supper? I thought I told you to bring the wee fucker his supper.' Grabbing one of the boys by the lug Junior led him bent over into the shadows.

The boy was weeping but in a short while he returned carrying a bowl of something. Bringing it close to my face he held out a spoonful.

'Eat it,' commanded Junior. 'Go on. You won't grow if you don't,' and too frightened to defy him I supped some sort of cold, sticky gruel, quite vile, really, the taste made even worse by not being able to see what it was exactly I was swallowing. They all watched as I persevered with the horrible, glutinous stuff. It had lumps in it.

When I'd finished Junior said, 'I can see you enjoyed that. Tapioca is what it's called, but we call it frog-spawn. If you don't behave yourself and be a good wee fucker we'll just have to feed you the real thing. No crying or pissing the bed now – *wee fucker*.' And, blowing out the candle, he departed with his little band of terrors as silently as he'd come.

That was to become my name from then on, always 'the wee fucker', as far as the big boy was concerned. None of the other children ever called me it except when they were angry or feeling hard done by and I happened to be the one closest to hand. And in time, like a pet dog, I answered to it without resentment or demur. It didn't bother me, why should it, when there were far worse things to contend with in that strange and nightmarish place.

One thing Junior Dinsmore never did, however, was come out with it if there were grown-ups around. Despite his adult swagger and the smoking which was openly tolerated, he was wary of those older than himself. A dog sometimes knows far more about his master than he's given credit for, and 'the wee fucker', while wagging his tiny, invisible stump, so desperately trying to please, was observing at the same time and storing up information to be used as ammunition later when his day would come. Which it would, for if you've learned anything about Hugo Dinsmore by now, it is that he has never forgiven or forgotten any slight or wrong. As a dish taken cold, revenge nourishes the spirit, strengthens the resolve, and genuinely does the heart good. I swear by it.

Some little while later when I had settled into my new role of household pet it seemed that perhaps some tiny reward for my patience might have come my way. We were in the vast potato-house at the time, sorting those tubers which had sprouted their pale shoots in the dark from those that had not. Junior was supervising us. Even I had a tiny task and my own tray to pick through. But I must have irritated him unwittingly for he took up a spud and viciously fired it at me, accompanied with the customary 'wee fucker'. He repeated the expression a few times for good measure. He genuinely seemed to derive satisfaction from saying it, especially that detonating, middle syllable which spat from his mouth like a plum stone, and just as he did so we all looked up to see Uncle Harry blocking the light in the doorway. He must have finished his creamery run early that day, although we hadn't heard the lorry come into the yard.

I remember that moment so very vividly, the setting particularly. Potatoes in the dark have this disturbing, massed quality – at least I've always thought so – lying as in some sort of charnel-house all of their own, yet still sending out those transparent, nerveless, soft feelers, inch by slow inch, towards any source of light, no matter how tiny, even a pinprick will do. A dead man's beard they say also continues growing, which always reminds me of those same slow tubers with a life of their own. Never a favourite place, the potato-house, and for another good reason as well, for this was where the children would be taken to be punished. I have to say it never happened to me personally, one or two close shaves, certainly, but I always managed to evade the lash of the great webbing belt with the brass buckle, one of the advantages of being so much smaller than everyone else. Size, of course, never held back the hand of any of the children themselves, although, as I've said, only Junior enjoyed tormenting me on a regular basis.

But that day it was his turn, for Uncle Harry took hold of him by the shaved neck, hurling him into a waist-high pyramid of Kerr's Pinks. He kept trying to get to his feet but couldn't, falling back time after time on to the rolling, slithering carpet covering the packed, earthen floor.

'Wash out your mouth,' growled Uncle Harry, stooping over him, his great behind looming up before us like the side of a mountain, hip pockets as big as soup-plates.

'Never let me hear you say that to him again.' And in a shocking gesture, which was not like him, Uncle Harry rammed a whole potato into his open, yelling mouth. A smallish one, I should make plain, which may well have been selected purposely for the size of Junior's gob. In that moment, seeing my enemy silenced in that way like a pig on a platter, I suppose I should have rejoiced. Certainly it was an image to cherish and I have never forgotten it, but a terrible fear of something I couldn't explain made me cry out, 'It's all right, it's all right! I don't mind being called a wee fucker!'

Uncle Harry turned to me and the look he gave me was far, far worse than any punishment meted out in that dark cavern of a place smelling like the grave. Shaking his head, he backed out into the light of the yard and was gone.

Oh, how craven I was in those days. If this were a happier story, like those in the cheaper forms of fiction, or up on a screen, my time from that day onward should have been much easier. Junior should have softened. He should, shouldn't he? After all, I had tried to protect him from further punishment. When moved to wrath, which was rare, my Uncle Harry could be a terrifying force, we all knew that, everyone did. Like his great lorry, once the brakes were off, he could crush and obliterate anything or anyone that stood upright in his path.

Once, on the Twelfth of July, I saw him fired up when he was fighting mad as well as drunk. Outside Lyle's roadside public house, it was. Four, no, five, maybe even six, Orangemen from some distant Lodge decided to set about him. They might well have been townees, outsiders who didn't know his strength or the awesomeness of his wrath once the blood flooded eyes and brain and the brakes came off. Standing well back in my first little Sunday suit and tangerine-coloured, junior sash, I watched his assailants hurl themselves at him with fist, boot and bottle. One after another he battered them senseless with great windmilling swings of his mighty mitts, the same clenched hands that held the silver and ebony flute – not in the procession, no, no, never there – but always off on his own, out in the fields somewhere quiet. Or, better still, sitting up against the base of a beech tree in McGookin's planting in the still of an evening, where I would steal up on him and listen, silent and still, like some shy baby rabbit in the undergrowth.

That was my Uncle Harry. And that summer's day of celebration and murderous drinking, when his foes had broken themselves on him finally, their city blood stippling the front of his best white shirt, he turned and saw me standing there among the legs of the crowd. But in that moment I realised he didn't, couldn't see me, for his gaze was still red and blinded. In head and heart the battle still raged, like the blood beating there. He stumbled off to find more of the yellow whiskey – that always made him crazy – and I was left there as if he'd disowned me. But I suppose I knew in my heart he had turned his back on me much, oh, much earlier than that, the day in the potato-house, to be precise, when I had somehow disappointed him so terribly.

At the risk of sounding like yet another of those pathetic penitents we get so many of in this place, always searching themselves like monkeys for fleas for deeper and deeper reasons as to how and why they 'went wrong', I suppose I've never really ceased trying to restore myself in my Uncle Harry's regard. Sometimes the cheapest, corniest axioms are what the business is all about. Gods, heroes, champions, we all want to die for them – we do, don't we? And I have to confess I turned out to be the most abject little cur imaginable whenever that great giant of a man happened to be close by.

But then he wasn't, was he, for his lorry and his run were almost his entire waking life. Mute, slow-moving, expressionless, he would appear each evening with his lunch-tin under his arm, to drop down at the table where his main meal awaited him. He always ate entirely on his own, the board cleared of everyone else's leavings. No one dared distract him once he started feeding, meat, gravy, cabbage, spuds, forked into his mouth relentlessly, while his free hand gripped a mug of almost black tea.

It was as if the entire household, that clutch of lesser satellites circling well outside his powerful orbit, depended on his strength and wellbeing for their own continued livelihood, for no one else – not Bob, nor Andy, Alec, Eric, Sid or young Tom – seemed ever to do a hand's turn between them save stand around gazing silently at stripped engines or gearboxes in the yard or in one of the many outhouses, occasionally delving into their oily innards with spanner and wrench.

On Sundays, having shaved and doused his head under the pump in the yard, keeping it there for a good full minute, as though refreshing himself, he would put on a clean, collarless shirt and mooch off up along the hedgerows with the flute inside the deep side pocket of his dungarees, the bright, ferruled tip of its black stem just showing like some giant fountain pen. After a time the notes would come drifting back to us, hanging in the air like silver droplets, but down at Larkhill we all went about our concerns as usual, pretending not to notice or hear, even, just as if it was only another day. Which it was, for we were a pagan bunch, quite proud of it, too, in our own way, wanting no truck with churches, Sunday schools or the rich farming folk who worshipped only a few miles away.

Later when I became much more fanciful, head filled with what I'd been reading, I thought of Uncle Harry as the great god Pan himself, piping away deep in our woods and fields, his melancholy call unsettling the faithful. In imagination I visualised the sound trickling through the open windows of Kilcarn Presbyterian meeting-house making the good folk praying there itch and fidget on their hard, waxed, pitch pine pews. But if they were aggrieved, and many of them were, no one dared complain, because the melodies he played were the ones they knew by heart, ballads of battle and the spilling of papist blood. But – here comes the irony – rendered like lullabies, soft as the coo of turtle doves, gentle as the Easter Lamb itself carved on their own great communion table. And later when my first real Twelfth arrived and I heard the fifes and drums beating out those same party tunes in martial tempo I could scarcely believe my ears, for Uncle Harry had tamed and transformed 'Dolly's Brae' and 'The Aghalee Heroes' into melting airs of lament and bitter-sweet yearning.

So, was he, perhaps, the great joker of our locality? Or is that just me? I like to think Uncle Harry was, and still is, laughing away quietly to himself behind that placid mask of his. Sadly I never got to share any of that inner mischief, if it genuinely existed, that is. The closest I came to it was on those fine Sunday mornings when I lay on my belly listening to the soft trickle of his Orange flute bubbling like spring water out of the very ground where he sprawled under that scarred, old beech tree.

That, then, was me, invisible, a sly, nervous presence in the long grass, and for most of the time, too, wherever I went, I might just as well not have existed. You see, after those first weeks my novelty value wore off and I was abandoned to the care of the children. I became their plaything. They dressed and undressed me, fed me, too. On one or two occasions the younger ones tried me with weeds and worms. I don't think any real malice was intended, more an experiment as to how I would react. Who knows, this new little creature with his curious, girlish clothes and ringlets might actually swallow the stuff. He didn't, of course.

They took it in turns to pull me around after them in an orange box on four pram wheels, my hands gripping its raw rim like some junior charioteer. At times they would harness the big black and white collie dog between the shafts. Buller was his name, after some obscure military figure. Only a Dinsmore would think up such a handle, for they were a most curious clan, wild and woolly, like something out of a western. Later when I started going to the cinema in the nearest town in earnest, I couldn't help but be struck by certain similarities. Ma and Pa Kettle and their own bunch of rowdies seemed like close relatives.

By this stage, of course, I was deeply ashamed of my own connection, and when laughter erupted in the dark I would feel my face go hot and would sink right down, which then cut off my vision even more than usual. Yet it felt good to be immersed in the darkness, and some of my happiest moments have been spent in that old country flea-pit, except when my gap-toothed, country cousins were up there being their ridiculous selves in black and white. In Technicolor the whole business would have been doubly unbearable. Eventually, I couldn't bring myself to go to see a certain type of film any more, which was a great sadness, for I dearly loved the movies despite the humiliation of being handed a child's ticket each time without having to ask for one.

But all of that is jumping the gun, reeling forward little Hugo's own film much too fast. Why be impatient, when where I am right now I have all the time in the world – well, a fair proportion of it – to let memories grow moss. No longer a rolling stone, more a beached minnow.

About a month or so after I had somehow become part of that strange, cluttered household of uncles, their wives and my cousins, whose precise blood relationship I still couldn't

65

disentangle for myself, without really being accepted – I knew by now I never would – Sinbad Scully appeared one evening. He came looking for me, making his way from room to room, stooping, smiling, peering into one face after another apologetically as if he were asking strangers for directions in a foreign country.

He found me sitting quietly in my own little chair which one of the uncles had fashioned out of a butter-box. Upholstery I had provided myself in the form of my folded quilt. Sprawled on the floor at my feet, Bessie and young Tom were playing a game of Happy Families, and although half that tattered old pack was missing, chewed up by Buller, no doubt, I hung on every move, memorising every painted, pasteboard face. I itched to take part, but knew I would have to be patient, as well as extra sly, perhaps, for some time to come.

The cards belonged to Bessie, she of the rust-red hair and russet freckles. Like specks on a thrush's egg, they covered every square inch of her, for she enjoyed me seeing her bare all over, not just at bedtime, for we all of us slept in the same great loft under the rafters, the smell of apples in their boxes sending us off to sleep half-tipsy, but in other places as well, out in the woods, mainly, which ever since I've always associated with illicit activities.

Already she had this tiny, curling wisp of something where her legs came together. Almost fluorescent in tint compared with the carroty crop on her head, the way it can be with certain women, it drew me like nothing else. Thus a tiny fetish takes root. Looking back, I suppose it was like parading naked before a favourite doll – what harm could there be in that? – me sitting there feasting my eyes on every detail of that skinny body, but especially that little tuft of chemical-coloured candy floss. Touching never entered into it. I was content to simply sit and watch, a habit which has remained with me ever since.

But getting back to Bessie and her solo performances in the buff, for I may have forgotten to mention she would often strike poses, bending and stretching acrobatically like a girl she said she'd once seen in Duffy's Circus. The pair of us, she whispered, would run away together and join it the very next time it came through. Better still, whenever I grew to be big enough. She would wait for me. Darling Bessie, my first love, for soon my affections were to radiate out from that first little downy bull's-eye to take in every part of her. Even then I think she and I were two of a kind, dreamers with a strong streak of exhibitionism. We both were in love with what we saw in the mirror, or in one another's eyes, for sometimes I performed for her as well, although never naked. Anyway, she had already made it plain how singularly unimpressed she was with my own little teapot spout, even when it performed its party trick of the golden trajectory.

Which brings me to another thing. When I arrived first, to my horror I discovered I was expected to do my numbers sitting on a chamber pot and in full view of an audience too, as if my puny efforts might somehow be miraculously different from everyone else's. Intense interest was taken in the operation. I was watched eagerly for the slightest change of expression as I sat there straining to oblige. But, of course, I couldn't, and word went back to Aunt Dolly who for a second time spooned into me the dreaded, dark brown draught.

All country people in that day and age had this obsession with evacuation. The entire family, even the women, would discuss their bowel movements openly in finest detail like it was some sort of daily marvel. But try as I would I couldn't share their enthusiasm. Early on Junior took every chance he could to humiliate me, holding up the chipped china pot, while loudly evaluating texture, quantity, colour and, particularly, odour, even though he happened to be gripping his own nose at the time. Eventually I graduated to the fields and the hedgerows like the other children who cheerfully dropped their offerings in the open or, if the weather was exceptionally bad, on the midden in the yard.

At the back somewhere was a three-seater privy which the grown-ups used, but I could never accustom myself to that unlit, noisome place with its rough wooden seats arranged over what seemed like a plunge to Hell. After dark, my aunts – at least, I believed they were, for I would remain confused about who was who nearly all of the time I lived at Larkhill – would go off holding a torch between them. Giggling would be heard coming from behind the boarded door which had cracks in it. Sporadically the light from the battery torch would shine through, but at the lightest footfall it would be switched off until the intruder had moved on.

In my own small and innocent way I was greatly intrigued by what might or might not be taking place behind that crude, unpainted door. All we boys were, including Junior, although he pretended not to be. Whenever I pressed her for inside information, Bessie would merely smile and perform another cartwheel. Somehow I always managed to bring the topic up when she was naked, associating this, I suppose, with the state of undress my aunties might also be in, while giggling in the dark. Of course it had everything to do with sex, sex, sex, which was another reason to talk about it with someone's little russet pom-pom the mere matter of a foot or so away.

When Sinbad found me that night watching for Mr Bone the Butcher and Mrs Bun the Baker's Wife, there was a lot I could have told him, but didn't. He had this syrupy grin on his face which made me grow cool towards him.

'Didn't I tell you you'd soon find your feet,' he murmured, an expression puzzling to me, as well as being a downright lie, like almost everything else he came out with. The collar-stud had never belonged to him. I was positive of that now. He had stolen someone else's story from them while they mumbled in a delirium in the bottom of a boat and that night he came seeking to filch something precious of mine as well.

But first he made it sound as though we were conspirators together sharing a private understanding.

'Come,' he whispered for my ears only, 'come and watch old Sinbad give the lovely lads a wee trim,' producing from the deep, inner pocket of his sweaty raincoat a pair of hair-clippers and going *snap-snap-snap*. Innocent that I was, dutifully I followed him, when if I'd had more sense I should have stayed with Bessie and her Happy Families.

When we got to the big main kitchen, drenched as always in smells of cooking and the constant washing of clothes, I discovered to my shock that most, if not all, the tribe were assembled there as though waiting for an entertainment to commence. This was the first time I had seen them together like this, men, women, children, as in some great family reunion, although there was no sign of Uncle Harry, and the sight was so unexpected that I hung back, feeling shy and awkward suddenly. But Sinbad propelled me forward. However, far more of a shock was seeing five of the boys, Junior included, sitting on chairs in a semicircle in the centre of the black and white tiled floor with tea-towels about their necks. They had their heads bowed with such an unvarying look of penitential despair on all their faces that I believed they must be about to be punished for some terrible joint misdeed. Part of me longed to know what it might be – perhaps I'd never find out, which was unbearable – but the greater part was relieved I hadn't been involved.

In the circumstances I began to feel much more relaxed, yet still edged into a dark corner where I could see without being seen, a position I had begun to seek out more and more frequently, willing myself to appear even smaller than I already was. The incredible shrinking Hugo. Or so I liked to fantasise.

Without preamble Sinbad advanced on Tom the youngest and, taking up a bowl which lay on the table, he placed it upside down on the lad's head like a china skullcap and holding it in position proceeded to snip-snip away at the hair under the rim. Tom had his eyes tight shut all the while and I could see him grimacing, but he made not a sound. Neither did anyone else, for that matter: complete silence reigned in that crowded room save for the click of the clippers, Sinbad's hand clenching and unclenching as if squeezing an invisible rubber ball. The fine young hair fell to the floor, some of it clinging to the tea-towel, and we all of us watched in awe as though weighing each curling strand privately in our own heads. Every so often Sinbad would stop and stand back to evaluate as well as admire his work. Satisfied, he would then blow softly on the fine teeth of the clippers to dislodge any particles of hair before resuming his human topiary once more.

Where the clippers had travelled Tom's bare scalp gleamed snowy white, while his face grew steadily redder in colour. The whole business seemed to be about humiliation, but it was impossible for me to turn away. When the bowl came off Tom looked different, not the boy I knew and played with, but someone now sullen and brutish, a younger version of Junior, it struck me, and suddenly I felt afraid as though Sinbad was turning out a fresh battalion of enemies for me to contend with. And so he snipped his way right around that unresisting circle, his victims slinking off the instant he took the bowl away like dogs after a whipping. Junior boiled and glowered, his great swollen fists clenched in his lap ready for battle but he, too, suffered the full treatment in silence, his thick neck livid already with the track of the shears.

Finally the chairs stood empty, a drift of dead clippings lapping about their legs. Up to then I had always believed everyone else's hair to be much the same hue as my own – except for Junior's flaming crop – but here was such variety, auburn to pale gold to the bright orange of the very last customer to sit in the barber's chair.

Wishing to creep away as unobtrusively as possible, I hung on in my corner beside the dresser waiting for my moment, but no one else seemed ready to leave and Sinbad was still intent on blowing on his clippers as tenderly as on a dandelion clock. On a more appropriate occasion I would dearly have loved a closer look, for the whys and wherefores of how things worked were tremendously fascinating to me just then. Sinbad, too, had been most impressive, holding us all in the palm of his hand like that same little silver instrument he kept half hidden there. I couldn't help but think of the undertaker at my father's funeral and the clever tool he, too, had employed so expertly, and there and then it struck me the world might well be full of intricate gadgetry for me to get my own hands on when I grew bigger and old enough to acquire them for myself.

Deep in such pleasant thoughts, suddenly I heard Sinbad speak my name for all to hear,

'Wee Hugo.' And then a second time, soft and loving as the very breath he had been directing towards his precious clippers. Made In Germany, he always loved reminding people, for everyone to marvel at as if at something truly priceless. How innocent we all were then, how easily impressed, imaginations as tenderly receptive as a Solomon Islander's.

Looking back, I must have been remarkably stupid. No, so wrapped up in myself that at first I didn't realise what was happening until I saw that everyone in the kitchen was looking at little me. Me, Hugo, the near invisible, all-seeing one. Only I wasn't. Not any more. It had all been in my head. No one else's.

With a yell I made a dash for the door, but Junior was

already there blocking my escape, a recharged Junior, even more malevolent looking than usual with his brutal, new redskin haircut. I heard myself scream loudly as he took hold of me and brought me back struggling in his arms to the warm chair he had just vacated, Sinbad looking on all the while with an expression I had seen before on Uncle Harry's face that day in the potato-house.

Leaning close, he murmured, 'Be a man.'

And in that instant I hated him, all of them, the entire Dinsmore clan, men, women, children, even dogs. Uncle Harry included.

But then I felt myself go limp. It was like the most exhausted feeling I had ever experienced, all the fight draining out of me like water from a pot. Surprisingly, not all that unpleasant either, reminiscent of that other sensation, an intense relief after holding back a pee for a very long time and then letting it all go as if it would flow on for ever until nothing would be left of one but a puddle on the ground. In truth it might well have turned out exactly like that but thankfully didn't. Closing my eyes as one does at such times, I felt that first icy love-bite of steel lifting up the hair on the nape of my neck.

Now I've no intention of diluting the horror of that experience, for it was necessary to keep its memory intact in my head until it would be time for those responsible to pay for what they had done, not just Sinbad Scully, but all of them. Still, to be completely fair, it could have been worse. For a start, I was spared the indignity of the bowl, and Sinbad didn't just run the clippers blithely up my back and sides as if he were mowing grass as he had done with the others. Even with eyes closed I felt I detected a certain anxious care, even reticence, in his touch, as though he was trying to recapture certain skills he once had as a ship's barber. For, yes, that had been his official position on HMS *Resolve* before it went down in torpedo-infested waters, all those heads he'd barbered bobbing like apples in a barrel before going under for eternity. I like to tell myself I received much more the officer treatment, as opposed to the rough and ready near-scalping reserved for your ordinary rating, like those five able seamen he shared a lifeboat with. Yet none of that could reprieve him. When I opened my eyes once, and once only, in the middle of it all, and caught that glimpse of my crowning glory piling up in instalments on the floor, as far as Sinbad Scully was concerned, sentence was passed.

When it was over I was trembling, head light in all senses, while Sinbad continued fussing around, flicking my chill, naked neck with the tea-towel as if every one of those old tricks of the trade had come back to him. Giving a final flourish with the cloth he stepped back as though expecting a round of applause, even a palmed tip. He was happy and smiling. But, looking down, I took in the full extent of what he had done to me – mirrors would have to wait – for there, lying on top of those other strands of, let's be honest, more ordinary hair, were my own beautiful golden curls now only fit for the brush and dust-pan.

It is said mothers often weep the first time their child gets its hair cut. They mourn the passing of baby innocence and frequently retain a lock as a keepsake along with that first little silver-plated pair of bootees, but I had no one to grieve over me or shed a tiny tear for poor wee Hugo. I continued to sit there, but it was as if I had become invisible. Sinbad was laughing and joking with the uncles while the rest chatted and gossiped away as merrily as crickets. Even Junior was intent on other distractions, squeezing the freshly attractive neck of one of his young cousins in a corner where he wouldn't be seen.

Clambering down from my kitchen chair, suddenly it came to me I wasn't invisible after all. Rather, the truth was, I now looked just like everyone else. Whether this would turn out to be a good thing was still too early to tell. But I must say, in all honesty, that was an exceedingly low point in the life and times of little Samson Hugo Dinsmore.

Making my lonely way back through that maze of a house and avoiding mirrors like a pocket-sized Dracula, for I had made a vow to put the ultimate moment of truth off as far as possible, I detected this terrible smell creeping after me like an invisible fog. In the half-dark I stopped, head raised, nostrils aquiver, trying to identify what it might be. Truly, truly horrible, once smelt never forgotten, it had to be only one thing, the stench of burning hair.

So with that nasty reminder still in my nose, and a cold feeling about the back of my naked neck, I sought out my bed in a box for another night at Larkhill. Life had delivered one more surprise package to Hugo Dinsmore. But, then, growing up can be full of shocks to the system, even to someone who has never quite mastered the knack of getting much bigger himself.

That night my pillow seemed strange and somehow scratchy, but if the others felt the same they gave no sign. Junior snored like a sawmill as usual, and long after everyone else was asleep Hugo lay on his back staring up at the rafters counting invisible knotholes in place of sheep. Far out in the darkness a night-bird kept repeating its eerie call over and over and over, the sound seeming to echo his name. But, as he listened more intently, gradually it began to change to something else which, although still recognisable, appeared to carry a message meant for him and him alone.

You-Go, it counselled ever so softly. *You-Go*.

But where? Where could he go?

FIVE

One of the first things I ever encountered at Larkhill was a skinned rabbit carcass. It was hanging from a hook on the back of a scullery door, head down, hind legs looped together, a solitary, ruby-red drop trembling at its lowermost tip. So many other impressions were swamping me at the time I have to be forgiven for not recognising what it was straight away, but under its fur it seemed it had been something else entirely all along, something horrible, in places transparent, like a misshapen, pale, pink balloon. The head was there, legs, belly, torso, but this thing could never have been one of the dear little creatures romping in frozen play over my quilt, or their livelier relatives observed from an upstairs window.

Over the days ahead I was to witness that swift transformation from furry bunny to rubbery sac many times. I won't say I became hardened to it – how could I – even though it happened so fast, so effortlessly, a slit made near the base of the belly, then a straightforward unpeeling down all the way and over the head as easy as unrolling a sock.

Certainly the uncles made it seem that way, offering to let me try out my own skills, but always I declined, moving back into the shadows where I belonged. Junior, as expected, turned out to be a dab hand, even had his own trusty tool for the job, a black-handled, ex-army clasp-knife, heavy as a cosh, which he had saved up and sent away for to Enfield, England.

That was a great Dinsmore passion, by the way, mailing postal orders for military paraphernalia advertised in the back pages of a paper called *Thomson's Weekly*, usually accompanied by a postage stamp drawing of the item in question. Straps, ammunition pouches, gas-mask cases – anything made from webbing, anything – badges, bayonets, forage caps, water bottles, map cases, viewfinders, goggles, camping gear – once a mosquito net – their appetite for such things was insatiable. They had a particular enthusiasm for German ex-army equipment, as I recall. Certainly it seemed always of superior quality. Is it my imagination or did one of the uncles not wear an Afrika Korps cap complete with desert-flap all year round? Rab Rommel Dinsmore?

I have to say I became infected myself and burned to possess a small, lidded compass, its tiny, red-tipped arrow-head swinging about and pointing directly at our nearest neighbour's delightful, pale cream, stuccoed house. By another bizarre coincidence their name happened to be the same as our own although, as I was to find out, to my deep disappointment, there was no family connection. That's what I was told anyway, but for a long time I refused to believe it, harbouring instead this fantasy of a blood-line, if not directly linking the rest of them at Larkhill to the folks on the hill, then most definitely me, young master Hugo Dinsmore. Mouthing my name to myself a dozen times a day, its very ring had me convinced I must be connected to quality. Where else could it have come from? No one of sufficient imagination among the Larkhill crowd could ever have hit upon it by themselves. It just had to be an ancient ancestral name, probably handed down from generation to generation, lovingly. Crooning it softly, I linked it with its equally classy surname. Such a harmonious pairing.

Naturally the next step was to investigate a possible family resemblance, although having suffered at Sinbad Scully's hands the mirror told me I looked more like Moe of the Three Stooges these days than a dashing young Prince Valiant. All the boys did, and because of it would return from school with the marks of playground warfare on them. But that was still ahead of me, the taunts, the nicknaming, the random cruelties, and so I spent my days instead creeping about the fields and woods near The Mount, as it was known, hoping to catch a glimpse of my fabled relatives.

In a cropped field close to the big square house three young children roughly my age rode fat Shetland ponies at low hurdles in a sort of scaled-down, gymkhana setting. They wore round, velveteen riding hats resembling furry acorns and I could see from the hair escaping underneath that two were girls, with pale hair very much resembling my own, which made me tremble all over. But I was too far off to make out their features, too cowardly to creep closer. Instead their merry laughter made me feel depressed and abandoned for some reason, like a scarecrow lurking there at the back of a ditch.

But making my way home my spirits rose again – they always did – and, imagination quickening, I invented a tearful reunion with the folks on the hill. Amid all the emotion, the cries, hugs, moist kisses, I heard those truly wonderful words, *Your old room has been waiting for you all this time. We kept your little nursery night-light burning in the window just in case. My God, would you look here, if it isn't the long-lost, Mopsy and Flopsy family quilt! Well, if that isn't proof enough, I don't know what is, even though he is the spitting image of Great-Uncle Oswald. We never gave up on you, believe me, we never did, darling little Hugo . . .*

There was more, of course. I had been stolen by gypsies. I

77

had been abandoned in a far-off place by a jealous cousin. I had been replaced soon after birth by some other cuckoo in the nest. The fantasies stampeded through my head until I had to lie stretched like a starfish on the grass and their fury abated. High overhead, white clouds passed by in calming formation driven by an invisible breeze from the western Lough. I smelt the sexual reek of the earth, heard the hum of a distant tractor accompanied by a dog barking, felt the damp soak stealthily up through my coarse flannel shirt and itchy khaki shorts.

For, yes, along with the pudding basin haircut I, too, had been kitted out from the back pages with someone's cutdown, hand-me-down trousers. Some boy soldier, obviously. Maybe even killed in battle, for always there were those mysterious stains and tears on nearly everything that arrived from that exotic English postal address. The shirt-tunic bore pale patches across the shoulders and chest where badges and epaulettes had once been, and the fly buttons were thin brass stamped with eagles' wings. In some other life they may have covered the backside of someone airborne. Who knows, perhaps someone as dinky as myself, a pocket navigator, say, with his own little cockpit all to himself and bank of instruments twinkling away in the night sky like the lights on a Christmas tree.

Such were the fancies that kept me company on those solitary rambles away from Larkhill. While the others were at school having tables and spellings drummed into them I filled my head with dreams of a life denied me. A favourite haunt was the old fairy fort deep in the fields, a single, protected thorn bush growing up out of its grassy dome like a sprouting hank of hair. People were a lot more superstitious then and I had already heard enough stories about the wee folk and what they got up to after dark to make me a believer too. Cheek pressed to the earth, I would listen intently for signals from below, messages meant for my ears and mine alone, for

I was forever seeking connections with some world other than the one I had been forced into. Convinced I had only to be patient, the time must surely come for me to be called home. Foraging among the fox and badger dens that riddled the mound, sometimes I would thrust a bared arm deep into their dark mouths, half hoping for a tiny, hot, dry hand to take mine and gently draw me down to an underworld peopled by beings much the same size as myself. But the only life stirring there seemed to belong to those same poor creatures which kept ending up on our plates at suppertime.

'Have some more of this lovely stew, wee Hugo,' Junior would say. 'God, how the boy does love his grub. And all the size of him, too. See, here's a leg, or maybe it's a bit of haunch, all to your wee self,' and he would reach across, transferring a dripping morsel on to my already heaped plate.

Worst of all, he had the rest of them persuaded I was a glutton for their chocolate brown messes. That was our diet, with the occasional treat of a fowl blanched and boiled to ribbons, or the odd trout or eel taken from the river. Where I managed to acquire this picky feeling for my food I'll never know, but then again it did fit in quite neatly with the changeling theory. In dreams, after all, I dined off only the very best china and silverware, while feasting on the finest fare.

But dreams couldn't disguise the reality that kept staring back at me from the shard of looking-glass suspended over the mottled brown sink in the scullery. That was where we performed our ablutions, not on a regular or daily basis like normal people, but every so often and always perfunctorily, a cat's lick, at best. Still in an agony over the state of my hair I studied its worrying lack of growth while the others went about their business somewhere else, instinctively realising I must not be discovered at this, for life would be a lot more unbearable if I got a new name, that of Wee Hugo the Jinny, never too far away from a mirror. For, I admit it, yes, I was vain and preening. I was. Or rather, I had been, drawn towards the nearest reflection in much the same way as that little compass needle veered true north each and every time towards the big white house on the hill. In vain I kept looking for some sign of softening in that jailbird image staring back at me, secretly plastering my scalp with sugar and water, lard, butter, even grease from the tins in the outhouse. Slicked back DAs were still very much in vogue just then but, of course, I couldn't lay hands on whatever it was those Saturday night Lotharios used to achieve their permanently wet look, Brylcreem, as a preparation, about as decadent for the males at Larkhill as French perfume.

But there was another reason for my obsession with the way I looked. Bessie, by this time, had lost interest in me as a playmate. In her eyes, you see, I had become merely another coarse-looking boy with manners to match, no different from the rest of them. I saw it when she looked at me. Rather, didn't, for no matter what I did, I was now invisible as far as she was concerned. No more Happy Families, no more playing wee shops or hospitals with me as patient, no more private performances in the raw. The betrayal, the injustice of it consumed me. As a cruel but invaluable lesson it should have left its mark yet, looking back, I cannot say it has.

Not all that long ago she travelled here to visit me, the only one of the clan to do so. I must say I took no satisfaction from the sight of her, for she had run to fat, hair frizzed and chemically degraded. She had four young ones now, she told me. Her husband was a bus conductor. They lived on a council estate which had been built not far from the old Larkhill. By the by, that had gone, flattened to make way for the new bypass and roundabout.

We looked at one another across the scarred table-top and I wanted to tell her how she had been my first true love, bare skinny limbs and little punctuation mark and all, as exotic in its colouring as a fishing lure, but the moment passed.

As she was leaving she said, 'Why, Hugo, oh, why did you do it?' But then so many others have asked me the same thing and always with that implication of waste and wilfulness that I don't try to give an answer any more. With a sideways shrug I simply smile, consigning the question to the darkest, most unused part of my mind where it belongs. It's something that hasn't overly concerned me for a very long time.

After she'd gone I returned to lie stretched on my narrow bed. It's where I do most of my remembering. So conditioned am I to the position, images rise like breaking bubbles on the bottom of a boiling pot the instant I lie down. Dreaming my life away, as people used to say, before I became that little lightning ball, everyone's match, and nobody's fool.

Looking back I often think Wendy Carnduff of Lebanon Lodge may have been the first real hardening influence on my young life, giving that delicate baby skin of mine its first proper varnishing. Certainly she put me through my p's and q's all right, not content until I became a suitable match for her own inimitable style. Wendy, dear Wendy, the name itself so impressive with its icy tingle of class and superiority, I can see you now in your tapered trews and angora turtle-necks. The trews were a constant – Black Watch – but the woollens rotated, a different, sugared almond shade for each day of the week, smelling of Lux and rosewater just like every other delicate part of you, darling Wendy.

We came face to face one late afternoon for the first time out in the fields in rather a shocking fashion. At least I was – startled, that is – barefoot, in my dung-coloured hand-me-downs and felon haircut, mouth dropping open at the sight of this trim vision with the small dog in tow. She stopped and the dog, a snuffling Scotch terrier, Pepper by name, promptly raised a hind leg, directing a feeble, lemon-coloured arc of piss up against a tall thistle. Overcome by embarrassment at the dog's behaviour and my own appearance I stammered something about taking a shortcut. It was the impression she gave, you see, so cool, so assured, so born to command, that I took it for granted that the land must surely belong to her, or to her people, rather. She could only be from The Mount – where else – although her hair was a dark reddish brown: eyes, as well.

She looked at me coolly, then said, 'Just who are you?' It was that 'just' which was my undoing, for instead of lying, as my instincts urged me to, I answered truthfully.

'Hugo Dinsmore.' I heard myself say it.

Those eyes, hazel, changing to gunmetal right through to near coal-black, then back again, they fixed me as though pinning me to an invisible board. Even the dog, oh, a surly little cur I never could take to, regarded me as though sniffing a downright lie.

'You're one of the Dinsmores?'

'Yes,' I said again answering honestly, for it happened to be the truth, although each of us had our own interpretation of what the words suggested.

Then she said, 'I'm Wendy Carnduff of Lebanon Lodge. Do you know it?' I nodded, for, yes, I did, having begun to carry the neighbourhood in my head by now through dint of tramping until it started to resemble one of those maps on the inside of my story-book covers, dotted lines for track and path and feathery tufts warning the unwary of marsh and bog. My imagination was only ever fired by the finest, most hesitant print. Never the thicker, heavier details, rivers, roads, churches and such.

The way I saw it Lebanon Lodge would have this broken, delicate line like Morse code leading up to it while, encircling it, back and two sides, would be empty space stippled with little rush marks. A wriggle of palest blue would further map out a stream, which would then billow out into a pond. Ducks were never signified, but I could well imagine them. In reality I had seen the house from a distance several times. Rust-red brick, with four barley-sugar chimneys, very like the ones on the house from which I had been cast out, it even had its name like ours cut into the lintel. Now I knew what those hazy, chiselled capitals spelled out exactly. Not quite as grand as its title would suggest, or as my latest friend always implied, still it had the power to impress enormously.

'My father's a retired railway official. He's on a full pension. What does yours do?'

I stared at her. The two of them, dog and mistress, studied me as if everything depended on my answer. There were fleecy white clouds in the sky, I remember, drifting left to right, as clouds always seem to do in our particular part of the world, slow as a line of icebergs. Cumulus. I wondered if she was familiar with the term. Almost certainly.

'He's away at the moment,' I heard myself say. 'He travels a lot.'

And in that instant the bond between us became set. Strange to tell, sometimes firm friendships can be based on mutual deceit, and ours seemed to flourish with each fresh morsel of invention we kept stringing together like pearls along a thread. For myself, I have to say I never felt the slightest remorse about what I was doing and with such zest, too, as I soon discovered for, as I saw it, my proper father could well have been a permanent, roving absentee forever traipsing foreign parts. He could. Frankly he could have been just about anything I cared to invent.

From all of this it should be clear I was now pretty well reconciled to the fact that those two dear boobies who had so thoughtlessly gone and died on me leaving me in this situation could not have been my real parents. Certain sidelong hints and sly references I had managed to pick up in my new home, for my little ears were always pricked as a young leveret's, merely reinforced the matter. But for the moment I had no real desire to go delving into my past. With a maturity far beyond my years I decided I should be a lot better prepared when I was older for the possible shock of what I might find lurking there like an apparition behind a door. Far, far more of a thrill was to go hatching fresh identities with my latest friend.

As I think I've mentioned earlier, the capacity to tell tall tales came easily. Sinbad Scully would have been proud. And here I had a new teacher, well, more a willing co-conspirator than mentor. Just like Bessie, in fact, for I must never forget dear Bessie and her naked arabesques, even though she had turned that skinny, freckled back on me. Wendy Carnduff, on the other hand, was someone I could never possibly imagine with no clothes on. This may seem perverse, but it may actually have been because of the very garments themselves. Maybe, for the idea, as well as image, of those beautifully checked trews – it was she herself who introduced me to that rare and wonderful word – and those fragrant, fluffy sweaters, boleros, twin-sets in lemons, pinks, lilacs and baby-blue, divested, as it were, from the rest of her, would have been just too shocking for me to imagine in my innocence. Which leads me to a further confession. Placing certain women on pedestals has become rather a thing for me, I'm afraid, and Wendy Carnduff came about as high in my estimation as most, although she needed no real help from me, seeing herself already, as she did, pretty far up there anyway.

She had this look about her that said it all, unwavering, unsmiling. I never saw her face soften once, never heard her laugh or crack a joke, and I became her slave. For life, at the time, I did believe, but, of course, things change, *we* change, although I didn't realise then that I would be the one to move on, not her. She had a way of fastening her gaze on you, head moving from side to side like a bird looking for worms, little Pepper, as well, which made the ordeal worse.

Soon after we met, suddenly she took hold of both my hands out in the fields one day, turning them over and over. I practically stopped breathing from the shock of those soft and scented fingers touching mine. For what seemed a very long time she examined them in minutest detail.

'Quite fine,' she pronounced eventually. 'For a *boy*,' and I took comfort from the fact that they still retained some of that pampered sensitivity from the old days when they dabbled in nothing more harmful than toilet-soap suds.

'This is called vanishing cream,' she said, taking a small white jar from her pocket, although I hadn't noticed any bulge up to then. 'No, it doesn't make you invisible,' she continued, unscrewing the lid, then dabbing some on both my palms. 'Although it would be nice, I always think, if it did have that effect on certain people.'

That was the way she talked, that I found so entrancing. Like someone in a book. And the Pond's, too, smelt so delightful, a cooling balm, that I closed my eyes allowing her to rub it in.

'I put some on my skin every night before bed. That's why it stays so soft and girlish. Although I *am* a girl. Touch, if you like,' she said, guiding my fingers to trace the outline of her cheeks. Like silk, or warmed bone china, to a blind person. Which I imagined I was just then.

'There's nothing wrong with a man having nice eyes and skin. You're quite lucky in both respects. I noticed it the first time we met. You're not like most other boys your age, are you?' And her head would go sideways in that birdlike way, those dark, shiny eyes of hers not missing an iota. And then out it came. *Oh-oh.*

'Quite small for your age, wouldn't you say?'

But, no, I wouldn't, wearied as I was of people making judgements, comparisons, mental measurements, based on one thing. Yet I will say this in her favour, she never referred to it again. Never. Just as I, in turn, refrained from mentioning the steel on her leg.

When first we encountered one another in the middle of that field that day with no possibility of retreat – she remained standing, while I advanced on her – I thought I detected a gleam of metal down one side of her shoe. Like a stirrup, almost, which I suppose it was, cradling the instep. As I have said, it was never brought up but, while taking care not to stare, it did rather fascinate me secretly, visualising the shape and mechanics of it under the trews. Of course it never did strike me that was the reason she always wore them. I know it must seem so obvious, but to my eyes they appeared so elegant, so beautifully cut, narrowing to perfect turn-ups, I couldn't imagine anyone ever wishing to put on anything else.

So enraptured did I become that I no longer noticed the glimpse of caliper, or the slight list to her gait, little hesitations at every other step. Tiny intakes of breath, it always reminded me of – that's if a leg could breathe. In no time at all I was walking in almost identical fashion, no mockery intended, the two of us moving across the grass in harmony, talking ten to the dozen, for it wasn't long before she had me as bad as herself, spinning yarns like a pair of old bar-room bores. Not that boredom ever entered it, certainly not for me it didn't. She had a habit of fixing one with those bright, burning eyes of hers before coming out with the unexpected.

'Can you sing?' she said one day as we traversed a wide pasture towards a gate which, like the little gentleman, I always opened and held wide for her. '*I* can,' launching into 'Jesus Wants Me for a Sunbeam'.

Her voice was unsteady, not as thrilling or sweet as I would have expected. She sang the piece in its entirety, choruses and all, and for the first time I felt embarrassed, critical, also, which was something new.

When she'd finished she said, 'Your turn now,' and I felt a terrific rush of blood to the face, ears especially, which felt like two swollen beets.

'I can't,' I told her.

'Don't be daft, *everyone* can sing. Try.'

By this time we had reached the iron gate and I put my hand on the bolt meaning to slide it to the side in the hope of distracting her, but she leant her weight hard against the rusted bars, preventing me.

'If there's one thing I cannot abide it's a Weary Willie,' she said.

So, fixing my gaze on a tree in the middle of the far field – it had a Union Jack flying from its topmost branch, so it must have been the month of July – I made a stab at the only song whose words I knew. Well, to be truthful, I didn't know I knew, but it happened to be the one Uncle Harry would sing off in the woods by himself between flute solos. Out it poured as if in a perfect parody from a stranger's lips, the words double-Dutch, as far as I was concerned, almost as mystifying as what a Weary Willie might be when it was at home. But the sound, oh, the sound. The notes seemed to fly like birds from an opened cage – my mouth, to be precise – although all had a shape and personality, as well as colour of their own. Yet it was as if I had them totally under control, directing them every which way I pleased, that's if I had a wish to do so. But, of course, I hadn't, so thrilled was I just to allow them their freedom.

Now if some of this sounds a little on the lofty side, it's not every day one discovers a God-given gift in oneself by purest accident in the middle of somebody's hayfield. Standing there on the already dampening grass, for it was about seven in the evening when Wendy liked to take Pepper out for his 'numbers', I listened to the silence following that last, drawn-out, thrilling note, as if a great shout had gone up, and then there was this hole in the air because of it. *Dear God*, I remember thinking, *the entire world has been listening to me. To me!* My singing had stopped everything in its tracks.

'You see?' Wendy said, with that rapid blackbird cocking of the head which I fought so hard not to imitate. To walk as she did was dangerous enough, but to start mimicking that twitch of hers as well might look a little like out and out mockery.

'With hard work and dedication you could be nearly as good as me. I do scales every day, of course, as well as piano practice. You do know what scales are, don't you?' And she climbed her way up through doh, ray, me, fah, soh, la, te, doh, in that less than perfect soprano of hers, ending, I'm sorry to say, on a high note that made my teeth ache.

But already I knew I would have no need for scales, or practice either. All I had to do was open my mouth and let the flock of notes fly, blessed as I was with perfect pitch and an ear that could hold a tune after a solitary hearing. So excited was I by all of this I could hardly wait to be off on my own to try out my next party piece. And it would be 'If I Were a Blackbird', for that was the other air Uncle Harry would sing after he had played it through on the flute. But Wendy had ideas of her own.

'Let's go to our secret place before it gets dark,' she commanded and so we set off.

Now why she felt drawn to this particular spot instead of all the others I could never understand, but I went with her none the less, the three of us navigating a couple of fields to where the solitary electricity pylon reared up out of its overgrown patch of no man's land like some ugly piece of giant Meccano. For, yes, it was forbidding, disturbing, too, in a way, with that constant low hum that kept the birds away. In a triangular, dead zone of rank grass and nettle, for no one ever took a scythe to the place, it squatted on four splayed, iron legs. In my head I had this fanciful notion they stretched down, down to the very hot heart of the earth itself which was where the power must come from. On a calm day you could hear it singing away to itself and, sometimes, first thing in the morning, even as far away as Larkhill, I would awaken to that distant drone like a low ringing in the ears.

'Now help me over like a nice boy,' Wendy would say on reaching the fence that was there to keep the animals out. Pepper, the dog, always found his own way, nosing into a tunnel of his own making in the long grass.

On the far side a track had been beaten right up to the metal structure itself, my handiwork, for always I was sent ahead to prepare the way for her ladyship, for she could be very demanding, refusing to budge until a flattened den had been freshly tramped for her in the grass. When it was to her liking, then and only then would she set herself down, arranging herself as though for a picnic and I would take up my position close by. As a matter of fact I do recall she may sometimes have brought along lemonade, and the two of us would sit there supping in silence in the fretworked shadow of that great thrumming, metal tower.

'Do you know why I like it here so much?' she said one evening as we sat ringed in by our ramparts of dock and bindweed. It was the very question which had been trembling on my lips for a long time, except I could never get up the courage to come out with it.

A few feet away a giant, rust-mottled stanchion reared up, diminishing as it climbed to where the wires carried the invisible electricity. That was what they did, I knew that, but neither of us was too interested in exploring the phenomenon further, our concerns rarely venturing above ground level inside our snug, grassy cockpit where Wendy talked and I listened.

'It's because no one would ever dream of looking for us

here, that's why. We could be dead for ever and no one would ever find the two of us. Wouldn't that be wonderful? Wouldn't they just be sorry for all the things they ever said about us?'

And then she ran through that roll-call of people she hated and who hated her in return, she said, enemies who one day would live to regret they ever talked about her behind her back the way she just knew they did.

It was the thing on her leg, really, she was referring to, not herself, for in anyone's eyes, but especially mine, she was a walking vision in her angora and tartan, even with that halting gait of hers. But she would never say it. Never. And I, of course, wouldn't dream of even hinting at what lay hidden under the green and black plaid. Even now as the dropping sun caught the gleam of burnished metal on her left instep I kept my gaze fiercely fixed on the pylon just feet away.

The list of enemies ran as follows. The postman who hated her on account of Pepper, that awful old Reverend Gillespie, always going on about the lame man in the Bible and staring at her every time the text came up, certain giggling, mindless girls in the church choir, a woman who did housework for them, her husband, who cut the hedges, a doctor who had once examined her with hands like two wet haddock, assorted shopkeepers and tradesmen in the nearby town, her aunt, uncle and fat cousin Roberta, three of the nosiest people alive. And, oh, that dreadful Elvis Presley person, even though she had never met him or had any desire to. Somehow I got the impression, I don't know why, her father and mother were on the list as well, although never mentioned by name.

Sometimes she would encourage me to scroll through my own personal list as well, and pretty soon I was reeling off names with as much gusto as herself.

'Yes, I know old Matt Scully all right,' she would say with

a bitter laugh. 'Who doesn't? Creeping about the countryside in the dead of night spying on people,' and suddenly the air seemed to turn chill and the hum in the overhead wires faltered as I thought of him out there knowing our secret place, and maybe what we talked about as well. But most times we became so excited with the idea of revenge and what form it should take we just sat there throbbing in harmony.

'Boiling in oil would be too good for them,' Wendy would say, although privately I felt that might be pretty hard to trump.

But there were also times, too, when her mood would change with a speed that terrified me sitting slavishly there by her side. Tears would flow and she would cry, 'Everyone hates me! Why?'

'*I* don't,' I would say, and she might perk up at that, looking at me through wet lashes.

'You're my only friend. You and darling Pepper here. You'd do anything for me, you would, wouldn't you?'

And I would answer, *yes, yes, of course, anything*, for I meant it with all my heart.

But one day she carried things a great deal further and I sat there numbed as I heard her say, 'Climb up there for me. All the way,' pointing to the pylon, 'if you're really my friend.'

For a moment I allowed my mind to go blank, lifting myself up and away as if on a magic carpet. I did that sometimes, like the boy in *The Arabian Nights*, riding out over our own green fields and hills instead of the turrets of old Baghdad.

But, drawing me down to earth, Wendy said, 'Please', a word I had never heard her use before.

'But why?' I said, feeling my life start ebbing away.

She looked at me with the utmost pity. 'Because *I* can't, that's why.'

'But it's dangerous,' I told her, hating the whine in my voice. 'I might get electrocuted,' that last word coming out like a betrayal as if I had been secretly hoarding it all along, a word I shouldn't even have known, let alone been able to pronounce.

'Oh, don't be such a cowardy custard,' she snorted, getting to her feet with a sort of sideways motion.

Never had she looked so entrancing standing there with me looking up at her like that, two little mysterious points pushing out the soft angora of her lemon-coloured sweater.

'I'll prove it,' she said.

And then she did the most amazing thing for, rolling up one trouser-leg, she thrust her bared shin against one of the supports. Metal on metal, I heard the sound it made, and kept waiting for a flash and a scream for, despite all that knowledge gleaned from *Arthur Mee's Children's Encyclopaedia*, I still had a superstitious dread of that great malevolent thing, always making sure I kept a safe distance from it. It also happened to be the very first time I got a proper look at the rod attached to her foot and so, in my mind, there was a certain distraction.

'Well?' she demanded, stepping back and swiftly rolling down her trouser-leg once more.

Bent over, she presented this lovely little bottom as though for approval, feminine perfection in two sweetly rounded halves.

'Are you my friend or are you not?'

We looked at one another. Then I looked up at what she was expecting me to climb. Narrowing as it rose to pierce the heavens, it held out two immense arms like outstretched wings, clenching in their claws the great cables that went loping and looping across the countryside from our pylon to the next, on, on, in a straight line as far as the eye could see.

'Well?'

But I was thinking: *Do I honestly care if I die or not? Perishing in a shower of sparks, or simply falling like a stone out of the sky, or perhaps both? What is more important, displeasing Wendy Carnduff, or risk killing myself?*

God help me in my state of crazed idolatry, but didn't I choose the second.

The first part of the ascent was nerve-racking, stretching upwards, then sideways, then up again to where the next two sections criss-crossed. But then, to my delight and amazement, it seemed to get easier and easier, my hands and feet conspiring almost instinctively to clutch and plant themselves with ease. Suddenly a foothold would be in front of me as if waiting there all along, most amazing of all, offering itself. In an instant of clarity it came to me the structure, the *thing*, wasn't an enemy, but my friend and, hugging it as one does a friend, I knew it was impossible for me to fall. The truth was it wouldn't allow me to.

Faster and faster I travelled upwards now, the air growing colder as I climbed, blowing on my face and hands, seeking out every part of me under my shirt and shorts. Those I felt now to be an encumbrance restricting me, for *Look at me, everyone!* I wanted to cry out. *Look at me and my amazingly perfect physique!* Like that man in the bathing-trunks with his promise of a body just like his in five easy steps if you sent off to his address in America somewhere. Mr Charles Atlas, with the world on your shoulders, I bet even you couldn't climb like this. *I bet no one could*, I wanted to crow, for everyone to hear down there in that world far below, the one I had climbed right out of as though through a trapdoor like Jack and the Beanstalk. And I wondered if I would be able to see the sea, the one Sinbad Scully had talked so much about and so, with this little eye, I followed the looping miles of cable as it marched eastward, for someone once told me that was where the power station was situated, facing out to Scotland.

Oh, but it was simply splendid the view from my iron

lookout tower, everything spread out for my inspection as on a great dish. Valleys, fields and hills, rivers and streams. Buildings, too. The church, manse and school – all in a cluster – the old ruined bleachworks with its race and dam, Lyle's pub, the post office at the Cross, labourers' cottages laid out in neat rows like dominoes, gardens front and rear, The Mount, too, the sun turning its greenhouses to mirrors. And, yes, Lebanon Lodge, and there in the hollow Larkhill itself. Good grief, there was even one of the uncles out in the yard with his head under our pump!

I couldn't begin to describe the excitement I felt, master of all I surveyed, and so I started to sing, for it seemed the natural thing to do. Lodged between two of the metal struts, I heard the big china insulators humming away above my head. They, too, had their own tune and we warbled along together in a sort of harmony, although I had words and they had not. And all the while I kept devouring the landscape and its wonders with my eyes as if I had been starved for a lifetime and might never get the chance of a feast like this again.

But in the middle of it all I heard Wendy's voice calling out to me for the first time, although she might well have been shouting all along for all I knew, so enamoured was I with my bird's-eye slant on things. 'What do you see?' she cried and the little dog barked along with her as if he, too, was curious.

'Everything!' I called down. 'Oh, everything!' feeling sorry for the pair of them, so diminished looking far below, two dots on the grass.

Then I heard her cry, 'You'll fall and kill yourself!' but I only laughed at her, knowing what she had no way of knowing, that I was as safe as in my own bed at home.

'Very well, then, see if I care!' came her voice soaring angrily and I just knew she intended to be hurtful and braced myself accordingly despite the distance separating us. And, sure enough, out it all came as if it had been there all along like a boil waiting to burst.

'I don't know why I ever bothered with you in the first place! Anyone could tell by looking at you you're not a proper Dinsmore! You're nothing but a wee corner-boy! Riff-raff! And, for your information, you'll never amount to anything else, for it's just not in you!'

After that she went limping off with much more of a roll than usual, it seemed. That's how it appeared, anyway, up there, looking down from a great height, but then maybe I hadn't really noticed it so much before below on the ground.

So I watched Wendy Carnduff and her little dog Pepper, who had never really liked me, walk off together out of my life and into the sunset, as they say in the movies. At least they were united now in despising me. At that point I didn't really know what or how I felt: badly, or nothing much of anything, really. Just what exactly was 'a wee corner-boy' seemed to be of far more import. Riff-raff I knew about, or could guess at. The very sound of the word – or was it words? – half explained itself. Rough, coarse, unwashed, shiftless, with ugly haircuts and clothes to match – but 'corner-boy'? The 'wee' part was an irritant I had long learned to live with, a bit like Wendy and her bad leg, I imagined. Corner-boy, I puzzled. Someone who spent their time huddled and hiding and peering around corners, perhaps? Devious, nervous and sly and small enough to get away with observing without being observed?

It was something of a shock to realise that someone had seen right through me, and quite so easily at that. Then I thought, I'm as good as Wendy Carnduff any day of the week, for even if I would always be the same Wee Hugo, she would always be what people called a cripple. The word, of course, was a horrible one – it had a sort of bitter taste to it, like alum or vinegar – and was also one I would never use to her face, let alone say behind her back, but she had gone and said some pretty terrible things to and about me. And that old father of hers was never someone high up on the railway, not in a million years, as she said he was, but had only been a porter, and that house they lived in never belonged to them either, but was only rented out from Alastair Dinsmore of The Mount.

Brain seething with all sorts of satisfying recriminations, by the time I had climbed all the way back down, landing on the trampled grass at the bottom, believe it or not I felt almost proud to be one of that awful Larkhill Dinsmore clan with their oafish, riff-raff ways. I did, I have to admit I really did, and off I went whistling like someone looking forward to a warm welcome home.

But, alas, as at so many other times in my career, the mood wasn't allowed to take hold. Someone, it seemed, had spotted me from the house, high on Electricity Board property, and so, instead of returning to the open arms of a family welcome, I received the first proper and sustained hiding of my young life, the uncle who had been washing himself under the pump deputed to wield the mighty webbing belt out in the potato-house while Junior and the gang watched the sport through the open door.

SIX

So Larkhill is no more. Obliterated, they tell me. Stone, brick, old mortar spread thin over some landfill site somewhere. Or poured into a quarry hole. The Kilcarn Roundabout, as it's now called, with its bloodshot pink sodium lights and Kill Your Speed signs, is what has taken its place on that map I still carry around in my head like one of those varnished, brown, schoolroom relics. On two wooden rollers. You know the sort. Whatever happened to Bohemia? Silesia? Moravia? Or Larkhill?

But just now and again I like to visualise an ancient piece of wall somewhere, intact still, distempered pale green and flaking, with certain faint, ruled, horizontal lines and what appear to be initials attached. The topmost one is J.D. – there are quite a few of those – and way below, my own. But whilst all the others have managed to climb that extra inch or so, H.D. seems to have stayed stubbornly where it is.

It was Junior's idea to keep a record of our heights on the wall of that scullery where murdered rabbits dripped silently. And very precise he was, too, lining up the stump of pencil level with the crown of our heads, then running the lath he used as a ruler through the mark made on the wall. Me, he always saved to the last, like a treat to be savoured.

'Your turn, wee fucker,' he'd say as, full of nerves, I'd approach the damp, scaly plaster.

'Both feet flat on the floor now.' Pushing me hard till the bump on the back of my skull connected with the wall.

Eyes closed and praying for a miraculous elevation, each time I would hear the same depressing verdict. 'Hard cheese, wee fucker. Shite, I do believe you're getting wee'er.'

One day I will never forget, Bessie, bless her, peered closely at the line he had just drawn.

'I think he *has* grown this time,' she announced. 'I do. Really. Look, everyone.'

But, throwing her down on a pile of old coats, Junior thrust a great red paw between her bare legs, while she bit and clawed, and we watched, feeling this layer of clammy sweat creep over us like a second skin. I know I did, along with that combination of guilt and arousal which was to become such a familiar accompaniment from then on.

'Who's for a sniff, then?' invited Junior, waving a middle finger at us while we backed away as if from something infectious.

Such incidents, some would say, have a formative – in certain cases, even damaging – effect on one, so if it's true, then I lay my curse on you, Junior Dinsmore, wherever you may be. A fear of the unknowable, something dangerous and threatening about the opposite sex may well have been planted there in those dark outhouses or lonely places in field and wood.

Much, oh, much later, I came upon Junior and Bessie one day in the open together up near the fairy fort and my confused state about the whole business took a further, worrying lurch forward. She was older then, we all were, but

98

unlike the rest of us she had blossomed into someone disturbingly grown up. In all those places now bursting through her still girlish clothes she seemed to have put on weight, she smelt differently, not a bit like the time I convinced myself her freckled flesh had the scent of trees after rain, she walked, talked, even smiled in an unfamiliar manner. And, with that knowing grin of his, Junior would refer to something unspeakable laying a curse on her at a particular time of the month, like a visit from a vampire, making her snappy and vicious. Hadn't we noticed?

That summer afternoon I came upon the pair of them on the far slope of the old rath, Junior once again was lying on top of his cousin. By this time I had started to lose much of my fear of him and what he might do to me and would bravely have championed Bessie even if it meant a beating. Prince Valiant still lived, even if he had grown wiser and more cautious. But something made me crouch low and spy on them instead of charging to the rescue. For one thing the damsel didn't appear to be struggling much, if at all, bare arms and legs spread compliantly as if lying in her bed back home with that old, slithery, salmon pink eiderdown on top instead of Junior. His trousers, incidentally, were concerti-naed around his ankles. The other unsettling thing was she wasn't crying out or making a sound of any sort.

But just as I was ready to race up the slope to the rescue like the true little knight errant, didn't I hear these muffled moans coming from her faster and faster the more Junior worked his bare backside, for, as if my poor brain could take in any more imponderables, how about that great snowy arse of his thrusting away like a piston-engine in overdrive?

When I think back on it, how could I *not* have made the connection between what I was witnessing and what took place in the farmyard on an almost daily basis? How many times hadn't I seen the bull labouring away, in much the same manner, on a heifer, or the boar, or Ussher Greer's great stallion, or the rooster, or the drake? For that matter, those dear little bunny rabbits out in the fields? And always the same dreamily docile state in the one being serviced. But then how could I possibly come to terms with the devastating image of Bessie having that great, engorged carrot of a thing pushed into her and her not objecting to it? And all for a single cigarette, too, because when he'd rolled off, hitching up his infantry pants, didn't Junior hand her one, and didn't she take it from him as casually as a square of Spearmint.

The business with the cigarette may well have signalled the end for me of Bessie's innocence. Mine, also, for I took up smoking a little later despite all the jokes about it stunting my growth et cetera, being persuaded that had to be the surefire way of getting girls to lie down for you. Just what to do when the tremendous moment arrived, I wasn't so sure of, even though the bull and the boar seemed to manage it as easy as slipping a finger in a glove. So I puffed away at the odd Woodbine which I managed to lay hands on, never thinking that an extra one might be needed at the point of surrender. Nicotine and the mechanics of the act had somehow become fused together in my mind, and as I studied the latest coupling in the fields or in the yard, a skinny fag between my lips, lower down my own modest prong would swell in harmony with the bull's mighty dripping weapon.

But then I had ample time on my hands to pursue my researches, for here I have to explain something about my schooling. Lack of it, rather. For although I had long passed the age for attending the place, no one ever insisted I go there. It was as if they had forgotten all about me, or didn't know my real age, or, perhaps, in their eyes, I was this perpetual infant, a bit like the baby Jesus, say, for in all the pictures I had seen of Him He was always the same, ballock naked on His mother's knee, little willy the size of a monkey-nut. Mine, on the other hand, already had a ruff of darkish down and could stand to attention without being ordered to do so. Even then, you see, I was anticipating all those happy hours of pleasure it was to provide for me.

But, of course, there came the time when I had to go to school with the rest of them. It was inevitable and natural and I found myself in a class where everyone towered above me, even the girls, but where I also happened to be the oldest, all of which I didn't find natural in the least. Sitting next door beyond the glass-topped partition with those they called the Infants the same size as myself, seemed to be a far more civilised arrangement, but no one else appeared to see it that way.

My teacher was a Miss Herron, Miss Meta Herron, and when I saw her for the first time I wondered if I was the only one to notice how apposite her name was, for she had these long, pipe-cleaner legs sheathed in beige-coloured lisle, while her head was kept cocked semi-permanently sideways as if on the lookout for something to spear with that great bony neb of hers. She wore rimless spectacles which she was forever polishing with a tiny, lace-edged hanky delicately looped through her watch-strap. I remember thinking at the time that had to be the very acme of elegance, that little wisp of femininity so daintily trapped there. But then what did *I* know? And, before I leave the subject, she always smelt of essence of violets.

'Well, Hugo,' she said eyeing me up that first day, 'I sincerely hope you're not going to turn out to be a chip off the family block. I've had four Dinsmores in this class at one time or another and all, without exception, have given me nothing but heartache. I must say you don't look the tiniest bit like any of them, so that may be a good sign. Do you know your ABCs? Your multiplication tables? Ah, well,' she sighed, 'I suppose that's just a little too much to expect.'

Head lowered to the lid of the desk in front of me, I concentrated on the initials carved there, while the rest of the class, those great overgrown gawks from the labourers' cottages, stared open-mouthed.

'Well?'

But I refused to provide an answer to such a question. Of course I knew the alphabet, for heaven's sake! Already I could read better than the rest of that lot at Larkhill put together, and in my head do long division, decimals, not to mention a smattering of algebra. Sarcastic, insensitive, plain woman, already I despised her.

'So,' she said, 'it seems we have a dummy in the class as well as a . . .' hesitating over *that* word, the one I would never allow myself to utter in case of scalding my tongue, even though, dear knows, I'd heard it enough times from others' lips.

But the damage had been done, and from that point on undiluted hatred coloured everything I did for her. Which was the bare minimum to ease me through each day in her class. I made a vow to never give her the satisfaction of either punishing or rewarding me, and so I set myself to seek out her weaknesses. Presiding up there behind her tidy table with those little treasures of hers spread in front of her like a line of defence against the rest of us hemmed in by the scaly, metal legs of our baby desks, she may well have imagined she had all the advantages and none of the shortcomings, but she had made a grave error in underestimating Hugo Dinsmore. *Master Hugo Dinsmore*, if you don't mind. Which brings me to another thing, for when Miss Meta Herron of Belmont, as she was always so fond of reminding us – as if it was somewhere in the Home Counties, for God's sake, and not some dreary Belfast outer suburb – when she disparaged my relatives in that way I felt the stirring of something which I never would have believed possible. Without realising it I had become infected with clan loyalty. Insulting the family name meant she was insulting *me*.

I have to say it was a shocking revelation, yet inspirational, too. There we were out at Larkhill living in the way that we did as if behind a moat or a high wall – well, we were, we were – different from other people, not merely because of our haircuts and khaki uniforms, but also because we smelt. Yes, we did. Other children refused to sit beside us in a double desk because of it and so, almost by necessity, we banded together. For the very first time that sense of being a loner, little Mister One-Off, began loosening its hold over me.

At lunch break, for instance, instead of munching my bread and jam sandwich somewhere off by myself, as I imagined I would be doing, I found myself gravitating towards our little tribe. Bessie was there and Junior and the rest of the crew and I slid up and joined them, drawn magnetically to the strongest force in the playground. Which was Junior Dinsmore, for he radiated the same malevolent energy away from home as he did at Larkhill, that cropped, burning, bullet head of his standing out like a warning beacon to anyone who might consider tangling with him.

On occasions he would parade provocatively about the cindered expanse, while we stayed close to him. Like being swung along on the tail of some slow-moving, yet deadly red comet, I liked to fantasise. Or, at other times, we would be his own personal wolf-pack with me the puniest cub tagging along. He ignored me completely, of course – nothing new in that – but then he ignored all of us, and so I began to feel as if I was a proper Dinsmore at last, not one of those namby-pamby pony riders who all went to some posh private school anyway, but just another of those roughs from that damp dump in the hollow where no one ever did a hand's turn except what he wanted to do and where we all lived like heathen savages, as someone once described us.

That may well have been old Principal Mooney, by the way. Certainly it sounds like him, for it was just the sort of thing he would say. A chalky-fingered, bald brute in a speckled tweed suit smelling of sweat, pencil parings and rancid hair oil, he held his tongue in check for no man. Two classrooms further up, along the length of Kilcarn Public Elementary School, we heard the swish of his cane, or the dreaded ebony pointer detonating on some unfortunate's skull and from day one, don't ask me why, I just knew Junior was his favoured target, even though he never cried out, swore, or ever complained to the rest of us once. All those scars on his scalp like tiny, pale, tick marks where the fuzz refused to grow, I convinced myself now, I knew where they had come from.

Once, I remember, as he stalked the playground looking for aggravation, the rest of us trailing in his wake trying to appear equally threatening, I caught a glimpse of old Mooney watching from one of the high, arched windows. That look aimed in our direction gave me the shivers, meaning only one thing as far as I was concerned. We were being measured up for future treatment as a family package, commencing the day we moved up into that senior class of his.

As I say, Mooney's tongue was almost as deadly as his favourite, hook-handled cane, the tip frayed like an old toothbrush. Even the minister took on this awful, cringing aspect when he came to put us through our catechism. Master Mooney would be drifting about the back of the classroom humming almost absentmindedly to himself, making the short hairs on our necks bristle, while the Reverend Gillespie would be stuttering on about Man's chief end being to glorify God or some such drivel. Poor, pathetic creature, he was to do himself in some years later over that sexual affair involving those Boys' Brigade campers. Drowned down a well, of all places. To do it like that took some guts, you could say, or a degree of despair hard for the rest of us to comprehend. Upside down like a human cork. Often it struck me there might well be some biblical precedent. Away off out in those desert wastes by yourself, after all, if the urge came upon one, what else was there but find a deep hole somewhere, with or without water at the bottom. Poor Eric Gillespie . . .

But any familiarity with the Scriptures I might have had was as a blank page. Old Baldy Mooney may well have been right about one thing when he called us heathens for, as far as I recall, none of us at Larkhill ever darkened a church door. Sundays were spent worshipping the god of combustion engines which no longer ran, or sending ferrets down rabbit holes, or taking trout from someone's stream while they worshipped unawares in Kilcarn Presbyterian church. It was as if there were this little pocket of godlessness ringed all around by piety and we were in it. As the sound of hymn-singing wafted towards us – it travelled on the still air like the wireless – unwashed and deliciously unkempt, we would go about our lazy pursuits much as usual. Uncle Harry would be off up among the trees somewhere with his flute, and if I wasn't there, too, flat on my belly, luxuriating in those bubbling arpeggios, I might sometimes accompany the distant church singers, a little choir of one, the only lark at Larkhill, for by now I found it well nigh impossible not to chime in with any tune as soon as I'd heard it. Even halfway through I couldn't help myself and, in school, despite my vow to get through the day with the least amount of application or attention, when singing lessons came round my resistance would crumble.

Most of the pieces Miss Herron taught us were like herself, sentimental and second-rate, for beneath that chill and beaky exterior she had this other side which I quickly homed in on.

For me nothing exemplified it more than the row of tiny, spun glass animals she kept ranged along the front of her desk. Oh, the purest kitsch imaginable. How my stomach would churn when some suck in the class, usually a girl, but occasionally a sissyish boy, would plead, 'Oh, tell us again about how you got your lovely wee seahorse, Miss Herron,' and then this look of utter skittishness would transform that old bitch's features.

'Well, if you're sure you're really all that interested, I suppose I could just tell you the story. Although, dear knows, you've heard it a hundred times or more,' she would simper, patting her bun.

Just try and stop me, I felt like saying, as she launched yet again into the account of her one and only trip across the water with her dear good friend Winnie Maxwell. The pair of them strolling along the front at Blackpool, for all the world like a couple of toffs, she would giggle. The longest promenade in the whole of Great Britain, would you believe! My beloved blue and gold *Children's Encyclopaedia* told a different story. Llandudno held that record. But, of course, how could I contradict her, no matter how I longed to do so? By this time I'd begun to notice, you see, how people's eyes would sharpen in on you if ever you happened to let slip some morsel of lore or information you weren't supposed to know about. No one liked a show-off, I'd discovered, even though, deep inside, was this secret raging exhibitionist, or would have been, given half a chance. The singing was another matter. There I could indulge myself to my heart's content, for everyone, it seemed, tolerated a boy soprano, even one with a convict haircut.

But, getting back to the glass menagerie, it was the first thing we saw when we looked up from our jotters, this miniature, petrified queue heading to, or maybe from, some invisible Noah's Ark, although there was no duplication. According to Miss Herron each animal was unique and individual and had a story behind it which we had re-told to us to the point of nausea. A sort of rage used also to seize hold of me at the rest of the class for pretending such utter fascination each time we heard about the giraffe from Newcastle, the elephant from Cushendall, the Bundoran hippo, the Portrush zebra, the Omeath tiger. God Almighty, was there nothing these two grown women ever got up to on their holidays by the seaside save trawl gift-shops bagging ornamental small game!

Her friend, the exceptionally stout Winnie Maxwell, for we had seen photographs of the two on safari, only collected cats and dogs. Early on they had agreed to specialise in different areas of the animal kingdom, untamed and domestic, so as to make the chase more an adventure. After all, Miss Herron would confide with a strange, sideways smile, they didn't want to ever fall out, now, did they? My imagination, being what it was, came up with a very different image of the pair, developing in my head like a negative in the dark, Mistress Beefy and Mistress Bony secretly loathing one another, the one eating herself into an early grave, and the other never putting on an ounce, while continually trumpeting the fact. Two sorry figures endlessly promenading on a wet fortnight together around the tail-end of every July.

But, as I may have mentioned, I didn't seem to possess a lot in the way of compassion in my make-up then. Quick imagination in abundance, certainly, but not much sympathy of any kind. But, then, again, why should I? And so, inevitably, my mind turned more and more towards reprisal every time the skinny one let slip yet another remark about 'those dreadful Dinsmores'. While busy with my crayons and Plasticine — a further humiliation for someone like me — I plotted away, inevitably fastening on the orderly little caravan marching head-to-tail along her table. Concentrating all my powers of spite, I willed one of them, *oh, just one*, to topple, for they appeared so fragile, so vulnerable, their tiny carcasses as see-through as a Glacier Mint. But by some mental force much greater than mine Miss Herron always managed to keep them anchored safely in front of her as though glued there.

Only one other person in the class was allowed to touch or go near them. This was a thin, intense girl with glasses and pigtails named Betty Cairns. She looked, in fact, like a younger version of the teacher, even acted like her, too, and so was entrusted to dust and polish each individual figure in the collection with a soft, yellow cloth kept in the drawer expressly for the purpose.

Stoking up the fires of revenge, I watched her at her work, pretending to be absorbed in colouring in a house or a tree or rolling a worm of Plasticine between palm and desk-top, something I loathed, the oily touch and smell of the stuff lingering until I could get to the outside tap and wash it away. So I watched and waited like a cat at a mousehole for the right moment to arrive and, strange to relate, it was indeed that very creature which was to give me my opportunity.

One afternoon while we were printing out the alphabet in our pale blue Vere Foster jotters – you may imagine how frustrating this was for someone already secretly halfway through *The Dog Crusoe* – suddenly one of the girls at the back of the class shrieked, pointing towards part of the wood panelling lining the walls.

'A rat!' she cried out. 'Oh, a great big rat! I saw it! I saw it, I tell you!'

She hadn't, of course, the silly goose, for it was no such thing, but instantly the entire class erupted, climbing on to their chairs and bawling for their mammies. For my part, I sat where I was. A mouse. What was a mouse to me, for Christ's sake? At Larkhill, my bedroom, if you could call it such, quickened nightly like a ballet performance with tiny harvest creatures the size of fluff-balls who had moved in for the winter. But then as I sat there, still centre of that storm of stupid terror, what did I see but Miss Herron acting like the rest of her charges. Waving her arms about, she had retreated to a far corner under the picture of little African piccaninnies at play in their village.

'Don't panic!' she kept yelling, 'don't panic!' while showing all the signs of it herself.

It struck me it was a bit like that scene from one of those same Bible pictures covering the walls, the one with the crowd fleeing before the Egyptians, and I was that lost boy in the middle of it all, stooping to pick up something. It looked like a pot or jar of some kind. And suddenly it also struck me, an opportunity like this might never come my way again.

So, under cover of all that yelling and milling about, I edged up to the teacher's desk and without stopping to think too much about it my fist closed around one of those precious little glass figures. In my hot and sweaty hand it felt just like a lump of ice, then, still without looking at it, into my trouser pocket it went. Glancing around I saw no one had noticed, particularly its owner still gibbering away in her corner oblivious to everything but the state of her nerves. That tiny, chill, awkward object seemed to bite through the lining of my pocket, the right, incidentally, which happened to have no hole in it. If it had gone into the other one, then it might have worked its way through to break on the floor at my feet, my crime apparent for all to see, a starburst of splinters instead of a puddle of piss, the usual manifestation of shame in that particular classroom.

Then it came to me, when all the fuss died down and the animal was seen to be missing, for surely it must, a search would be made. First, the insides of our desks, then schoolbags. Finally, our pockets turned out in front of us. One half-chewed apple core, the key from a Spam tin, a small German coin, one spent bullet, a horseshoe nail for boring chestnuts with, a blown wren's egg, an army Fusilier's badge. Roughly my usual tally. But now, a miniature glass camel, a present from Ballybunion as well.

Simply swallowing it did cross my mind, just as I'd done with my collar-stud all that time ago, both objects nestling companionably together somewhere deep inside. But the notion passed. Torn between hanging on to the little humpbacked creature or quickly hiding it, I looked about me, for, yes, I admit I did consider planting it in someone else's schoolbag, the saintly Betty Cairns coming to mind. But then that would only mean Miss Herron would get her prized piece back again, when what I intended was to prolong her punishment. Indefinitely, if possible. Oh, the rapture of revenge. Sexual, too, in its way, for to my great surprise didn't I sense my little charley come to attention, poking his way unerringly through the hole in my empty pocket as though determined not to be left out of things. Cupping the little rascal in my left hand, I grasped the camel from Kerry with the other, edging through all those bawling idiots towards a windowsill where a geranium grew in a big brown pot, its soil still moist from Betty Cairns's nurturing and, taking a last good look around me, and with my back to it, I pressed my plunder deep down into the earth, burying it far below the surface.

Eventually, for it had to happen, Old Baldy poked his head through. Spotting him there, Miss Herron appeared to shake off her hysterics for the moment, moving to meet him, hands outstretched and waving slightly like somebody about to be punished. Which, of course, was what I had in mind all along.

'A rat,' I heard her lie above the din. 'Oh, the most awful big rat, Mr Mooney. You should have seen it. Oh, as big as a cat.'

Old Baldy looked at her. Then, as if hearing the clamour for the first time, he brought his cane down hard on one of the desks, raising a chalk storm, the detonation cutting through the racket like a pistol bark.

'Be quiet!' he roared, and we dropped into our chairs as if shot.

Striding to the door, he yelled 'Dinsmore!' and I felt as if I really had been pierced by a bullet. But then in a moment Junior appeared, grinning, hands in his pockets as if interrupted in his favourite pastime of pocket billiards.

'Go and fetch the pointer, boy,' ordered Baldy, and after another short interval my relative returned with it in his hand.

Standing there, gripping that polished rod, he looked about him as though determined to make the most of his brief moment of celebrity. Oh, I have to say I felt so proud of him, of me, of all the Dinsmores, in that instant. And, to make my moment even more complete, didn't he give me a great big wink.

'There. Behind the coats,' piped old Skinny Legs, yet another lie, pointing to the low row of hooks where all the children's rainwear hung almost to the floor.

Slouching across to the rack, Junior proceeded to belabour the coats for all he was worth, whereupon some of those ninnies began to blub anew at seeing their best Burberrys being abused in that way and with such obvious relish, too. After a time when nothing ran out from under the barrage with fur and a tail Mooney called his beater off and Junior returned the way he'd come, the pointer under his arm like a swagger-stick.

'Back to work,' ordered Old Baldy, giving Miss Herron a look that made her grow pale. 'Not another peep out of the lot of you,' he said glaring at us. Her, as well.

I looked at him standing in the doorway there between the two classrooms, jaw jutting, eyebrows twin tufts of harness hair, and *brute* and *brutish* were the words which sprang to mind. And if that comes across as another of those clichés, for so many of our country teachers then seem to have been like him, then forgive me, but that was how it was. To get their jobs in the first place they had to grovel and bootlick, humiliated by a bunch of pig-ignorant, farming folk on some school committee or other. I was to see this in action myself later on but, recalling what they would soon turn into once they got their great feet planted on a schoolroom floor and were free to vent all that ingrown spite and resentment on a bunch of poor kids like ourselves, sympathy took a trip.

But getting back to that day when I discovered the thrill of thieving allied with sweet revenge – after the door closed the class returned to some kind of normality, while a trifle tense still and softly humming like a motor running down. One of the girls occasionally would give a smothered gasp and a little babyish cry and quite a few asked to be excused to go to the toilet. Being something of an expert on such matters, Junior said nerves, pure and simple, made them want to pee like that, they couldn't help it. In the connecting wall between both sets of outside lavatories he had loosened a brick with the spike of his clasp-knife and would crouch there with his eye pressed to the hole in pursuit of his researches. Sometimes, too, he told us, for the fun of it, he would poke his prick through just to hear them shriek. Secretly, of course, they loved seeing it appear in that way like another inflamed peeper spying on them as they sat on their wooden seats making their water. On our side we had to make do with chipped, bare china, chill as an iceberg.

So I waited for the moment to arrive when Miss Herron would notice the gap in her display of seaside souvenirs. And, sure enough, didn't it come a little while after she had dropped down at her desk, face still white from her ordeal with the imaginary rodent and Master Mooney. Under cover of my *Golden Pathway Reader* I saw her eyes widen and her mouth fall open. Then her head came forward until her spectacles practically brushed the line of animals, glass upon glass.

'My dromedary!' she wailed. 'Who's taken my lovely wee dromedary?' the class becoming agitated all over again as if the room had become infested a second time, only on this occasion with something they had never ever heard of before, as foreign-sounding to those dumbos as *mammoth* or *mastodon*.

And I was right, too, about the searching of our schoolbags, desks and pockets. Naturally nothing was found and a perfectly good half-hour of lesson time squandered. At the end of it all Miss Herron laid her head sideways on her desk and wept. We watched and listened in horrified silence, for the sight, but especially the sound, was so strange, this odd gulping like the rasp a rusty old pump might make before it's primed with a bucket of water. Because of the state she was in Master Mooney was brought into the investigation and yet again we were made to turn out our belongings in front of us, overcoat pockets as well, this time.

Old Baldy stood up straight at the front of the class while Miss Herron sat crushed and wilting at her desk, balled wet hanky pressed to her lips. Her eyes were red, as was her nose. But you could tell he was fed up with the whole affair, animals too, for he kept glaring over Miss Herron's shoulder at them, yellow teeth showing like the Bengal tiger might well have done if ever it were to come alive. Earlier he had gone amongst us prodding at our spread treasures with the furry tip of his cane as if he might catch something. Close up he smelt pretty contagious himself, the old bastard, even an arm's length away, as he picked through my own scattered little hoard. Well, he finished off my lovely bird's egg, I do remember, but without a word of apology or regret. Bound to happen, of course, a miracle it had stayed intact so long, anyway, but I hated him for it and added him to my list of present and future enemies.

The whole sorry business ended some little time later with Junior being blamed, even though his pockets yielded nothing save his beloved clasp-knife and a creased photograph of Jane Russell lying back in some Hollywood hay barn or other. You know the one. The consistent whack of the cane accompanied by old Mooney's synchronised gruntings carried through to us over on our side of the partition, and in one way I felt pleased with myself for having somehow managed to dole out a double dose of retribution to both my tormentors. Then I experienced an unsettling and unexpected moment of guilt at having got a fellow Dinsmore into trouble in that way. But that passed quite quickly. As it always does.

As far as I was concerned Junior and I were now quits and some time later the gap in the line of glass animals was closed up almost as though, as a species, the dromedary, a little like its name, had never existed, except that I and I alone knew where he was buried head down in the dark in the rich earth, just like poor Reverend Gillespie in his well, except that he had been disinterred and the camel hasn't. At least, to my knowledge, it hasn't.

It was my little secret and secrets can be so satisfying, so comforting, especially when people are being rotten to one. I discovered that then, along with something else about myself as well, namely the thrill of petty thieving and how exciting it could be. While still at school, I pilfered a pearl-handled penknife belonging to Master Mooney, a confiscated magnifying glass and, once, his playground whistle, all objects which could be transferred swiftly and without trace to a handy flowerpot. In every case the theft was a reaction to some slight or injustice, as I saw it. In this way Betty Cairns managed to mysteriously mislay a tortoiseshell hair-slide of her mother's, a favourite, German-made pencil sharpener and a small perfume bottle which Miss Herron had given her. So, in a way, you could say the school became a veritable storehouse of buried knick-knacks and only I had the treasure map inside my head. Even so I never felt any desire to go digging them up. To gloat, magpie fashion, over my hoard held no appeal for me. No, the thrill was in seeing my enemies' response when their loss was brought home to them. All the same, if I so wished, if the notion ever took me, I could always go back and restore those hidden objects to their owners. Seeing their reaction to that might be interesting. Not quite as satisfying, perhaps, yet still intriguing.

Once, I remember, when Junior reverted to his bad old ways – it may well have had something to do with those marks on the scullery wall again – I decided to bring punishment to bear on him by pocketing his beloved clasp-knife. Deep in the woods was an old oak tree, last relic, I suppose, of what must once have been some ancient Irish forest, and it had a hole in its trunk just big enough for me to get my hand inside. So I dropped the knife in and then went back to wait and watch for the reaction, which was extremely noisy and violent as expected. We all suffered for, oddly enough, Junior smelt conspiracy, don't ask me why. Even Bessie got blamed, which caused me some distress as I was still in love with her at the time. It was before she sprouted breasts or had broadened in the beam end or got what Junior called her 'monthlies' on a regular basis.

A couple of days later I returned to the hiding place, for I couldn't bear to see Bessie abused so, and discovered to my horror that when I reached into that dark, woody mouth I couldn't get to the knife. There it lay buried for eternity and the squirrels to make of it what they would, unless, of course, someone was to come along and take an axe to the trunk which enclosed it. For the very first time my little schemes had backfired on me and not a thing was there I could do about it.

Now if this were someone else's story I imagine there might be a change of heart at this point, some sort of redemptive rubbish in the narrative, but if that's what you are expecting, then I'm sorry. Hugo Dinsmore is not your man. For, of course, the swiping continued, or the magicking away, as I preferred to think of it, as the speed at which my hand moved became faster and faster the more adept I became. The mystery of all those disappearing, dinky, personal objects continued throughout the rest of my schooldays in Kilcarn School. All those buried little relics pushed deep into the earth of flowerpots.

Sometimes, since, I've often wondered if anyone ever noticed or realised how the haunting seemed to cease the day Hugo Dinsmore left at the age of fourteen. And the day he went through those gates for the last time, emptying his schoolbag as he raced all the way home, as though on a paper-chase, brought the end of the first part of his life as a young animal to a close. The next and most exciting sequence was about to commence.

SEVEN

The first time I ever sang in public was at a Young Farmers' hop in Drumard Orange Hall and the song was 'Love Letters in the Sand' so, reading back from that, I must have been sixteen, although how I got to be there, or found myself up on a stage alongside Gordon Johnston and his Swingtones I cannot be certain, which seems strange coming from someone with such fanatic recall of all the important milestones in his life.

Still, why do I have the impression Sinbad Scully may have had something to do with it? Certainly he was there all right, that I do remember, greasy grin, buttoned-up raincoat with its lingering scent of wintry damp, even though it happened to be August and the dancers sweltered, as though he felt duty bound to remain constant in a world where a Sputnik had been fired off, somebody had just run a four-minute mile and a submarine had slid like a whispering wraith under the North Pole.

That last item, incidentally, had fired my imagination like no other. Not that a Pathé newsreel camera had been present on the voyage, or if it had, no one considered pointing it *upwards* at that slow-moving, ghastly dome of ice. Instead we got arrowed charts, rear-admirals, and a shot of the USS *Nautilus* itself, streaming wet and khaki-coloured to the surface in Boston harbour. In my head, naturally, I had this other image. Men prematurely aged with the horror of what they'd seen through a periscope, yet forbidden ever to talk about it, even to wives and loved ones, a mixture of Jules Verne and that last U-boat picture, my brain still pinging with the Asdic and the cries of actors left to perish behind trapdoors of sweating steel.

In a kind of private chant I kept repeating *watery grave, watery grave* to myself, as Bessie and the rest of us trailed home together. We always went to the cinema in a family group, with or without Junior, but usually without these days, he having got a job for himself. The unthinkable, yes, I know, breaking the Larkhill tradition like that, but it was true and we moved about in this little, nervous huddle because of it, as if we might be ambushed on the long, dark way back from town by the dreaded Cogry boys at any moment.

How could he do it to us? But he did, fetching up in a bloody, striped apron and spattered rubber boots at the back of the town's butcher's dismembering streaked carcasses of meat. Happy, contented, each night he would come home to us with the smell of dead animals about him, and for the first time I came to realise the significance of that dread word Flesher printed over McCabe's shop in big red letters. No more rabbit for us. Now it was chops and liver, oxtail and tripe, and something called skirt and, of course, those famous peppery sausages people were said to walk miles for. *Watery grave, watery grave.* Still the refrain continued to haunt me, refusing to go away. And then it came to me whose lips I had heard it from back in that old house of ours as the clock ticked and the fire draught roared behind its little postage stamp of flameproof glass like a trapped demon, and I was back once more in my high-chair listening to a tale of shipwreck, drowning and a collar-stud sliding to oblivion through a hundred and fifty fathoms of clear water, finishing up, not at the bottom of a sea with an unpronounceable, foreign name, as it turned out, but inside my own stomach.

And there was the one responsible for that particular fairy-tale. From my vantage point on the platform I could see him clearly at the back of the hall near the door along with all the other riff-raff who congregated there as if ready for retreat if ever one of those red-faced farmers' sons decided to take exception. Which could happen so easily, for it was their big night after all, and our lot from the labourers' cottages and assorted holes and hollows like Larkhill were something of an underclass as far as they were concerned. They distrusted us and we, in turn, despised them for their ruddy, moon faces and hands like shovels but, particularly, on occasions such as these, their truly terrible dress sense. Even someone like myself in plain, white shirt and shiny, Terylene trousers, the best I could manage in the circumstances, felt like the young Elvis amongst them. Same greased quiff, too, for my hair had long since been nurtured away from that awful prison cut. Even Junior had a be-bop now.

He went to an old barber's in town, Moses Mullan, who drank methylated spirits out of a cough-bottle and had a tremendously shaky hand because of it, yet always seemed to have a full house. Later I discovered a hoard of dirty magazines was kept flattened under the cushions where his customers sat waiting their turn for the big revolving chair which carried you back by slow degrees as in a George Raft movie. Completing the gangsterish illusion, hot towels were also part of the service.

But Bessie was my private, my personal hairdresser, the two of us slipping off together somewhere quiet where I would sit with bowed head and closed eyes, an old tablecloth knotted about my neck, just about long enough to cover the flagpole which elevated from the recumbent to the perpen-dicular in my trousers the instant she leant over me and I felt the soft pressure of those splendid young breasts rubbing against me. And afterwards, I would rise shakily with a light head, as if I just had not merely a haircut, but sex, as well, while Bessie shook out the tablecloth. To be honest, there were times when I did reach climax – why deny it – for I was growing fast then, more outward, as opposed to the vertical, you might say, and wet dreams, waking or otherwise, were about as common as coughs and sneezes.

Thanks to Junior's tuition I was lucky, I suppose, being spared much of that anguish and self-disgust which normally plagues young people round about that time in their lives. Cocked, primed and bursting to perform, I was ready to put all that valuable lore he'd fed me into practice. Going to dances in Drumard Orange Hall seemed the logical place to start, so there I was in my button-down, poplin shirt and tapered Terylene slacks. Women wore slacks, men wore trousers, but in the movies that was what they were called, so I wore slacks. I had also, I remember, white, shortie socks teamed with black, tasselled loafers, another imported expression. Surrounded by all those agricultural students in heavy, tweed sports jackets and hairy grey flannels I felt like a visiting tourist. And if so many people hadn't known me for a Dinsmore I might well have been tempted to put on an American accent.

One discovery I did make, however, that night. When you sing, you can get away with it. Truly you can, and when the time came Pat Boone and I sounded as though we had gone to the same high school together. Not that he was ever a particular favourite of mine. Even then you could tell how he would end up, bland, born-again, boring. But then that was what my public demanded of me, the sweetly sentimental, when what I longed to give out was Fats Domino, Chubby Checker, with a bit of Eddy Cochrane thrown in for extra heat. Alas, it was not to be. No screaming bobbysoxers for Hugo Dinsmore, no tearing of his clothes, no lipstick traces, not even a solitary swoon.

That night when I looked down on my audience, I suppose I realised that what I'd seen on television in black and white or, better still, in Technicolor in the movies, could never happen here in Drumard Orange Hall. My audience, they stared up at me, fiery red faces scorched by the sun – it was haymaking season – and I made them look and listen to me, *me*, holding them to the very last note, even though the two faces I kept returning to were right at the back of the hall. But Sinbad and Junior I even managed to ensnare too, for, by the end of the song, they weren't grinning any more. Instead they had that same look on their faces as everyone else, a sort of befuddled, vacant expression, I can only describe it, as if away off in some private, sweet-tempered realm all of their own, access barred to every other person there but, specifically, me, up on stage. It's something most people don't ever properly appreciate, that essential loneliness, the *apartness*, of the one giving out, if you care to think about it. To be frank, I didn't, then. Too much to expect from someone barely shaving. Bum-fluff, Junior called it.

After I had steered the number to its conclusion there was this sort of hush in the hall, catching of breath, almost, and I was fearful, genuinely so, caught up there as in the still centre of some awful storm about to break over me. Hurricane Hugo. Why had I allowed myself to be pushed up on stage by Sinbad Scully like that, that terrifying introduction of his – 'Wee Hugo Dinsmore for his pleasure!' still ringing in everyone's ears? Like an invitation to an execution, with me blithely mounting the steps, scorning the offer of a blindfold. So I waited for my just reward for being so forward. Oh, a very bold boy, indeed. Worst of all, not knowing his place. Then the clapping, whistling and foot-stamping crashed about that bad boy and, in that precise instant, he knew where his place had to be from then on, in a hall packed full of people looking up at him, and not the other way around.

Only one incident occurred to mar my moment. Oh, a small thing, really, I suppose. But in that clear and blinding instant of anticlimax as the racket ebbed, I couldn't help but notice people congratulating Sinbad, slapping him on the back, grin across his face even broader if possible. Junior, too, seemed to be getting his fair share of friendly punches, although he had the decency to raise his fat, butcher-boy's thumb to me, winking as he did so.

And so that's how I came to be a regular at the local dances, making guest appearances, unaccompanied for the most part, although the blind accordionist, whose band it was, might occasionally busk softly away in the background, milkily glazed eyes directed at the same spot on the floor. A gentle soul, who lived for his music, he rarely spoke. I don't think the two of us ever exchanged a word. However, the other three, the fat old bus conductor who played the alto sax, the fiddle player, and the ancient drummer, would hand me cigarettes and call me young Mario after Mario Lanza. That's how out of touch they were.

But then so was the crowd who followed the band from country hall to country hall. And like the Swingtones I also learned to give them what they craved, a nightly serving of something sweet and sickly like the speckled buns they devoured when the great metal teapots and loaded trays came round at the interval. God forgive me, but it wasn't long before I was milking 'Nobody's Child' and 'A Mother's Love's a Blessing' to the last saccharine drop. But then if I hadn't done so I suppose I wouldn't have met the Eggman. Still, that's getting ahead of myself.

Flushed from my solo performance, I would thread my way through the dancers to the rear of the hall where the malcontents and outcasts congregated. They rarely took to the floor, this line of silent starers, for that was their sole purpose in coming, it seemed, to look, but never touch, disdain written on every feature. Junior was there, of course, but usually too busy smoking and skylarking, with frequent trips outside to refresh himself from a row of stout bottles he had lined up on one of the windowsills. In the midst of that bunch of sharp dressers, in his stiff as card jeans and too tight Ben Sherman shirt, sleeves rolled up to within an inch of his armpits, he looked like a lumberjack who'd gatecrashed a fashion parade, for these were serious devotees of cut and style, looming over everyone else a good three to four inches by virtue of their rockabilly haircuts and thick crêpe soles. If ever they did converse among themselves, it was invariably about collar lengths, precise button formation and the right and wrong way to tie a Windsor knot. They had this ritualised way of standing, I recall, stork-like, on one leg, perhaps to protect their gabardine and sharkskin, the other bent at the knee, thick, sponge sole flat against the sweating plaster. Like a row of Masai. Soon I was propping myself amongst them in that selfsame manner, puffing away on a Gold Flake, while pointedly ignoring the swirling dancers just as they did.

Yet even though no one ever referred to it, inside, despite my celebrity, I still was acutely conscious of what I must look like amongst all these silent giants. That extra four inches they had created for themselves seemed such a cruel injustice and I couldn't wait to get my first pair of brothel-creepers, even though I don't suppose any of us there knew what that first word meant. If anyone did, then it would have to be Junior, for he talked of huers, kip-shops and french letters with all the assurance of one who practised what he preached. On Saturday nights he would set off on the butcher's bike which he used for deliveries when he wasn't wading in blood and guts at the back of McCabe's. As tightly encased in shirt and jeans as one of his employer's famed, freckled sausages, skin pink and bursting, too, he would beckon me outside.

'Open your mouth and put your hand on my cock,' he'd order, and, not daring to refuse, soon I would sense a massive disturbance beneath the denim.

Laughing like crazy he'd thrust a cigarette between my lips then straddle his waiting roadster, just like that same old 'pro', as he referred to her, later that same night up by the railway station. The town only had the one and Junior promised to take me with him to be initiated when I grew big enough. *Oh, so funny, Junior.* But I didn't relish the notion, no matter how desperate I was. Bella Badger, her name was, or that may have been her nickname, an enormous, waddling whale of a thing with a tiny, painted, rosebud mouth and short, dyed, black bangs like a china doll's. I kept imagining how her eyes might roll right up into her head while Junior gamely mountaineered away on top.

So while I dreamt of the unattainable with someone my own age I sometimes danced with the younger ones, or, rather, they would coax me into dancing with them, arriving in giggling relays, even though there was only one Ladies' Choice each night. I have to say it was a real eye-opener being clasped by some of these same little minxes, especially during the slower numbers. Swaying to a foxtrot, or revolving to a waltz, I would keep a nervous eye out for their mothers watching from the sidelines. The first few times, frankly, I was apprehensive as to what their reaction might be, seeing their precious pigeon in the arms of someone so much older, despite the match in our height, but to my surprise, instead, I received only smiles and nods, even little fluttering waves of encouragement.

It wasn't all that long before I got to be an expert in controlling myself and my expression, as wee Betty, Norma or Alice kept flattening that aching bulge in my groin with the sweet, bony, little mound of her own. My dancing skills improved no end as well, for by now I was seldom off that bumpy, beeswaxed floor. The way I saw it, my dinky partner and I were like two youthful stars in our very own musical, surrounded by a horde of clumsy, sweating extras, an invisible spotlight trained on us whichever way we turned or twirled.

The real truth of it is, my head was beginning to swell alarmingly, along with the image I had inside of the rest of me as well. For the very first time my size no longer was a disability. The opposite, in fact, for, miraculously, it had opened up a delicious new world where it constituted the exclusive qualification for admission. That other world, the one away from the dance hall, where I had always striven so hard to know my place, suddenly seemed no longer worth fretting over. Of course I was heading into dangerous territory, I realise that now, and who knows where I might have ended up if Junior − yes, Junior − hadn't been the one to alert me. But before that happened I basked in a haze of my own celebrity, letting myself be pulled about by all those sweet, sticky little paws, head swimming with the scents of Palmolive and tiny dabs of talc and Tabu as if in a microcosm of what was taking place all about me, except that this was infinitely more dainty, far more refined.

Compared to their sisters, cousins and aunts, my female flock of little darlings, in their gingham and ankle socks, were like another race of beings entirely. Occasionally, between dances, I would allow myself to be persuaded to go outside with one of these poppets. For a breather, you understand, or a shared bottle of Appleade, which inevitably led to closer intimacies. As far as I was concerned any tiny fumblings and nuzzlings taking place in the dark around by the side of that old Orange hall were entirely innocent despite the demon in my pants. Wide awake at the merest touch, he continued to be a great embarrassment to me, and away from the floor I kept one hand half clenched in my pocket nearly all the time now, which I hoped might add to that air of casual sophistication I was so keen on promoting. In the dark there was no need, and even when it did get in the way in one of those clammy babyish embraces of ours none of my partners ever showed the slightest distaste. Oddly enough, it seemed to make them thrust themselves at me, and *him*, even closer. This was genuinely confusing to me but I was enjoying it far too much to want to question it. I may even have been a little in love, not with just one, but several at the same time, for, a further puzzling thing, there never appeared the slightest sign of jealousy or rivalry among my new girlfriends. It was as if they were perfectly content to share me amicably like a favourite plaything, their very own walking, talking, dancing boy-doll, despite that jutting appendage, and I have to say their wee Hugo adored every moment of it.

Meanwhile Junior watched with a grin on his face, never saying a word.

'Come outside for a fag,' my rough relative whispered one night after a particularly strenuous quickstep, and I followed him along the back passageway lined with Orange regalia leading to the night air. The stars were out in a twinkling rash, I remember, and for a moment I felt a little light-headed still reeling from the ferocity of 'Lady Be Good'.

Around the side of the hall Junior led me and as I stood there in the dark I heard him take a piss against the pebbledash. In the silence it sounded like the din a horse might make, invisibly steaming there, not a bit like my own efforts, and even though I felt like joining in I held back. I don't know why it was, but even with both of us invisible in the darkness I had this prudish notion about being discovered by one of my little playmates. They, too, came out here to relieve themselves. Everyone did. I knew that, and the idea of them in a companionable circle, hunkered, hissing in that way, had often excited me, yet I didn't care to risk damaging the image they might have of me as that Little Lord Hugo who never went to the toilet. Like one of their own dolls, I suppose. All in my silly head, of course, for Junior could have set me straight about what they really were like, knickers lowered, tinkling away in private. But, of course, I would never have wanted to believe him anyway, preferring my own rosy fantasies.

After shuddering and shaking himself, I heard him open one of his lined-up stout bottles, snapping it down hard on the edge of the stone window-ledge. To my great surprise he tore the cap off a second one, handing it to me. I drank and the foam rushed straight up my nose making me cough and splutter, much to his amusement.

'Tell me,' he murmured, coming up close, 'what's it like with them wee hussies?'

'Like what?' I answered foolishly.

'Don't play the innocent. Tell me, is there any hair around it yet? Did you get it all the way in?'

I drew back, denying any such thing. But he only laughed.

'I don't blame you for keeping them all to yourself. Mind you, take care you don't get caught. If one of them wee huers ever tells on you, you'll be for it. Some of their das or big brothers will cut your crigs off. Well,' he sighed, 'I'm away back in again. I just love to watch them two Hoy sisters dance with one another. I'd gladly drink their water just to have a poke at either one of them. Preferably big Deirdre.'

After he'd gone I stayed where I was, gripping the chill neck of the Guinness bottle. I can't remember whether I finished it or not, that dark stuff was never really to my taste anyway. So, I thought, that's that, then. No more juvenile frolics for Hugo Dinsmore, no more clinches in the dark, no more sweeties passed from mouth to mouth in lieu of kisses, no more Hollywood musical nights, no more the young Mickey Rooney, for, yes, I fancied an affinity there, despite the puggish features and ginger hair. Back to being a junior stork again among all those silent, senior specimens. Too bad, but then it outweighed the loss of both balls. It did, didn't it?

So I went back inside again once more and even though the stout provided a certain degree of courage it was hard standing at the back pretending indifference, particularly when I had to refuse every single invitation to get up and dance. How their sweet little faces smote me as my former partners were made to return shamed and dejected to their places on the far side of the hall. I even thought I detected tears at one point, which was probably the worst part of all, for then everyone else started staring at me, not with the admiration I had become accustomed to, but distaste and extreme disappointment. Even Sinbad Scully looked as if he had changed his opinion of me.

Soon I began to feel convicted of a crime which Junior had put into my head and of which I was completely innocent. Yet again my size had turned out to be the real villain, the one cruel factor which had people judging me. It might as well have been branded on my forehead for all to see, *chaser after wee girls*, when what I longed for more than anything was contact with someone my own age and what passed for normal height. Was that such an impossible demand? Was it? Evidently it was, and for quite a few Friday nights afterwards I stayed at home gazing mournfully into the fire.

Once or twice Junior offered to take me with him on the bar of his bike to see the fat, old prostitute up behind the railway station. She entertained clients in a disused carriage propped up on concrete blocks. Junior said it had curtains, even photographs still, of all the principal seaside resorts, above the double seats where the action took place. First class, obviously.

But I declined each time. It was the business of riding side-saddle on the crossbar, you see, legs dangling like some infant's, which dissuaded me, not having to face Big Bella in her compartment boudoir. Only children travelled in such a fashion – or some pathetic half-pint like Hugo Dinsmore.

For the first time I was in real and proper danger of facing up to the reality reflected in other peoples' eyes, not that other image I had always carried within, like a snapshot in a wallet, of someone well-proportioned from the better favoured side of the family. Something else, too, which I had always shied away from, as from a past apparition, crept into my thoughts as I gazed into the hot heart of our grate.

From what I had pieced together, and using a little basic arithmetic, I decided I might have been conceived on VE Night. I also reckoned my real father might possibly have been an American soldier, a GI. And, as for my proper blood mother, not that sweet, elderly creature who had so tenderly cared for me like her very own up until her death, she must have been a Dinsmore relative, a daughter, cousin, niece, of some kind, part of that whole sprawling connection. All these must haves and might have beens frustrated me, for no one, not even Junior, ever cared to talk about what was clearly a buried family scandal. Even the Dinsmores, rough and ready as they were, apparently had certain tribal taboos about what people thought of them. Part of me took satisfaction in what I saw as my romantic origins, but another side picked up some of that same family shame as well. A constant reminder to them of something better forgotten, there I was, and they were stuck with me. More to the point, I was stuck with them, poor Hugo, squeezed like a torn tennis ball between two warring states of mind.

In my less depressed moments, of course, I realised just how ridiculous I was for being made to feel ashamed of my parents and what they might have got up to before I arrived on the scene. Anyway, why should that crowd at Larkhill make such a big thing of it with their less than spotless record? Take Uncle Harry, steadily drinking himself out of a job by this stage. Then there was another brother Sid who had served time for stealing a load of tractor tyres, Cissie who had taken up with a Catholic, a publican at that. And who was truly to say just who had fathered three, maybe, four, of the young ones running around the place, even though such affairs, just like mine, were kept strictly in the family, so to speak?

Thinking along such lines I willed myself out of my despondency, that old inflamed Hugo imagination taking over yet again. An image of an impossibly handsome man in uniform with perfect teeth and a drawl began taking form like a negative coming alive in a darkroom tray. Someone very like Alan Ladd suggested himself, for obvious reasons, I suppose, for it was common knowledge then just how tall, or perhaps not, he was. But then such attributes rarely count for much in the movies anyway. In real life, unfortunately, they did. Around about this time I considered seriously setting my sights on becoming a film actor. But before such dreams took hold, Deirdre and Doris Hoy entered my young life, that hot, perfumed reality of theirs managing to eclipse any further fantasies I might have had.

Two raven-haired sisters, they lived with their widowed mother in Posy Row, as it was known, that huddle of labourers' cottages just a little too convenient for Lyle's pub, and in reality must have been no more than a year apart, if that, yet they looked like twins, dressed, talked and, above all, laughed, in duplicate. Every man I knew was smitten, including Junior, and I reckon that flock of gaudy flamingos standing along the back wall as well, for they were something of an attraction, the Hoy sisters, at every country hop and hooley in the locality.

The thing that set them apart, aside from their ripe, Italianate looks, was the way they always danced together.

No one else ever got a look-in. In a haze of scent and hair lacquer they would arrive as a couple, then waltz, jive, mambo, samba and tango together – the Latin American medley was where they truly excelled, never ever any of those terrible, communal thrashes for them, like the Pride of Erin or, God forbid, the Gay Gordons – and, of course, after 'Goodnight Sweetheart' and the national anthem they left together.

Despite being so wrapped up in one another they must have been aware of the terrible toll they were taking on us. A space always appeared for them on the floor almost as their right as if they were putting on an exhibition, which they were. Oh, the way they danced, laughing into each other's eyes as they swung out, then in, to a quickstep, or clinging almost indecently in a slow foxtrot. Which one led, we kept trying to work out? Perhaps, more importantly, who took the woman's part, as though that might provide some clue to the divergence in their personalities. But was there one? Doris, at a guess, would have been the older, Deirdre the younger, but like everyone else I regarded them as the Hoy sisters, a fused entity pointless to try to separate, even if one could. Identical hairstyles, same tight angora sweaters show- ing off deliciously downy forearms, nylons, pencil skirts, strappy shoes. Each also wore a fine gold chain about one ankle, as I recall. Junior swore it meant they were mad keen for *it*, but he knew, and I knew, that was wishful thinking. We all did, eyes ravening on the sweet braille of suspender bumps, the bite of rubber roll-ons. Above all, that double image of twin, proud peaks gently colliding in mid-dance.

For some strange reason, I don't know why, I began experiencing a personal affinity with these Hedy Lamarrs of the dance-floor. And when Junior gave a running commen- tary behind his hand to those other wooden Indians, I would edge out of earshot not wishing to be disloyal. Concentrating all my feelings in a single, prolonged, burning glance, I willed them to look in my direction. But they never did, never would, or could, it seems, appreciate Hugo Dinsmore's finer points, just dying as he was to be recognised, not as he appeared, but from the inside out.

One night as I was in mid-flight – the song, coincidentally, was 'If I Were a Blackbird' – I picked them out sitting on a bench together by themselves sharing a mineral and a single straw. They were both passionately intent as ever, giggling over some girlish secret or other. Perhaps Junior was right. Perhaps they did talk dirty all the time to one another, just as he said they did, but even though that was the way it looked from up there, still I refused to believe him and his pals. Two mischievous angels, that's what they were, misunderstood and bad-mouthed just like Hugo Dinsmore, and as I sang I aimed the notes directly at them, no one else, putting every atom of ache and longing into the words, for the first time really appreciating just what that sad old ballad really was about. Never had I sung better, I knew that, perhaps because of it, and gradually the wheeze of the accordion ebbed away into silence and I was on my own, voice soaring like the bird in the song.

Afterwards the reaction was everything I could have wished for. Some of the old dears in hats and aprons who helped with the tea could be seen rubbing their eyes. As the young farmers stamped and catcalled I looked out over their heads for the sisters, but they were nowhere to be seen, a cruel blow, for I felt positive something had travelled invisibly between us, and not just on a one-way current either. At which point there was a lull, the band taking a break for a smoke in the small room at the back of the stage. Climbing up, the Master of the Lodge announced the raffle was about to be drawn and having no interest in such things I mooched off outside for the piss I should have taken earlier.

The night was still starry, perhaps even a little more so, and looking up at all those pinpricks in deepest space – who knows, one of them with a solitary Russian on board – it left me feeling more insignificant than ever. Standing there with the only warm friend I could rely on in my hand like that, I became aware of the tip of a cigarette glowing in the surrounding darkness and as I watched a second joined it. Someone gave a laugh, light, mischievous, and because it had to be who I thought it was, instantly my cock shrivelled as though taking it personally.

'Hugo? Is that you?'

Now I can't properly remember whether I answered coherently or not, some sort of gasp or grunt would be nearer the mark, so overcome was I by the combination of shame at being caught like that, and shock at the Hoy sisters actually knowing my name. But I must have recovered sufficiently for soon, even more of a surprise, I was smoking one of their cigarettes. Craven A turned out to be their preferred brand, I discovered, in the elegant red packet, and the one I myself was to favour from then on.

'Are you staying to the bitter end, Hugo?'

And the second voice came chiming in breathlessly, 'Anyway, there's only one other old dance to go, Hugo.'

'Bet it's a request, too.'

'Aye, a moonlight saunter. Ugh!'

It was like being buffeted softly from two sides at once for, in tone and pitch, their voices seemed identical, and it was impossible to tell which was which – more exciting in the darkness, who was who. And each time I heard my name uttered like that a sort of shiver would take hold of me. Under the Terylene my left leg still felt damp and prickly, but I don't think that could have been the only reason for it.

'Say you'll walk home with us, Hugo.'

'Oh, please say you will, Hugo, for we don't like to go on our own, do we, Doris?'

'No, Deirdre, we don't.'

Of course the whole idea, as well as proposition, was

laughable, but so desperate was I to believe them I embraced the suggestion eagerly. Imagine it, me, Hugo Dinsmore, all four foot ten or so acting as protector to this same pair of strapping blades. And if there lingered the merest element of doubt or cynicism in my mind, then I was their property, every inch of me, the moment one of them said, 'Sinbad Scully, he's always following us.'

'Do you have a coat, Hugo? *We* haven't.'

Even if I had, I would gladly have forfeited it.

And so we set off for Posy Row under the stars. The road was neither dark nor eerie for, in the light of the moon, stretching ahead of us, it was as white as salt, but they pretended it was, clinging and tightening their grip on lucky little me at every rustle or squeal in the hedge.

And one of them would say, 'You know, you've got the most beautiful voice, Hugo. Has anyone ever told you that? He has, hasn't he, Deirdre?'

'Oh, you have, Hugo. As good as anyone on the radio.'

'Records, too.'

Then, 'Hugo?'

'Aye.' Me replying like somebody regaining the power of speech after some colossal shock to the system, which in a way it was.

'Would you sing for us? Just to keep us company.'

'Go on, say you will, Hugo.'

So, raising my voice to the stars, I did sing for them and doing so felt that combined, soft pressure on either side of me, yet somehow pulsing individually as well, as if each was making a private bid for my affections. 'Walking My Baby Back Home' was what I gave them and rapture seemed well nigh complete when after a time both sisters joined in. And their voices were not bad at all, surprisingly sweet, childlike, even, I decided, as arm in arm, we went strolling along just like the words in the song.

134

When it was finished Deirdre asked, 'Do you like Johnny Ray, Hugo?' and I told her, yes, I did, which was true, even though his appeal was more to girls, but I didn't feel embarrassed, and they hugged me to them even more tightly if possible, and I knew it wasn't because they were still nervous about someone in a dirty old raincoat leaping out at them in the dark. After all they had Hugo Dinsmore to protect them and the way he felt just then it was as if he was gaining in height with each step of the way. Looking back, such an innocent period that was. People did sing together like that then, walking along country roads late at night, and innocent was what we all of us were. I know I certainly was, allowing myself to be taken in hand by Doris and Deirdre Hoy, a willing lamb being led ever so gently towards instruction in the ways of older women, something I've never ever regretted, by the way. Never.

Of course we arrived at Posy Row eventually and as the first gable-wall came into view my companions cautioned me to silence in the sweetest way imaginable by pressing cool, scented fingers to my lips. A wakeful dog barked once, and giggling, clutching me close, in their dancing shoes they tiptoed past that first sleeping house. Not a solitary light showed in the entire row and, stopping there, we listened to the awesome quiet, and it was as if the three of us were the only ones left alive in the whole world.

'Will they be waiting up at home for you, Hugo?' whispered one of them and, with just the right amount of adult unconcern, I felt, I signalled a no.

'Would you care to come in for a coffee?'

In how many movies had I heard the identical invitation with everything it implied so, imagination quickening, I gulped, yes, I'd love to.

The house we arrived at was right on the end of the row and, unlike all of the others, it did have a faint glow showing through the drawn curtains of an upper window. Now one of Junior's favourite calumnies was that the Hoy sisters kept a red light permanently burning upstairs as a sign of their availability. He had seen it many, many times, he swore. *Liar*, I thought. This was nothing but an ordinary bedroom lamp somebody might leave on if they couldn't sleep, say, or if they were waiting up for someone. Thinking of it in that way I experienced a pang of something difficult to put into words, yet connected, I feel sure, with the gypsy life I was still leading out at Larkhill along with that other load of transients.

'Mind the step,' came the whispered warning as a key was turned and, completely blind, but deliciously so, I was led into a house of women for the first time. Only much later was I able to appreciate just what a privilege it was, for I may well have been the first, possibly last, male to be invited into that mysteriously thrilling domain.

Still in the dark, I let myself be drawn into a room which, because I could still only touch and smell at this stage, seemed overpoweringly exotic. Enfolded by unfamiliar textures and breathing strange scents, I allowed myself to be lowered on to something furry and immensely yielding. Knees pressed almost to my chin, I crouched there, listening to those two goddesses giggling in the dark. I could hear rustling and unmistakable soft, muffled little grunts that meant only one thing, and as I visualised them undressing for me, *me, Hugo Dinsmore*, and at such a thrillingly early stage in the proceedings, too, sure as hell didn't my trusty little friend down below swell predictably. Then a dim light snapped on in a corner of the room and I saw each had slipped on some sort of silky kimono affair in the dark, pulled tight, but showing bare legs and matching slippers below, very like the ones, I couldn't help thinking, I had once worn myself all that time ago as a young bunny in an old house called Endeavour.

Sitting on a couch facing me, they watched for what I took to be a reaction on my part, and I stared back unprepared as yet to deliver one. The right one, it came to me, trembling inside in case I just happened to come up with something that might be a disappointment. But my face must have showed what they wanted to see, for Deirdre said, 'You don't mind us like this, do you, Hugo?' as though apologising for their new state. 'Being more comfortable, I mean.'

And Doris said, 'Please don't look too close, Hugo, it's a terrible mess.'

'Don't blame me. *I'm* the tidy one.'

'Indeed, you are not,' and then they had this darling little spat right in front of me like a couple of kittens pawing harmlessly while I looked on already irretrievably smitten.

'Do you take milk, Hugo?'

'Sugar?'

Nodding rapidly in quick succession I looked from one to the other, which was to be the pattern from then on, me switching attention back, forth, like a tennis umpire, as each in turn vied for my regard.

'*You* make the coffee.'

'No, *you* make it. I want to talk to Hugo.'

'Oh, very well, then. But *I'm* having him next, remember.'

Was there ever such a delightful tug of love? I don't think so, and naturally I indulged myself shamelessly, taking pains never to betray favouritism if I could help it. But then my affections rarely strayed towards one sister over the other, for I worshipped both equally as if they were joined at the hip. Or anywhere else, for that matter. To tell the truth, this constant vigilance did take it out of one and there were times when all I longed for was to sprawl back in that big slithery

beanbag chair of theirs and let them come at me simultan-
eously. As indeed was the way it happened one memorable
Sunday afternoon when all three of us got drunk on a bottle
of sweet sherry together while Mrs Hoy slept through it all
upstairs.

But that's getting ahead of myself. In between there was
this slow, exquisitely paced period of courtship – some might
call it prick-teasing, but let them, I don't mind – with me the
one being wooed, even though I had all the proper
equipment in my trousers for carrying the campaign to them,
not the other way round.

But that first night while Deirdre – yes, it was she – was
boiling a kettle somewhere down the hall, Doris continued
smiling at me and I smiled back. Taking advantage of this
lull, I was able to absorb a lot more of my surroundings for
the first time, even though the lamp with its tilted, purplish
shade in the corner seemed to throw more shadows than
light on the room and all its unbelievable disarray. On the
evidence I'm certain someone else would say the people who
lived here must be a right couple of trollops. Slept here, as
well, for, yes, there was a bed and a great double affair at that
which only excited my feelings the more as I visualised my
two dark angels cuddling up in the warm together.

Heaped with pillows and scattered with satin cushions, it
was strewn with all manner of clothing, as if simply flung
down there like that in a rush for the door when the two
temptresses headed out for the dance. But then I was no
objective outsider, was I, now that they had thrown a net
over me. A veil, too, for what I saw was not sluttishness, but
merely thrilling evidence of their disregard for dull people
and boring convention. Compared to the ravaged rooms I
was used to back home, I now found myself in a virtual,
female Aladdin's cave. Everywhere I looked was excess.
Tottering piles of magazines and paperback books, records,
hats, gloves, scarves – hanging from every hook and upright

stand – drifts of shoes, jars of face-cream, perfume bottles, lipsticks, dolls and teddy bears in abundance – oh, lots of them. Even more decadent, last year's Christmas decorations coated with half a year's dust, and, of course, the back of the door papered with pin-ups. I took comfort in seeing no proper competition there, no Rock Hudson, no Elvis, no Brando. Instead, all the fabulous movie-star brunettes smouldering and pouting, Gardner, Hayworth, Taylor, Tierney, even the peerless Ruth Roman, all berry-lipped and luscious, obvious choice, the more one thought of it, for two such dreamboats.

Head already swirling with the mixture of scents that drenched the room, I did at one stage actually imagine I might have strayed into a Hollywood apartment to have coffee, instead of someone's front parlour in Posy Row. What an innocent I was in those days. Proper greenhorn. But, then, they were too, in their own way, I suppose, despite the head start they had on me in age and experience and, being women, unfairest advantage of all. Everything was magical about the Hoy sisters as far as I was concerned, their coffee included. Of course I had tasted such a thing before, but never like this. Always the Camp variety with the Highlander on the bottle, as if any self-respecting kiltie would ever have been caught dead sipping a beverage so effete, not to mention vile.

'Another cup, Hugo? Doris and me couldn't survive without it. Correct, honey-bunch?'

They talked to one another like that all the time – *sweetie-pie, babe, toots* – and I adored it, sunk there in my beanbag, dazzled as if the Nescafé was making me see double.

'Tell us, what do you think of this place? Go on, be truthful now.'

But before I could get a word out, even if I could express my awe, the second one giggled, 'Bobbie would have a pink fit if she saw the state of it. She would, wouldn't she, Doris?'

And then it was explained to me how their mother, Bobbie – for always they referred to her like that, but not in any malicious fashion, I should explain, more the way one would talk about a slightly scatty older sister – hadn't left her bed above a year this coming Hallowe'en with what I took to be some mysterious female complaint better not gone into.

Still I couldn't help but look up at the ceiling as if registering the weight and presence of the invisible and, so far, silent one overhead. My face must have betrayed my nervousness for Doris hastened to reassure me.

'Don't worry, she's out for the count. You'll probably hear her snoring in a minute.' Both going into a fit of the giggles.

'We always slip a drop of Hennessy's in her cocoa before we go out,' explained Deirdre.

By now I felt I was beginning to get my bearings. Doris was the younger, and Deirdre had a tiny mole at the side of her mouth as a further aid to identification. A beauty spot. But what if it wasn't the real thing? What if it had been applied by brush? Then where would I be? Women, I'd read somewhere, were known to enhance their appearance in that charming fashion, but the book, like myself, was hopelessly old-fashioned. I have to confess I do have this irritating tendency of pursuing fancies inside my own head like that, even in the middle of a conversation, so when one of them addressed me I was a little put out for a moment.

'Well, what?' I stammered, for that had been the question I thought I'd heard put to me.

'What do you think? Of all this?' A hand holding a cigarette waved languidly in the air. She was lying sprawled on the bed, showing a leg, as they say, which didn't make it easy to look her in the face.

Yet somehow I managed what I thought to be a neat answer. 'Hard to tell, for I've never been in a lady's boudoir before,' and they clapped their hands at such a wonderful word.

After that we chattered away freely, smoking, drinking coffee. Indeed, in typical romantic fashion, I fantasised that there might well be some secret connection between the three of us, so easy was it for me to anticipate, then share in all those charming little secrets of theirs. Imagine my surprise and delight to discover that they, too, never had a proper father either in the respectable sense. Laughing, Deirdre would often say they must have hot, foreign blood in them somewhere because of their looks and sense of rhythm, for Bobbie had been a McLennan, a redhead at that. Crouched at their feet on my beanbag throne, I felt like a tiny god while they prattled on about such things, so much for one little man's brain to take in at a single sitting.

But, finally, Deirdre stretched and yawned. 'Beddy-byes, boys and girls.' And obediently I rose from my nest.

'I hope we haven't got you in trouble. It's awfully late.'

But I only laughed at the very idea of anyone even daring to chide Hugo Dinsmore for being out to the scraik of dawn, as people say in these parts.

At the door I received a kiss on both cheeks, dry, hot and scented, in rapid succession, and as we said our farewells on the step I felt still in a daze, but happier I think than I'd ever been in my entire life.

Outside it was almost light, that luminous, eerie interval just before dawn, and the birds were making an unholy racket. All this, too, was a first for me, for I'd never been abroad so early or so late before.

A good hour it took me to get back to Larkhill along those whitening back roads, my legs nearly as light as my head. As I came through our gateway the rooster was crowing and a light showed in the scullery where Uncle Harry would be

141

eating his solitary breakfast before setting out for the creamery. For a time I stood there taking all of it in, that silent ruin of a house, the jumble of outbuildings thrown up almost by chance about three sides of the bumpy old yard, and it was as though I'd never seen it properly before. How depressing. How awful. Certainly no place for Hugo Dinsmore, someone still throbbing after a night with two such dreamboats. Perhaps the most beautiful in the entire county. Country, even. Ireland, Great Britain, Europe, the World, the Universe . . .

The coffee may have had a lot to do with it, caffeine still fizzing in my veins, for my brain crackled with such notions and would go on doing so well into the daylight hours like the insulators on the pylons I could see marching mistily across the fields at the back of our house. Up the stairs I crept, although, to be truthful, it really wouldn't have bothered me too much if someone were to discover me coming home reeking like a harlot, convinced as I was that the scent of that room and of those two lovelies still lingered, impregnating every part of me, and love-sick already, before lying down in my box of a bed, I resolved never to wash again because of it.

And that is how a beautiful friendship with the Hoy sisters began. Not another soul did I tell either, not even Junior – especially Junior – although I would dearly have loved to have seen his reaction. It was my secret. Theirs, too, for I didn't need to be told they felt the same way about our discreetly ordered trysts as I did.

Sunday afternoons became our regular time to meet. As two dedicated pagans they found our Northern Sabbath as profoundly depressing as myself. By this time it had become clear to me I was growing away from all that yawning inertia which constituted the uncles' day off. What am I saying? Every day for them was like that, and it grieves me to sound so superior after all those happy hours I had spent idolising those great silent gods in their oily overalls, but they had become tiresome to me. More importantly, engendered the fear that that's what happened to everyone, even Hugo Dinsmore, if they allowed the curse of Larkhill to take hold. A sort of malaise hung over the place, I convinced myself, which would turn one into someone who would occupy his hours dopily gazing at two rusty pieces of metal which had never been made to fit, or the carcass of a car that wouldn't, couldn't run, or any of the other useless items of junk that littered the yard.

Marking time, that's what it seemed to be about, and the more I thought of it, of me, too, ending up the same as the rest of the Dinsmores, even, God forbid, Sinbad Scully, in his damp old ruin among the trees, the greater my anxiety grew. So, on Sunday, when the hammering on metal, punctuated by lengthy periods of weary introspection, proved far too painful to bear any longer, I would take myself off to walk the country roads as if training for a marathon. Arms and legs working briskly, I would cover six, seven miles, more, sometimes, brain roaring away. Elaborate scenarios of sweet retribution was what it came down to mainly, for I regret to say I had a lot of that in me then still. But when most permutations had been exhausted, for there are only so many ways of causing your enemies to suffer pain in your imagination, my thoughts inevitably would turn to matters of sex. It didn't take much to set me off. Underwear on a line, a used French letter, a torn scrap from the *News of the World* impaled in the hedge, a pair of young bullocks vainly trying to mount one another, almost as frustrated as I was. And then when it became too much, what else but retire behind a ditch, or into a thicket somewhere, and drain off some of that surplus overflow leaving me bleary eyed and much less energetic on the way back home.

But the Hoy sisters, Doris and Deirdre, saved me from

143

much of that, making my Sunday afternoons thrilling again. Timing my journey to a T, I would arrive at the house well into the afternoon, for they rose late, receiving me, yawning, in their dressing-gowns and slippers, which for me only added to their allure. And soon my heart would be racing even faster as the coffee got to work. They liked theirs dark and strong and soon had me drinking it that way as well. We would chatter on about film stars, fashion, music, all the things I never got a chance to discuss with anyone else, and they would play records while I sprawled there pampered like a little lord.

Sometimes, too, they would apply make-up to my face, dressing me in their clothes, even stockings and high heels on one thrilling occasion, me submitting with eyes closed, only opening them when they felt satisfied with my transformation and manoeuvring me with much giggling in front of the tilted mirror. Ever so coyly this red-lipped dote stared back and for a moment I held my breath, the room going suddenly very still, everything suspended, as though this stunning creature was waiting for me to make the first move. But before I could make her acquaintance, one of the sisters put a record on the Dansette and, seizing me, threw herself into a cha-cha-cha. Xavier Cugat, if I remember, he of the frilly sleeves and maracas, hotter than a chilli pepper, while beyond the drawn curtains the long Antrim afternoon steadily darkened, growing more drear if that were possible.

To tell the truth I never wanted to return to Larkhill ever again. Right here in this hot, scented cave was where I longed to stay, almost as if I had found my real family at last, and if they preferred having a sister instead of a little brother, then so be it. In time, who knows, I might even learn to like it. I should explain the word *kinky* hadn't yet entered popular usage, at least not in the way it was to some little time later, associated mainly, if I recall, with a tall, tight type of boot, so if what we got up to all that time ago behind closed curtains was indeed *kinky*, then no one told me about it. Like that earlier brief involvement with under-age girls at dances, it could have got me into a lot of trouble, I suppose, and once I remember Junior did detect traces of Tangee on my lips, as well as a partial glaze of Panstick when I got back home. Pulling me close he breathed me in as avidly as if I had been an orchid and I felt certain my secret had been discovered, but he only laughed, saying, 'You've been dipping your wick again, wee fucker. You have, haven't you?'

But, of course, I hadn't. The very idea of doing such a thing with my two dark angels never crossed my mind and even when on that magical afternoon when I did lose my virginity in Posy Row with their assistance I was relieved of it so pleasurably, so expertly, I don't think I was even fully aware it was happening to me. Being drunk might have something to do with that and many times since I have wished I could relive the experience, in slow motion naturally, without the complication of a third of a bottle of Croft's Original cream sherry this time.

The occasion in November of that year when I was still sixteen is something I've no intention of going into in crude or needlessly graphic detail, for that would only tarnish something very personal for me. I may well have lost something, but I also gained something immeasurably precious as well. Still, I don't suppose the memory would be too damaged if I sketched in the bare outlines of how it came about.

The day was bitterly cold, I remember, first frost of the year cloaking everything in a salty skin as I strode to meet my new friends. Breath smoking, I listened to my heels ring out on the dry, hard road, teeth chattering occasionally. By the time I got to their house, my feet, hands and face felt numb, and when they saw me both sisters exclaimed I would surely catch my death, dressed as I was in such awful weather. Some

145

sort of misplaced vanity always made me wear the same basic combination, white shirt and dark peg-leg trousers, for I thought it made me look like one of those American teenagers perpetually hanging around soda fountains, or cruising Main Street six to a car, outline of a pack of cigarettes showing through the rolled up sleeve of their T-shirts.

'I don't know about you, Hugo Dinsmore, but I just can't seem to get warmed up,' said Deirdre.

The beauty spot was real, I had decided, and because of it she had just that very slight edge in terms of allure. Despite her complaint about being cold, however, she was wearing her usual patterned, silk kimono, and from what I could make out, from past as well as present observation, not much else underneath.

'The coalman didn't come this week, you see,' explained Doris, pointing to the empty grate. Then, giving a laugh, she added, 'We both stayed in bed until about ten minutes ago, didn't we, Deirdre?'

'Oh, we both love our beds, so we do. Are you that way too, Hugo?'

Lying, I told her, yes, I was a terrible sluggard as well, for I wanted to agree with them in everything, no matter what, even about lying late, which was something one could never do at Larkhill. But then such a room as this seemed purpose-made for lazy self-indulgence, with its solitary lamp shedding a soft, reddish glow over all that rich disarray scented through and through by their feminine presence. In imagination I pictured them stretched there, duplicate bumps beneath the salmon pink eiderdown and its plump, diamond stitching, gorging themselves on soft-centres.

'Would you care for a wee drink of sherry wine, Hugo? Even if it is a Sunday?'

So we sipped the sticky, sweet nectar out of the gold-rimmed tumblers Deirdre brought back from that mysterious domain in the nether regions of the house, for in all my visits there I never once ventured beyond that front room of theirs. As for the upstairs part where the old mother moaned softly, dozing her life away, that was as forbidden as Tibet. To ask to use their lavatory, wherever that might be in the geography of the place, was unthinkable. Miraculous feats of control I endured until I got out the door and then and only then did I let go in a rush, putting even Junior's Niagara to shame.

Thinking back over that magical afternoon I've often tried to recapture the moment when I ended up under the covers with the Hoy sisters, but the actual, the precise instant remains a blank. We must have got tipsy – in my case considerably more than that – and the chill of the room may also have had quite a lot to do with what happened, but who suggested it, or even if they hadn't, who climbed into that big unmade bed first? I feel convinced it couldn't have been me. Then again, maybe, just maybe, emboldened by the sherry, for the first time in his young life little Hugo Dinsmore started ordering events instead of letting others take charge. Who knows? But whatever the whys and wherefore of it, there he was, softly bolstered by two deliciously warm, perfumed bodies, hardly knowing if he was still completely clothed or not under the weight of the eiderdown, or even if they were, with all the blood in his circulation seemingly concentrated in that one part of his anatomy with its own stubborn ideas as to what should happen next.

Taking me in hand, literally so, the pair applied themselves to my education into the mysteries of the female form with all its delightful curves and crevices. Under the eiderdown in our heated cave of slithery satin we nuzzled and explored, never knowing where the next touch or caress was coming from, or from whom, taking refreshment every so often from the bottle of Croft's until it rolled empty across the carpet.

At one stage I remember Doris, or it may have been Deirdre, for they were interchangeable by now, stretched out a pale, freckled arm to switch on the cream-coloured radio beside the bed and then, as the three of us resumed our experiments in the dark, the Amami Hour from Radio Luxembourg murmured softly from a few feet away.

That particular wintry Sunday in late November was to mark the true beginning of my dalliance with the Hoy sisters and each time I kept returning it was for more of the same, another little extra nibble of the cake of experience in weekly instalments. I have to say I was a most quick and eager learner – still am, I like to believe – and will always be grateful to my two teachers. They taught me so much, not just about what goes where and how, and can be relied upon to give pleasure, but certain things about myself as well. For instance, that women liked me just as I liked them. I discovered they were comfortable in my presence and so felt able to confide in me because they felt, I suppose, I posed no threat to them. How often have I been called 'cuddly', 'pet', 'wee dote', and quickly getting used to it I turned my proportions to my own advantage, for the truth was my height, or lack of it, allowed me access to regions and areas of delicious experience denied to other more ordinary men. But then, I suppose, most of this was something I should have picked up earlier, anyway, in my encounters with those younger ones.

The truth of it was I had all the proper makings in me of a little ladies' man, and a naturally talented one at that, and each Sunday I spent behind closed curtains in Posy Row with my two tutors brought me ever closer to what I might have become if this particular story of mine hadn't taken a darker turn because of the one called the Eggman.

BOOK TWO

EIGHT

Calling up the past, I often think, can be a little like looking through the wrong end of a telescope, for when I try to remember who or what I was in those far-off days, all I seem to see is this foreshortened figure resolutely marching along country roads in all weathers so immersed in his own thoughts he felt himself to be invisible. And if anyone ever did call out to him or give a jerky nod in passing he would push swiftly on, head lowered, as if suddenly naked and exposed.

The simple truth was I didn't have much aptitude for passing the time of day with people, and while part of me envied those who had the lazy gift of it – Junior, for instance, who would gab happily away with total strangers for an age, soaking up tittle-tattle – another side asked why? Why bother? To me it all seemed like so much ballast holding back the pure ascent of the imagination. I do believe I had this preposterous theory that the brain could handle only so much information, and if it became overloaded with dross there mightn't be room left over for all the important stuff, like the meaning of life and how one should deal with it and

– well, basically, sex, I suppose. All this, of course, was before I met the Hoy sisters.

So as not to come upon other people while out walking, I would stick to the most remote back roads well away from houses or, even, fields, where animals might be, with the chance of someone tending them. Cars presented more of a problem, not that there was ever much in the way of traffic in our backward parts. But if ever I did catch the sound of an approaching motor I would drop down into a ditch, or match myself to the girth of a convenient tree until it passed. To be gawped at from some deliberately slowing vehicle would have been intolerable, country people being that way, I've found, with a need to imprint one like a Polaroid. In my imagination, already, I felt I had been tagged mercilessly and started listening behind doors hoping to catch the particular nickname I had been saddled with, something devastatingly apt, say, which would be with me for ever. Still, at the back of my mind, I kept this tiny glimmer alive that maybe, just maybe, I would get away with plain Hugo. And do you know, for some crazy reason, it does appear to have turned out that way. On first acquaintance people are inclined to make jokes, people who don't know me, but then, as they do, the wisecracks fade away and they end up addressing me by my proper name, which is as it should be, for it does have a certain ring to it. Hugo Dinsmore. At least I've always believed so, with a certain nobility, even gravity, as though its owner is not someone to take liberties with.

But there was one motor car which passed over our rough roads that for some reason drove me into the ditch more frequently than all the others, even though there was always plenty of warning, for its throaty purr could be heard for miles. Among the dead leaves and bracken I would crouch with a vividly realised image of it and its occupants inside my head. Long, low-slung, an outrageous blush-pink in colour, it careered along the country roads as though in unstoppable slow motion, a great, dusty, metal and chrome-finned monster, swollen sump brushing bumps along the way. It may well have been a Chevrolet, or a Cadillac. In fact I'm fairly convinced it was the only one of its make and model in the country.

The people riding inside rarely numbered more than two, three at a push, but the driver never concerned me for, like the car, it was the passenger by his side who impressed himself indelibly, like the profile on a medal, for that was all that could be seen of him sliding past, that large, oddly babyish head covered in short, blond hair, almost ovoid in shape, and I have it for a fact certain people who don't know him well enough still think that's the reason for his nickname. And the rest of him could reinforce the belief, for he was, still is, round, in every other respect, except for his hands and feet, dainty, almost girlish, some might say, although no one would ever dare suggest such a thing, drunk or sober. Certainly not to his face.

Everyone knew the Eggman or, at least, his reputation, which preceded him like an invisible current driven in front of that monstrous radiator grille. In his wake, people stopped what they were doing to stare after the receding, exotic number plates as if they had caught a whiff of something noxious in passing. It was said his money came from his old man, the original Eggman, who during the war got rich on the black market selling the commodity that gave him his name. Poor people from the city bought the cracked produce no one else wanted which he hawked from the back of a cart, an old bent country man dressed almost as badly as themselves. And, like all the best self-made men, wealth hadn't changed him. The family continued living in the same dwelling, a raw, red roof of tin replacing the original one of scraws only gesture towards modernity and the banknotes people swore were stuffed in ticking mattresses deep among the horsehair. Much of this, of course, was – still is – fanciful.

153

People enjoyed creating stories about the Ritchie family – that was their real name – yet, as it turned out, Hugo Dinsmore was soon to be in a position to separate fact from fantasy for himself as he got drawn into the strange world up at the Hillhead, their house on the hill. Or Humpty Dumpty's Castle, as I would refer to it secretly whenever I was feeling hard done by. That came later. At the start when everything still seemed heady and exciting it was as if all my dreams of finding my rightful place had come true, that finally my banishment was over.

But the first time I had a clear and unobstructed view of the Eggman was in the Ezra McGladdery Memorial Hall. I was on stage at the time about to be called to the microphone. The band had acquired one by now, ostensibly for announcements, but I liked to flatter myself placed there for my solos. Steadying the cool, metal stalk, I would twist the knurled band, adjusting it to my singing height as deftly as Perry Como or an Eddie Fisher, and holding on to that moment became a sort of dangerous, but delicious thrill for me, for when the hall was hushed, then and only then would I begin.

That night, looking out over the sea of upturned faces, and beyond at my two newest fans at the back of the hall, for Doris and Deirdre were there, I decided to give them 'Danny Boy'. Now whether it was because it happened to be the first ballad he ever heard me sing, I don't know, but certainly it was to become the one the Eggman always requested later when he and his business cronies were maudlin, although I will say I never once saw the man himself even verging on the sentimental, let alone drunk.

That night he appeared just as I took hold of the microphone. The back door opened – I suppose I was the only one to notice – and there he was, almost filling the frame, for he was a massive figure of a man, accompanied by two strangers, a man and an older woman. He was wearing a

154

caramel-coloured overcoat in camel hair, I remember, draped about the shoulders in vaguely continental fashion, certainly unusual in our parts, sleeves empty at his sides like an amputee's. His companions appeared half-cut, a couple of townees slumming it. In contrast, he, I noticed, had on a pair of livid tan drover's boots.

So I sang, while he watched, which put in such a way might sound a trifle odd in a hall of about a hundred or so other people all gazing intently at me as well, but that peculiar look of his, which I was to get to know so well, seemed to carry far greater voltage than all the rest put together, even my two dark angels on their favourite bench against the back wall. Let me describe the famous Eggman's stare for you. Colder than ice, eyes a washed-out blue, same colour gin takes on after tonic water has been added, it seemed never to waver, creating the impression he knew more than he did. In all the time I was with him I never once saw him lose a hand at cards, any sort of bet, either, because of it.

Already it starts to sound as if I was a little in love with the Eggman. But then, awe and adoration are pretty close relatives, and fear, which was to enter the equation some time later, can be a component as well. Falling in love came easily to me then. Desperate to impress, I performed shamelessly, and after the song was ended – he didn't applaud as everyone else did, simply stood there, as though those empty sleeves of his were the real thing – I continued making an exhibition of myself to 'Rock around the Clock', jiving with Deirdre Hoy while people gathered around, clapping on the beat.

When the last note had sounded I looked towards the door but the man in the camel hair crombie had disappeared into the night along with his two hangers-on. That was the way he operated – in, out, then on to the next port of call, perhaps half a dozen in a night's trawling, always restless, always unsatisfied, wringing out the essence of a place and the people present with a roving glance or two from those fish-dead eyes of his. Hardly an ideal object of affection, but to me he fulfilled all those longings to be in with the right crowd.

In the days that followed I kept hoping for another glimpse of the big pink car. I would listen for its hoarse roar in the distance and prepare myself to be recognised, but it never appeared. I began to question people about its owner.

Junior looked at me. 'That gangster? What are you asking about *him* for?'

'Oh, nothing,' I told him, trying to appear casual. 'I just saw him at the dance, that's all,' and left it at that, not wishing for him to catch a whiff of something he might use against me.

With the Hoy sisters I could afford to be more open, but to my surprise a strange sort of awkwardness set in at the mention of his name. Doris left the room and Deirdre began rapidly leafing through a pile of old *Picturegoers*. That day the sweet sherry bottle remained unopened, as did the bed covers, and I made a resolve never to bring the subject up again.

But my fascination with the man in the movie star's overcoat and cattle-jobber's boots refused to go away. Swallowing my pride, I contrived an accidental encounter with Sinbad Scully.

'I didn't see you at the big dance the other night,' I threw in as an ice-breaker.

'No,' he replied, tapping the side of his nose in that suggestive way of his, 'a wee diversion unexpectedly came up. An old heart-throb.'

He was looking at me hoping for a reaction but I kept my gaze firmly fixed on the passing hedges. We were strolling along in leisurely fashion like two contemporaries taking the air.

156

After a pause he said, 'A wee birdie tells me you've found a playmate of your own. *Two*, to be precise,' and instantly my relaxed mood evaporated, leaving this empty cavern in my chest.

Forcing a laugh I told him, 'Not much escapes you, Matt,' for I knew there was no point in denying it. Our secret was in the open and that was the end of it. As things were to turn out it was to mark the finish of the Hoy sisters and yours truly as though Sinbad's greasy touch had somehow managed to soil the precious thing the three of us once shared together.

'The Eggman was there,' says I, persevering.

'Was he now?'

We walked on. It may very well have been a Sunday. There was that stillness in the air as if the land itself was resting after a hard week of pushing up the crops just to have them cut down again over and over, endlessly.

'Do you know him?'

'Know big Lyle?' he exclaimed. 'Me and him go back, oh, a long way. And the father before that, as well. Ah, the times we've had together. The things I could tell you.'

But I was in no mood for a fresh dose of Sinbad Scully's tall tales. Realising it had been a mistake, a humiliating one at that, I told him I had to go back, and swung around.

'Well, if you must, you must, wee Hugo,' he said. 'Don't be such a stranger. Think of all the times I dandled you in front of your mother's fire. And you only knee-high to a grasshopper. Still are,' he added with a malicious grin, 'dearie me.'

No, *dearie me, you old fraudster*, I thought to myself, walking off. My face was smarting.

I have a feeling that may have been the very day Doris Hoy met me at her door and told me her mother had been taken poorly during the night so play was cancelled. Of course she didn't use those words, but that was what was implied, and being the sensitive person I am I wished her mother well and walked away as casually as I could. Then, again, it might have been a week later, perhaps more. Maybe it was me just being me, conflating what I took to be a run of bad luck, for I've always felt those rarely arrive singly, a bit like those famous London buses, although I haven't had too much experience of them, I have to say. But then, mercifully, a break, even what seems like a reversal of all those blows to the ego, occasionally comes along. Mine happened this way.

One night at Larkhill while listening to *Sing Something Simple* on the wireless – Junior was there as well with his feet up, for the meat business fairly took it out of you, he said – we both heard a car pull into the yard. Its headlights raked the window, illuminating the inside of the kitchen and our startled faces, for we frequently sat in the dark with only the dial on the radio showing, waveband tuned to the Light Programme.

'I wonder who the fuck that can be,' grunted Junior, hauling himself up out of the old settee and going across to peer out. I heard him give a sudden cry and next thing he had dragged on his unlaced boots and was heading for the door in what can only be described as a high old state.

'Jesus! Sweet Jesus!' he kept exclaiming as he stumbled outside.

By this time whoever was in the car had switched off their high-beam and, creeping to the window, I, too, put my face to the glass, but all I could make out was the vague outline of something big on wheels, pale-ish, but nothing concrete in the way of make or registration. It was an exceptionally dark night, I remember, starless, with a moist west wind thrashing the stripped trees.

When Junior returned he looked shocked, and something was strained in his delivery too.

'It's the Eggman,' he said. 'Asking for you.'

158

'For *me*?'

'Yes, you, you sly wee fucker you,' he snarled, taking hold of me with those great red maulers of his like two lumps of raw meat. Smelt like it, too, for he could never quite rid himself of the reek of the slaughterhouse no matter how hard he tried, even when he set off in a haze of Old Spice on those visits to Bella Badger, although why he concerned himself with her crude sensibilities was a mystery.

'Just what the fuck have you been up to, then? Having him come out here after you.'

I stared at him. 'Nothing! I don't even know him!'

'Then why the fuck were you asking about him only the other day? Eh? *Eh*?' each monosyllable reinforced with a shake that made the bones in my jaw rattle.

'I don't know, I tell you!' my voice cried out, and at that someone in the car pumped the horn twice, loud, lingering blasts that set the dogs barking in the outhouse where they had been locked up for the night.

'You go out to him, you hear? Right now, wee fucker. Whatever you've done, nobody here is going to lift a hand to save you.'

God help me in my gullibility, but already I was half convinced maybe Junior was right, that somehow I had managed to upset the man outside in the big American car, although how or why I had no earthly idea. Choking back the fear, I went outside, for what else could I do?

Ahead of me I could make out the dim bulk of the Cadillac squatting in our old yard like something landed from a far galaxy. In my head I kept thinking – *spacecraft only exist in the movies. You can make it disappear. You can, Hugo, if you close your eyes and will it to return from whence it came* – but a voice, a recognisably human one, spoke from one of the darkened windows.

'Get in, young Dinsmore,' it said, rear door swinging

159

silently out towards me, and so, sleepwalking forward, I prepared to be abducted by aliens.

Putting my head for the first time into that cavernous interior was like entering a foreign territory. That's how it seemed to me then and each time I rode inside the more it felt as if I had diplomatic immunity, Cuba, for some crazy reason, always coming to mind. Perhaps because of the smell of cigars and bay rum which, of course, was what I was to discover it was called much later. I mustn't forget, too, the scent of new leather from those great bench seats. That never seemed to lose its pungency, even when spiced with the tang of cow dung on the boots of the people travelling inside.

Sniffing up all of this like some marmoset, I slid along the enormous empty banquette, longer than our own settee at home. In front of me I could make out two heads above the rim of the seat, the much larger one belonging to the person who had addressed me as 'young Dinsmore'. Still tingling a little from the thought of the great man himself actually addressing me by name, *knowing* it, even, I waited to be told just what I was meant to be doing here.

'Will you sing for us?'

Another shock, for the tone was polite, respectful, almost, as if he was asking if I took milk in my tea or not.

'Here? *Now?*'

The one behind the wheel laughed at that, sounding young, not much older than myself, and it's curious but sometimes simply an intonation can make you dislike someone intensely and from that moment on I hated J.J., the Eggman's driver. Or – bum-boy – as I was to refer to him privately whenever I was in one of my more smarting moods.

'No, at a wee party. Don't worry, we'll bring you back in one piece afterwards.'

Sitting there in the dark, palms pressed to the cool leather, I tried to take in just exactly what was being proposed.

Already it must have been about ten o'clock and although I was able to come and go much as I pleased I had always set myself certain private limits regarding staying out late. In some strange fashion, deep down, I suppose, I still did secretly long to be treated like any other normal person my age, even in a crazy setting like Larkhill. Uncle Harry, too, had to be a consideration, not that he even seemed to know who I was any more these days, what with his solitary drinking and all.

'Well, how about it, young Dinsmore?'

The Eggman's voice sounded tired, as if he didn't greatly care one way or the other, and his companion, pretty-boy there, I sensed, couldn't wait to get me out of the car anyway, so I thought, to hell with it, him, in particular, and said, 'I'll need to put on a shirt and tie first,' although why I suggested the tie I don't really know as I didn't possess such an item anyway.

'Five minutes,' said the Eggman. 'No more,' and I slid back out along the seat as if it had been greased.

Junior, poor old Junior, was on his feet, mad with curiosity, and more than a touch of the jitters, too, I couldn't help noticing, when I got back.

'Well?' he whispered.

'Well, what?' said I, taking a risk, but it was just so satisfying seeing him suffer like that.

'What did he want, fuck you?'

I looked at him. Had I the guts to tell him, none of his equally fucking business? Had I? Instead I told him the truth. Why complicate matters?

'He wants you to sing at a *party*?' he exclaimed, making it sound like a reception for royalty.

'Yeah, some old do or other,' casually I informed him. 'I'll need a clean shirt. How about that one you said was too small for you? The one with the green checks.'

161

And, amazing as it may sound, he went off to fetch it, sweet as pie, him, Junior Dinsmore, his precious houndstooth Ben Sherman, even though he'd outgrown it by about four sizes. He stood there watching me pull it on and, continuing to astound, said, 'Here, you can't go looking like that. You don't want people laughing at you,' giving my cheeks a rough rub and lick with a flannel, even combing my hair for me. 'You don't know where it might be.'

I have to say I felt strangely touched, submitting myself to being tugged and patted in that way, like being groomed by a big brother, an almost caring one at that.

'Tell me all about it when you get back, wee fucker. You can hang on to the shirt if you do. Deal?'

And that, I suppose, had to be one of the finest moments I'd ever had at Larkhill and, leaving the house, I vowed to bring back as hotly coloured an account of my night out as I could cook up on the way home. I was quite expert at that, I'd discovered, quite the little embellisher. But the way things were to turn out I needn't have bothered too much about embroidering my recital anyway, reality requiring no additional brushstrokes from me.

The drive we took that night became something of a mystery tour, our headlamps transforming every bend in the road, every passing house and gable-wall, every bush, tree, into something starkly lit, alien, even, as if we'd lifted off into space after all. Perched there in the middle of the back seat, my feet barely touching the carpet on the floor, I kept watching the dashboard, diamond-studded with lights that flickered occasionally, off, on, green, red, amber, and once blue, as if the monstrous, wheeled brute we travelled in followed a career of its own choosing through the night. The Eggman looked as if he was asleep, great head lolling, while the driver by his side held the wheel as lightly responsive to the touch as though it was whipcord, hands blanched by the glow from the dials in front. My own face burned, though whether from Junior's attentions earlier with that musty old flannel or the fierce heat which blew about my ankles, I couldn't quite decide. For a good twenty minutes or so we drove without a word and then J.J., it was, who broke the silence.

'Smoke, kid?' he enquired, and in a rush I told him, yes, yes, I did, ignoring the sneer in his voice and that word 'kid', and up came his hand holding a cigarette. Taking it from him, I got the impression of a ring, a certain almost girlish softness in his touch, also, which made me feel a lot better. And then this stubby tube thing like a lipstick, its tip a red-hot glow, was passed back. Having little if any experience of cigar-lighters – cigars, even – of course I allowed it to die on me. J.J. laughed and for the rest of the way, like a fool, I held an unlit Camel in my hand.

Such were the sort of little tricks J.J. liked to play, some more vicious than others, especially when we were alone together. Whenever the Eggman was present he always made it appear as if we were just having a good laugh, pair of young cubs horsing about, but always the laugh seemed to be on Hugo Dinsmore. But that was some way off. Meantime, he rode in a car as big as a bus, on upholstery that must have swallowed an entire ranch, while other more ordinary mortals slept in their beds, unaware that the young Dinsmore was gliding past like passing nobility. Never hesitating once, never needing direction, J.J. seemed to know exactly where he was going. I envied him his mastery, his American tobacco smoke drifting back into my face. *Some day*, I told myself, *I'll be behind a wheel just like that, rolling past in profile*, for it came to me how cars make everybody appear equal in the eye of the beholder, no matter who they are or what height they might be. Some a little more so than others, depending on the make and model.

163

On first sight the house we came to that night looked like one enormous, transparent box, for it seemed to be made entirely of glass, save the roof, although even that had been generously skylighted. Picture windows, those truly glorious modern creations, had the people inside as though on display, moving about in full view, talking, laughing, with drinks in their hands, as we climbed to meet them, the pierced emblem on the prow of the car tilting alarmingly, and me staring through it in awe.

Cairndhu had been built on the side of a hill for its panoramic views of what people claimed were five of our six counties, although I have to say I was only ever there after dark and could only make out fairy lights far below. A distant town showed up as a miniature Milky Way, hamlets a little less so, while a solitary homestead became a fixed star.

Bumping over a cattle-grid, we passed between pillars topped by a pair of rough-cast eagles, a distinguishing feature of our part of the world, I've noticed, as if a job lot had gone cheap once upon a time, or there had been an inexplicable fad for the things. In a sweep we drove right up to the front of the house where a dozen or so other cars were spread about the gravel as though simply dropped here. Even I could tell they were parked pretty erratically, and later when I had been inside a while it became obvious that most of those present had arrived plastered. Straight from a race meeting at Fairyhouse, I discovered, and judging by everybody's mood, more than a few winners had been marked on their cards that afternoon.

The front door had been thrown open wide to the night air and I followed J.J. and the Eggman inside, the pair of them walking straight ahead as if it was their own place. On the facing wall I saw this portrait of what looked like a woman with two eyes on the same side of her face. The rest of her was pretty outlandish as well, all heavily outlined planes and angles, but if you stood well back it did become a lot clearer, so that after a time she became quite recognisably female right down to the breasts and fuzzy dark arrowhead. I mention all this because I spent some considerable time in the hallway later studying her at close quarters because I didn't know what else to do with myself and she was the first thing I had seen at Cairndhu. Later on somebody told me it was an original Picasso – not a copy – but then nothing about that house would surprise me. Like most of the goings on there.

But let me sketch in some rapid, first impressions of the scene when first I sidled into that enormous, glass-walled lounge, although a word like lounge cannot do justice to such a magnificent chamber. A record was playing at full volume. I'm nearly sure it was Acker Bilk, for the owner of the house, the alcoholic judge, had pretty mediocre tastes when it came to his record collection. Anyhow, he wasn't there, as he spent a fair part of the time passed out upstairs. Later, when the noise from below finally began to pierce the whiskey mists in his brain, he would appear, bare-legged beneath his robes, wig comically askew on his bald head and everyone would applaud enthusiastically as if witnessing the spectacle for the first time. Everybody called him plain Alec, which at first seemed very shocking to me until I came to realise that all the people there, including Justice Dunwoody, had two very separate lives. Tonight the private one was on display without restraint or inhibition, for who there would ever think of ratting on the others? For the first time I witnessed that privileged chapter of the rich and powerful, and if you've learned anything about Hugo Dinsmore so far you'll have guessed that he just couldn't wait to be part of it, even a little part, like a dog wagging his tail and waiting for the first titbit to fall.

In that great aquarium of a room all was noise, laughter and banter, the radiogram belting out 'Stranger on the

Shore'. People stood in groups or sprawled on low leather and chrome furniture and all were throwing drink into them as if it was about to be rationed. There were loads of women present, smelling extravagantly to high heaven, and every one seemed to be laughing with her head thrown back showing off superb necklines, as well as lots of upper chest. For the most part, the men were a disappointment, fatter, older, coarser. But then that may only have been me projecting all the green arrogance of youth. J.J. was the best looking there by far, gliding about like a young Dean Martin, all that slicked back, oiled hair, even the same dimple cleaving the chin. For some reason the Eggman seemed to have disappeared and, lost and embarrassed, I stood near the door until a woman with a roguish glint came over and asked, 'Whose wee man are you, then?'

She was wearing something excessively low-cut, dazzling to the eye on account of all its encrusted diamanté, expensive, certainly, but overdone. Even I could see that, poor little Hugo Dinsmore from Larkhill. But then I've always been lucky enough to possess this innate sense of what is classy and what isn't.

'Have you had anything to eat yet?' she continued, and not waiting for an answer led me across to a table laden with all sorts of curious delicacies I'd never seen before.

'Here, let me fix a wee plate for you,' she said, diving in with a spoon, and I had this curious sense of *déjà vu*. I was back at my mother's funeral being pampered all over again by those aunties of mine, one in particular, her perfumed heat making my head light, although, to be fair, Aunt Patricia hadn't been near as pissed as this one.

That was her husband over there, she told me, out for the count on the sofa.

'Sleep, sleep, sleep, that's all he does,' she confided. Her breath smelt of onions. 'Or work, work, work. I don't know why he even bothers coming to Alec's do's.'

And then, her voice sharpening, which was a tremendous relief to me for I felt sure tears might not be far away, she said, 'He could buy and sell this lot here. Some of them look down on him because he left school at fourteen.'

Without thinking, and with my mouth full of chopped greenery, I heard myself say, 'Me, too,' and she looked at me as though only properly for the first time. There was this terrible pause, or so I thought anyway, the shirt I had borrowed from Junior clinging to my back like some hideously patterned batch of curtain material instead of the acme of cool it had seemed in the mirror when I put it on.

'What line are you in, then?'

Acker Bilk was now playing 'Little Flower'. *God*, I thought, *it's an LP*, distracting myself with foolish irrelevances to avert that great, hovering pile of cow-shit overhead, a recurring image of mine when things go wrong, and she stuck a finger into the mess of runny stuff on my plate, then put a dollop in her own mouth, sucking the finger clean, slow as slow.

'I sing,' I told her, reading the signals, for what is it about Hugo Dinsmore that brings out the mothering instinct in these women? Frankly I'm quite happy to keep it that way, not wishing to tamper with Nature or a good thing while it lasts. J.J. had some talents in that direction, too, it would appear, as I watched his oily progress about the room, dropping a smile, a whispered word here, a fleeting touch on a bare arm there.

'I know what *you* need,' my newest auntie said before making her unsteady way to where the drinks were, me watching nervously as she poured something clear with ice into a tall glass, filling it up from another much smaller bottle.

'I'm Fiona, by the way, Fiona Delargy,' she introduced herself, handing over the drink. 'And the thing on the settee there catching flies is my Dermot.'

'Hugo Dinsmore,' I replied. First sip of the mixture tasted like nectar, the ice striking my teeth like a frozen kiss.

'One of the Kilcarn Dinsmores?'

'Very distant,' I told her. Not bad, considering the geography separating Larkhill and the folks at The Mount.

'Did you come on your own?'

'No,' I replied, 'with Lyle.' I nearly said 'the Eggman' but, laughing loudly, she said it for me and, lowering my eyes, I let it pass as if I hadn't heard.

A little while later she left me as abruptly as she had come, going straight across to a jolly group on the far side of the room and I felt as if a light had suddenly been switched off leaving me standing in the dark, then, seconds later, as if one had come on instead, drawing all eyes towards me, caught there like some hick intruder in that room where the dense blackness outside made a mirror for everyone within. That, I think, was when I went out into the hall again to finish my appraisal of *Woman with Pitcher*, although I couldn't detect anything resembling pot or pail. *Woman with Marked Deformity*, more like. But, to be fair to old Pablo, I did rather admire the colours and wacky composition generally.

Behind me I could hear the roar of raised and rising voices pierced by the screech of Acker Bilk's clarinet. Except for a solitary ice-cube the glass in my hand was now empty. When it melted completely I would go back inside and look for the Eggman. That's what I told myself. But what would I say to him? *When are we going home?* More to the point – *where the hell are we* – thinking of that black night beyond the glass and all those unfamiliar roads, and the strong possibility of being stranded here with a load of drunks.

I was watching the ice-cube dwindle and die on me when a voice said, 'What the hell are you doing out here?' It was J.J. I looked at him foolishly.

'Just where the fuck have you been hiding yourself?' he

hissed. 'Lyle's been asking for you. He wants to know why he hasn't heard you sing yet.'

'Nobody asked me.'

'Nobody asked me,' he mimicked.

He looked at the glass in my hand. 'What's that you're drinking? We didn't bring you here to get pissed, you know. These people here are way, way out of your class, *yokel!*'

I may not have mentioned it before but J.J. happened to be a townee, yet, despite the natural, inborn contempt which that entailed, I couldn't help wondering just why he seemed to dislike me so much. The odd thing is he didn't make me feel as bad as I should have done. All that venom was so overwrought, you see, it seemed almost comical. Even though I kept my feelings to myself, he may have sensed it, which only made him even more unrelenting in his campaign against me. But this is not the time to go delving into J.J.'s pathetic psychology. Later I would find ample opportunity to pick the scabs off that delicate skin of his, for when you're constantly on the receiving end of someone's spite you sometimes start getting an unfair advantage, simply by being more objective than the red-faced one doing all the roaring.

'Come on, Doris Day. He's in the kitchen,' he said leading me back into the mêlée again.

I noticed how his face seemed to settle back almost instantly into the smiling, ingratiating mode. What a creep – an exceptionally good-looking one, admittedly – but a shit all the same. *Creep, creep, creep*, I kept repeating to myself and it carried me through the crush right up to a door at the far side of the room and beyond.

'Here he is,' announced J.J., closing the door behind me.

We were in a beautifully appointed kitchen, modern, gleaming, functional, like the rest of the house. Surprising, really, for the alcoholic judge had never been known to cook anything other than the odd boiled egg and then the whole operation was perilously fraught due to that early morning tremor of his.

The Eggman and three other men in suits were sitting playing cards, a pile of soiled notes crumpled in the middle of the table. He didn't look up but, spreading his poker hand in a fan, reached for the pot. A perfect run of face cards. High hearts.

'I've brought the budgie,' said J.J. brightly, but the Eggman didn't appear to find it all that amusing. Neither did the others around the table but, then, perhaps they were still in mourning for their losses. Realising he'd made a mistake, his face said as much, J.J. went pale, and seeing him like that, craven, more than a little desperate, too, I felt my first real boost of the evening.

'Well, young Dinsmore,' the Eggman said, turning those pale, steady eyes of his on me, 'are you ready to give us a wee song or are you not?'

Then, to the card-players, he said, 'The lad here I want you to know is a proper young Caruso. You have to hear him. You're about to hear him,' and, rising to his feet, his great toffee-coloured overcoat seemed to fall from his shoulders almost to the tiled floor. The belly on him, I saw for the first time, was immense, forcing out the waistband of a pair of striped, suit trousers supported by red braces, and his white, none too clean shirt was open at the throat.

'How about one more hand, Lyle?' one of the men complained.

'Aye, you've given us a right hammering and no mistake,' another said.

'Something of a rarity,' sighed another and there was general laughter at that.

'I suppose it beats being burgled,' someone else added in a resigned tone of voice.

Throughout, J.J. had this sickly smirk on his face. He kept

170

looking from face to face in a desperate pretence at being part of this proper men's club, but fooling no one, especially me.

'Tell them to turn that racket down out there. Tell them the lad here is going to treat them to some decent music for a change,' ordered the Eggman, and obediently J.J. went to the door.

But as I made to follow, the big man said, 'Hold on there, young Dinsmore,' and to my amazement plucked a note from the winnings spread in front of him and pushed it, folded, into my breast pocket. After a moment, sighing, the others followed suit, dipping into their own depleted funds as well, until I had this rustling bulge where a hanky should be and which I didn't dare think about examining or counting, even in my head, as though it might all turn to used bus tickets. As a matter of fact, the rest of the night it would stay exactly as it was, even though I could feel its itchy burn through the thin cotton of Junior's shirt. And even when I did manage to get home I still felt a trifle nervous about taking a closer look.

Naturally I hid it all, along with those few other little mementoes I'd managed to save from my earlier life, and gradually that wad of well-thumbed notes was to thicken considerably between the pages of my old *Golden Treasury of Fairy Tales* with the picture of Rumpelstiltskin on the cover. And as my nest egg grew, so also did my own attitude towards the stuff in general. Easy come, easy go, seemed to be the name of the game, as I became infected by the Eggman and his cronies' casual way of pulling fat bundles from their hip pockets without having to count or, sometimes, even, look at them. Of course, silly me, I had got it completely wrong. Money wasn't something to be tossed about carelessly, even in the smaller denominations. Money meant power, life itself, better even than sex, for you could always buy that. Happiness? What was that, anyway? Something women went on about when drunk at parties.

Happiness, if you really wanted to get down to it, simply meant making more of the same. Only fools abused, mishandled it, and there were always plenty of those around at the late-night poker sessions, usually young idiots with sports cars eager to throw Daddy's hard-earned wealth across the table at the Eggman.

Here I'd love to be able to tell how, in the end, I came to despise all these people and their thick wads of readies – every transaction I witnessed only ever involved cash in hand, as if cheques, cheque books, above all, receipts, had yet to be invented – but then that would be a lie. The truth was I itched to emulate and imitate, in my own small beginner's way, the longer I spent in that company and titbits from their table kept falling my way. That night in the judge's big glass house marked a turning point for young Hugo, for once he'd had a taste of the forbidden fruit, how could he ever dream of going back to plain porridge again?

When it was time for me to sing for my supper my first choice, naturally, was 'Danny Boy' – or 'The Londonderry Air' as my own tribe prefer it to be called. Either title, I have to say, suits me. But tonight I was in very different company. Mixed though it was, no one seemed to care a jot. And why should they, indeed? What they kept moulded to the shape of their hip-bone, after all, was the commonest currency going. No politics, no religion, no mention of Pope or Prod, the unspoken rule. That was back in those innocent days and, if that sounds much too good to be true, all I can say is young Hugo Dinsmore was there and he should know. Then, again, maybe not.

After I'd finished the number, to a fair amount of raucous applause, someone shouted, 'For God's sake get him something to stand on! Let the dog see the rabbit!' and there was a deal of laughter at my expense, but not unpleasant or hurtful in any way. J.J. promptly hauled forward a coffee table and helped me up on to it with a sort of limp-wristed, mock gallantry. The top of the table was made of glass, like so much else in that house. I could see the rug beneath and felt nervous about performing on what seemed like a transparent skin, reinforced though it may have been. My voice wobbled on the opening notes to 'The Blackbird' because of it, but I made it to the end.

While not as responsive as what I'd become used to in the various Orange halls, the crowd was manageable, I sensed that, not all that different, considering their money and the amount of drink in them. Scanning the faces, as I always do, I concentrated on those who seemed more receptive, but after one of the songs someone bawled out a request for 'The Eton Boating Song' which threw me badly, and halfway through another a woman began laughing hysterically, not because of the number and the effect it may have had on her, but because of drink again. The Eggman, who was standing in the kitchen doorway, told her to shut her trap – yes, as crude as that – and the room went quiet.

'Now, now, Lyle . . .' someone admonished in half-hearted fashion. Then, next minute, a man sitting beside the woman slapped her across the kisser, not a particularly hard or vicious slap, as in the movies, just enough to administer sufficient shock to keep her quiet. I supposed him to be her husband, but he may not have been, for my later experience of such gatherings was that not too many married couples attended, at least not with each other.

After that things seemed to go downhill as if something had been released, even more drink being downed and Acker Bilk reversed on the turntable with the volume up. I saw J.J. slip upstairs with the woman who had come over to me right at the start, Fiona something or other, with that better half of hers still open-mouthed and out for the count on a distant settee. He owned a chain of hotels, but there were far more interesting notables there that night.

Since then a lot of people have begged me to name names. What have I got to lose, they say, given my present situation? But why should I? Why should I satisfy them and their eagerness for the sniff of scandal? But, without mentioning anyone specifically by name, some of the people there that night were – a certain well-known barrister with shortly to be realised political ambitions, an off-duty superintendent of police, a BBC announcer with his young friend, several actors and actresses, a viscount with a thing for make-up and woman's underwear, a louche divorcee who had buried three of the wealthiest men in the country, a heart specialist, a couple of university lecturers, a well-known boxer and fitness expert, along with various horsy people and those associated with the betting and public house trades. And, of course, my very own big cheese himself, although the Eggman was always a man of mystery when it came to what might be described as the precise nature of his occupation. Even after knowing him as long as I did I never was quite certain just where all that money kept coming from.

'Time to go, young Dinsmore,' I heard him say just as the party was entering another and even more relaxed stage. One of the younger women, a redhead noted for her Sabrina-like bust, had peeled off her sweater and was encouraging one of the men to join her in a game of forfeits, the loser stripping to their underpants, possibly beyond. Aching to be a fly on the wall, I would have given anything to stay, storing up visions to dream about later.

Instead I got J.J. breathing in my ear, 'Adults only. We don't want to stunt your growth, now, do we, sonny?' I noticed a streak of pale, pink lipstick by the corner of his mouth and tried matching it to the drunk hotelier's wife he had disappeared with earlier.

Life can be cruelly unfair, I kept thinking to myself, as I followed him and his master across the gravel and into the night and the mundane countryside beyond. At my back I could hear the unmistakable cries of grown-ups having fun, more fun than I could ever imagine, although even I had heard of the famous ritual of car keys in the dish, exotic as a Zulu fertility dance, although Junior talked casually about it like someone *au fait* with such goings-on, even though if his own lucky number ever happened to come up his only offering to the proceedings would be a pair of bicycle clips. That image, I have to say, did cheer me up, and made me wonder if just maybe some miraculous night it might be my good fortune to drive home with someone else's drunkenly obliging wife. Part of me thrilled to the idea, then, in the way it always does, another voice whispered – *what if it turned out to be that stick-thin chain smoker in the corner?* For there's always one, isn't there, a sort of law of nature, like pretty and plain invariably turning up on that double blind date together. In that moment in the dark there I thought of the Hoy sisters, those two superb exceptions to that rule, and wondered what they would say if they could see me here like this.

Our return journey to Larkhill was as silent as the one going. More so, if possible. Lying back against the sighing leather, my brain bubbled with everything I had seen earlier, and I took scarcely any heed of the route we were driving. J.J. navigated as masterfully as before, and no one spoke, or seemed to smoke, either, I noticed. I kept wondering if the two in front were thinking along the same lines as myself, re-ordering and evaluating the evening's events. But then why should they? I wondered what it must be like to take everything in one's stride like that, even on a night like tonight. Was that what the business of being a grown-up was really all about? Never getting excited, or making sure one never showed it? Would I, too, get to be the same, eventually? For the first time, surprising as it might seem, I

175

didn't feel quite so enthusiastic about being in that same club after all, despite all my earlier eagerness to be a paid-up member. But the sensation was one of those short-lived ones, like a hiccup in the ambitious scheme of things.

I made it clear to J.J. I wanted to be let out some distance away from our ruined old pair of pillars, for I believed he might drive straight into the yard, headlights blazing, as a final act of malice on his part. But he didn't. He pulled up by the side of the road near McGookin's plantation as requested. The harsh white beam lit up the wall of beech outside as I slid along the seat. A touch of westerly light rain was in the air. Standing there by the side of the road I could feel the light spits on my face.

Rolling down his window the Eggman said, 'J.J. will call up for you on Saturday.'

'Another party?' I blurted, and the moment I said it could hear J.J. laughing away over on the driver's side.

'Don't be greedy, wee man,' was his comment and the Eggman gave a sort of low chuckle as well, which was unsettling, for it was the first time I think I'd heard a sound like that coming from him since I'd been in his company.

'Don't worry, young Dinsmore, I'm sure we'll find something to keep you entertained. Just come up to the house with J.J. here. That's if you've nothing too big on,' and the great car pulled away and off into the damp night in the direction of Drum Cross, tail-lights contracting to fiery dots as I stood there watching and waiting for them to disappear. Maybe, even, for ever, for all I knew.

In the trees an old owl was going *to-whit, to-whoo,* as I tiptoed between our pillars. In books that was always the sound they were supposed to make, and I kept repeating the refrain over and over in my head all the way inside and up the dark stairs to the loft with my shoes in my hand as if I had made this truly wonderful discovery, like the reason why you always wake up with a boner in the morning combined with the urge to have a slash. I suppose I should have anticipated that in the light of all the evening's excitement, or maybe the notion was still in my head as I slept, for that particular night, in about ten years or so, I pissed the bed, which was something that didn't quite tally with the new image the young Hugo Dinsmore had now in mind for himself.

NINE

The following Saturday early I was up nervously scanning the sky for rain almost as though the weather might have some important bearing on what lay ahead. No one had said anything about being in the open, it was simply something that had got stuck in my head for some reason, like deciding to put on my best clothes, as well as scrubbing my face, hands and neck raw. At this hour the entire place was graveyard still. Even the rooster seemed to have given up on his morning obligations. But then nobody ever got out of their beds much before noon, anyway, except Junior and, today, despite all those promises to tell him about my big night out, I was off the hook yet again, for he had pedalled merrily away on his butcher's bike some considerable time before.

For him this was the busiest day of his week. Once, when the shop was full, secretly I had watched him through the window among the festoons of speckled sausages and swags of hanging beef, that familiar, cropped head bent almost studiously over the grooved block, while his hands sliced and filleted with a knife whose curved blade edge had been fined to a pointed crescent of steel. It was like watching a stranger at work and at one point, I remember, he made some typically sidelong remark to the couple behind the tiled counter in their starched white coats, so unlike his own bespattered one, both laughing unrestrainedly, and moving back among the shoppers I experienced this curious sensation of family pride, almost, at how popular he seemed to be in that precise moment. Yet, shot through, too, with an odd sense of betrayal as though he'd been holding out on us and it would only be a matter of time before this new life of his with its shared jokes and grown-up camaraderie would take him away from us.

Does any of that make sense? Probably not, coming from someone so desperate to fly the nest himself. To actually wish to hang on to Larkhill and the life we all of us lived there, keeping everything exactly as it was in suspension, seemed perverse. But perhaps the truth was I wanted to be the one to go first.

Someone else, however, was to beat us all to it and in a manner so terrible none of us could ever have imagined possible.

And so that morning I sat alone shivering in our stone-flagged scullery where the shot rabbits used to hang, gazing out the only window in the entire place overlooking the yard and the stretch of road up which the Eggman's car must come. I have to say my wait was a long and nervous one, racked as I was with the worry J.J. mightn't turn up at all. But, then if he did, our band of sleeping beauties within might be up and about to witness the Cadillac's arrival, as nightmarish a vision on our cobbles for drowsy innocents like them as a pale, pink double-decker bus.

But then at about eleven or so didn't I hear that familiar, six-cylindered, throbbing growl in the distance and rushed out to show myself. I was wearing black Sta-Prests and a sand-coloured windcheater, something new which I'd only had about a week. Tapered neatly at the waist – perhaps too

179

neatly – it had elasticated cuffs that left weals on each wrist and was in a child's size. Most of the clothes I wore then seemed to fall into that category, with me working extra hard to disguise the fact. Like turning up a collar or rolling back cuffs, generally allowing the garment in question to hang loose, open, seemingly casual. Yet no matter how hard I tried, why did I get the impression I was fooling no one, least of all me, primping away in a mirror, while sleeking back that embryo teddy boy cut, sugared water on a comb working best, then pushing up the collar just far enough to cover the DA hairline at the back.

As expected, J.J. drove straight into the yard, sweeping the car around full circle to pull directly up in front of me. Someone was with him in the front seat, a stranger with a crew cut as close as you could get without actually abrading the scalp.

'Don't forget the golf clubs, wee man!' was J.J.'s opening crack but, ignoring the jibe, I pulled the rear door open and slid in. *That damned windcheater*, I was thinking.

As we were pulling out between the leaning pillars something made me turn and look back over my shoulder. Through the dusty glass of the rear window I could see this figure materialise in the far doorway, a wreck in a torn vest and old army trousers held up by baling twine. It was Uncle Harry, barefoot, eyes a-glare, clutching a Ross's lemonade bottle, for he invariably awoke with one beside the bed to slake his morning-after thirst. He seemed to stare directly into my eyes as if bypassing the car entirely, zeroing in on the real, the proper focus of his displeasure. I watched him stand there swaying. Then, as he raised the already half-empty bottle to his lips, I didn't feel quite so bad after all, knowing he had something far more pressing to preoccupy him, how to blunt the edge of the hangover and get him halfway on the road towards the next.

'That your old fella back there?' enquired J.J., and

although I told him no, no, it wasn't, which was strictly accurate, yet there was still this hard-to-explain pang of betrayal.

'This is Rocky, by the way. He eats wee lads like you for breakfast. Don't you, Rocky?'

Rocky was wearing a tight white T-shirt, sleeves rolled up high over tanned biceps, the rest of him, as far as I could make out, almost gypsyish in colour, too. Later I was to discover he had another nickname, Darky, because of it, although no one ever called him it to his face. He smelt of stale sweat, Capstan full-strength, and a touch of Uncle Harry's own morning-after odour in addition, as opposed to J.J.'s customary scent of Tabac and that barber's preparation he liked to rub into his scalp. Withdrawing into the recesses of the back seat, I gave my own armpits a rapid once-over, deciding Junior's shirt might get me through another day. Just.

There was a radio in the car and while we drove J.J. tuned it in to Radio Éireann. I think it was *Hospitals' Requests*, all those oddly named sanatoria and their equally unfamiliar-sounding patients' names a hundred miles away. A lot of it was opera or John McCormack. People in the Free State, it did strike me, seemed to adore Italian opera for some reason as if they were from Naples instead of Navan or Nenagh. The sound issuing from the speaker in front of J.J. was vastly different from that which trickled or, occasionally, spat in bursts from our own old Cossor Monarch, still wired to its two wet and dry batteries. It was like being in the best seats in a concert hall with Jussi Björling bawling away in your ear, but after a time Rocky reached forward and turned the volume down to a soft drone.

With a laugh J.J. enquired, 'Bit of a head, eh, big fella?' but the other ignored him, staring straight ahead at the road like something carved from inked oak, for he had all these writhing tattoos coiling up each arm. I have to say Rocky did

181

rather fascinate me, and that feeling had a touch of trepidation about it as well at the start, although gradually disappearing the more time we were to spend together. That first day, however, it was like staring at the back of a broad-shouldered totem, topped by a bullet head criss-crossed by pale battle scars, similar to Junior's, but with more of a violent pedigree, I decided.

Meanwhile J.J. kept making all these cracks, incapable, it seemed, of keeping his lip buttoned for longer than a minute, sarcasm his favoured weapon, and he had two sitting ducks close by, the big man in jeans and T-shirt on one side, and me in my schoolboy's zipped-up jerkin trapped in his rear-view mirror. As for himself, that day he may have been wearing a beautiful gabardine jacket, smoke grey, with patch pockets, over a pair of lean-legged, canary-coloured cords. And, yes, his shirt, I recall, was maroon. As far as appearances went, J.J. was becoming something of a template for me, and I continued to study him the way one would a photograph or an advertisement, convincing myself one day I too would cut a dash like that. And by the time the car arrived at the Hillhead I managed to persuade myself of something else as well, that, unbelievable as it might seem, the silent Rocky and I were on the same side, and if we had an enemy in common then it had to be J.J.

'Sit where you are,' ordered the foe when we pulled up at the house and I made to slide out of the car, 'till I hear what Lyle has to say. Wouldn't be a bit surprised if he hasn't forgot all about you. He's like that, you know.' And then a final refinement. 'You just might have to walk all the way back home.'

But it seemed I was right about the big man in the passenger seat and our new alliance for, opening his mouth for the first time, Rocky told me to get out of the car, while turning a look on J.J. that said, *mess with me at your peril, pal.* Me, too, I flattered myself into thinking. Me, too.

His voice was curiously light for someone of his size and appearance. I could detect that slightly whiney, city note there as well but, of course, could never, ever hold that against him, not Rocky Devine, hardest nut ever to come out of that place they called Tiger Bay. Recalling what J.J. had said earlier about him eating boys like me alive, it appeared he would have no trouble whatsoever in dealing with friend J.J. in similar fashion, and slipping out of that back seat I felt buoyant as a balloon.

'Come with me, kid,' he commanded.

Following the big man I kept thinking of all the prize-fighters who had that same nickname, even a few heavy-weights, and puffed my chest out accordingly, mentally shadow-boxing all the way across the concreted yard and up the front steps of the farmhouse.

A couple of dogs came rushing furiously from an outhouse at our approach, but Rocky calmed them down, patting, talking to them in a manner more like a country person than someone coming from a brick jungle. Still I noticed he was wearing those same tan drover's boots like everyone else connected with the Eggman, even the piss-elegant J.J. I wondered if I, too, would get to own a pair, for already I greatly admired the look of them. They lent a touch of swagger, a certain freebooting dash which I was beginning to find attractive.

The Hillhead, as a structure, was long and low, with two wings extending at right angles from either end of the dwelling proper, as if added on without much pride, or even plan. Less of an eyesore than Larkhill, it may have been more of an affront to the neighbours, snug and well-doing in their own neat, Snowcemmed farmsteads. But then the people, like the place, provoked unease. Why with all that money

183

could they not be bothered to give the place a decent coat of paint, or fix the fences and outbuildings, or put on a new roof instead of that old tin one? Best of all, tear the entire place down to the ancient footings and rebuild, as so many other folk were doing these days, pebbledashed bungalows complete with south-facing picture windows the favoured option.

After all, they did no real farming as such. Admittedly lorries did seem to come and go at all hours disgorging loads of untagged and ravenous store-cattle, which after a day or two of fattening were then loaded up again to be sent off God knows where, but that was only a low form of huxterism much along the same lines as that old egg business. The Hillhead over the years had become a kind of rough and ready outpost bounded by respectability and order, a source of constant resentment as neighbours' fences were trampled flat, their pastures invaded and lanes and byways churned to a muddy, khaki soup. And, ultimate reminder of all that aggravation and downright vulgarity, wasn't there this great brute of a Yankee car trundling along the roads like some enormous, browsing, rosy beast.

Forgive me if I appear to dwell on this in extra fine detail, but the Ritchies came to play an important part in my young life, and like Larkhill, the place, too, assumed the same sort of relevance, almost as if I had swapped one gypsy encampment for another nearly as disreputable. In fact it didn't take too long for me to feel at home in a place where everyone had the same attitude to those outside the immediate family. We were here, they were out there, and if they despised and distrusted us, then we in our turn pitied them, although I have to say those at the Hillhead had a deal more assurance. Knowing our place was far more ingrained. Even I had to recognise that.

'Head on in,' said Rocky with a shove, sending me up over

the front step and along a low and narrow dark entrance hall, a few pictures on the papered walls, dogs and curly-haired children for the most part, and I smelt damp. From what I could immediately make out there seemed to be no upstairs, the layout remaining unaltered since when it had been your traditional cottage with thatch and windows about the size of a draughtboard set in two-foot-thick, fieldstone walls. Groping my way along this dim passageway I came to an open door and, hesitating, felt Rocky's paw on me once more as he sent me stumbling into the Ritchies' kitchen.

Now I will always remember that very first entrance of mine, not because of the interior, which was what I was used to anyway, black and burgundy tiles in the customary diamond floor pattern and a range roaring away in an alcove, but for the reaction of the folk present. Put quite simply — not a solitary, stirring glimmer of attention or interest. An oldish woman with bent back and a silvery bun bustled between a dresser and something spitting on the hob, while the lounging male company continued with their timeless masculine pursuits, a bluish tobacco haze filling the low-ceilinged room, tongue and groove pine the colour of strong tea.

I stood there, the thick fug catching me at the back of the throat. Rocky had disappeared off through a door and I wondered whether to follow him, but then the old lady murmured something.

'Are you hungry, son?' almost in passing and before I had time to reply, using her ample backside, the only part of her free, she shunted me over to a table against the wall where three men in dungarees and caps were silently wolfing down mountains of fried grub.

I sat myself down in the only, the narrowest space available, no one paying me the slightest heed. But then I was almost getting used to all of that by now, relishing it in some odd way, too, nearly, but not quite, at home already in that household where nobody had been known to make a fuss of anyone, simply proceeding about their concerns in that silent almost morose manner I've always associated with hard manual work and the people involved in it. Thinking of J.J. outside dab-dabbing away at the bodywork of the Cadillac with a cloth like some girl not wanting to get her clothes messy did give me this pleasant little stab of vindication knowing he would never feel at home here among all these rough types.

'Eat up, son. Plenty more where that came from.' The softly spoken old biddy in the black dress and flowery pinny had dumped a plate in front of me piled high with bacon, eggs, sausage, three varieties of fried bread.

After she'd shuffled back to the range for more relays of the same, the man on my right asked, 'You want your black pudding?' and overcome with a sudden rush of gratitude I passed over my own three dark, glistening rounds.

'You can have my tomato, if you like,' volunteered another of the men. Then this same one enquired, 'Are you the wee jockey?'

I looked at him. Surely he must be confusing me with someone else. Or could it be his discreet, countrified way of commenting on my height? Yet it did leave me with a distinctly odd feeling, for the truth was I had never seen myself in such a role before, despite it having a certain indisputable glamour. Bantamweights, juvenile actors, gymnasts, boy sopranos, certainly, but never a star of the turf in quartered silks and riding-boots.

'See him over there?' pointing with his knife to someone curled up in an armchair in a corner, someone I hadn't properly taken notice of before, a red-faced character in sheepskin jacket and herringbone cap. He looked half asleep, or drunk, perhaps both, cigarette burning down carelessly between dangling fingers.

'That's McCourt the trainer,' my immediate neighbour

said, leaving it in the air as if I was expected to put two and two together, or simply let pass something so blindingly obvious it scarcely warranted a reply.

When I had polished off what was on the plate in front of me – I hadn't realised just how hungry I was – I sat where I was picking my teeth along with the others. To tell the truth I didn't know what else to do with myself, even why I had been brought here in the first place, and when my companions eventually rose, belching and groaning, to leave the way Rocky had done earlier, I sat on at that big, scrubbed, white table trying to give the impression I was part of the furniture. A smallish, carved newel post, say. Or maybe some sort of human hatstand. Invisibility would have been a blessing, yet the desire was very much there as well to be a part of what went on in this mysterious household where people came and went as though following unspoken orders from an unseen source. Cocking an inner ear I tried listening out for it but could hear nothing save the sound of my own blood circulating.

And then someone walked into that room, a blonde vision in apple-green pulling on a pair of white gloves as delicate as little lambs' tails.

'Have you seen my charm bracelet?' this looker demanded. 'I left it on the dressing-table in the shell box where I always keep it.'

'No, I certainly did not,' said the elderly woman, still not taking her eyes off the smoking pan.

'Mammy, you know I never go out of the house without it. And, anyway, where's Lyle? He promised to drive me into town.'

'J.J. will give you a lift.'

Picture this stranger sitting there, little me, H.P. sauce-smeared plate in front of him, suddenly appearing unspeakably gross in the presence of such a creature. Acid-green sharkskin two-piece, pencil skirt clinging to her lower curves as though poured into it. Not a crease, blemish, ripple or indentation breaking the entire silky flow. A miracle of feminine tailoring, truly – in as well as out – for how could I not help comparing it with the Hoy sisters' own particular brand, the indent of suspenders and bite of perforated Playtex no longer quite so arousing or exciting as once it had been.

Standing there smoothing those dainty little piqué gloves of hers in that low-ceilinged, smoky, old farm kitchen, she continued to exude such an intolerable air of sophistication I wondered how she could bear to even be here. Then I remembered someone had said the Eggman had a sister – it may well have been Junior – and it came to me this had to be the one. Watching her at close quarters was like devouring a sundae, better still, knickerbocker glory, with both eyes, but then to my consternation I heard her ask, 'Who's *he*?' and even though she wasn't looking in my direction I was convinced she must have read that disgusting little mind of mine.

'What's he doing here?' she continued, quizzing the old woman as if I hadn't a tongue in my head.

And then the mother, for, yes, it was Mrs Ritchie, in soft, almost confused tones, enquired, 'Yes, who are you, son?' as though only seeing me properly for the first time despite having set me down and fed me barely five minutes earlier.

'Hugo Dinsmore,' I told them both.

At this the young snow queen stared at me long and hard. 'From The Mount?'

Oh, no, I thought, *not that again*. But the gaze she fastened on me told me she wouldn't be fooled anyway, not her, so I held my tongue hoping for the moment to pass. She had the most exquisite legs, enclosed perfection in forty-denier. Already every last, fine detail of that figure I just knew was imprinting itself for future reference when I would be able to think of nothing else.

But the same question came again, the one with no answer. 'What's he doing here?'

The old lady looked at me and I looked at her while the clock ticked. There was this ancient wag-at-the-wall alongside the dresser, vaguely Tyrolean in design, its *tock* seeming to mimic the very sound my heartbeat was making.

'He's with me.'

The voice came from the man in the corner, the one who had appeared to be asleep all along, well hidden, too, behind the wings of his old armchair, for Miss Ice Maiden gave a kind of startled gasp, but it may have been false for all I could tell, and said, 'Oh, I didn't see you there, Mr McCourt,' in this queer little girl's voice.

'Come and give old Malachy a wee birdie, sweetheart,' said he, rising stiffly to his feet, a round as well as paunchy individual, with a face that glowed like a tail-light, a whiskey drinker's face, nose bulbous and pitted as an over-ripe strawberry.

Dutifully she moved across to grapple lightly with him and I saw his puffy hands rest for a fleeting moment on those silky buttocks. In some odd way the sight disturbed me far more, I do believe, than his earlier lie about knowing me. They continued flirting for a minute or so, even I could see that, young as I was, beauty and the beast, and surreptitiously, so that only I could see it, he slipped what looked like a pound note into one of her gloves, and then in a swirl of scent she was gone. Without her precious charm bracelet, I noticed.

'Is the big man out in the paddock, Mrs R?' the stranger in the sheepskin coat enquired, but the old lady shook her head.

'Sure, I'm only his poor mother, Mr McCourt.' But I could tell from the way she said it she wouldn't have it any other way, wearing her martyrdom, like so many of her kind, with a sort of rueful enjoyment.

Over the weeks and months ahead I was to study her performance closely as she shuffled back and forth across those checkerboard tiles in a pair of worn-down felt slippers. Her feet were pure torture, she kept reminding us. Bunions as big as Spanish onions. That was her one little joke and we were expected to smile, then commiserate, as the fries piled up in front of us, relays of that same combination, the eggs, the sausage, the streaky bacon, three varieties of dipped bread. Where that tomato came from, I will never know, although occasionally one of the men would bring in a capful of mushrooms he'd foraged for in the fields.

The great black frying-pan seemed like a personal weapon almost, which, two-handedly, she wielded like some mighty, cast-iron racquet. When out of service – rarely, mind you – the lard in the bottom would congeal in a white, sickly pale layer, up to an inch thick, speckled with the crumbs of former meals and bits of rind. But all of us lived by and for the skillet then, often three times a day, for we knew no better. Occasionally someone might happen to encroach on her private domain close to the range by accident and she would wave it almost dangerously about until the interloper had moved back where he belonged. And if ever one of the dogs managed to slip in unnoticed, belly trailing, eyes darting, those same runny eyes would stay fixed on the pan in her hand, never herself, as if remembering some former nasty experience connected with spitting fat.

'Well, young buckaroo, time to let the dog see the rabbit,' breezily announced this stranger who appeared to know much more about what I was doing here than I did. He moved with a limp, I noticed, favouring the left leg, as, dutifully, I followed him out of the kitchen and through the same door the others had taken. I wondered if they would all be waiting for us on the other side as if in on the great secret too, for in my head this preposterous notion had started taking root, some tremendous surprise waiting to be sprung on me which could go nice or nasty, either way, depending on just how my luck happened to be running.

The pair of us emerged on to a patch of jungle-rough ground, dock weeds pushing waist high through a tangle of rusted machinery, harrows and bits of old ploughs and the like, and Mr McCourt in his sheepskin lurched ahead of me along a path that eventually took us out on to a deep and winding lane. The early winter sun was full on my face as I kept slightly to the rear of this roly-poly stranger as though out of habit, even though we had only met up about half an hour earlier.

He was puffing quite a bit. Perhaps a few too many of those colossal Ritchie fries in his time, I caught myself thinking, and then, stooping to catch his breath, one hand on a corduroyed knee, to my utter amazement I heard him say, 'Never get up in the saddle on a full stomach, I meant to tell you that. It's not just a matter of the weight, you understand, it's a question of being in peak condition. A horse can always tell if you're not at your fittest, and take advantage. But, then, you're still a bit of a novice at the game, aren't you, laddie?'

For the briefest instant that word 'novice' was like a reprieve, a solitary raindrop on a thirsty man's tongue. But what consolation is that to someone dying in the desert?

Please, Mr McCourt, a truly terrible mistake has been made here, I felt like blurting out. *You seem like a nice enough man and I hate to think of someone taking a hand out of you, but, please believe me, I've never even approached, patted or barely looked at a horse, so I have to tell you if you think I'm going to get up on one you might as well ask me to commit suicide right here and now . . .*

And so that is how, in sharp contradiction to what my head told me, and heart still beating, some short time later I found myself being hoisted on to the slippery back of Lagan Lass, the Eggman's four-year-old.

191

'Most likely you're a wee touch rusty,' I remember the trainer reassuring me as we went up the lane. 'But, then, it's like riding a bicycle, I always tell people. Once you're in the saddle again it all comes back to you.'

What, I couldn't help thinking to myself, *what comes back to you? What if it never was there in the first place?*

Then he said, 'As soon as big Lyle took his first look at you he had you down as jockey material. Made for it. His exact words. Told me so himself.'

Well, that clinched it, of course. Insane as it may sound, I do believe I actually started convincing myself he might be right. Perhaps I had all the sleeping potential of a fledgling Lester Piggott. Come to think of it, had I really known I could sing until I tried, or had a terrific head for heights? Now there was a thought. If I could clamber a hundred feet or so up an electricity pylon as blithely as a steeplejack, or one of those famous Mohawk girder-walkers in Manhattan I'd once read about somewhere, just how high stood a horse anyway? Anything measured in hands, not feet, couldn't be much of a trial for someone like me. Could it?

And so, finally, when I got to the field where Lagan Lass was grazing as docile as if she'd just emerged from a pair of milk-cart shafts, in my head already I was hearing that racecourse roar in my ears, while sensing the caress of a thousand pairs of trained field glasses on my speeding, silken torso heading for the home stretch.

Over in a far corner of the field I caught my first glimpse of the Eggman that day in his camel hair, standing out from the group of men surrounding him like a bright, russet oblong. All appeared intent on something on the ground and for a moment I felt vaguely upset they weren't paying sufficient heed to me and my big moment.

Meanwhile, without a word, Mr McCourt had headed straight for the browsing filly while I stood there. For the first time it struck me how damp the grass was, my trouser bottoms soaking up the morning dew like a pair of lamp wicks.

Remember the youthful Lester P., I kept telling myself. *Remember those Red Indians on top of their skyscrapers. Oh, for Christ's sake, remember the Alamo while you're about it, what difference does it make?* And I cut across the field to the man in the sheepskin coat now waving to me while holding on to the horse's head, sliding feet making wet ski-tracks in the grass.

The closer I got to the animal the bigger and more alarming it became, so that by the time I was at its side it appeared truly enormous, a vast, tawny-coloured beast with nothing to subdue it save a halter. No saddle, no stirrups, bare-backed as a redskin pony.

Mr McCourt held it on a short, tight rein while its wet breath whistled through flared nostrils. From where I was standing I could see right up those twin, fleshy, pink caverns and the smell was something else as well, a high, old sweaty stink that would soon be all over me too, I felt certain.

'Let her have a sniff of your hand, so she can get to know you,' Mr McCourt instructed. He seemed different some-how, steelier, as if he would brook no nonsense from me or Lagan Lass. 'The way you would a dog.'

Now, no one had ever imparted that particular morsel of lore to me before, about dogs, I mean, but I did as I was told anyway, with the fervent prayer that a horse was also able to make a simple distinction between a bunch of baby carrots and an outstretched human hand.

'Here!' the trainer yelled across to the men gathered at the distant end of the field. 'Give us a hand, one of you, to lift the lad up!' and slowly the group began to disperse, making their way towards us in leisurely fashion as if still digesting the meal they'd had earlier. The Eggman stayed put. But then I'd started to realise this was his style by now, never involving himself too closely in anything if he could help it, like one of those story-book generals on a hill directing operations through a telescope clapped to his good eye. And always with loads of underlings around, for, another thing, I can't recall seeing him on his own, ever, in all my time, someone always with him to fetch, carry and generally facilitate. Later on I used to manufacture an image of him lying sleepless in bed at night, vulnerable, with no one within call. It was, of course, wishful thinking on my part, a way of taking some of the sting out of my own resentments. But, then, I did find out the Eggman really *did* suffer from a form of insomnia, and so made certain there was always someone to keep him company, usually in the card sessions that would often stretch on into early light.

While Mr McCourt held the halter one of the men swung me up and on to the horse's back as effortlessly as if I'd been a bale of saved hay. Perched there, I gripped the animal's withers between my knees, the way I remembered seeing those painted braves in the movies do it. The distance from the ground presented no particular problem, but this sensation of resting on something so terrifyingly hot and muscled did. It was like straddling a living, breathing tree-trunk that was about to move off under its own steam with me stuck to it. At least I prayed it would be that way. The crazy notion seized me, I don't know why, that if somehow I could manage to harmonise my own body heat with that of the creature beneath a sort of bonding might occur, and Lagan Lass and I would become as one.

But while I was concentrating on some form of revolu-tionary, chemical breakthrough, Mr McCourt put the reins in my hands and stood back as if excusing himself from further involvement or responsibility, and the man who had helped me mount and had seemed like a sympathetic enough soul, slapped the horse's flanks and immediately it went into motion. Not in any startled or jerky way, as I would have expected after such a smack, but with a resolute, almost leisurely action. I could sense every muscle of that great, slippery frame flex and ripple beneath me, but then more and more of them started unexpectedly coming into play which I tried desperately to accommodate.

Gradually the pace beneath me accelerated from a plod to a brisk stroll to the beginnings of a canter and by this stage I had given up all pretence of going with the flow, even if there was one. Shame or no shame, I simply wrapped both arms around that great, ridged, throbbing neck as far as they would stretch and clung on for dear life.

As we headed for the far end of the field I thought I heard someone call out, '*Ride 'em, cowboy!*' but if they did, it never registered properly, for I was gripped by a new and even greater terror that my mount would attempt to take off like a steeplechaser once it arrived at the hedge which kept coming up at an alarming rate, while looming higher and denser the closer we came. There was a lot of wind by now and my eyes watered freely as the horse's mane, tough as fuse wire, whipped back into my face.

But, suddenly and quite miraculously, in almost prayerful fashion, didn't there appear a gap in the hedge as if the Great Pilot in the Sky had indeed decided to let a lifeline down in His infinite mercy – no gate, which would have been the end of me – and Lagan Lass went pounding through and into the next field, where the nightmare continued. This one had cows grazing in it, black and white milkers, who stared stupidly at the odd spectacle. Something small, red faced and human clinging desperately to another animal's back, was what they saw, and they carried on gaping at our double progress all the way across their pasture and into the next field of fresh corn stubble. Which was where I fell off, long after I should have done, dropping down on to the yellow bristles, boneless as a baby.

Lying there I watched Lagan Lass. Instead of trotting on now that the irksome weight had been removed from her, she had stopped and was looking over her shoulder at me as if to enquire, *just what are you supposed to be doing there, flat out on your back like that?* with the same uncomprehending look those cows earlier had directed towards me. The reins hung slack almost to the ground and there was some sort of white stuff coating her muzzle. *Christ Almighty*, I remember thinking, *what if I've damaged her in some way*. Like riding a bicycle in the wrong gear, or with the brakes on, a valuable piece of horseflesh like that maybe laid up and out of action because of my incompetence. They were delicate creatures, so I'd heard, susceptible to colds and colics, often wrapped in rugs and blankets like ailing children.

'Come here,' I said softly, a little lost after that, for what do you call a horse anyway?

The eyes were brown and soft and definitely reproachful and I thought, *how could you ever have misjudged this creature so?* And then I had this fantasy, the pair of us continuing our ride across country together where no one could ever find us. 'Into the sunset', was the sentimental expression which suggested itself, even though it was about noon. But how could I manage to get myself back up there unaided? The horse seemed to realise it too, for there came that look again. *If only*, it seemed to say. The cruel truth we both had to face was that Hugo Dinsmore's day as a jockey was over almost before it had started. The whole world had witnessed his humiliation, including a bunch of stupid, grazing Galloways, and at that point I wondered just what was left to do next. So, rising from my bed of stubble, I went over to my sad-eyed, docile friend.

'Good girl,' I murmured, 'good, good girl,' taking the reins in one hand and stroking that amazingly delicate and glistening head of hers with the other. It really did seem an awful shame to give up so easily now that she had got to know me, for if everyone fell off that bicycle Mr McCourt had talked about first time round and never attempted to get back on again, where would that leave us? With millions of rusting Raleighs and Humbers just lying there, all for the want of exercise and that little bit of perseverance on the part of their owners, that's where. But what if there happened to be a convenient gate I could use as a makeshift mounting-block?

Just as I felt sure I'd spotted one, about the right height for my purpose, too, in the farthest corner of the bare cornfield, I heard the impatient pumping of a car horn, and over the distant hedge didn't I see the long, low outline of the Eggman's car. It had pulled up silent as some great rose-coloured hearse in a by-road bordering the field where I now was standing with Lagan Lass at the end of its halter. Instantly visions of retribution started racing through my head, and I'm ashamed to confess it, but I let go the sweaty, leather strap in my hand as if up to no good, even caught in the act of a possible horse-napping.

I saw Rocky rise up from the car, recognising him by his white T-shirt and shaven scalp, and in a moment he was striding in a straight line across the stubble towards me. When he got up close, without a word, he took a long, hard look at the horse as if examining her for possible maltreat-ment while I stood there dreading the worst. To receive a roasting from Rocky of all people would have been pretty nigh unbearable.

'Did she throw you?'

Then, looking me over just like the horse, he asked, 'Are you OK?'

For one breathless instant I felt like acting my way out of it but, instead, 'No, I fell off,' I told him, and after a second or two he laughed.

'You're lucky you stayed on as long as you did. It was somebody else's stupid idea in the first place. Anyway, no

197

harm done, kid, I'll take over from here.' And like one of those same Indian bareback devils I'd been fantasising about earlier he grabbed a handful of tawny mane and in what seemed like a single movement swung himself up on to Lagan Lass, appearing to rise up off the ground in an almost floating motion as if those tan leather boots of his had springs instead of nails in the soles.

'They're waiting for you back in the car,' he said, looking down on me. 'You'll get a lift back to the house.'

With a final laugh he dug both heels in and the horse broke into what can only be described as an effortless, galloping action, dispensing with all those tedious successive stages she had gone through with me earlier, like some four-legged E-type going from nought to sixty in as many seconds. Rocky, as I got to discover, came from one of those legendary waste-ground, gypsy families racing semi-wild, shaggy ponies over cinders from when he could barely walk, a rough-rider, something of a city-bred centaur, a bareback, wild man, everything, in fact, and in total, I myself would have loved to be, given half a chance.

But the car horn sounded another impatient salvo, a shade angry now, I couldn't help thinking, as I sloped across the field to face the music, for there had to be some of that surely, knowing full well not everyone would be as sympathetic or as good-natured as the great Rocky Devine.

'Well, at long last. Mr Fucking Steve Donoghue. Don't hurry yourself,' was J.J.'s greeting as I got to the driver's window. Donoghue, I assumed to be some other turf figure, although I hadn't heard the name before, but then I never had too much difficulty in getting J.J.'s drift anyway, so heavy was the sarcastic tone it usually came with.

'You smell like you've been rolling in shit,' he exclaimed the minute I climbed into the back seat, which was probably true, causing me the most intense embarrassment, not, I have to say, on account of J.J.'s delicate sensibilities, but because the Eggman's sister, Heather, happened to be sitting alongside him, something of a shock.

'Can we go now? *Please?*' she said and J.J. took off with a screech of rubber.

They were in a foul mood, the pair of them, that was obvious and, pressed as far back against the leather upholstery as I could get, I could feel the emanation of all that rancour wafting over me as if I was sitting in a hot draught. She kept on telling him she was going to be late, late, *late*, although for what was never spelled out.

'Take me into town. You hear me, J.J.? Right away. Now.'

'I have to drop our young bareback rider off first.'

While all this was going on I felt like the invisible man, yet knew that couldn't be so, for there was that same old mug in the mirror looking back at me, even more pathetically eager to please than usual.

'Why's everybody making such a fuss of *him*, I'd like to know? What's he doing here? Who is he, anyway?'

'Has nobody told you yet?' said J.J. 'That's our yodelling cowboy back there. Oh, yes, sings too, you know. Your big brother likes having him around, so he says. You know how he loves collecting weirdos.'

'Like you, you mean, J.J.?'

That seemed to shut him up, which was something the beauty in the apple-green costume was good at when she felt like it, turning people off and on like a tap, so smitten were we all with those cool, Arpège-scented charms of hers.

'Oh, come on, J.J., be a pet and run me into town,' says she, changing tactics, while moving closer along the big front bench seat. 'It won't take you more than twenty minutes the way *you* drive. Lyle won't say a dicky-bird. Honest. I promise.'

You could almost feel J.J. turn to something soft and

putty-like as he felt her warm, wheedling breath in his left ear. Although I couldn't see properly I felt certain she may also have laid a hand on his thigh.

'What's the big deal about going into town anyway?' I heard him ask. His voice seemed to have gone all weakly tremulous.

'I don't want to miss my two o'clock appointment with Frederick, that's why. My hair's an awful mess. Just look at it,' she offered, running her fingers up that delicately tonsured nape.

'Looks terrific to me. Like Audrey Hepburn,' he said, and she moved even closer.

'You really think so, J.J.?'

It was like sitting behind two Saturday night lovebirds in the cinema balcony, that same sensation of trying to concentrate on the action on the screen while hotly imagining what Romeo's paws were getting up to in front in the dark. Hers, in this case, for the back of J.J.'s neck was getting redder and redder, always a give-away the circulation somewhere much further down is throbbing at full pelt as well. I couldn't help wondering just what the Eggman would say if he knew his baby sister's fragrant little mitt was inching closer to J.J.'s covered cock, maybe even resting on it right now. Lucky J.J. Lucky cock.

By this stage we were barrelling along at a fair old lick. Evidently J.J. had given in to the pressure – and who could blame him – and was heading for town after all, so I simply sat back to enjoy the ride. This stretch of our route was familiar to me. In fact we passed Lyle's pub, its half-door open, and I had this sudden image of Uncle Harry inside in a corner on his own as usual, the black bottles steadily lining up like skittles on the table in front of him, while the people within let him get on with that slow, remorseless descent towards complete and total stupefaction. For the second time that day the same puzzling sense of betrayal affected me like a nagging ache somewhere in the chest, and I slid down deeper into the soft American cowhide, even though no one, especially Uncle Harry, could possibly have seen me rolling past in splendour like some returned Yank brat on a pilgrimage to the old country.

Continuing, about a mile on we came to a crossroads where five roads met, a source of immense local pride in our neck of the woods for some baffling reason and, lo and behold, I spotted Sinbad Scully. He was sitting on a low stone wall in conversation with Kitchener McClung astride his beloved, red, Italian scooter as usual. Certain malicious folk said he actually slept with it beside the bed, humping it up and downstairs twice daily like some fragile, family relative. Polished to a ruddy brilliance, it came complete with all the trappings, the racoon tail tied to the end of the long, whippy aerial, the battery of badges and lamps across the front, enough wattage to illuminate an entire village, that's if they worked and weren't there for the pure look of the thing. An obvious obsessive, he had become something of a local joke in his ex-army parka with its fish-tail, not simply because of the Mod thing, although that was sufficient reason to set him apart as eccentric, but because he was close to forty years of age with an aged mother who indulged him like the teenager he so obviously felt himself to be.

I often watched him buzz past on my long, lonely walks, the whine of the Italian two-stroke hoisting bird life out of the trees and the reek of Esso mixed fuel lingering long after the sound had faded. While I envied him madly his Vespa, I had this other image of him forever vainly searching the country roads for some other lonesome Mod like himself to make contact with, all the while yearning to be wreaking havoc on those rockers and greasers in faraway, seafront Hastings or Brighton.

Of course it didn't do to identify too strongly or openly with someone like Kitchener, so if his name ever did come up and the customary cracks were made I would hold my own with the best of them. Deep down, still, I always had this feeling of kinship with old Kitchener and if it hadn't been the ruin of a carefully wrought reputation I would have loved to have been invited on to his pillion, in imagination the pair of us curving along that Riviera Corniche, white-socked and summer-suited, like Cary Grant in *To Catch a Thief*.

As we slowed down at the Five Corners Sinbad and Kitchener gaped at the car and those inside in customary hick fashion and I gave them a languid wave – I couldn't help myself – and saw their eyes widen in disbelief, especially Sinbad, who came down off his stone perch to get a second and better look. To make my moment even sweeter, Kitchener followed us for a good mile or so, riding close to the bumper as if to carry back verification of who really was riding large as life in the back of the Eggman's big American motor. Eventually he did fall back and away, while J.J. carried on steering with two fingertips, apparently oblivious to who or what had been on his tail.

I have to say when I look back on that day I ask myself why I didn't just get him to stop the car then and there and simply let me out. But, then, what makes someone that age keep stumbling on hopelessly, as well as hopefully, from one humiliation to the next? What gluttony for punishment. What capacity for abasement. And so I stayed in the car. And all because of the fear of missing out on something that might make all the insults worthwhile, that might suddenly appear among all that slurry of contempt like some precious nugget of sheer brilliance, a reward for perseverance. Like the priceless look on Sinbad's old face, for instance, and what he would be sure to be broadcasting to the entire neighbour-hood within hours about young Dinsmore's new and elevated status. Taken up by the Eggman. Latest pet and protégé. Admittedly a bit of a failure as a jockey in the junior stakes, but still pretty nifty in the voice department. Which I have to say I was itching to show off as the radio kept playing one favourite after another.

The pair in front seemed to be listening as well, as we spun past all those tin-roofed squatters' shacks on the High town Road, dropping down into the city. J.J. kept tapping the steering-wheel in tune with the tempo, an instrumental version of 'Moon River' and, shamelessly, I began to hum along too.

To my intense delight, after a short while, the princess in apple-green said, 'Well, are you going to sing properly, or aren't you?'

'Oh, Christ, does he have to?' complained J.J. loudly but, ignoring him, I slid into those middle bars as silkily as if I had been Henry Mancini's missing vocalist.

When it was over and the radio voice started announcing the next request I waited for a reaction, but none arrived. I must say I was greatly disappointed in the Eggman's sister and her lamentable lack of manners. Instead of praising my performance, something I was well used to by now, she took out a mirrored compact and began dabbing at her brow and cheeks. As the hot, dry scent of cosmetics filled the car, disturbing and arousing in equal measure, I studied the down on the nape of the perfect neck in front and had a terrifying urge to lean forward and blow ever so gently, just to see those blonde, dandelion hairs quiver and change sheen.

'How will you get back?' J.J. asked as the first red brick, suburban villas started slipping past, and I saw her give him a sly, sidelong glance.

'I don't suppose you could wait for me by any chance?'

'While you get your hair done? No way!'

But in spite of his fine words that's just what he did do, dropping her off on the pavement outside the salon with all

203

those lavender-smocked girls inside bending over their clients under hooded driers as if their brains were being sucked out of them.

For a moment J.J. sat on behind the wheel smoking one of his fancy foreign fags and watching her progress towards the glass doors. We both did. Oh, that superbly moulded chassis, the head held high, the burnished legs, the olive-green shoes tapping like tiny hammers, heels barely the diameter of a sixpenny piece. A kind of perverse, proprietorial pride filled me as if already we were related in some way. People in the street were staring at her as well, I noticed, and then as their eyes switched to the car and the two of us inside it came to me it would be very hard to give up this new life before it even got properly started and however it was to turn out.

'OK,' said J.J., tossing his butt out the window, 'one hour. That's it. Finito,' sounding like some dago film star, and swung the car into the traffic.

Sitting behind that sleek, dark head I was ideally placed to gape about me to my heart's content. Strange as it may sound, I'd only been into the city one time before and remembering that occasion was like trying to hold steady a blur of impressions. Unrelenting noise, the reek of traffic, those great clouds of wheeling starlings over the massive domes of the City Hall never seeming to decide where to settle. Like the people themselves. Even on this day of all days I felt safer with a quarter-inch of toughened glass between us. This, of course, I know is only me, with all my bred-in-the-bone country bias. But that afternoon I noticed a change in J.J.'s demeanour which seemed to bear out my theory, for he appeared to soften and visibly relax the more he travelled over city tarmac, elbow resting on the window-sill, fresh cigarette on the go. The truth of the matter was the country set J.J.'s sensitive nerves dreadfully on edge, all that muck, dirt and stink of manure, not to mention the deadly dull unfolding of the seasons. In town you had a permanent roof over you. He'd often say things like that, while calling us a right bunch of yokels, and even though there was kidding in the air I sensed he meant it.

So I watched him become almost human for a change, that ferocious tongue silent for the moment, with nothing more dangerous to curl around than a wad of gum. To my amazement he passed me back a stick. Juicy Fruit, I think it was, which as always tasted terrific those first six chews or so then became so much boring cud.

In our great growling limo we moved out from the city centre and away, too, from its swarms of shoppers, punctuated every so often by solitary men already weaving home with a skinful even though it was only two o'clock on a Saturday afternoon, and now we started travelling past red brick rows of identical houses with painted front steps and the same sort of china ornaments facing outward from their parlour windowsills. One of a curtsying child daintily holding out a corner of her frock between finger and thumb appeared to be in tremendous vogue for some unaccountable reason. At least a dozen of the simpering little horrors I counted before we reached a better class of dwelling where figurines were kept dusted and locked away in china cabinets, never on a sill for the ignorant to gape at.

On a peaceful, tree-lined avenue we slowed to turn into the gravelled approach to a grand-looking house where several young boys were tending its front rose garden. One or two were my own age, yet I couldn't help remarking how all wore short blue trousers of the gym variety and singlets, even though summer had long gone. J.J. braked the car with his usual showiness and called one of them over.

'Is Gus about?' he asked this boy who had fair hair, bad skin and was carrying a rake.

'He's in his wee office. Will I get him for you, mister?'

'No, that's all right, son, I know the way,' replied J.J. climbing out and stretching lazily like a sleek cat in the sun.

The other youngsters had stopped their work and were gazing at him in open admiration, so, true to form, he posed some more for the poor saps' benefit before sauntering towards the stone front steps with a final, two-handed backward sweep of his Tony Curtis. The massive front door of the villa was wide open and he disappeared inside.

The boy standing by the car window waited until he had gone from sight then, opening the door, slid swiftly into the driver's seat. Stunned by such outrageous behaviour I sat there, more than a little frightened, too, for it was like being caged with a wild animal, one who smelt like one as well, I couldn't help noticing.

'How many gears has this yoke got? Is it an automatic? How fast can she go?'

The questions, unanswerable all of them, tumbled from him as he twisted the wheel with a savagery that paralysed me even more. The shaved and pitted neck dropped from sight and, ultimate horror, I realised he was rifling the glove compartment.

'Has your man got any fags in here?' he was muttering. Then, 'Oh, fuck me!' I heard him exclaim. 'Jesus Christ, look at this, would you!'

Coming forward in a rush I saw the dark, framed opening below the dashboard, mouth of a small, oval-shaped cave – a treasure cave – for it was literally stuffed with notes, handfuls crammed in like so much engraved waste paper, crumpled wads in every denomination. We both stared at something quite awesome in its effect on us, almost certainly something we would never, ever clap eyes on again in our young lives, something which both of us also realised instantly we should not have seen in the first place. Blondie gave a gasp and slammed the flap shut.

'Oh, Christ, don't tell your man. Don't tell Gus. Promise?'

We stared at one another across the plumped-up leather but my eyes, I knew, said it all. Forgotten. End of story.

Then he said, 'Sure you haven't a ciggy? I couldn't half do with a drag,' and I would have given a lot at that moment to have obliged, the two of us sharing a calming puff together, like a couple of grateful escapees from some awful near-catastrophe.

'What's your name?' he asked.

'Hugo,' I told him.

He deliberated for a moment. 'Is that a papish name?'

Then he said, 'Are you the new intake?' and I looked at him in bewilderment for this had left me almost as stumped as the previous question. In fact I was still pondering it. Could Hugo be what he said it was? Quite a shock for someone who had never doubted or questioned that particular aspect of his origins before. Could there be an actual Saint Hugo somewhere? All Catholics, so Junior said, had to take some old saint's name as a form of identifying mark, like that dirty fingerprint the priest dabbed on their foreheads at Lent. They couldn't be baptised otherwise, he said.

As we sat enclosed there in the still, stuffy confines of the car, faces suddenly appeared at the windows and we were surrounded by the rest of the gardening detail. Peering in at us they had a raw, impoverished look, given a threatening edge by all those institutional haircuts. One of them tapped on Blondie's window, mouthing something, but was ignored. Then another hammered on the glass on my side and Blondie rolled down his window and instantly all the cropped heads were trying to force themselves through that narrow space and into the car.

'Did you lay hands on any smokes, Burnsie?' one of them demanded breathlessly as if he knew what his mate had been up to.

'Ach, come on, share and share alike. Don't be a shite, Burnsie.'

'How about a French letter?'

Then someone asked, 'Who's the wee cunt in the back?' which for some reason seemed to enrage Blondie more than all their questions put together for, shoving his way out against the press of bodies, I saw him grab one of the younger boys savagely by the throat.

'Fuck away off, Macker,' I heard him shout, 'or I'll shove the end of my rake up your tight wee arse!'

'Instead of Gus Gilmore's prick, you mean?' one of the others said and they all went silent looking at him, except the young boy who was weeping and rubbing streamers from his nose.

'Here comes the other one!' came a warning cry, all moving back as J.J. appeared above on the front steps. With a grin on his face he strolled back down across the gravel towards the car.

'Well, my little chickadees,' he said, 'I hope you're all behaving yourselves. One of these days somebody I know just might have a wee job for some of you lucky ones.'

'Like the last time?' Blondie enquired, returned to his old cheeky self.

'Mebbe. Mebbe not. Depends on whether the big boss inside thinks you've been good boys or not. Have you been good boys?'

I sat in the back seat watching and listening through the open window to all of this. Secrets seemed to be in the air, private connections arcing between J.J. and that rough-looking bunch out there in their shrunk-in-the-wash uniforms, information not meant for other people's ears or comprehension. Least of all someone like Hugo Dinsmore, green as green and twice as cabbage-looking.

Now, of course, the whole wide world, I imagine, knows about that place, its covert ways and what went on there.

You've probably read the stories for yourself. It's been in all the papers, even some English ones. But that day in J.J.'s company the last thing to cross my mind was that I myself might narrowly escape being back inside that house where all those terrible things took place, forever associated in people's minds with the name on the board at the entrance to its driveway.

As J.J. was preparing to drive out past its ornate Celtic lettering, there came a final clamour of young voices above the sound of the engine.

'Let us clean your car for you, mister!'

'It won't take a minute, honest!'

'We'll do a good job, mister, no kidding!'

'How about the windscreen?'

But J.J. told them, no, no, he was in too much of a rush even for that and, letting out the clutch, allowed the car to roll forward. At the last minute he tossed away his packet of Gauloises and I saw the boy with the blond hair pounce before any of the others could get to it, holding it high in the air the way you would a tasty bone above a pack of yapping curs. I couldn't help wondering to myself whether it might have been empty, for, yes, it did seem the sort of little trick J.J. might love to pull on the unwary. Then, again, probably he would derive almost as much satisfaction from leaving some largesse, no matter how meagre, for that lot back there in their Home For Working-Class Boys, to give it its official title. Either way, J.J. appeared to be in a rare good mood as we made our way past all those solid-looking, brooding houses where no one seemed to live or work despite the gardens being so well cared for.

'Well,' he said, 'what do you think of Glenrowan and the bad, bold lads, eh?'

For the life of me there was nothing I could think of in reply to that, but it didn't seem to matter for he kept on with the same old line of caustic banter.

'Anyway, young Dinsmore, just you see and behave yourself, that's all, or you might end up there yourself.'

Then he gave an explosive laugh. 'Gus Gilmore, for a fact, I know, would love to make a fuss of somebody just like you. Who knows, you might even make his famous Best Boy of the Year Award.'

Happily he let it drop after that and the rest of the way into the centre of town we drove with the radio on. But, to tell the truth, I wasn't paying much attention, or wanting to sing either, for there was something about the things he had said that left me uneasy as if some new and nasty encounter only J.J. knew about might be lying in wait for me like a shadow at a dark turn of the stairs.

But then everything seemed to brighten wonderfully almost as though I was back in people's good books again, where I have to say I had always felt it my right and proper place to be. Travelling back to the Hillhead with the Eggman's sister in the car trailing an almost Parisian intoxication from Frederick's beauty salon in her wake, I allowed the new feeling of near rapture take over. And if a word such as that, rapture, seems a trifle excessive, why not, for it was what I felt, for she had slid in beside me instead of in front with J.J., as both of us had expected her to do. And yes, I feel certain he did as well, even though he drove on as if nothing untoward had happened.

'So, big boy, tell me all about yourself,' she kicked off with, fixing me with those piercing, blue, Ritchie eyes of hers, and for an instant there I thought I really was in some sort of movie heaven after all, with Lizabeth Scott or, maybe, even the divinely glacial Alexis Smith alongside, while in front our chauffeur for the day discreetly attended to his business.

Well, straight off, I was shy and tongue-tied as expected, but that soon wore off just like it had with Deirdre and Doris

Hoy, and soon I was babbling away about my young life up to that precise moment in the back seat of the Eggman's car with his apparently intrigued, glamorous sister by my side. Even so I did take care to paint a proper sort of picture, glossing over the rawer aspects of life at Larkhill. No Junior. No dead rabbits. No bed in a box. God forgive me, no Uncle Harry, either, which was to rise up to haunt me in the light of what would soon take place. Instead, more than I should, I suppose, I concentrated on that earliest time of all, in an old, russet-coloured house at the end of a winding, gravel drive with a pink, fairytale nursery and two devoted darlings who, nevertheless, did abandon me to an existence for which I was cruelly unprepared and which I really never got used to, not even now.

All of this I built up with little embellishments, many of which were manufactured, for I realised I had forgotten quite a lot about that particular period of my life. Images occasionally flash past like something momentarily seen from a moving train, but never in any sort of continuity or sensible chronology. I mean, was that really me riding a cock-horse up our old, carpeted hallway? Did I once wear a little woolly hat and cream-coloured pull-ups? Did I actually swallow a collar-stud, and if so where was it now?

The more I spun my embroideries the more I became aware I had two listeners in that car and not just the soft, scented presence further along the seat from me. J.J. was listening, too, it came to me, not saying a word, and I had this new desire to impress him almost as much as Heather Ritchie with details from a past he couldn't possibly have known about just like her. Best of all, couldn't contradict or query, even if he wanted to. Still, the risk was there, for he had been to Larkhill and must have been able to put two and two together. Yet for some reason, which I still cannot fathom to this day, he held back from the interjection that might have rumbled me.

211

And when we arrived back at the Hillhead I discovered the magic still held, for even if the business with Lagan Lass earlier hadn't been forgotten – far from it – it didn't appear to have harmed my reputation in any way. On the contrary, I had become something of a hero in my absence in everyone's eyes, displaying commendable pluck for my size and years in staying on for as long as I did like that. Sort of a rodeo star in miniature, you might say. Rocky may well have had something to do with that, of course, but all the rest of them in that kitchen, eating voraciously for a second time that day, made this great fuss of me, calling me the young Roy Rogers.

The horse trainer, Mr McCourt, who was drunk, deep in his armchair all over again, kept shaking his head. 'Ah, well,' he would murmur sadly. 'Ah, well, you stick to the singing, young fellow-me-lad, for you either have it or you haven't,' and taking him up on it I asked him if he would like a request.

'Mother Machree,' I have a feeling it may have been, for the tears started coursing down his cheeks. Even the old woman by the range stayed what she had been doing, staring off into distant space as if at something from her past. Oh, that dark cavern behind the eyes no one else can ever enter, even when it happens to be you who's making those memories flow. A bit like Bertie Beggs, high in his projection box in the cinema working the magic machine, sending out those same sort of images down that long, smoke-filled funnel of light on to the screen below for people to dream and fantasise over. But then Bertie has his own secrets, too, I suppose. Like all of us. Like Hugo Dinsmore.

Yet certain folk, it also struck me that day in the Ritchies' big kitchen, would seem to possess more of them than others, the cave deeper, blacker, more closely guarded, for silently, in his usual, unannounced fashion, the Eggman

212

appeared in the doorway to watch, listening with that air of his of seeing and knowing everything the rest of us could never know. He looked across at me and I looked back at him leaning against the door frame there and I wondered whether I would ever get to learn anything about him that he didn't care for another to discover. Everyone else in that room, J.J., Rocky, old Mrs Ritchie, McCourt in his armchair, even the beautiful sister who looked in at us all enjoying ourselves, I felt were transparent to my little eye. But not him. Never the Eggman.

At one point he gave a kind of sigh, hardly more than a low intake of breath, yet instantly the party started to break up, the room emptying as if on some secret wavelength a signal had been transmitted and received. Even his old mother went back to work at the hob while Mr McCourt submerged sighing into the recesses of the armchair, a fixture with his whiskey bottle. For my part, I followed the men outside where they stood around for a moment in deep, individual thought before disappearing into various out-houses.

A little while later Rocky drove me home in his old Ford pick-up with its shifting load of scrap iron in the back that drowned out any possible conversation between us. Not that we had much more to say to each other, and I was relieved in a way for my first day at the Eggman's seemed to have taken a lot out of me. More than I realised.

'Well, kid,' he said, as he dropped me off at the end of our lane, 'be seeing you,' and I got the strong feeling the words were meant to be taken quite literally, instead of being just the customary expression of someone's first and last goodbye.

TEN

In my head there's this map of Larkhill still which every so often I get the urge to set down on one of the lined sheets of paper they supply us with here, red for roads, blue for water, and a wriggly, black caterpillar for the old railway line before it closed down, although I'm sure it exists in its cutting still, a rusty relic under a bushy jungle of crab-apple, ash and sally willow.

I think I may have about a dozen versions. Yet in all of them the line of blue meandering across the page throws up more fragments of recall than all those other symbols put together, for it follows the course of the Moylena river. *Place of the rushes*, the derivation, I once was told. Pretty humdrum, really, compared to others commemorating massacres and the like. But then our own stream, I imagine, never saw much in the way of skirmishes, ancient or otherwise, except when we played there, Bessie, me and the other kids – occasionally Junior, although he saw water more as a medium for torture, Gestapo style.

In those days the river was our dawn to dusk playground. Our clothes carried the permanent reek of it. Fount of all our fantasies, it was where I caught my first shocking glimpse of

Bessie's little vertical pubic stripe in clear outline when she waded into what we called the Big Pool, skirt tucked into her knickers.

The Moylena was our private Amazon, Zambesi, too, for 'Sanders of the River' and Tarzan were our two favourite heroes then, whose personalities we took it in turn to don the moment we arrived at that sandy overhang where kingfishers shot from their holes like neon bullets. Getting to the far side was never a problem, for as well as stepping-stones there was a high, old, single-file bridge that swayed under you like the one Johnny Weissmuller raced across pursued by headhunters when there wasn't a hanging liana handy.

Stumbling back from Lyle's public house after midnight, for he was always the last to leave those darkened premises, or so people said, Uncle Harry would use it himself as a shortcut. And it was from that same old Goat Bridge, as frail and rickety as a string skeleton, that he fell one Friday night towards the end of January. It had been snowing all day so the walkway must have been more treacherous than usual, on a black night with the wind creating drifts that curled and eddied. Anyone sensible would have stayed close to their own fireside but my Uncle Harry had a pathological horror of missing out on his nightly skinful. He would have been pretty far gone by the time he got to the far side and so I see him swaying there in that giant's, double-breasted, army coat of his which was to be his undoing, with its cargo of a dozen Red Heart weighing down its deep poacher's pockets. And him along with it, for when he landed in the torrent below, the skirts of his greatcoat must have floated out like water wings at first, then becoming sodden, until finally the dark, liquid ballast in the tintops took him lower and lower, till by the time he fetched up in a khaki, sodden ball against the floodgates, sucked there by the pull of the race, he would have been a goner.

Still, who knows, the initial fall may have done for him straight off. Yet I always visualise him being carried down the Moylena borne on the current like the sleeping girl in that picture, *The Lady of Shalott*, Uncle Harry buttoned into his old ex-army greatcoat instead of a nightdress with a posy in his hand.

Of course most of this is speculation and a degree of fantasy on my part, for the time between lurching through the pub's back door and being found next day by Joey Baines, the water bailiff, jammed tight between two teeth of the floodgates, will never be accounted for, which for some reason has always been the most troubling aspect of the entire business for me.

The news was brought to me by Junior. I was up at the Hillhead at the time for I had practically moved into the Eggman's place by now. There was nothing or no one to keep me at Larkhill any longer, except, perhaps, who and what Uncle Harry had once been, but that was only a memory now, it seemed.

Someone called me out to the yard at the front of the house where Junior waited leaning on his butcher's bike. I half expected to see him in his blood-stippled apron with a brown paper parcel of deliveries sitting in the front carrier but, to my surprise, he was all dressed up as though off for a night of it with that old tart of his up at the railway sidings.

'Uncle Harry's drownded,' he announced, just like that, while feasting his restless eyes on all about him, but especially the Eggman's car sitting there like a giant, pink jujube on the scored concrete.

'Where? How?' I gasped, but already I knew, seeing him descend in slow motion in my head like some great, ungainly, flapping bird into the brown rush below.

'They found him above the first weir. Sinbad Scully says

mebbe he done it himself, like young Aggie Beresford, her and the baby that time.'

'Fuck Sinbad Scully! What does that old cunt know about anything?'

He looked at me with a shocked expression, as if seeing as well as hearing me for the first time. And with new respect, too. *Not before its time*, I couldn't help thinking.

'Will you come home?'

Somebody was whistling 'Bobby's Girl' in one of the outhouses. You couldn't tell who from the sound, and we both listened intently as if waiting for the first bum note to occur, and somehow I just knew if whoever it was started to sing the words that stupid song would stay with me, going around in my head for the rest of my days, pinpointing the exact moment when I heard the news of my Uncle Harry's death and, perhaps even worse, that maybe he hadn't put up too much of a fight, if at all, when the time came.

'Stay here,' I told Junior, oh, quite the masterful gent all of a sudden, and I sensed him staring after me, possibly thinking along the same lines himself as I went inside to ask J.J. to run me over to Larkhill.

There was no easy, no practised way of breaking my bad news to all of them eating at table, so, like Junior, I came straight out with it, for it had to be done. A deep sort of respectful and, yes, embarrassing silence settled over the kitchen and I experienced those first dry pricklings behind the eyelids because of it. Yet it was more a matter of feeling sorry for myself, rather than the great, drowned bear I once so idolised. The Eggman wasn't in the kitchen but someone got up to go out to tell him and I really did feel that proper tears might not be so very far off after all when he came in and pressed a fistful of warm, crumpled notes into my hand, followed by him telling J.J. the car was to be at my disposal for as long as I needed it.

Looking back at that time it strikes me my reactions were a trifle peculiar in the circumstances, some might even say warped, for while feeling incredibly grateful – I was, oh, I was – I kept on thinking to myself of the proprieties involved in rolling up to somebody's funeral in that sort of transport and one of such a lurid hue as well. When the time came, of course, I need hardly tell you nobody relished the occasion more than Hugo Dinsmore, arriving in proper James Cagney fashion in a sharp, three-button, made to measure, light-weight, barathea number in pale charcoal. God forgive me, but I have the impression I had also on a pair of sunglasses just in case those hayseeds present missed the connection and my new status as the Eggman's latest protégé.

But before that came about, when J.J. and I emerged together as if dressed like a couple of mourners already in our near-matching suits and slim-jim ties, Junior's face, for a second time, said it all. Mouth half open, he stood there, great purple hands encircling the handlebar grips, and I felt certain J.J. was bound to say something insulting and terrible. But he didn't, merely going over and getting into the car without a word, while I stood there tortured by a new quandary. What was to be done about Junior now that he was here, for I knew J.J. would never countenance stowing that great ugly machine of his in the car's boot – or trunk, as it was known – even though it could swallow it with ease. And Junior, in turn, would never leave his precious bike behind, no matter how much he would love to be seen in just such a motor. Alternatively, I could always ride home with him on the bar, I could, couldn't I, legs dangling like some overdressed puppet for everyone to have a great laugh about.

From the car J.J. called out, 'Well, are you coming, wee man, or aren't you?'

So I went. Of course, I did. What else? – leaving Junior standing there in the middle of the Eggman's yard like the delivery boy I suppose really he was in everyone else's eyes except mine, for I still saw someone who had only ever known me as the 'wee fucker' with an ingenious line in persecution, including more than once, I recall, getting me to place a hand on his burgeoning cock. All of this came flooding back, yet not in a bitter or vengeful way, but as if already I had abandoned him just like Uncle Harry and the rest of them back at that ruined old warren in its hollow between weir and railway line.

'Let's go,' said J.J. and we took off. I didn't dare look back once.

For some time we drove in silence. Then he said, 'What happened? Could he not swim?'

'That's right,' I told him. 'Just tripped and fell in. Didn't stand a chance.'

'Jesus! The country's one dangerous fucking place, I tell you. Worse than fucking Vietnam.'

Pulling out the fag packet he asked me to light a couple from the lighter in the dashboard while the car rolled on towards Larkhill on four massive, fat, whitewall Goodyears. Dragging on a Disque Bleu I could feel the numbness which Junior's news had brought starting to wear off, which in turn made me keep expecting some of those first warning aches and pains that might signal the onset of proper grief of the sort other more normal people are supposed to experience, even people like Junior, who probably was pounding hard on his pedals behind us right now. How embarrassing if he managed to beat us to it, showing up at some crossroads ahead, red-faced and grinning, like one of those rustics who make a habit of racing alongside cars just as their dogs do.

I kept watching out for him but, instead, an equally dreaded figure materialised on the road in front, not on two wheels, but on foot, as usual. Striding along, head high, as if with the scent of carrion in his nostrils already, Sinbad Scully was eating up the tarmac and I didn't have to be a fortune-

219

teller to know our destination was the same. Passing him by, I felt like reaching over and pulling on the wheel, so ridding us of that malevolent old buzzard for keeps.

At the house everyone was sitting around in deep silence in the biggest and gloomiest room staring in front of them as if waiting for something to happen. *Someone* to make it happen, more like, and it came as a shock to realise that someone was meant to be me, little Hugo Dinsmore. A coffin straddled two chairs in the far room, but not open to accommodate the passing gape of the mourners as was the custom. Later Junior said Uncle Harry's body – I find it hard to use the word *corpse* – had swollen to such an extent, because of its being in the water, as well as other transformations of an horrific nature, that the undertaker had advised against having the lid up. But all the time in my head I had this surge of images of mutilation and rapid decay beneath the varnished oak, the eyes gnawed from their sockets by the great eel, as black and thick as a car's inner tube, reputed to lurk waiting for just such offal in its lair deep beneath the weir.

J.J. came inside with me. I think he was more curious about the set-up than wishing to pay his respects, but I felt in no mood to dissuade him even if it meant loads of cracks later about hillbillies and inbreeding. Already he had started referring to Larkhill as Dogpatch. Strangely enough his muted commentary did have the effect of lifting my spirits.

'Who's the old biddy knitting in the corner?' he whispered. 'Looks like Whistler's Mother-in-law.'

It was Aunt Dolly, and not a day older looking, despite J.J.'s comment.

I could see her glaring at me in my up to the minute gear – lording it, in her opinion, I felt sure.

'You still haven't grown much,' was her only comment when I went across to her.

In retaliation I made a great show of giving one of the

uncles money to buy drink for us all. He didn't seem to mind
– it was the jailbird, Sid – but I could see Dolly clacking
away with those needles of hers like angry chopsticks as if to
say *we have no need of your easy come, easy go riches*.

'Are these all your *relatives*?' J.J., again. He made the word
sound like shit. 'The redhead's quite tasty in her own way.
It's all right to have a poke, as long as she's not your first
cousin. Or did no one ever tell you that before – Abner?'

Bessie was sitting apart by herself, head lowered, dressed
demurely in a black and white, spotted, pinafore number
with a peek-a-boo collar and, I like to think, grieving in her
own way, for I know she had loved the man in the closed
coffin almost as much as I had. She was his pet, anyone could
see that. He would bring back sherbet packets and liquorice
sticks for her each time he went out on a Friday night, even
when she was long past the age and the taste for such things.
For some time I have to confess I was intensely jealous, and
later, when I caught her and Junior spread-eagled that time
up at Taggart's old rath, I hugged the secret to myself as a
reserve against a time when I would be ready to usurp her
place in the big man's affections. But looking at her now,
sad-faced, lost in thought, in her little dress, I was glad I'd
kept it to myself. Anyway, how could I have ever brought
myself to put it into words without destroying my own
innocent image, as well as hers? The shock would have been
too great. Someone like J.J., of course, would have found no
difficulty whatsoever. *The butcher boy's been hiding the
chipolata, just thought you should know*, I could hear him
announce without preamble, *with little Gingersnap more than
happy to oblige*.

'How are you, Bessie?' I said. 'How have you been?' as if
I'd returned from overseas and not four miles up the road.

She kept her eyes downcast, twisting a hanky in her lap,
but, persisting, I told her, 'I like your dress', hoping, I

221

suppose, she might reciprocate, for it really was an exceptionally snazzy piece of tailoring I had on my back.

The Eggman had taken me to his own man in town and sat watching like a great, blond Buddha in a leather armchair while Terry Nugent – 'Tailor to the Elite' – measured me, his mouth full of pins. The suit had everything. Five-inch vent, ticket pocket, four-button, mother of pearl cuffs, under-arm sweat pads, a lining of Italian paisley silk. I had three fittings and the finished product staring back at me from the full-length mirror was perfection. Hugo Dinsmore, junior fashion plate and man of the moment, Ulster's own Paul Anka, take a bow. Which I did a lot of afterwards when no one was around to catch me miming to a glass.

While I was endeavouring to get a reaction from Bessie, J.J. came oiling his way over towards us, drawing up a chair, setting himself down on the far side of her. Snaky as some dago lover-boy, he promptly pulled out two Du Maurier and for a terrible instant I felt convinced he was about to light both in his mouth before offering her one with his foul spit all over it. But he didn't, holding it out to her unlit, instead. Modestly she shook her head but I noticed a glint in her eye, a lightening which hadn't been there before.

'Well, well, well,' said he, 'Hugo's certainly been keeping *you* well hidden, I must say, missy. Now I wonder why that could be. Hm?' fixing me with a greasy grin on his face. And as if to say, *yes, just why is that, Hugo?* Bessie glanced at me as well and, put on the spot, Christ knows why, I snatched the spare cigarette from his hand and stuck it in my own mouth. Wrong end and cork-tip foremost, unfortunately, which really amused the pair of them.

'Here, let me show you how it's done,' cooed J.J.

He had one of those flashy American college rings on his fourth finger, groovy, I suppose, if you care for that sort of thing, and I noticed Bessie eye it avidly. Right in front of me, as I watched, the person I once idolised as the very

222

essence of girlish innocence was changing back into that same hussy I had caught groaning under Junior like a heifer in heat. *Oh, Bessie, Bessie, how could you have allowed yourself to do such a thing*, I kept thinking, when what I meant, I suppose, deep down, was – *and not with me*.

Some time later the bold Romeo himself appeared, lobster pink, and in a sweat from cycling like a madman so anxious was he not to miss anything. Scully was with him. They came into the big sitting-room, the one, effusive and bent on mischief as ever, and the other like some grief-stricken scarecrow. I could hear him sighing tragically right across the room as he went from person to person, palms piously outstretched, as if he had taken orders since last I'd seen him. I ignored him completely. Even though it was a time to bury the past, like the man in the far room, I could never forgive him for putting the story about of Uncle Harry giving himself up to the Moylena's embrace in that way. Even if it was as he suggested, what earthly right had he to voice such an opinion? Instead, it should have been buried and forgotten along with the drowned man himself, when the time came to slide what was left of him, as full of gas as an old pig's bladder, into that trench in the poor people's part of Kilcarn graveyard, deep among the dock, the nettles and leaning headstones.

And so we sat staring at one another in that musty old parlour, if one could call it such, with its crippled, bog oak furniture and wallpaper once vaguely floral, but now practically indecipherable under years of grime and neglect. A blaze of sorts, fed by anthracite and damp wooden blocks, guttered in a fireplace and for the first time I noticed a calendar hanging from a nail above a sideboard with the date 1937 on it, under a picture of an impossibly young and melancholy-looking King George and his merry, dark-eyed, new bride.

I could sense depression starting to seep through me like the damp behind the faint cabbage roses on the walls. I imagined it held in some sort of suspension there in the plaster, just biding its time to break forth in sweat as soon as someone put the first match to that bundle of old pre-war newspapers and dry sticks in the grate, visualising, too, what must have been that first great, billowing back rush of smoke on account of the old crow's nest wedged high in the chimney. I kept wondering, also, just how much longer I would be able to hold out on this uncomfortable kitchen chair, chosen in the first place for fear of messing up my new trousers with their knife-edge creases and half-silk linings. Hitched high above oxblood loafers, they showed six inches of fine cotton lisle stretched tight as a dark second skin. Cheap, corrugated, teenage white might be all very well for the likes of Junior and his pals, certainly not for the newly imaged Hugo Dinsmore.

Putting all of this down, as I do now, I blush, for I can just see myself perched there on my slatted, wooden throne slumming it like some visiting sprig of nobility. But then Junior came across, thrusting his great speckled kisser right up close to mine. His breath smelt sweetly rank as if he'd been at the Bushmills laid on at my request in the next room.

'You come along with me,' he whispered and, forgetting all those earlier, grand delusions brought on by an expensive new outfit, I did as I was told as if nothing had changed between us and I was back to being the meek and dutiful slave once more. Along the dark passageway I followed him. It smelt of baby wee even though all of us had long since grown up from those days when we would let loose in running spurts when we couldn't manage to reach the outside air in time.

'In here,' commanded Junior, pushing me into a room I'd never been in before, small, dark, airless, with a bed, a chair and a press in the corner, and instantly I knew it was where

Uncle Harry had slept all those years, for it still carried the scent of him and his clothes.

Beside the bed, rumpled just as he'd left it that last morning, stood a half-empty orangeade bottle, the contents flat and acid yellow, and as my eyes grew accustomed to the light I made out the pale form of a brimming chamber pot, the piss identical in hue to the orangeade. For some reason, I don't know why, this fact registered with tremendous force, as if I'd stumbled on some hitherto unrecognised chemical axiom, and I was still staring at the two containers, clear glass and china, when Junior pulled open the door of the old press and took out something in a flat, wooden case. Carefully he carried it over to the bed and opened the clasps and I saw the gleam of silver keys inside against soft, greenish velvet.

'This is for you,' he said. 'Old Harry would have wanted you to have it. Anyway, none of the rest of us is musical,' putting the flute into my hands.

For a moment, stupidly, I felt like saying, *but you know I can't play*, but, thankfully, something made me hold my tongue. Sitting alongside on the unmade bed Junior watched intently as I fingered the cool intricacy of ebony and chased metal, as if I might somehow put the instrument to my lips, filling the room once more with the sound we would all listen to of a summer's evening, drifting down from McGookin's wood.

'Now come and have a drop of the hard stuff. On you, wee man, on you,' and, laughing, he put an affectionate, beefy arm about my shoulders.

'See your man back there?' said he, squeezing as he did so. 'If he gives you any oul' buck just say the word and I'll knock his pan in. Feel that.'

Rolling up his shirt-sleeve he proceeded to pop his bicep for my diversion before taking my hand and laying it on a freckled bulge the size of a cricket ball. Sensing the sudden rush of blood heat, for one awful instant I thought sure the next area for my admiration might be that other engorged muscle further below but, thankfully, he drew me to my feet and we went back down along the dark passageway, arm in arm, like a couple of long lost buddies.

'I'll tell you something else,' he confided breathily, holding me fast in the selfsame grip he had once employed when measuring me against those pencil marks on the scullery wall. 'I don't give two flying fucks for your Eggman. He might well be the biggest gangster going, but he doesn't scare me one bit. Him, nor any of his hard men. You hear me, wee fucker?'

'Sure now, he's not so bad,' I responded weakly. 'He's been very decent to me.'

'Mebbe so, but always you remember you're every bit as good as any of them up at that place, even if you are wee. The Dinsmores have nothing to be ashamed of.'

I could swear there were tears in those bloodshot eyes.

But before he let me go there was one final thing he wished to confide and as I heard him out, with all my heart I wished he hadn't.

'Me and Bella's thinking of getting spliced.'

I peered at him in the half-light of that pissy, old rat-run of a passageway of ours. What could I say? I knew something was expected of me. But, somehow, an image of the pair, Junior and his monstrous bride-to-be in a church setting instead of writhing together in that old, beached railway carriage, him with his jeans at half-mast and her with her barrage balloon bloomers down about her enormous ankles – that's if she ever wore any when doing business – kept getting in the way.

'She's saved up a fair wee bit. Enough, she says, to get me started in my own shop.'

'But not here.'

I could hear the quibble in my voice, I couldn't help it, and he stared back at me. Then, rolling his head from side to side as if to disperse some of the alcoholic mists in his brain, he muttered, 'Both of us wants to make a new start. Mebbe even across the water. You understand? You do, don't you, wee fucker?'

And, oddly enough, that wee fucker did, for, still in his grasp, suddenly he was seeing them in a shocking new light, actually *talking* together, and in all seriousness, too, across from one another on those ancient, worn, plush seats, old, dark-toned, sepia photographic views of tourist attractions – the Glens of Antrim, the Giant's Causeway, the famous swaying rope bridge – gazing down on them, Junior and Bella, like that pair in the nursery rhyme, the couple Sprat.

'What do you think?'

'Think?' I said.

'Yes, think.'

For a moment I looked at him. Then, shutting off my brain and instincts along with it, I said, 'Why not?' which seemed to satisfy him, for he gave a vast sigh like some lovesick bullock while loosening his hold on me.

Back in the main room somebody had made tea. There were ham sandwiches, even a cake, and in a grand gesture, for the Eggman's money nestled fat and reassuring against my thigh, I sent out for more drink from Lyle's pub, two dozen stout of the brand the dead man had always favoured. Sid set off at a gallop, grinning, and in the short time he was gone – he must have commandeered Junior's bicycle this time round – an atmosphere verging on the convivial seemed to develop, which was an eye-opener as much to me as seeing that chocolate sponge sitting in the middle of our old table. At one stage, unprompted, I sang 'Jeannie with the Light Brown Hair', Uncle Harry's favourite, and the one he would always sign off with up among the beech trees. Bessie snivelled, even Aunt Dolly suspended her knitting, while Junior sat with a young one straddling each knee, a look of extreme soppiness on his face. Probably thinking of the patter of tiny feet himself, the crazy thought did cross my mind, for the sentiments of that old ballad had worked their magic on me as well.

In the silence that followed Sinbad Scully was heard to announce, 'Beautiful, just beautiful,' in what I construed as a proprietorial tone of voice, which broke the spell, taking me out of my warm and generous mood. In an oddly perverse way it felt good to be able to detest someone again, like an acid antidote after so much cloying sweetness. Like Aunt Dolly's chocolate layer cake. I've always been that way, I don't know why, and a short time later when J.J. and I made our escape, driving off together, it felt good to pass that same old hypocrite by, ignoring his outstretched hand signalling his desire for a lift. J.J. slowed down fractionally as if the mood of cordiality still lingered but, 'No, no,' I told him, 'drive on,' and he glanced sideways at me as he accelerated past, with a knowing expression on his face.

'Friend of yours?'

The day of the funeral the Eggman came as well as J.J. They sat in the car with the heater running while the family shivered around that raw, open wound in the ground. There was a foot of khaki slurry in the grave and the coffin made a squelching noise as it was lowered to rest. Some young clergyman – God alone knows where they found him – stuttered and stammered his way through the burial words. To be truthful, I felt nothing save an intense and irritating boredom. Any grieving to be done had long since run its course. I wanted nothing more to do with funerals, ever. Three was more than enough for someone my age, I kept telling myself. First my parents, now Harry.

I was wearing a new, three-quarter-length sheepskin coat the Eggman had just bought me, I remember, and deep in its soft, thick, fleecy innards I shrank until I was like a tortoise with only my head showing over the orange hide of its collar. Looking around it seemed everyone else except myself had on the wrong, out of season, apparel, Junior, in particular. Jeans, sleeveless pullover, same old lumberjack shirt, uncovered arms like corned beef. Bessie, too, the only woman present, looked pathetic also, I felt, in a short, almost mini skirt and bare legs. Both possessed identical flesh tones, I observed, as if for the first time, Dinsmore skin, the cold accentuating every goose bump, spot and blemish.

As I studied the assembled clan standing there gazing into the grave I had a presentiment this would be the last time I would ever see them again. And as the first ochre clods bounced off the coffin lid I walked back to the waiting car, head lowered, hands buried deep in the soft deep pockets of my new, beautiful and eminently desirable overcoat. J.J. gunned the engine as I approached, a throaty, impatient roar that sent the rooks boiling up out of the yews. Behind me, heads turned at the sudden racket, crude, intrusive, like the man inside. But I closed my ears to it, as well as to their sensibilities, sliding into the sudden shock of heat in the back seat.

To say a chapter, or something similar, closed in my young life is what people always say when looking back with hindsight, but I knew it, one of the rare and startling certainties in a period always associated in my memory with confusion and doubt. Nothing was said as we drove and I was glad of it, content to lie back in the folds of my fabulous animal skin while breathing in the heady scent of all its amazing newness.

'About here?' enquired J.J. at one point, slowing the car to a crawl and glancing across at the big man as if they had something prearranged in mind. We were passing Posy Row at the time and I gave a gasp, realising I, too, was to be involved in their scheme, whatever it was, and whether I liked it or not.

229

'So, wee man, tell us which house your two lady friends live in?' asked the Eggman and leaning forward I pointed at one of the cottages. Unkempt privet hedge, cracked concrete path, green front door and maroon curtains drawn across, as always, as if in perpetual mourning.

'They mightn't be in,' I told him.

'Try them anyway. Just say Lyle Ritchie wants to know if they'd like to come for a spin and then on to somewhere nice. Tell them we'll wait.'

'But not too long,' J.J. cut in cheekily.

It was coming up to four o'clock on a Thursday afternoon and I had really meant what I said about them being out. Curiously enough, I had never asked if they had jobs to go to, yet I suppose they would have volunteered such information if they'd cared to, or thought it any of my business. *I* certainly didn't, my head filled with other things unconnected with boring reality like what they got up to when I wasn't around being indulged like some little junior pasha.

When I got to the front door I had a fit of nerves. It seemed an eternity since last I'd been inside, a sort of cooling-off period having set in just about the time Sinbad Scully had got wind of our Sunday trysts. Breathing deeply, I thought of all the reasons not to go through with this. So, what if I pretended to knock, then after a plausible period of waiting simply turned away? But the Eggman's car was drawn up right across the gate mouth and I knew I hadn't the guts to carry off such a scheme, not with that deadly blue stare of his drilling through the layer of thick sheepskin covering my back.

Deirdre answered the door. She was wearing cerise toreador pants and a tight, fluffy, peach-coloured polo neck. Her hair looked shorter, cut neat and close, in a dark, glossy helmet very different from her normal page-boy.

230

'Well, hello, stranger,' she greeted me, leaning up against the jamb of the door like Ava Gardner in her latest movie, but without the cigarette, and a warm treacle of gratitude and renewed ardour slid over me just like the first time.

'Well, look at *you*,' she said, eyeing me up and down. 'Come to visit your poor relations, are we?'

'No, no, no,' I protested, sweating, and in a stammering rush blurted out my message.

She looked at me coolly, then, leaning close, plucked an imaginary speck of something off the fleece of my lapel.

'I hope,' said she, 'the Hugo we know and love hasn't fell in with the wrong company,' and I realised then she had spotted the car straight off, but was pretending it didn't exist, along with the occupants. Just the two of us on her doorstep the way it had been before, as if nothing had altered or been damaged in any way, and in another warm rush I longed to reassure her I hadn't changed either despite the get-up and the two people waiting for me.

'Do you want to come in? Doris is lying on the settee like a big fat whale.'

'I can't,' I told her, glancing over my shoulder. The engine had quickened, picking up more revs.

'Well,' she said, 'I know Doris would dearly love to see you, and I'm bored to bits. Both of us are. Sooo. . .'

She left the final word trailing tantalisingly in the air, carmine lips funnelling her warm breath into my face. It smelt sweetish, vaguely alcoholic, and remembering that day spent passing the sherry bottle under the bedclothes, I felt a stirring down below through a couple of layers of sheepskin and fine worsted.

'We won't take long,' she said: 'just enough to get the war-paint on,' disappearing inside.

'Well?' enquired J.J. when I slid into the back seat, the Eggman saying nothing.

231

But it was him I was trying to impress when I announced, 'No problem. They'll be straight out,' with the implication that, let's face it, how could it be otherwise with Hugo Dinsmore on the case?

But time passed and passed, the car filling with tobacco fumes, and I could sense impatience emanating from the Eggman like an invisible haze. J.J. kept glancing sideways for the signal to put his foot down and just when I thought that moment had arrived I heard the front door slam followed by the rapid heart-stopping tattoo of stilettos on the concrete path. Then the rear doors swung out and I moved across to form the filling in a sandwich, bolstered right and left by a matching pair of the most delightfully, freshly perfumed and powdered creatures imaginable. Basking in the warm feeling of having pulled off this stunning coup single-handedly, I felt the great car shudder then accelerate away in a cloud of exhaust smoke towards its mystery destination.

Before we had reached the open countryside, which wasn't all that long for Posy Row sat in isolation surrounded by farmland, J.J. started passing back the fags, always a surefire ice-breaker I had learned, but as yet hadn't much chance to practise. But it was he and Deirdre who did all the talking. The Eggman – or Lyle, as I kept reminding myself to think of him now in company – spoke not a word. Nor did Doris and I. She had slipped a soft hand into mine deep in my coat pocket and as far as I was concerned J.J. and that bad, bold sister of hers could laugh and kid away together for ever just as long as those deliciously cool fingers remained secretly entwined in mine.

'Tell me, girls,' J.J. said, although it was obvious the question was addressed to only one, 'what's it like living out in the sticks? How do you stand it? Nothing but moo cows, sheep and horses. What do you do for fun?'

'Oh, you'd be surprised at some of the things we get up

to,' replied Deirdre, directing a puff of smoke at the back of that perfect, brilliantined, Roman head of his.

Sliding a bare, bangled arm about my neck, she teased, 'Wouldn't he, Hugo?' and I felt myself go all hot thinking our little private pastimes might be about to be made public, even though I relished the idea of having done things with the sisters in that big double bed of theirs which, if he'd known about, would have driven J.J. half nuts with envy. At least I liked to believe so anyway, hugging our back seat secrets to myself in a rapture as we all drove on together to the famous Burnfoot Inn.

Newly opened little over six months or so, already it had become the talk of the country, a byword for sophistication and glamour, the very first roadhouse anyone had ever seen in our part of the world, that very word *roadhouse* epitomising, somehow, a dream palace where film stars might congregate over cocktails. Some said it even had a swimming pool and palm trees like something out of 77 *Sunset Strip*, on Sunset Boulevard instead of the Drumskeagh Road. And when J.J. casually let slip the name of the place the girls gasped involuntarily and I felt Doris's perfect little paw contract in mine. Naturally I betrayed no emotion one way or the other, just like the Eggman, silent as a gravestone, yet still wondering what must be going through that mind of his, if anything. Perhaps there was this dead, dark space back there somewhere, like an emptied attic. Perhaps all his impulses originated some place else, maybe in his stomach, say, or his womanly chest, for he had breasts, most definitely, or in the region of his dick, even though it was difficult to imagine anything with a life of its own in the shadow of that enormous belly of his.

But then as we passed an arrowed sign – Burnfoot Inn 200 Yards – above a picture of a jolly fisherman holding a salmon in one hand and a spilling tankard in the other, he seemed to stir, the great, camel hair shoulders shifting slightly.

'Now, remember, girls,' we heard him say, 'this party's on me. J.J. and Hugo here will see you right. Order what you like.'

'Don't worry, big man, we will, we will,' retorted Deirdre, always the cheeky one, and I thought for a moment she might have said the wrong thing, but he only laughed.

'Only the very best for any friend of Hugo's,' he told her and there was something almost elegant in the way he put it, as if maybe I'd misjudged him all along, not recognising an aristocratic layer lurking under that, at times, country-rough, gangsterish exterior. And some of that same stylishness seemed to have rubbed off on the rest of us, for we swept into the place as if an invisible net of superiority had settled over us the moment we stepped out of the car.

Just inside the front door there was this massive mirror and, catching a passing reflection, I thought to myself, *now there's a classy party, if ever I saw one* and, indulging the fantasy to the hilt, continued, *I wonder who they might be*, the two stunning brunettes, that giant in the unbuttoned crombie, the other one laughing and showing his perfect teeth. Last, and most intriguing of the entire bunch, the elegant young guy in the sheepskin coat.

J.J. kept holding doors open. It was definitely a 'ladies first' thing with him, I noticed, although my instincts told me he was much more interested in getting a good rear-end view of those retreating, tightly corseted, perfect, twin chassis. Each arse chewing a caramel, as Junior would have phrased it, if he had been here instead of bouncing up and down on that great human trampoline he seemed so set on taking up with. I still couldn't take it in. How could I, given the wealth of sweaty detail he had supplied me with about his courtship, the act so outrageous, crazed, even. Yet the more I thought of it – fearless, too – confounding everyone, not only at Larkhill, but in the entire locality, once the knot was tied and

234

the word got out. A strange, warm gush of sentimentality was gathering in me towards the once much feared Junior. Might he ask me to be best man, I even found myself wondering, and if so, would I say yes? Damned right I would, damned right. . .

'What was that, Hugo?'

It was Doris sliding up unawares as I waited for her and her sister to emerge from the Ladies' Room. It was the first time I'd ever set eyes on those dainty little cut-outs before, confusing at first glance, for the female version looked exactly like a man in a kilt. J.J. and the Eggman had headed straight ahead as though totally at home with the layout of the place.

'She'll be out in a tick. So she says. You know what she's like. Late for her own funeral.' Then she stopped, a look of horror on those pretty features.

'Oh, I'm really, really sorry, Hugo, I forgot all about your bad news. Was it awful for you, pet?'

And cupping my cheeks with those cool palms of hers she planted a kiss on my mouth, the taste of her lipstick pleasant in a vanilla-ish sort of way, yet vaguely repellent, too, leaving me wondering what the etiquette might be concerning how long one should decently wait before wiping it off. But then Deirdre emerged in a haze of scent, for the first time making me realise just why they called it a powder room. Grabbing hold of me she brought her face up close and I felt certain I was about to be imprinted a second time.

'What do you think, Hugo?' she giggled. 'Isn't it great? This joint, I mean? I don't know about you two, but I'm going to have champagne.'

'Oh, Deirdre,' said Doris, 'you can't!'

'Just watch me. Anyway, the Eggman's loaded.'

Then, 'Oops,' she said, looking around her, 'I mean Lyle,' and at that point I realised she was already somewhat loaded herself in her own way.

The place we walked into together was much less festive and far gloomier than I'd expected, but then I suppose it was still too early for the night's fun to get going properly. We were in a big dining-room full of empty tables all set with sugar-pink tablecloths and red candles in bottles waiting for a waiter to come round and put a match to them. I could also see a horseshoe-shaped bar backed by an impressive, lit array of hard liquor, and there was a piano as well, raised above a polished dance floor about the size of somebody's front room carpet. It had little lights set into the margins, a reassuring detail which I had noted in countless night-club movie settings.

J.J. and the Eggman were sitting at one of the tables talking to a man in a dinner jacket, which in my naive way I interpreted as a further sign of sophistication. He rose as we approached, beating J.J. to it, pasty pale, dark dyed hair combed sideways in inky strings across his scalp instead of back. 'Ah,' he said, 'here comes the glamour! Welcome to the Burnfoot!' He had an English accent, not posh, more Northern industrial, I'd say, and the name of the place sounded awkward, foreign even, coming from his lips, as if he hadn't stepped off the boat too long.

'I'm Ronnie. Ronnie Hoffman. But my friends all call me Ronnie. Like Lyle here.' As he spoke he laid a hand lightly on that broad, camel-hair-covered shoulder, removing it almost immediately with a nervous smile as though he'd touched something dangerously hot or electrically live.

'I hope you're all going to dine with us. We have some excellent, freshly caught Coleraine salmon, or steak, if you prefer it. But, first, something to drink?'

'Bring us a bottle of bubbly, Ron. Four glasses. Right, Lyle?' It was J.J. acting Mr Big Shot, but fooling no one, especially me. Deirdre giggled and the men all looked at her with that same, sudden expression on their faces as if getting to know her on a more intimate footing was a distinct possibility for the very first time.

'Make it two bottles,' said the Eggman, and Ronnie bustled off, returning in under a minute with an ice bucket, the champagne and glasses. We watched intently as he stripped the foil, then bent back the little wire cage. Twisting the cork slowly, he grinned at Deirdre who gave a screech the moment it popped, then shrieked some more as foam filled her glass. Everyone laughed, except the Eggman who kept staring at her with those Reckitt blue eyes of his while cramming his mouth with nuts from a bowl on the table in front of him.

Champagne tasted dry in the throat and prickled the hairs in your nose. Those were my first impressions, not the seductively explosive sensation I had expected. Doris sipped hers slowly, a look of extreme caution in her soft eyes, Deirdre half emptied her glass at the first gulp, J.J. left his untouched, and the Eggman drank nothing, a rime of salt from the peanuts ringing his lips. He watched the four of us, as did Ronnie Hoffman, who leant on the back of one of the chairs. His hands were the palest I'd ever seen, the nails perfect with a soft, almost pearly sheen.

'Enjoy,' he said, 'it's on the house,' then left us.

J.J. filled Deirdre's glass again, which was to be the pattern from then on as if she was being readied for sacrifice or doped for the operating table. Doctor J.J. with his oily bedside manner. And all the while the Eggman kept staring as though waiting for the anaesthetic to take hold. I think he drank orange juice, but there may have been something else there as well, clear, colourless, like vodka, or maybe even gin, but it was impossible to tell as his glass was brought to the table each time without him lifting a finger or having to say a word.

For the life of me I can't remember what we talked about, which is strange, because we were in the Burnfoot for a very long time. I suppose I would have remembered if it had been of any consequence, but then J.J. did nearly all of it. I do recall him smoking a lot and shooting his cuffs to show off a set of flashy links he seemed very proud of – a gold Dunhill lighter, as well as tie-pin – and as the champagne started coiling up through my veins – it seemed to start at the feet for some reason, which struck me as distinctly odd – across the table from me I kept seeing these little reflected points of light as if J.J. had turned into an expensively decorated Christmas tree. Doris and I sat there, hands joined under the pink tablecloth. Once she got up to go to the Ladies and I felt a distinct pang of abandonment as our palms disengaged.

By the time the subject of food came up we were on our third bottle of Bollinger. Folding menus the size of draught-boards arrived, in French as well as English, but the Eggman asked for a sirloin steak, well done, nothing on it, as did J.J., while I dithered along with the girls. Finally Deirdre plumped for prawn cocktail followed by beef stroganoff which appealed to me as well because of the name, which sounded like something Franchot Tone might have ordered at Sardi's, and Doris, who was picky at the best of times, decided on a mushroom omelette.

Halfway through our meal the pianist arrived, a little, prematurely grizzled guy dragging a clubfoot. No sheet music, just a drink in his hand aimed for the distant lid of the baby grand. He looked so serious, so businesslike at first, limping across to the raised stand, settling himself on the stool, flexing his fingers one by one, but then, starting to play, a look of rapture crept over his face. All night, despite everything that was going on at our table and all around us, too, my attention kept returning to our little maestro in the old-fashioned tuxedo, the standards pouring from him, 'Laura', 'Deep Purple', 'Misty', 'Where or When'.

Meanwhile we ate, drank, smoked – sometimes simultane-ously, it seemed to me – and people started arriving in couples, the candles coming on, pricking the dimness one by one, as did all those little dance-floor glow-worms in shades of magenta right through to palest violet. I suppose I must have started getting drunk. Well, of course, I did. Was there an alternative? I think, too, I switched from champagne to rum and Coke at some point, the sweet trolley having approached like a silent, charged chariot. Black Forest gâteau, sherry trifle, crème caramel, something amazing called a *sorbet*, followed by cheese and biscuits. J.J. and Deirdre by this stage were drinking brandy out of balloon glasses while the Eggman yawned and picked his teeth, but I no longer cared.

'Does he take requests?' says Deirdre. 'Your wee man at the joanna?'

'Is the Pope a Catholic?' replies J.J., lighting a cigar, an open box of fat, banded torpedoes having appeared amid the debris on the table. 'What do you want him to play, babe? Just say the word.'

'Hugo,' says she, sweetly fluttering her thickened lashes while turning an open-mouthed, glassy stare on me, 'tell J.J. here what you'd like to sing for us all. Better still, be a pet and go up with him yourself.'

So, with the Eggman's silent blessing – at least, I took it to be so – that is how I found myself leaning up against the side of that piano in the Burnfoot Inn in front of a crowd of flushed businessmen and their lady friends giving them 'Moon River' followed by 'The Shadow of Your Smile', and finally, 'Stranger in Paradise', for I had learned three was the magic number when it came to requests, one being never enough, but more than three laying yourself open to a charge of having a big head. Which, of course, was the case, but which I had learned to keep only between myself and the mirror.

The applause seemed heartfelt enough and Bobby McBride the pianist gave me a wink, which I took to be approval and, of course, Deirdre couldn't keep her paws and lips off me when I got back to the table. I have to admit I was starting to get quite blasé about the whole business by now, cultivating the sort of world-weary, yet always polite reaction to compliments I had seen the professionals use. Like that wee guy playing the piano up there, smiling, always smiling, even when the racket from the tables drowned out some of his best flourishes. The two of us had much in common, I found myself musing, sipping my Bacardi and Coca-Cola, and not merely in the stature department either, give or take a few inches here and there, of course. But then again he had a bad leg which, thank God, I hadn't. This was the sort of pathetic guff travelling through my head when one of the other diners approached our table.

'It's my young sister's birthday,' he broke in without preamble. 'Georgie, her name is. Sing "Happy Birthday" for her.'

A big, meaty, rugby-playing bruiser with a number-two crew cut, he was glaring fixedly at me as he spoke. Blazer-boys, we called them. His was navy blue with gold buttons and a yellow and purple crest, the striped tie, clearly club, as well. For a moment everyone stared up at him standing there, shoulders a match for the Eggman's.

Then J.J. said, 'He doesn't do requests. It's not in his contract,' and Deirdre laughed.

The big three-quarters went even redder in the face if that were possible. Quite conceivably a young farmer, too, which made him even more of a cunt.

'I'm talking to the wee guy, not you,' he said and it was one of those moments when I felt fear and excitement in equal parts, sensing trouble, yet exhilarated by the certainty I would be safe on the sidelines if and when it were to break out. It was a sensation I was to experience quite often after that, the way things were to turn out for me.

'You heard what he said. Push off now and don't be bothering us.'

Suddenly it was the Eggman's turn, and listening to his voice like that after such a lengthy stretch of silence came as something of a shock. But then that was the effect it usually had on a lot of people anyway, so sparing was he with anything he did say. Those who knew him tended to fill in the blanks, a bit like joining up the dots in one of those kiddy pictures, and the odd thing was just how remarkably adept everyone became at it. In this particular instance, for a change, no one had to do a thing – the jigsaw was already complete – least of all our friend the baboon in the blazer. Yet there was that brief interlude while he hung over us all not yet totally convinced in his mind if he had been insulted or not and how, before finally going back to his friends to brood on it some more.

'Would you believe it!' said J.J. 'What a creep! I hate those big fucking gorillas, don't you?' and for a moment we seemed to be united in our contempt for the breed, drinking bubbly, while over at that far table of theirs they made do with pints of Guinness and Babycham for their boring girlfriends.

After that things became a trifle hazy. Certainly I can and do recall incidents in isolation, but not in any proper or connected pattern. People started dancing, I do know that, including Deirdre and J.J. who, as expected, turned out to be pretty nifty, the pair of them, putting on an exhibition when the floor cleared for 'Jealousy', the other couples not having the necessary nerve for a tango. Hand in hand, Doris and I sat watching with the Eggman as they swooped and jerked like swallows over the postage-stamp, polished floor, the low-level lighting drawing attention to all that terrific footwork. To get up myself to dance with Doris might only take away from the perfection of the moment for us both, I convinced

241

myself, or at least suspend it in some fashion. I remember feeling sorry for the Eggman sitting there like a rock having no one to play pat-a-cake under the table with. That tells you just how drunk, as well as far gone, I must have been, I suppose.

At some point, however, I did have to take a piss, and disengaging myself from that sweetly perspiring clasp I went to the toilet and was washing my hands with the Burnfoot's plentiful hot water and scented soap when J.J. breezed in as merry as ever I'd seen him. Drawing out a small steel comb he proceeded to work on his hair even though it didn't look as if it needed it. Then he examined his teeth, his tongue, and the invisible hairs in his nose, finally brushing away imaginary dandruff from the shoulders of his gabardine jacket. I watched him out of the corner of my eye, for it was fascinating to see someone as vain about his appearance as myself, although I must admit I could never be so relaxed about it in front of another person as he appeared to be.

'Here, wee man,' he said, holding his cupped palm out for my inspection, 'have a sweetie,' and I saw a handful of glistening pills of various shapes and colours nestling there.

'I've got mandies, black bombers, bennies. Be my guest.'

Deep down I think I realised, then, this might be another of those life-turning points. But I had a choice this time or, rather, I felt I had, fooling myself, no doubt, that when I did select a single, blue, baby beauty I was doing it of my free will because of its innocent colour, or, not, more to the point, because I didn't want to look a total greenhorn.

'Excellent, excellent choice, my little friend. Big Deirdre's been eating them all night like Smarties. Any more and she'll be cleared for take-off. Which is the way I prefer my women, don't you? Airborne. Totally airborne, man,' and, arms outstretched, he made several swooping passes about the tiled floor of that Men's Room, laughing crazily as he did so. Then, unclenching his fist, he picked daintily through the assortment until he had settled on the desired combination.

'All together now,' he said, closely watching me, and for that moment I felt I still had a choice, either joining him, or slipping my own little robin's egg number into my pocket like an after-dinner mint for later.

'On second thoughts, not one of those,' said J.J., peering down at what I held in my palm. 'Far too rich for your young blood. Have one of these instead,' exchanging the pill for something that looked like an Aspro only bigger.

'Now be a good boy and do as Doctor Feelgood says. Ready, are we? Good. Down the hatch,' and we swallowed together. The taste was indeed like something you would take for a headache, bitter to the tongue and dry-sticking in the throat. Grimacing, J.J. gave a shudder, washing his own mixture down with a mouthful of water from the tap.

'Tell you what,' he said, leaning close to the mirror, 'we'll go back to their place and make it a foursome. How about it, wee man?'

I looked at him preening himself in front of the glass and felt whatever it was I'd just swallowed turn to bile in my stomach.

'Their mother's bedridden,' I told him, to which he reacted by giving a great laugh.

'Just the way her daughter will be, if I have any say in it. While *you're* on the job with number two. That's if you haven't been at the cookie-jar already, you sly wee shite you. Matter of interest, what's she like? Hot, is she? Run in the family?'

I could see he was getting excited, leaning in hard against the basin's rim. And was it my imagination but did his eyes seem hot and slightly staring, too, suddenly?

Endeavouring to bring the temperature down, I asked, 'What about Lyle?'

'What about him?'

He had turned around to face me, fixing me with his gaze, and over his shoulder I could see my own mug staring back at me, a look I despised, showing everything as usual. Again he laughed.

'Don't you worry your pretty little head about the Eggman. I'll let you into a secret. He can't get it up. Likes to watch, mind you.'

'I must remember to tell him you said that,' I heard myself shoot back without thinking and his expression changed from nice to nasty as he reached forward to take me by the lapels of my lovely new suit.

But just as I had decided I had gone too far this time didn't the door bang open and there stood one of the blazer-boys from the far table as if he had been waiting poised outside for the perfect stage entrance. Which certainly had the desired effect all right for J.J.'s hands flew from me as, pale as a ghost, he backed up against the basin.

'So,' said the bruiser, 'not so high and bloody mighty now, are we, all of a sudden,' obviously taking note of the rapid alteration in J.J.'s complexion. Mine, too, I felt positive, although I didn't dare risk a glance in the mirror to find out.

'Listen, mac, better have a care. You don't know who you're dealing with here.'

'Too fucking right I do. A fruit merchant and a midget.'

After that there was this tremendous silence broken only by the slow hiss of water escaping in one of the cubicles. Then someone flushed the cistern and, as one, we all turned to stare at the middle door, the only one closed, I realised for the first time, which seemed a shocking oversight on my part, yet now the noise of that lever being depressed sounded as welcome as a cavalry bugle to a wagon train of homesteaders. For some reason Big Chief Red in the Face in the rugby blazer appeared momentarily distracted by the presence of another person, for he headed straight for the row of urinals, unzipping his flies as he went. J.J. and I exchanged quick glances and made for the door. But before we could escape unscathed we heard him say, 'We'll settle this in the car park outside later.'

I have to confess my legs were shaking as we sat down at the table again, and was it my imagination but had the atmosphere in the entire room undergone a change in our absence? For a start the pianist had packed up and quite a few of the couples were on the move too, leaving money behind in saucers on the tables. Deirdre was still as sportive as ever, but I was seeing her in a different light now because of what J.J. had said. Her mask of make-up had lost much of its perfection. She had a strange, overwrought look about her, also, her ringing laugh an irritant, and I could sense the Eggman had started losing interest and patience not only with her but the rest of us as well.

For a time J.J. toyed with his drink, then, leaning across, he whispered something briefly in the big man's ear. He looked at him, then at the corner table where our crew-cutted sportsmen were in a menacing huddle along with their dumpy womenfolk. They were staring hard in our direction, specifically at the girls, who must have been a source of upset all evening, but, in particular, Deirdre, whose every antic was aimed at causing outrage.

'Did Rocky say he'd show up or not?'

'Not exactly.'

'What do you mean, not exactly?'

The Eggman and J.J. were now having this dialogue over our heads, but I wasn't paying much attention. The blond brute who had made threats in the Gents earlier was now back with his friends and I could see that trio of close-cropped scalps in a huddle as though some sort of battle strategy was being hatched, like the ones, I suppose, they were used to in the locker room just prior to laying into the opposition. Instinct, aided by imagination, somehow told me I would be the one to get thumped first in any scrimmage.

The next time Ronnie Hoffman appeared bearing someone else's bill on a tray the Eggman called him over. 'Any sign of Rocky?' he asked and the other told him, yes, as a matter of fact, he was in the public bar having a drink on his own as usual. Should he call him?

'No, no, not to worry,' replied the Eggman. 'Just tell him there's a wee job for him.'

I was watching and listening to all of this and saw the bold Ronnie's face go pale as if something unspoken and ugly had surfaced suddenly.

'No trouble now, Lyle,' I heard him murmur. 'Please, not in *here*. Promise me.'

'Relax, everything's under control. Tell you what, send a drink over to those young people in the corner. Say it's from Lyle Ritchie and his friends with our compliments.'

The man in the dinner-suit looked down at him for a moment. There was sweat on his upper lip and a tiny, inky snail track had appeared from nowhere just below his hair line. Turning, he walked back to the bar.

'What's happening?' asked Deirdre. 'Where is everybody, for God's sake?' Her voice sounded slurred.

Reaching over, J.J. patted her on the cheek. 'Everything's under control' he told her, echoing his master's message. 'Relax, honeybun, you're in safe hands.'

'Well, just keep them to yourself, that's all I say,' she retorted with a laugh.

Under the table I could feel Doris's hand contract in mine.

'Let's get her home,' I heard her whisper. 'Please, Hugo.'

Soon after the Eggman got up and we rose along with him, with barely a backward glance at the debris on the table, all that lovely food and drink apparently already only a memory. Out of the corner of my eye I could see movement at the distant table and yet again felt my legs quiver as if in anticipation of what might lie in store outside. Yet the Eggman appeared in no great hurry, taking his time, exchanging business pleasantries with Ronnie H., who shook hands with J.J. and myself, after giving both girls a fleeting, little continental-style peck on the cheek.

'You take care now, you hear?' I remember were his parting words, pretty ironic, really, considering what my fevered imagination had been busy cooking up for us all.

Halfway to the car, which stood out from the few remaining ones still there like some sort of great slab of raspberry ice-cream, we heard a shout behind us. Turning, I saw our three sporting types from the dining-room heading in our direction. Already one of them had peeled off his blazer in readiness, his shirt dazzling as a Persil ad, but the Eggman didn't falter or betray the slightest indication he had heard a thing.

'Hey *you*! What's your hurry, big man?'

For my part I kept on going, taking my cue from the one in front, in the hope he knew something I didn't, namely, that by some miracle of acceleration we would be able to get to the car and drive off intact before the trio caught up with us. J.J. seemed to be thinking along the same lines, dragging a reluctant Deirdre by the hand, although I noticed that he kept glancing from side to side. Anywhere, in fact, but over his shoulder at the rapidly overtaking, opposing team.

At my back I heard the crunching sound of another's feet and almost instantaneously a figure stepped from behind our Cadillac, T-shirt a pale glare in the dark. Momentarily the footsteps ceased as Rocky, for it was he, came round the long, pink snout of the car while we piled past him into the sanctuary of that leather-scented, expensively padded interior. Except for the Eggman, of course, who seemed as heedless as ever to the drama he had set off back inside about an hour earlier. With a sigh and a grunt he settled his great bulk into the passenger seat, followed by a whirr as his window went down like a glass curtain rolling back on what was to turn out to be an open air performance of some kind, the outcome of which the man in front of me appeared familiar with.

Outside, the glare from a sodium lamp high in the branches of a tree cast a yellowish wash over the gravel. As I watched, as though taking their cue from the solitary figure already standing there, arms folded, blocking their way, those other three actors moved forward slowly until they, too, were centre stage and conscious of an audience.

Plaintively, Deirdre was heard to enquire, 'Will somebody please tell me what the hell is happening?' but the Eggman held up a hand and she fell back mumbling into her corner.

Trying to recapture just what took place next beyond the confines of that car in any precise or ordered fashion has been one of the hardest things I've found, for some reason. Which is baffling, for at the time I did convince myself I would be able to re-run the events in slow motion whenever I wished, lingering pleasurably over each progression in the action. So why, then, is so much of it a blur, as if the camera in my head was out of focus, or not even functioning properly? Anyhow, this is my personally edited version of events, which I tell myself is the way it happened.

At the outset, the tough who had discarded his jacket advanced on our solitary champion, fists raised, as if any contest was to be settled quickly, man to man, by civilised rules. Theirs, I imagine. Certainly not Rocky Devine's, who held his ground until the very last minute, then kicked his adversary on the kneecap with what seemed like amazing accuracy, using that great, swinging, yellow right boot of his. The sound of the impact, reinforced toe on thinly covered bone, travelled through the glass, followed seconds later by an agonised scream as the downed man rolled on the gravel clutching his bent leg to his chin.

One of the women who was standing well back with her friends at the edge of the battleground echoed the sound with a high, keening wail of her own. From her reaction I took it the two must be closely connected, possibly even brother and sister. Not that that made me in the slightest bit sympathetic or compassionate towards her. As far as I was concerned, she was this great country heifer who may well have instigated all of this just because I had refused to sing a stupid song for her. I hoped she was satisfied now seeing him on the gravel like that making an unholy mess of that nice whiter than white shirt of his. I couldn't help thinking also it was just as well he had the sense to hand her his blazer like he did.

As those sibling cries rang out on the night air in harmony, the remaining bruisers seemed to freeze, their brains trying to react to what they'd just witnessed. Then, arms outstretched, scalped heads lowered, they charged to mete out punishment like a pair of full backs at the man running with a ball. Only there was no ball, was there, for both his hands were free, and he didn't even attempt to feint or dodge in the slightest degree either. For a moment there I almost felt I could share something of that icy logic in Rocky's head and when, eventually, he did sidestep, balletically almost, at the last heart-stopping second, chopping down hard on a shaved nape, then kneeing the other crouching runner in the face, the perfectly controlled and economical beauty of the whole operation left me breathless with admiration. Surely it deserved applause, approval, at least, but the Eggman remained immobile and I could tell, without seeing it, that his face had stayed expressionless throughout.

Rocky gazed down on the vanquished threesome the way a craftsman might run a cool, practised eye over his most recent handiwork. One of the men who had got to his knees now appeared to be throwing his dinner up. The other two still lay writhing and groaning, and all the while the one I took to be the sister kept screeching like a foghorn, yet still making no move to go forward to give succour to the one she so obviously had an attachment to. One thing for certain: this particular birthday she would remember for a long time to come. A Sagittarian, it came to me.

Eventually the Eggman said to J.J., 'Give those women back there something for the damage. Wear and tear.' Which to my mind I took to be humour, yet his tone, as ever, stayed irony-free.

'What if they won't take it?' J.J. asked.

'Leave it with them. They're not going to just stand there and watch it blow away. Now, are they?'

It seemed to me one of those genuinely surreal nuggets of conversation but one I did feel I probably was going to have to get used to from now on, like watching people being pulverised in pub car parks while I looked on from a ringside seat.

Sighing, J.J. climbed wearily from behind the wheel and I watched as, almost delicately now, he took the long way around the casualties. Not once did he look in Rocky's direction, who remained rooted, face and arms gypsy dark against the shocking pallor of his T-shirt. I realised it was hardly likely, but was there even the remotest chance I could ever be like that, I asked myself, like him, an Eastwood or a Bronson figure – well before they were invented, of course? Then it was still Victor Mature, who I always had this soft spot for, on account of his being marked down for martyrdom right from scene one.

I couldn't be sure whether the sight of a wad of notes in J.J.'s hand had anything to do with it or not, but the hysterics appeared to die right down. Maybe life was like that, I told myself. Maybe you could buy almost anything if you were brass-necked enough. Certainly it seemed that way whenever the Eggman was in charge, dispensing the stuff like sweetie coupons.

When J.J. got back into the car again he glanced across at the Eggman, then asked, 'Happy now?' The big man nodded and the car coughed softly into life.

'What about Rocky?' I blurted out. I couldn't help myself, for he was still standing there in a world of his own. As the headlights came on full I saw his T-shirt was spotted with something dark which hadn't been there before. The blood of an Irishman. Three, to be precise.

Misunderstanding my concern, J.J. said, 'Don't worry about Rocky. He enjoys his work. He does, doesn't he, Lyle?'

'Cuts it a touch fine sometimes, mind you,' said the Eggman and J.J. laughed, as I did myself.

And so we drove away from the Burnfoot and our night of drama, and some way along the road J.J. had to pull over for Deirdre to be sick. Whether it was the delayed effect of all that open air carnage or too much drink and little pale pills, or a combination, I'll never know. Anyhow we sat there in the car listening to her retching her guts up on to the grass verge as the light grew progressively pinker in the east, while Doris hid her head and sobbed for shame on my shoulder.

We dropped the pair of them off at the entrance to Posy Row just as someone's backyard cockerel sounded reveille. Out of the back window I saw them take off their high heels together, then, supporting one another like a couple of dowagers, limp towards that end house, the only one with a light still burning behind its curtained top window.

ELEVEN

The following March, right at the beginning of the month, we had that famous snowstorm, you may recall, nearly two weeks of continuous blizzard, blinding, then paralysing the entire Province. The city kept on functioning, of course, a soot spot in a milk-white sea, but where the street-lights ended and the Corporation buses turned about, reversing their destination boards, and the dark of the countryside began, muffled under all that remorseless precipitation, it was Siberia for the rest of us.

The Hillhead got the brunt of it. Because of its elevation, there was always a wintertime blockade of sorts anyway, usually a day, maybe two at most, when the lane filled up, but never like this, they told me, not flat to the tops of the hedges, a fleecy mattress the depth of a car. In adjoining farmsteads people managed to keep a way open to the foot of their avenues and the road, but at the Hillhead no one lifted a shovel or a spade. In the yard outside someone had tramped a cinder path to the coal-house and back, but that was the end of it, the outline of the Eggman's Cadillac Eldorado furring over until it resembled a giant, abandoned, soft toy.

Not that I was able to look out and gauge that slow

transformation for, along with Rocky and three others, I was marooned about half a mile away in an old out-farm connected to the main dwelling by a deep and twisting loanen now choked with snow too. My gypsy existence, sleeping on a broken old settee here, in somebody's spare room among all their junk and cast-offs there, had brought me to this place, a halfway house for the rough types who did jobs for the Eggman, usually at dead of night, shifting livestock from truck to byre and back again, as if stealth and speed by the light of headlamps was essential.

Rocky remained a constant. The others came and went, reeking of dung and diesel oil. They had accents from other, sometimes remote, parts of the country – the island itself. Most had nicknames, just like Rocky himself, but theirs seemed variable, vagrant, not like his, which fitted him, I always felt, closer than a proper handle could ever do.

A heavy, choking fug filled the place, becoming visibly bluish at times because of the vicious down-draught from the ancient, cast-iron stove. We lived on tinned goods, Scotch broth and a sort of meat and vegetable stew at almost every meal. One of the Southerners, Packy the Rat, attended to the cooking – if you could call it that – slapping down ladlefuls of sticky, brown gumbo on to chipped, enamel plates. It was all very much what I always imagined bunkhouse life to be, and soon I was referring to our quarters as the Bar-K just like the rest. Strange to say, it turned out to be one of the happiest times of my life, listening to tall tales of drinking and mighty fights and wild, wild women – villainy, too, for the place was crammed with stolen goods encased in new-smelling cardboard, radios, television sets, a lot of electric irons, kettles and toasters, oddly enough, judging by the illustrations on the cartons.

At night we watched *Gunsmoke*, *The Fugitive* and *Sergeant Bilko* on one of the brand new fourteen-inch TVs. The picture came and went, as snowy as the world outside, and when the power went off eventually, all those drooping lines buckling under their weight of white, we played pontoon and twenty-one by candlelight while the snow inched ever upwards on the far side of the pitch black window pane. Just beyond the back door was this permanently fresh, yellow stain where we would relieve ourselves, the shape and outline of South America – or India, for some curious reason – which we all secretly tried to embellish. I remember each time I stood there trying to push its boundaries out in much the same way we once would send a trajectory over the wall at school dividing the boys' and girls' sides of the toilets. Such were the innocent pursuits that passed the time for us: cards, boastful talk and television for a time, and me admiring the orange tracer-trails my own piss made against all that bright, outdoor pallor.

But one morning I awoke to find everyone gone except for Rocky and myself. During the night they had been called away, as often happened at the Hillhead, perhaps through some form of telepathic communication from the Eggman, for it looked as though we were still cut off by deep drifts. Looking outside I could see their tracks leading off into the glare of the wilderness and after we had eaten what was left in the big, blackened saucepan Rocky and I set off as well, sinking to our knees in the dark, gaping holes left behind for us.

It was a bright, crisp day, I recall, with a flawless sky of almost duck egg blue, and silent everywhere, the only sound the dry, sucking crunch of our feet. I must say I felt sad at having to leave the old Bar-K behind and my new-found, cattle-rustling, cow-punching friends, missing them already and their jokes about the wee Prod for, without labouring the point, it became pretty obvious early on that all of them, including Rocky – although he never, ever referred to religion – dug with the other foot. Up to that time I don't think I'd ever even met a single Catholic, let alone spent three days under the same roof with four of them. This may seem strange to have to say, but the community I grew up in then was like that, as tribally exclusive as if we were Bantus.

Rocky's home life, that's if he had one outside the Hillhead, was a complete mystery to me. I knew he came from somewhere in the city, but which part, or what his people were like remained equally obscure. That morning we must have appeared an odd pair ploughing silently through the white wastes together. I think I had one of those out of body experiences – I believe that's what they're now called – as, for a brief moment, it was as if I was tracking our progress from a point overhead instead of down below with the smell of snow in my nostrils, airily floating like one of those plump, sky-diving cherubs you see in old paintings. *Just who could they be?* the cherub was wondering. *And what possibly could be the connection or relationship between them? Uncle? Nephew? Father? Son?* Closer to the truth might be master and apprentice. At that particular stage in my life it was as if I was destined to be always the eager disciple following in others' footsteps. Like right now, literally, as I sank deep in the tracks left so thoughtfully behind by my old bunkhouse pals.

I have no proper or vivid recollection of how it was when the pair of us finally got back to the Hillhead that frosty morning like a couple of returning explorers. No one made any kind of fuss of us, I do know, which shouldn't have been a disappointment, but was, for I tingled still as if I had been through a lot and had a mighty tale to tell. So, as always, quietly I edged into a corner in that big smoke-filled kitchen, taking care not to draw attention to myself or speak unless spoken to. In the back of my mind I still had the notion that at some stage, one of these days, someone might notice me and my presence properly for the first time and I would be

255

banished as an interloper, a fraud, impostor. Yet running alongside that feeling was another almost contrary belief that all this might continue for ever. Why not? There was nothing really odd or unnatural about any of it, the money, the clothes, the non-stop meals. Most of the time now I never questioned it, just like J.J., I suppose, putting all of it down to the pleasing appeal of my personality and sparkling blue eyes.

The weather softened, an almost temperate clamminess now in the air, the snow melting to grey slush, then to running streams that filled every watercourse to overflowing. On the surrounding farms there was sudden activity as drains were cleared, hedges laid, walls and fences mended. Men were out ditching furiously as though the weather had set them back badly and precious ploughing and planting time must be made up for in other ways. But up at the Hillhead life's tempo remained unaltered, the seasons meaning little to the Ritchie family and their tribe of hangers-on. Me included, for yet again it struck me how my new existence mimicked the one I'd led at Larkhill. No one had any sort of regular occupation or routine, yet money appeared to flow in from somewhere and never looked as if it was worked for, as far as I could make out. Not that I had ever any deep or aching desire to go into all that. It was like that Sunday school text I'd always been so taken with, the one about the necessity, nay, obligation, to neither toil nor spin. That could be me, I decided, a regular lily of the field in my bespoke hopsack with its covered buttons and multitude of pockets.

About this time J.J. melted from the scene, a bit like the snow, but not entirely, as in the case of the white stuff. That would have been wonderful, for he was hard work to be around, touchy as a snake at the best of times. Then a day or two shortly afterwards the Eggman, too, went on a trip. I don't believe there was any connection, but then again there might have been, for nothing ever was explained or elaborated on in that household, people appearing, then disappearing at the instigation of a silent semaphore of nods, winks and sideways jerks of the head. London was mentioned and Rocky drove him to Nutt's Corner airport which was not all that far off. When he got back around lunchtime I was mooning about in the yard kicking a tin, feeling conspicuous, even more fraudulent than usual.

'Hop in,' said Rocky through the Eldorado's open window and, heart beating rapturously, I climbed in beside him. He was smoking full-strength Capstans and the interior smelt like a pub back-room after the night before. He hadn't shaved either, a blue-black stubble pencil-dotting cheeks and chin and continuing right on beneath the collar of his T-shirt. One hand resting on the wheel, the other holding a cigarette on his knee, that was how he drove.

Neither of us spoke, although after all those hours of communing on my own I was burning to hear a voice, especially his. But I held my tongue, for I knew that was how he wanted it, my hero, with the cigar-store Indian profile, although where I got that image from, God alone knows. Instead, I consoled myself with the notion of the bond I believed we'd formed that day tramping back in the snow together with never a word between us to mar the mood.

I sat there staring straight ahead through the slightly curved, American, shatter-proof windscreen, the pair of us like a couple of human specimens in a travelling, drained aquarium, although so far we'd only raced through the tiny, restricted world of a flock of sheep, a dog pissing by the roadside and a man up a telegraph pole repairing the ravages of our big snow. As diversion, I pretended I was some sort of detective, restricted to a combination of observation and intuition to tunnel a way into the head of my silent subject. Everyone had secrets, I told myself, and everyone at some point would air them to someone else if that person happened to be handy and the moment ripe, as when under sufficient pressure or tension. But Rocky would never go in for confession like that, never, it just wasn't in him, he wasn't the type. That was my first inspired piece of deduction, as I thought of it, already warming to the task of getting to know him better than any of the others at the Hillhead simply by being with him, a sort of silent human camera, you might say, turning over at his side.

Our destination that day was Belfast as it became clear, for soon we were heading up, then over the Black Mountain, down around the Hairpin Bend, then past the first terraces of ruddy brick. The houses I noticed kept getting closer together, shedding their gardens, any form of growing, as though Nature had no business to be here. It's a bit like that, our capital city, short-changed as regards parks and greenery, as if all that open, useless space might give rise to wasteful fantasies of lotus-eating. Remember this was the town, after all, where playground swings were chained up on a Sunday like so many trussed gibbets.

Our mystery tour took us first to one of the poorest, most desperate places I think I've ever encountered. By comparison it made Larkhill look like the Pope's summer palace. We turned into the permanent shadow of the mighty hulk of a disused mill like some soot-stained, brick-built, beached liner, every fragment of glass across its front starred by a generation of stone throwers and catapultists, blotting out the light from the terraces huddled at its base. The moment we entered the area swarms of children poured from every house, attracted to our presence as if we were riding in something marshmallow pink and edible. Yelling, they ran alongside, touching the paintwork in an ecstasy, while shawled women with babies came out to stare silently from the dark rectangles of their doorways. Rocky drew the car to

258

a halt beneath a lovingly crafted graffito exhorting the neighbourhood to Fuck The Royal Family and, turning to me, cracked a joke, possibly the first I'd ever heard from his lips.

'Sound the horn if the Comanches start attacking the wagon train.'

I looked at him for confirmation, but he was gone, striding across the street, the kids calling out his name as though he was some kind of visiting celebrity – prize-fighter, conceivably – and I watched him dip into his pocket, then throw a handful of coins in the air like someone sowing seed.

While the urchins scrabbled in the dirt I followed my bodyguard's progress. I had a clear view of his destination, one of the houses directly across from me. The door was wide open like all the others in the street and I could see straight into its cave-like interior. Shocking as the general rundown state of decoration was, what really shook me was the floor, or rather the lack of one. No boards, nothing, simply beaten earth. Later I was to discover this wasn't such a rarity in Jamaica Street. Precious wood in any shape that could be salvaged, in the form of banisters, cupboards, skirting, mouldings, would be fed to the fire when times were rough.

As I continued to watch, a tableau started to unfold, a woman moving forward to embrace the visitor. She looked old. Careworn, came to mind. Then I saw a man hunched in a chair, a rug covering his knees, who had the appearance of being even more spent and frail if that were possible. Already, in my head, a touching scenario was beginning to develop. The returned prodigal. Aged parents. One even crippled, just to add to the pathos. I kept waiting for money to change hands surreptitiously, perhaps slipped into an apron pocket so as not to cause embarrassment.

But there came a scratching on the car window and, turning, I saw the street children had re-formed on the far side of the Cadillac and were now peering in at me, an exhibit, protected, but only just, by a sheet of glass, from their attention, like that day at Glenrowan. Their heads, too, had been shaved against lice and all had that same darting look as if anxious not to miss the slightest chance of larceny. One of them – a cast in one eye, and thoroughly scabby – came right up close and examined me sitting there in my suit, tab-collared shirt and knitted tie, and I could have sworn his nostrils flared as if trying to get a scent of me through the clear Triplex. I don't know why or how I did it, but I lunged suddenly at him behind the glass and he drew back, a terrified look on those pasty features. On the instant the others scattered as well, and seeing them like that I just knew that the merest pressure on the horn would send them fleeing like a flock of starlings.

Rocky came back to the car after that, sliding behind the wheel without a word or flicker of expression on his face, as I suppose by now I knew he would. Yet I still was deeply curious about the two old people I had seen him with earlier in that dark den of a house back there. I felt convinced they had to be his parents and burned to question him, for it wasn't easy keeping up that tight-lipped, junior sidekick routine all the time.

We were climbing into a district now of red brick, terraced houses, a grid of identical streets, drives, avenues and – oddly enough – crescents, according to the signs. Meaning nothing to me, the names flitted by. But then we pulled into one of those same sloping streets where the children looked a little less feral. Far below us the sea glittered like an enormous metal lid and across on the distant side of the great Lough pale patches of affluence showed against the cultivated green where the rich lived and played. Bankers, businessmen, architects, accountants, becoming weekend yachtsmen, gardeners, golfers, rally-drivers. Where we were was the raw northern curve of the city where houses with clay floors could still be found and people hid from predators like us slowly cruising in our pink, purring American chariot. Debt-collectors, tick men – for that's what we were, as I was to discover that day – were what everyone dreaded. Our clientele couldn't afford the luxury of despising us. That was much too strong, too independent an emotion.

The first house we stopped at had a pot-plant in the window, a searing red geranium like a blood burst. The garden grew cabbages, kale and leeks instead of fancy blooms, the only cultivated one in the entire street. The others held tin cans, bottles and bicycle frames, even discarded, ruptured mattresses. Rocky switched the engine off and lit a Capstan. He stared away up the rising street, a faraway, musing look in his eyes.

Then a woman came out, smoking fiercely herself, a man's lovat green cardigan pulled over her meagre chest. Hair-curlers, those wire mesh ones like miniature rolls of netting wire, bunched out her headscarf. Writing this, I can't recall exactly why I paid so much attention to her appearance – and yes, she did have on down-at-heel, purple, pom-pommed slippers – unless she was my very first customer ever, for, to my shock and surprise, she shuffled around to *my* window, not Rocky's, silently pushing a handful of money at me. I stared down into her cupped palm, silver mixed with coppers, then up at her. A passing freighter's siren hooted mournfully away down below on the glinting Lough, although the sea lanes that day were as clear as glass.

'Do you want that wee woman to catch her death?' Rocky said. He was grinning. 'Go on, take it.'

And so I did, feeling the weight of transferred coins heavy in my hand, slightly greasy, too, I couldn't help remarking in my fastidious way.

'See you next week then, missus!' called out Rocky,

switching on the engine and pulling away from the kerb, still leaving me holding a handful of warm change I didn't know what to do with.

'Put it in the bag,' he said, pointing towards the glove compartment. As well as the leather pouch there was a school notebook in there, cross-hatched pages lined with names and addresses with amounts ticked off in columns alongside.

At our next stop the woman enquired, 'Who's this?' pointing at me sitting there with my two hands folded. 'Where's that other well-dressed, young gangster, then?'

'Having a rest cure. The job was getting on top of him.'

'Like me and that drunken bum of a man of mine on a Friday night, you mean?' riposted the woman, a gamey old thing with bottle-blonde locks and ruler-straight lipstick. Mulholland, her name was, according to the address in the book. Fifteen bob weekly interest on an outstanding debt of twelve pounds ten shillings, which didn't take a financial wizard to work out she'd still be paying off well into her seventies. I may not have mentioned it before, but figures never were a problem for me at school. The place, the teachers, yes, but not that adding, subtracting and long-dividing lark and so, looking at the open notebook on my lap filled with J.J.'s surprisingly neat copperplate, it was as if I was reading the history of these people, as well as the Eggman's, pounds, shillings and pence translating to something far more alive and intriguing.

'Think you can handle it, kiddo?' enquired Rocky as we went searching for our next victim. He didn't seem to have a system, as far as I could make out, simply cruising the neighbourhood expecting people to appear, dinero in hand, at our approach, as if it was an ice-cream van we travelled in and not a big American car.

Yes, I thought I could, I told him. Already I had started ticking off names and corresponding amounts while endeavouring to match the existing handwriting as if I might be called to account when my predecessor returned to his duties.

On that score – 'What about J.J.?' I asked, as we drove on with both windows rolled down.

'What about him?' replied Rocky.

'When'll he be back, I mean?'

'J.J.'s all washed up,' he said. 'You're Mr Cash and Carry from now on.'

I looked at him aghast. 'Fuck me,' I said. I couldn't help myself.

'Big Lyle found out about him and young Heather. He took a powder. She's staying with an auntie up the country somewhere till it blows over. For her, maybe, but not for lover boy. You'll miss him, I take it.'

I looked at him. 'You're right,' I told him. 'Like a hole in the head.'

This time he laughed and it was as if a weight had been lifted from both my shoulders. Perhaps it had been J.J. all along, it came to me.

'Who's next for the treatment?' Rocky asked.

'Lynch,' I told him, scanning the notebook. 'Number forty-two.'

'Here comes the bit I hate,' he sighed, drawing up to the kerb outside a house with the blinds drawn as if for a death in the family. 'Now I've got to get out of the fucking motor, so I have. Why can't they just divvy up like all the rest?'

I watched him snuff his cigarette out between finger and thumb then stride off up the path to a house looking that little bit more run down than its neighbours, mildewed cardboard masking several of the panes in the bedroom windows.

Rat, tat, tat, knocked Rocky on the door, then stood back to stare at the upper storey. I thought I saw a blind twitch. Then, ducking down, he moved with sudden swiftness around the side of the house where there was a narrow entry

263

choked with rubbish. As I watched I saw him grapple with a small man dressed only in trousers and vest who dropped from a window overlooking the alleyway. Rocky's face looked dark and grim as he frog-marched his victim out into the street for everyone to see, although nothing living moved, not even a dog or a child at play. But I knew, just as the man himself must have done, behind every curtain lurked a presence, waiting and listening there.

'Not out here,' I heard the debtor plead. They were only a few paces away in front of the car. 'Not in front of the weans. Please, Rocky.'

From my front row seat I saw my T-shirted companion hesitate over what course to take, and it came to me almost instantly, instinctively, as if we were in tune, the precise, professional dilemma he faced. Whether to create a vivid example here for all to witness as well as remember – even though the street was still dead as a desert – or show a degree of mercy to the barefoot little creep he held by his scrawny shoulders. At that precise moment I did wish for the latter to happen. It was the still unreformed softie in me, I suppose, but that was to change and much faster than I would have believed possible. In fact after Rocky had herded Lynch back up the entry out of sight again, returning after a minute, maybe two, which was all that was needed for a dose of correction, most, if not all my sympathy had taken a hike, to be replaced by something very different indeed.

'Sleekit wee shit,' grunted Rocky, climbing in beside me. I noticed a drying rime of red across the knuckles of both hands on the wheel. 'How much does he owe us now, the wee prick?'

'The whole lot, or just the weekly repayments?'

He gave me a sideways glance.

'Weekly repayments?' The phrase sounded impossibly pretentious, not to mention distinctly fruity, coming from his lips like that and I felt my face go red.

'How many weeks is he behind?'

'Three,' I told him. 'Today makes four.'

'Next time it'll be the casualty department,' he said, and looking down at the notebook with its lack of crosses opposite one name in particular I felt a sudden and irritating resentment start to fester, even though I knew next to nothing about this person called Lynch.

'How many punters to go?'

'Eleven,' I told him and he slid the car out and away towards our next call.

And so we continued to graze our dense little patch of red brick pasture, the Eggman's own personal land of never-never, and I sat back alongside my protector feeling more and more at ease in my new role as the afternoon drew on. In the notebook gradually all the ticks became crosses, while the weight of money in the chamois leather bag in the glove compartment grew accordingly. My hands were getting grimy, I noticed, with all the transactions, yet it didn't seem to matter any more. I began to feel a distinct sense of my own importance, a swelling of self-esteem, as all these wee women kept coming up to my open car window with their outstretched offerings. Other tick men – for the first time I realised the word must be connected to the marks I kept making with my biro – had to demean themselves by knocking on doors, the man from the Co-op, or the Pru, for instance, but not the likes of us, languidly serene in our upholstered, mobile counting-house, the Ted Heath Band Show pumping softly away on the Light Programme.

By the time our day's work was done I was filled with contempt for these sorry cases who had somehow got themselves into our bad books. There was no hope for them, no escape, I could see that, for they were stuck there as if by some inherently weak, human glue in their make-up, binding them to those same ruled pages for an eternity, and it was nobody's fault but their own.

'You did just fine, kiddo,' said Rocky as I closed the accounts on the last sucker, shutting the notebook away safe alongside the bulging moneybag in the hinged compartment in front of me. 'Where did you learn to keep tally like that?'

'Sort of a family gift,' I told him. A total fiction of course. 'All the Dinsmores are great at figures.'

'Like horseback riding, I suppose?'

I fell right into that one, but didn't mind, for the mood between us had become light and playful. Indeed, Rocky's entire demeanour seemed to have undergone a steady change as if he, too, had felt something lifted from his brawny shoulders as it had from mine earlier when I heard the news of J.J.'s banishment. *So, I hadn't been wrong after all, he had been poking Heather, lucky bastard.* And so full of myself was I just then, I nearly kidded myself I might even have been in there with a chance too, risking the Eggman's wrath just to get a feel at the lovely Heather. But then the thought of those glacial blue eyes, that great brooding bulk, made any premature interest in the subject between my legs go soft on me like a slow puncture. Yet I still was curious about J.J.'s disappearance and some time later raised the topic again, feeling a lot more confident now about having a head-on conversation with Rocky.

We had parked the car and were in a club he had brought us to in the Markets area. Dark, noisy and smoke-laden, it was filled with men, a lot of them hard and formidable just like Rocky, but laughing, drinking, playing cards. He had introduced me to several of them, something I hadn't expected, and quickly I had become Hughie, but the variant on my name was rather to my liking. Already several full glasses sat in front of me. I could feel the moneybag clamped between my thighs under the table like a small, round

266

football. At my elbow Rocky was lowering pints of stout and Power's chasers.

'Who knows where the wee cunt is lying low. Maybe England, maybe even with his rich mammy and daddy in Bangor. You didn't know that, did you? Grammar school boy with posh parents?'

I looked at him. J.J. in a blazer and cadet corps haircut? Maybe even piano lessons? He saw me grinning.

'Out and out fucking waster. Loved being in with the wrong crowd. The hard man. Pretending to be Legs Diamond. More Legs Chicken.'

This was a new Rocky, witty, relaxed, among his own kind. Drink kept coming to the table, but I had long since lost the notion of keeping abreast. Someone started singing in a far corner, the song deeply republican I realised almost immediately, but mournful and soothing in some curious, almost hypnotic fashion. Did they know I was a Protestant? But any unease was fleeting, barely registering. By now Rocky had a faraway look in his eyes. What was he dreaming of, I wondered? What were they all pining for, as the words and the drink loosened their senses? Green glens, a white-washed cottage by a lake, an Irish colleen humping home a creel of turf? Images from an unattainable and maybe mythic past that had been filched from them by people like me and my lot – or so I was led to believe. Yet I didn't feel like a usurper somehow. Never had. Never would. So what did that make me, then? Different, maybe, but not all that different, and as the foam in the glass went down in front of me, so did any remaining feelings of being an intruder.

Anyway, Hughie wasn't such a bad name, was it? A lot more cosily traditional than Hugo, with its formal Teutonic tone. So, how about O'Dinsmore then while I was at it, softening the hard surname? Everything about me seemed to be losing its sharp outline fast, even my very own name, for Christ's sake, but before that happened and I became as soft and pliable as Plasticine Rocky brought me back to reality and that bundle of money I gripped between my legs like a girl guarding her virginity.

'Declan will change it into readies for you. Won't you, Dec? Give the lad a hand, I mean?'

Declan was about sixty with a drinker's face, watery, weary eyes, rosacea-tinted cheeks and an impressive tremor in both hands.

The pair of us sat down at an empty table out of the way and I spilled the day's takings on to the damp mahogany. Then we set to stacking the coins in ordered little pillars of copper and silver alloy. As he laboured my companion sighed with the effort of calculation and the slowing effect of alcohol in his system. His tongue stuck out from the side of his mouth. Thick beads of sweat broke on his forehead with the intense concentration. I was never to see him again and all the time we didn't exchange a single syllable. A serious alcoholic, down to the last twitch and tremble.

When we'd finished sorting the proceeds, with a finger he wrote something on the wet surface of the table for my attention and I recognised a figure which seemed to correspond roughly with the one which I decided myself should be the grand total. He stared at me and then when I nodded razed our neat little grove of coinage, scooping the ruins into his outstretched barman's apron with those mottled, bluish paws of his. After he'd gone back to the till I looked down at my own palms, grimy as a coal-heaver's, reeking of metal, and when he returned with a wad tied with a rubber band the notes seemed equally soiled.

I went to the toilet to wash away the scent and residue of my first day's work as apprentice debt-collector, settling into the job as easily as if born to it. Hugo Dinsmore, tickman to the Eggman. Staring at the face in the bit of cracked mirror over the basin I wondered if other people had begun to notice the change in me already. I thought of J.J., that permanent air of disdain, specifically, how his hands always seemed so spotless compared to everyone else's. Now I thought I understood why. How he must have hated all those transactions through the car window. And now it was my turn to take over where he'd left off. I wasn't absolutely certain I could carry it off or not, but I would give it a damned good try.

When I got back to the bar again, hands soap-scented and tingling, Rocky was still staring off into space as if searching for an imaginary break in the tobacco haze, something out there far, far beyond the confines of the room, its smoke and its din. A fresh singer was hard at it. Something about a highwayman on the moor was all I could make out as I slid down beside the man in the white T-shirt, although not quite so snowy by this stage. No blood, as yet, like that night in the car park, but ketchup from a hamburger one of the barmen had rustled up earlier, cigarette ash and a tan spillage of Guinness.

I was thinking to myself the ravages to the T-shirt might somehow turn out to be an indicator of the gradual deterioration of Rocky himself: the greater its wear and tear the more drunk he seemed to be getting. Part of me felt alarmed, disappointed, too, at watching what was happening to my hero in front of me, but some other part quite liked the idea, for I felt liberated, free to ask as many questions as I liked, having him in this state. And so I started to probe, gently at first, but gradually stepping up the rigour of my interrogation while the ballad singer warbled away off in the background.

'J.J. says you really enjoy your work.'
He looked at me out of bleary eyes. 'He did, did he?'
I nodded.
'You mean duffing up people?'
'Yes,' I told him, tingling nervously at my own boldness.

'Only when they ask for it.'

'Like those three apemen at the Burnfoot?'

He grinned. 'Yeah, you could say that.'

'What about the wee guy today, the one who didn't cough up?'

'That was different,' he said.

'Did you enjoy that?'

This time I thought I had gone too far for he stared at me as if seeing me in a new light, as inquisitor, maybe.

'Listen,' he said, 'never you get too cocky or smart or you might end up the same as J.J.'

'What's going to happen to him?' I asked.

'Getting the Liverpool boat would be the smart move.'

'Before you manage to have a word with him, you mean?'

He grinned. 'You catch on fast, wee Hughie.'

After that came a lull. We drank some more and stared off through the smoke haze as if seeing the same vision of a magical, rural heartland instead of the walls and decoration of a back street shebeen. But I couldn't help myself now, the itch for more confession was too hard to resist. So then I asked him about the tattoos. Ex-army, it turned out. Palestine, Kenya, Suez.

Had he ever killed anyone? 'In action, I mean.'

Rocky toyed with his glass. 'Nobody keeps score. Only a rookie would ever talk about something like that.'

'Why did you quit?'

Came another pause. Then he said, 'You know, for a country boy, you ask one hell of a load of questions. Not such a great idea in a place like this. Somebody might just be listening and take you for an undercover cop or something.'

I looked at him. *Me?* With *my* stature? He mustn't have been as far gone as I thought he was, for he laughed. We both did.

Then I heard him say, 'What about giving us all a bit of a

come-all-ye yourself, kiddo? That's what you're good at, isn't it? But, not "The Sash". OK?'

Well, I did perform and it was like old times, the minstrel boy himself bringing down a hush on that rough speakeasy, little corner of rebel Ireland in the heart of our own true blue city. I thought of Junior and the rest of them back at Larkhill. I usually did at such times. What would they say if they could see me now? By the time I'd run through my party piece, every number hand-picked for sentiment and pure mush, I don't think I'd ever seen so many hard cases rubbing their eyes. More like a church hall of old ladies than a hard-bitten crew of dockers, street fighters, jailbirds, and slaughterhouse-men, for, indeed, there was a distinct whiff of freshly butchered meat coming from somewhere, which, of course, only reminded me of Junior.

Climbing down from the chair I had been hoisted up on to — why didn't it bother me to be still treated like a boy soprano in that way? — I saw the table below covered with more topped-up glasses than could humanly be disposed of by two mortal drinkers. Death by alcohol poisoning would seem to be the only escape route from such a place. That, or some miraculous, external intervention. Like a police raid, for instance. Dives like this, I imagined, must have their doors kicked in on a regular basis, the air of illegality something you could practically inhale along with the tobacco fumes. I looked at my watch at some point. It seemed to be fast, not by minutes, but by an hour. *Hours* even. Panic taking hold, I looked across at my companion. He was staring straight ahead, glassy-eyed, like some character in a horror movie. Too many draughts from all those steaming beakers finally messing up the old brain, making him look like an Igor instead of a Rocky. Both names straight from a comic-book, come to think of it.

Why I did it I will never know — I must have been mad —

for I heard myself enquire, ever so softly, 'Tell me, what's your real name, Rocky?'

He mumbled something in near-coma fashion. I leaned closer.

'Eugene,' I could have sworn he said. Yes, Eugene.

The last thing I remember after that until the following morning was something pinned to the wall of that place. Among all the nicotine-stained portraits of unknown martyrs – at least, I supposed that was what they must be, for all had that same desperate look of impending finality about them, a bit like the faces on a Wild West wanted poster – was something very different, advertising a trip to Lourdes. All those alcoholic palmers taking the bitter-tasting waters of Bernadette's grotto. Perhaps a busload of them singing their way south through France, 'Kevin Barry' instead of 'Ave Maria'. The word 'pilgrimage' on the poster seemed somehow very shocking to me, like a solitary, electrifying epithet in an otherwise mild run of graffiti, and I kept on staring at it even though it wasn't in any way accented, except in my own head.

Then it faded from consciousness like a light bulb going out and I awoke in the back seat of the Cadillac with the birds singing outside the steamed up windows. I was alone in the car and my head hurt. I rubbed where the pain seemed to be concentrated, but after that initial reaction my first instinct was to dive across the seat and pull open the glove compartment. The leather money pouch was still there, but empty and squashed like an animal carcass, and for an instant fear turned my sweat to an icy sheen until I remembered the club and the exchange that had taken place there. Deep in my inside pocket I detected the reassuring, papery feel and thickness of the precious wad gripped tight by a rubber band still there from the night before. Lying back against the ribbed leather, I breathed in a more human fashion, deep, slow gulps of air with the windows rolled down to their fullest extent.

From inside the car I could see a hedge, then trees, then a glimpse of dew-covered fields. We were deep in the heart of the country and it looked like we had ended up in the middle of a lane, stalling right there as if the ignition had cut out, just like whoever was behind the wheel at the time. I was lucky, I told myself, to be still here in one piece. Yet although I hadn't had time to get out I somehow convinced myself the car must be okay as well, for it always felt that way, armour-plated, I don't know why. Just like the people who travelled inside.

Rubbing a hole in the misted glass, I saw Rocky up ahead. He was standing taking a long and leisurely morning piss with his back turned to me. For the first time, in the dawn silence, I recognised the sound it made as it hit gravel. I watched as he went through the customary shake and shiver routine, then, buttoning up, he turned and headed towards the car. I don't know what I expected to see. Something lingering from the night before and all its excesses, perhaps? But he looked much the same old Rocky, same deadpan warrior with a head carved out of something akin to a wooden gatepost.

When he got into the car there was a reek of sour drink, spent cigarettes and stale sweat but, then, I imagine that made two of us. Nothing was said or mentioned, but he did pull out a flat quarter-bottle of something to put to his lips. He passed it over to me. It tasted like vodka or white rum, clear, odourless, heart-stopping. It might well have been poteen, for that place from the night before seemed just the kind of joint where something like that would change hands in unlabelled bottles.

After that we drove home in silence, for even I had learned other people's hangovers are strictly their own affair.

Sitting there I watched the early morning countryside roll past with coated tongue and a head throbbing like a tom-tom all the way back to the Hillhead and the first rooster's midden call of the new day.

TWELVE

The Eggman came back from London in a startling new rig-out. Tommy Nutter three-piece in chocolate brown, butcher striped shirts from Lord John, Chelsea boots by Lobb. He'd had his own last made for him, so rumour went. Gone the crombie camel hair, in its place a creaking, leather trench-coat. With the blond hair and glacier-blue eyes, it made him a dead ringer for an overweight Curt Jurgens.

I looked at Rocky for confirmation that now we worked for an SS man, but he steadfastly ignored me. Ever since our day and night together he had remained aloof and I had felt hurt and neglected, not having learned the lesson as yet how men like that invariably resent those who have seen a more naked side to them. Just when I thought I had gained a confidant, as well as protector, along comes a boozy night in the Butchers' Club to mess things up.

Travelling in the Cadillac now, the three of us, was more like riding in a funeral car than previously. At least J.J. exercised his vocal cords. I thought of him across the water busily bullshitting a widow in a pub somewhere. It was an image that lingered, then remained fixed, I don't know why. She would be in her fat forties, vulnerable, inclined to weepiness when the gin flowed. Somehow I always knew J.J. would find a soft touch to exercise his charms on, before, too late, they discovered what he was really like underneath.

I had a lot of time on my hands just then to think along such lines, drawing parallels, maybe lessons, too, for I had this terrible feeling my own appeal might be on the wane. For a start, nobody invited me to sing any more, which I realise must sound pathetic, made even more so by my behaviour at parties, for there were still plenty of those about where I would hang around practically panting to be asked to perform like a dog wagging an invisible tail.

There were many moments of despair in strange, lavish, over-lit bathrooms, much staring into mirrors for revelations of what had gone wrong. To be made redundant, as well as invisible, at seventeen, by a hi-fi system, what a fate, for suddenly I began to notice how every house now seemed to have the very latest in equipment, gently strobing turntables, brushed metal amplifiers, speakers the size of meat safes. No more Mantovani or Acker Bilk spinning on a beer-stained radiogram. Now it was the Modern Jazz Quartet chiming away like icy chandeliers, or the Swingle Singers softly moaning in descant, while people lounged, staring dopily at the latest furniture from Heal's or the Op Art on the walls. Alcohol, too, seemed to be losing its appeal to joints and something small, round and white in tablet form.

But then maybe it was because the Eggman was mixing in a different, much more hip set than I had become used to. I put it down to the London trips. There were more of those now, many more, almost every weekend by plane from the airport nearby. Rocky would drive him there, then turn up to wait for him on his return coming down the aircraft steps blinking in the lights like some great disorientated bear in his glistening leather pelt. The new clothes, still in their labelled West End carrier bags and wrapped in beautiful pastel shades of tissue paper, would be stowed carefully in the boot and we would drive home to the Hillhead in gloomy silence.

After each weekend in the Smoke he appeared to be in a lousy mood. It didn't take a genius to recognise how dissatisfied he was with our own sad wee bog-hole after the hotspots of Knightsbridge and Soho. What he got up to there in those famous night-clubs where each table had its own individual little red-shaded lamp as well as cream telephone, ordering champagne for his new business buddies, filtered down to me only gradually, a drip here, a droplet there. I kept ears and eyes wide open, making myself as inconspicuous as possible, but then that posture, as well as pretence, came easily.

Then one evening he came off the late plane from Heathrow and there was a change in the man I now secretly referred to as Herr Eggman. It made me feel a little better about being treated more and more like a dogsbody, for, yes, it was always me who had to take charge of his Bond Street purchases, laying them out side by side and upright like so many precious papooses in their plastic bags in the boot of the Cadillac. J.J. would never have been asked to do such a thing, I told myself, dishonestly, perhaps, for, of course, he *had* been ordered about like a skivvy, why fool myself, and as I fondled all that sumptuous gear swaddled in tissue paper smelling of extravagance and cologne I plotted how I could get my hands on some of it for myself. My one suit was beginning to show signs of wear, the trouser seat especially.

That night the Eggman looked flushed, possibly high from all those little courtesy miniatures they handed out on the flight. He began to talk and, of course, we listened intently – at least I did, I can't speak for Rocky – to all the stuff about some club called the Colony and, in particular, twin brothers he had met there the night before. They seemed to be pretty influential, very big wheels indeed, although I certainly had never heard of them. Reg and Ron. The Eggman seemed thrilled to be on first-name terms with them. Champagne, the very best, never stopped coming, to be plunged into ice buckets, although the quieter one of the pair only drank ginger ale.

As I listened I couldn't help wondering what they might think if someone were to tell them what the big, florid-faced Irishman's nickname was back home, the one sitting at their table and matching each round and slap of readies on the pink table linen with his own. But, then, from what I was hearing, huddled there in the dark of the back seat like that, I did rather get the impression that nearly everybody there, except the brothers, had a tag of some sort anyway. It was very much that sort of gathering, the place bursting with celebrities who kept drifting over to share a glass and chat with the twins.

'Look at this,' said the Eggman taking something from his wallet and passing it back to me. He switched on the little overhead light so I could see what it was, a book of matches with a big C and a gold crest on the cover. I realised I was meant to be impressed and after a proper interval of respect passed it back to him.

'No, look inside, dumbo,' he told me testily, and indeed there was something scrawled there in blue biro. 'Do you know what that is? That's Christine Keeler's fucking phone number, so it is. I'm going to give her a buzz next time I'm over. How about that, then?'

Rocky and I, we didn't say anything, and he seemed perfectly satisfied with our reaction.

Well, the following weekend he did travel across to London but whether he connected up with the famous young scandal queen I'll never know. In fact he may well have been rebuffed, not only by the lovely lady herself, but by his new East End friends as well. Something had gone seriously awry with his plans, that seemed obvious, as he sat in the front passenger seat like a great, pale, sulking, leather-clad lump of lard, for that was how I saw him now, no longer the formidable, princely figure who had driven up to Larkhill and taken over my young life, but someone wearing clothes that would have looked perfect on Hugo Dinsmore's youthful back, not his. My feelings towards the Eggman were changing, and speedily at that. It came to me J.J. must have gone through the same transformation, finishing up the way he did, secretly loathing the man who had turned him into a well-dressed messenger boy. Getting involved with Heather might just have been his way of getting even with someone who made him do everything bar wipe his backside for him.

It was the strangest thing, but even though I could see clearly, as through glass, an image of the path I was heading down, the same one, no doubt about it, J.J. had taken, except, of course, in his case riding young Heather along the way – lucky stiff – how could I stop myself? I couldn't. And, anyway, where could I go, even if I managed to bundle my courage together and simply took off down the lane one fine day away from the house on the hill and the people in it?

One afternoon I did set off, not in any kind of rehearsal or dummy run for the real thing, but basically out of sheer boredom. I drifted rather than strode. The hawthorns were in full blossom and there were lambs, even, stumbling around the fields on woolly, pipe-cleaner legs. Their cries filled the air, mewling, bewildered, baby cries. There was the screech of seagulls, too, following a lone ploughman on a tractor. Behind him the furrows parted in slow motion in glutinous, gleaming, cocoa-coloured coils, falling miraculously straight as teeth in a comb.

Like some townie I began to gulp in lungfuls of the hardy, April air. Fresh dung, wet grass, the tremulous, pale scent of early blooms. Leaning on a gate I felt as though I'd escaped from somewhere damaging to the health. All my senses were thrumming as if up to now I'd only been functioning on half-power. Under my spread palms the rusty iron of the gate felt scaly, painful, almost, to the touch. I could hear running water, one of those shy, little, crystal, country streams trickling away secretively at the base of a hedge nearby. I got a picture of it in my head, nosing through the flags of watercress under green locks of mermaid's hair. And here, too, a slow, calm pool where water-boatmen sculled and dragonflies flirted dangerously close to the surface. I had this intense longing to be like that boy Tom in *The Water Babies* having all of his wonderful, aquatic adventures. Whoever wrote a story like that knew what he was on about, for, whether under water, or ice, or in a burrow far below ground, wouldn't it be terrific to be able to escape to such magical places when the real world gets too much?

And then I thought of the pylons, for, you see, I had almost forgotten about that other windy, upper-storey world where everyone and everything looks like toy soldiers in a nursery landscape. I wondered if I had the knack and nerve still to climb up there. Hugo Dinsmore and his magic beanstalk. Looking off into the blue-green distance I thought I could just about see one, which must be where Larkhill lay, I told myself, for I couldn't imagine the idea of them existing in any other part of the countryside other than there, I don't know why.

That day I continued on in the same dreamy state, reliving bits of an earlier life. But when I got to the end of the lane and the main road, quiet and all as it always seemed to be, I found myself unable to take a step further for, quite suddenly, I felt shaken and nervous, the sight of all that scoured tarmac leading off straight and undeviating in two directions starting off a fear of the consequences of taking one in preference to the other. And beyond that again more and more choices, routes of escape proliferating, a bit like all those different wires inside a radio or a TV set, it came to me, and pursuing the image, dangerous, too, if the wrong decision just happened to be made. I stood there where the lane ended and the county road began, seeing myself as somehow alien, not quite cut out for the country life, the suit, the shoes, the entire ensemble singling me out as an interloper for all to see.

But then in the distance a car materialised, racing towards me. Pale in colour, it gave the impression of being high-powered, eating up the road, so, not wishing to be spotted marooned there like some overdressed oddity far from home, wherever that might happen to be, I moved into the lane mouth again. I started walking back the way I'd come.

The roar of the approaching car deepened, then seemed to falter as it neared the turning to the Hillhead. Moments later I heard it swing in behind me and as I stood aside to let it pass, a big, whiteish monster – a Daimler, I was to find out, that ticked over as discreetly as a clock – a voice called out, 'Hello there, young man!'

Behind the wheel, grinning out at me, was someone well-known at that time in the Province, often snapped by the press. And, of course, I should have recognised the car straight away, for it also appeared in the same photograph, with him inside, like right now. In those innocent times of ours what one drove marked one out as a celebrity, all the notables in our little backwater becoming associated in the public mind sooner or later with the particular make and model they went in for. According to what I'd heard the only other such motor in the entire North now purring beside me was one owned by the Duke of Abercorn himself, although his flew a stiff, little royal emblem on its prow.

'Tell me, friend, is this where Lyle Ritchie lives?'

By now my gaze had moved on from the lovingly Simonized bodywork of the Daimler, fastening instead on the canary-coloured, yellow driving gloves resting on the steering wheel. They seemed to epitomise the very grandeur of the man wearing them, a touch of decadence there, not just in the tint but in their soft chamois leather and perforated palms as well. And, of course, always a fresh buttonhole winter and summer, usually a violet, another of his trade-marks, not forgetting the handkerchief tucked inside the left cuff. I ate up all of these details, the oiled black hair as sleekly sculpted as a bathing-cap, the eyes equally dark and glistening, the smooth, slightly sallow cheeks.

'Is he at home, do you know? The big man?' He grinned as he said it, trying to draw me into the ambit of his charm.

I told him Lyle had left some time earlier.

'Still driving the pink torpedo?' he enquired. Then, 'Haven't seen you before. You're new, aren't you?' with a look that seemed to encompass every solitary thing about me even though we had only just met.

'J.J. along with him, I take it?'

What a lot of questions. Already I felt as riddled as a colander. I told him J.J. had gone from the Hillhead. He raised an eyebrow.

'Wee falling out, was there?' Then he said, 'Just tell him Jack Laird dropped by,' and I managed to keep myself from blurting out that I didn't need to be told who he was, sure, everybody knew.

He backed the car out on to the highway, then with a wave of one brightly coloured, gloved hand, accelerated smoothly away. It may have been my imagination but the lingering smell from the tail-pipe seemed different to what normal petrol left behind, high octane, very expensive, like the scent of the man himself.

Walking back up the lane I kept thinking, what an amazing encounter, someone like that just dropping out of the blue like a visitor from another galaxy and about as exotically removed, too. I looked around me. The man on the distant Fordson was still ploughing, the moist, chocolatey tilth spilling out behind the harrow as if squeezed from a tube. He would be doing this, or something similar, day in, day out, for the rest of his natural life. I felt a kind of pity for him moulded up there to the curve of his tractor seat. Very possibly he might well feel something of the same for me, mixed in with a certain amount of contempt, if he happened to turn in his iron saddle, catching a glimpse of me between a pair of gateposts. *Another low-life, gangster specimen from the Ritchie place*, I could almost hear him observe to himself, *up to no good as usual*. The idea of it pleased me, making me feel at one with the man in the big white motor car for, from a distance, to someone like that on a tractor, it might look as if the pair of us were close associates and, given the extent of his prejudices, almost certainly planning something shady together. Think of it. Hugo Dinsmore and the great dance-hall king himself, Jack Laird, thick as thieves.

When the Eggman returned home later that day I told him of his visitor and his mood took on a remarkable change. If someone like that could be said to be almost animated, then he was. For the past weeks he had been shuttling in and out of town with Rocky, a face on him like a thundercloud. The London trips had ceased. Something had obviously gone sour there, a financial deal, maybe *deals*, falling through, for he started taking a new and unexpected interest in the debt-collecting business. Up until then he had treated the whole thing almost jokingly, the accumulated amounts garnered from all those wee women's snap-purses small beer compared to the sums he was expending on flash gear for his great, fat, broad back. Still, I got the impression it might not have been his tailoring bills he resented so much, more the large paper white ones he had been lashing out on his so-called buddies across the water and their doxies.

Once or twice I heard him refer to 'those fucking English' and their la-di-da, mouthy ways. Naturally this was so much music to my ears, for Rocky and I, we could have been able to tell him, couldn't we, never trust anyone with an accent designed for the specific purpose of making your own sound like pig-shit, although the idea of two East End barrow boys doing so did upset the proposition rather. For the briefest of moments I felt a twinge of sympathy – but only a twinge – for the big, perspiring Irishman sitting there surrounded by sharp-suited smoothies. Closer to home, of course, Jack Laird himself sounded as Anglo as they come, maybe more so, but that didn't seem to count now that he and the Eggman started being seen out and about together in each other's company. And this development I feel certain led to a change in my own status.

One day Rocky called me over to the car and told me to get in. At first I thought it was to be one of our tick-collecting trips and instinctively reached towards the glove compartment, but Rocky told me to forget it.

'And you can put your wee notebook away as well.'

I looked at him knowing he had no intention of saying another word, but for once I wasn't going to indulge that silent cat and mouse routine of his. 'Just tell me where we're going,' I said.

He gave a sigh. 'Lyle wants me to learn you to drive.'

'You mean *this?*'

'What do you think? You're far too well dressed for a cattle lorry.'

'But I've never ever driven anything before.'

'Jesus. H. Christ, that's the whole fucking point!'

Then, relenting, he said, 'Relax, it's an automatic. Them fat, Yankee bastards are far too lazy to change gears. Anyway, they drive for days over there. Route 66? Remember?'

He took me to this disused airfield, flat as a concrete football pitch, in the middle of the country somewhere. During the war lots of these places were laid out for the Big Push, humming night and day with Spitfires and B40s landing and taking off, but after 1945 they were just left like that, so many barren, archaeological wastelands surrounded by farmland. Rocky drove out into the middle of this cracked, grey expanse, then parked there. We must have looked about as conspicuous as if we were on an ice floe.

'Okay,' he said, 'now change places.'

In the distance could be seen a couple of blockhouses and the remains of what just might once have been a control tower. Hay bales were piled against its outer walls and a file of sleepy looking pigs emerged blinking to take a mildly curious look at us. I got in behind the wheel but to my embarrassment, too late, realised I could barely see above the padded dashboard. Rocky lit a cigarette, ignoring my predicament, which as far as I was concerned seemed about as mortifying a beginning as one could wish for, then started talking me through the controls, pointing to each knob, button and lever and explaining what its function was. To my surprise he turned out to be an unexpectedly considerate teacher and when the moment of truth finally arrived he produced a torn, old, leatherette cushion from the trunk of the car for me to sit on.

'Now,' he said, 'give her the gun.'

And I did so, feeling the engine fire into life. It was a scary moment, remembering only too well when someone else had tried putting me in charge of a ton of horsepower, the real McCoy in that case. I felt certain I would disgrace myself this time around as well. But I didn't and Rocky had been right, the gears presented no problem, for the car, it seemed, did the work. All I had to do was keep the front wheels on an even course. I began to enjoy the sensation of flinging that great weight of finely tuned, Detroit technology all over the place, accelerating, swerving, braking, even reversing, with nothing or no one to get in my way. At one point one of the pigs stupidly strayed into the path I had set myself, but instead of avoiding it I put my foot down. Porky began to trot, then gallop, then squeal, the shriek of the tyres on the ribbed concrete a match for the cries of the fleeing sow. Whoever it was said the pig is one of our more intelligent animals must have got it badly wrong for our particular quarry finished up running in ever-decreasing circles, a spume of white froth dripping from its snout.

'Enjoy that, did we?' said Rocky as I rolled the car finally to a halt.

'Yes,' I told him, 'yes, I did,' which happened to be the truth.

'Well, just make sure you don't do it when you get on the open road, okay?' he replied handing me one of his evil Capstans.

We sat there gazing out across the bare, almost bone-bleached expanse. It seemed to stretch all the way to the horizon, foreshortening as it neared its far perimeter point, a glimpse of still water breaking its path where the great Lough lay. All that wartime, lend-lease concrete poured in sections and left to set, simply acres of it, just handed back to the elements like that. And us learner drivers as well, for, as I was to discover, I was not the first to come out here to take over the controls of someone else's car. At weekends, Sundays, for the most part, there might be as many as half a dozen warily circling one another, forming their own intricate paths and patterns across the cement like a stately procession of Dodgems in slow motion. Girls with their fathers and boyfriends mostly, which made me glad we had the place to ourselves, for I wouldn't have cared to be seen as some kind of sissy taking instruction at the wheel of such a tremen-dously masculine motor.

Still flushed with my success, I enquired, 'What about a licence?'

He laughed. 'When you work for the big man you don't need to worry yourself about wee things like that.'

We continued to park there, admiring the lunar landscape, all those shades of grey, the interior filling with Capstan fumes.

'Well,' said Rocky after a time, 'it looks like you're number one driver now.'

'What about you?' I asked with some alarm.

'I'm heading off. England, I think.'

I sat there trying to imagine life at the Hillhead without him. First J.J. – although he was no great loss – and now Rocky. Did I really wish for all this sudden isolation? Being number one at anything was more than a little daunting.

'Care to come along?'

Of course I knew he didn't, couldn't, mean it, but I toyed with the notion for a crazy moment or two.

Then he said, 'You wouldn't be a lot of use with a pick and shovel navvying on the M4,' and that was the end of it.

He made me drive back to the Hillhead some time later and although we kept to the back roads, meeting little or no traffic along the way, I was sweating fiercely by the time I jerked the Eggman's Cadillac, still unscathed, on to the yard to a halt alongside the gable-end of the house.

True to his word, Rocky did slide out of our lives after that. I was never to see him again, or hear anything further about his progress across the water, if that's where he ended up, labouring, I suppose. Unlike J.J., whose prospects I could well visualise, he simply left a blank which I didn't even try to fill in, allowing him to fade away like that disappearing dot in the middle of a television screen.

One thing he did leave me to remember him by, however. As usual we were sitting in the car together in the customary haze of cigarette smoke, which was something about him I wouldn't miss, with him in the passenger seat, for that was the way of it now.

'A wee word of advice, kiddo,' he said to me. 'Don't ever cross the Eggman.'

It struck me it may well have been the first time he had ever referred to him in that fashion in my company before. Maybe it was because he was leaving, but, anyway, he had my attention.

'I wouldn't recommend it.'

'Oh, but I never would. Never,' I protested. The moment I said it I knew it sounded girlish and craven in the extreme.

'Well, you just never know,' said he. 'The day might come.'

Looking back, in one way I wish I'd taken his advice at the time, then, in another, what's done is done, to hell with it. Here I am to prove it, and paying for it. But mostly I think to myself the alternative would have turned out a lot more punishing in the long run. I console myself with that particular line of reasoning, holding it tight like a private talisman to get me through the bad times.

The other day one of the Bible-buffs – you might be surprised at just how many of them are serving their time in here – slipped me a tract. Where they get them from I'll never know. I suppose they're not seen as any threat to officialdom, although some of the guys do, I know, use them for rollups, which *are* against the rules, because of what they tend to fill them with, Glengormley Gold, as it's jocularly known, being the hot favourite right now. It arrives here in all sorts of guises, passed from mouth to mouth at visiting times, mainly, for a certain amount of conjugal necking is permitted, or so I've been told. Anyway, the printed text read *Be Sure Your Sins Will Find You Out*, a wee bit close to the bone, surely, I thought, in a place like this where the reason we're here is because we did get found out. It gave me a laugh, and then it didn't, recalling, as I did, just how easily I allowed myself be seduced.

THIRTEEN

If I were to pinpoint a time and place where my downward slide began in earnest I suppose I should describe one night when the Eggman and I were the guests, yet again, of Jack Laird at what he liked to refer to as the 'flagship' of his fleet of dance halls, for at that particular period he had, I reckon, at least six. He made it sound like the SS *Carinthia*, and looking down on the dancers, packed, yet circulating below, we might easily have been at the heart of some great, gently sprung, pleasure-palace anchored for the night. As a matter of fact the real sea was not so far away, for Marino's had been built originally on the shoreline facing the lights of the city across the Lough where most of the dancers had travelled from.

We were high in Laird's office suite at the time with its one-way windows overlooking the floor below, another of his tricksy little notions. Feet apart, he liked to stand on the deep pile, mushroom carpet, whiskey and water in one hand, the other thrust deep into a pocket of his spotless white tuxedo, surveying the customers sweating and shoving thirty feet below. A bit like a captain on the bridge, too, it came to me, for I was a little drunk at the time and in one of those moods when I saw myself as the cleverest, most perceptive little shitehawk imaginable, half afloat on the tides of his own vanity.

Across from me the Eggman was sprawled in a beige leather armchair a match for my own. The all-over colour scheme was in shades of cream and ivory but the decorator, whoever he was, hadn't made allowance for the man planked facing me, for tonight he had on a hideous, pistachio green linen jacket, blueberry slacks, pale blue shirt and brown knitted tie. Every time I looked at him my eyes watered. Our host, on the other hand, looked like David Niven.

In a glass-fronted case were all his trophies, for in his time he had been all-Ireland ballroom champion. Indeed, he still gave demonstrations, specialising in Latin American rhythms. There were framed photographs everywhere of him and his partners, all brunettes, as befitted the culture of the mambo, rumba and samba, I suppose. For some reason they looked much the same, ageless, forever flashing-eyed and provocative in tight satin and Cyd Charisse hairstyles. For his part, he seemed to get just that little bit older in each one.

It was common knowledge he had married four of them, one of them tragically doing away with herself by putting her head in the oven. That was when we had our own city gasworks, of course. She didn't feature in any of the black and white photographs, but her tragic presence refused to go away, leaving a slime trail of unpleasantness on his reputation still. Alma Bickerstaff, her name was. He had seen her one day dressing a downtown shop window, stopping the Daimler then and there, and calling her out from among all those amputee dummies with bald heads. Of course, how could she refuse such an offer, his promise to make her one half of a winning combination of the ballroom circuit, including that Parnassus of the terpsichorean art, the Hammersmith Palais. Jack Laird always said he could make anyone a prize-winning professional, providing she was

290

pretty and could move gracefully, both qualities he must have spotted that fateful day he happened to drive past C&A's big window. And even though he must have been well into his fifties by the time we met he still had an eye for fresh talent, although that word could take on a separate and rather more free and easy meaning when it came to what might be required of the shop girls, typists and trainee hairdressers he called up to the captain's bridge.

'That one there. See? In the yellow mini-dress?' he would say to his manager Gerry, pointing down into the heaving mass below. 'And while you're at it, her there with the yokel at the bar with the crew cut in the John Collier suit.'

Gerry would screw up his eyes and stare hard in the direction of his master's pointing finger, a nervous individual with thick, bottle glasses, not young or trendy, as might be expected, but in the business with Laird a very long time.

Meanwhile I sat there enjoying every minute, and in the process learning an awful lot about women as well. What struck me most forcibly, I suppose, was that no one ever refused to come upstairs with old Gerry, not even those with boyfriends, or the ones who seemed far too respectable to be at Marino's in the first place. And once they got there and saw the cream and blond grandeur of the office they didn't want to go back down again. It was hard for me not to fall in love at least five, maybe six times in the course of an evening. While pouring the drinks, for that was very much part of the ritual, I would feel myself tremble in the presence of so much playful, home-grown young beauty sitting there downing Bacardi with silken thighs pressed together, or crossed, which inflicted even more damage. They giggled, they pouted, they stretched out their sleek, dark, seal-like heads for Laird to light their cigarettes for them. He had this trick of holding one of their wrists lightly as if taking a pulse, whilst bringing up his lit, gold Dunhill with the other. I watched in awe vowing to learn and never forget any of it. The ones he

291

fancied were invited to stick around after the last number, the others he eased downstairs quickly and painlessly and always with a kind of lubricating charm that left them not quite realising they had been rejected in the first place. But the darlings kept on coming, my God, how they kept on coming, in relays, giggling up the stairs, borne on a rising current of Blue Grass and Pagan.

'Gin and tonic? Vodka? Bacardi?' I would offer. Then, reading the labels in Laird's drinks cabinet, 'Dubonnet? Cointreau? Pernod?' all women's drinks and never, not once, getting turned down, just like Gerry. And so I got this crazy notion in my head – it may still be there – that there was no such thing as a teetotal brunette which, of course, led me to think of the Hoy sisters which, again, only served to strengthen the theory.

Throughout it all the Eggman sat staring silently straight ahead of him in his armchair like some Technicolor human dessert in pale green, red and blue, threatening to melt and run over the sides of his chair at any moment. At one stage when Gerry had escorted the last dolly bird back downstairs – I felt genuinely sorry for him, he was really panting by now – the Eggman grunted, 'For Christ's sake, Jack, how about a blonde for a change? Just one. Or maybe a redhead, even.'

I did think he had a fair point, but Laird would have none of it. 'My dear chap,' he drawled, 'blondes are common, they're most definitely cheap, and invariably they're frigid. A bit, I imagine, like your good self, old bean.'

There was silence, broken only by the vocalist through the almost but not quite soundproofed glass. The number was 'Now or Never' and he was giving it the full Elvis treatment. I looked at the big man opposite, terrified as to how he would react. Once again his outfit continued to obsess me, I don't know why, racking my brains as I did to remember which country's flag had all those particular primary colours in them. Some central American republic more than likely, like Panama or Puerto Rico – or Belize, maybe? I took another swig from my rum and Coke. But then he laughed. The Eggman actually guffawed. I suppose the other knew he would all along.

'Tell you what,' Laird said, 'seeing as this happens to be your birthday,' – certainly news to me – 'I'll relax the house rules and the preference of a lifetime this once. OK. Choose. Be my guest.'

Ponderously the Eggman rose from his armchair, his spread palms making a sucking sound as they left the pale leather. He lumbered to the window, staring down for a moment, then, 'Her,' he said, pointing. 'That one. Blondie smoking like a train beside the pillar,' and Gerry shuffled to his side, craning in the direction of his finger. It struck me as a tremendous shame that someone of his years should be made to puff up and downstairs like that even though he was as slim as a whippet in his old-fashioned, double-breasted tuxedo with the shiny, wide lapels.

'No,' said the Eggman, turning, 'no, let young Hugo here talk to her. The women like Hugo, so they do. Don't they, wee Hugo?'

They were all looking at me, even old Gerry, so what was I to do but go across and take a look myself.

'Where?' I asked.

'There. In the kinky white boots, with the big knockers.'

In the background I could hear Laird utter a deep sigh of resignation.

'Talking to the big guy in the sports jacket?' I insisted.

Through the glass and fifty or more yards beyond that again, right at the back of the hall, I see, even smell trouble, for already the scent of her hairspray and his Old Spice seem to be in my nostrils as an alarming accompaniment to his bodybuilder's girth and her equally Amazonian proportions.

'Now, you're sure that's the one?' I enquired, playing for time.

293

'Positive. Now run along,' and so I did, padding down the thickly carpeted stairs with the low-level lighting like the approach to some casino or night-club, and into the din of the dance hall. I felt a bit unsteady on my pins. Perhaps I had been rather reckless with the Smirnoff. I also felt distinctly aggrieved at the Eggman treating me the way he had in front of the others. Gerry, I could tolerate, but not Jack Laird, for I had seen him looking at me in that sly, sideways, smiling way of his. This was meant to be some kind of humiliation, I felt convinced of it. Why set me up with two of the toughest looking eggs in the entire place otherwise.

The noise hit me like a thump in the solar plexus the instant I set foot on the edge of that glistening, maple wood floor. The showband – it was the College Boys – were bouncing in their own raw, choreographed style to 'The Hucklebuck'. Hugging the clammy walls, for there was no way I was about to venture into the middle of that maelstrom of jerking bodies, gradually I began edging towards my quarry. They were having an argument of some kind, that seemed pretty obvious, one of those Saturday night, dance hall tiffs usually associated with jealousy, or being slighted in some fashion. Real or imaginary, it didn't matter, it was all part of the weekend ritual, ending in tears, being sick, or getting thumped. Sometimes, on occasions, all three. Thank God I wasn't involved in any of that any longer, I told myself, but, then, to be strictly truthful, I never had been, I supposed, never even having got to that stage in the courtship rigmarole.

I stood there, observing the pair of them. What I would say when I got up close remained a blank. *My fat boss up there fancies your girlfriend* not even a remote possibility.

Her escort had on one of those nubbly, oatmeal, sports jackets with patch pockets, and any padding in the shoulders was definitely all his own. I thought I recognised the tailor's style, that wee cripple bloke on Peter's Hill where all the bodybuilders went for their bespoke gear. My entire attention was focused on the bruiser for, as I saw it, he was the one posing the biggest threat by far. His hair was cut close in a flat-top and the Windsor knot in his tie was about the size of my hand. Glancing down I detected a definite tremor there, so, sticking the offending mitt in my trouser pocket, casually, I thought, I sidled up to them.

I was right about one thing – a couple, actually, her hair lacquer and his aftershave. Even in a place such as this which smelt like the biggest tropical hothouse in the universe they appeared to have gone overboard in the toiletries department.

Right, thinks I, *here goes. After all, it isn't me who's doing the actual propositioning, I'm just the humble messenger boy.* And at that point, for the very first time it hit me that I was being observed all along, every gesture, move and expression scrutinised and analysed from high up behind a wall of tinted glass, like something struggling feebly under a lens, every embarrassing gesture and tic magnified, even at that distance.

'Hi!' I said cheerily, the sweat breaking out all over me, 'Mr Laird has asked me to ask you both how you're enjoying your night out together at Marino's.'

Mr Universe lowered his great ox-like head to look down at me. 'Who?'

'Mr Jack Laird. The proprietor. It's our regular policy to check with the patrons.'

'Our?'

'Yes,' I said. 'I'm part of his team.'

For a terrible instant I felt convinced he was going to fire that last word right back at me again like some Martian who so far had only mastered a series of single syllables.

But then she came butting in with, 'Is this some sort of questionnaire thing?'

Her boyfriend looked at her suspiciously as if she might

have been hiding something from him all along, namely a knowledge of far bigger words than he himself had ever come across.

'Absolutely!' I cried excitedly, suddenly seeing a light shining somewhere that might lead me out of this. 'Absolutely. We're running a competition. All you have to do is answer a few simple questions.'

'OK,' said the boyfriend, 'fire away, sonny.'

'No, no,' I said, waving my non-existent clipboard, 'we're conducting the survey upstairs in Mr Laird's office. First, the ladies. Then their partners. It won't take a minute. Honest.' My voice sounded cracked, for I had been practically shouting all along because of the noise from the band, but suddenly the number came to a finish, that word 'honest' ringing out like a desperate cry for help above the low buzz of the dancers. One or two close by turned to look at us and the big guy glared back with an aggressive squaring of his Charles Atlas shoulders.

'I forgot to mention it,' I said, lowering my voice, 'but it's for the best-dressed couple here tonight. The questionnaire part is only routine.' I could see I might have struck gold for, as he put a hand up to straighten the knot in his tie, she patted her bouffant in a similar gesture. The hair, I noticed, refused to budge, as stiff and unyielding as burnished Brillo.

'What do you reckon, doll?' the big gorilla asked, but before she could reply I cut in with, 'First prize, a trip to London for two. All expenses paid.' By this stage I was starting to enjoy the fantasy I had created, particularly the look on their faces. Let the Eggman handle the upstairs side of things,

I told myself, I had done my bit down here more than valiantly, for by now I felt confident she had swallowed the bait.

'OK,' I heard her say, 'I'm game if you are. I won't be long. OK?'

He nodded. The deed was done.

After a deal of pushing and excusing myself we got to the foot of the stairs leading to Laird's office and I turned to her. 'What's your name, by the way?' I asked, although why I should be interested at all from this point on I had no idea.

'Rosaleen,' she replied, 'but call me Roxy. Everybody does. What's yours?'

'Hugo,' I told her.

There was a pause. Then she said – I swear it – 'Hugo first, then,' giving a great, brassy-sounding laugh that echoed all the way to the head of the stairs. In fact it lingered on and into the room beyond and, hearing it ring out like that, like a hooligan cry in the street, the laugh of a proper, common as dirt scrubber, I got the uneasy feeling this one meant trouble. Something else, too, told me she'd had a head start on the rest of us when it came to hitting the hard stuff.

'This is Roxy,' I said, introducing her as she stood there in her knee-length, white, patent leather boots and mini-frock looking about her, but not in the least awed or overwhelmed by it all, it being immediately obvious she was different from all the other sweet little darlings who had trotted in previously. I could also see the way the Eggman was staring at her. Like one of the livestock back on the farm, it did rather strike me, and I thought, not for the first time, what a brute the man was, no style, no class, no breeding, even though she herself had all the finesse of a streetwalker.

I poured her a drink, Johnny Walker, ice, Coca-Cola. A whiskey drinker, no less.

She toasted us all from her low armchair, affording a perfect sighting of her robust, Tanfastic thighs, and the tantalising glimpse of something cerise, silken and triangular in shape further up. Throughout, the Eggman's eyes never strayed, not once, from the floor show and she stared back, bold as brass, the rest of us in the room forgotten.

'Hey,' she said, 'I know you. You used to come round our street with Rocky Devine, didn't you, in that big American car? Still got it, have you?'

'It's outside. Care for a spin? How about a lift home?'

She threw her head back, giving another brazen laugh, and I could see Laird flinch. But I was much too intrigued by what was going on, transfixed, even, at the sight of the Eggman actually being flirtatious, albeit in elephantine fashion, and just as outrageous, being encouraged by the look of things.

'Well, how's about it?'

'How's about what, big guy?'

'A ride.'

There was an audible intake of breath. It came from the man at the window in the paler-than-pale tuxedo with the pretty blue flower in his buttonhole. Gerry looked shaken as well, taking his specs off, then holding them out and staring hard through their thick, bottle glass as if inspecting them for a speck of something.

'Oh, I wouldn't know about that,' replied Roxy. 'My boyfriend's downstairs. He has his own car. Tell you what, though, wouldn't mind another refill.'

'Hugo,' ordered the Eggman from his armchair, 'give young Roxy here a wee top-up while she's making up her mind.' I swear he was smiling, a nauseating grimace that transformed his massive mug into something resembling a hollowed-out, Hallowe'en pumpkin head.

'Yes, be a good boy and do what you're told, Hugo,' countered our guest. 'Know what I call him, everybody?' she announced to the room. 'Do you? Hugo First. Get it?'

The Eggman slapped his thigh. 'Hear that? Jack? Gerry? We've got a new name for the boy here. What do you think, eh?'

'Aye,' said Laird drily. 'Though vaguely Germanic, I'd say, wouldn't you? Hugo Furst? Not bad, mind.'

'Not bad? Dead on, Roxy. Dead on!'

And for the rest of the night he took immense delight in introducing me to newcomers as 'our visitor from Hamburg' or, alternatively, 'that teenage Berlin singing sensation' although no one seemed to want to try me out in that capacity. Of course I hated it, needless to say, and drank more and a lot faster than I suppose I should have done. But then everyone else seemed to be racing down the same path by now: it was developing into that sort of night. Laird himself started opening bottles of champagne, drenching the mushroom carpet, uncharacteristically, I thought, more and more with each one. And the brunettes began arriving in relays once more, although by this stage mine host, who was swaying just a little, seemed unable to make his mind up as quickly and as decisively as he had done earlier as his penthouse office filled up with all these dark, sleek, bobbed heads and one defiantly, bleached blonde one, for the bruiser boyfriend, it would appear, had well and truly got the push. I kept waiting for him to come pounding on the door, but he never did, which was a pity, for I would have loved to have seen how the Eggman would handle fourteen stones of angry, pumped up muscle with no Rocky to step in the way.

The party was really starting to take off big time when Gerry, the soberest one present, went across to whisper something to his boss who burst out, 'Shit and corruption!' then started for the door.

'What's up, Jack? What is it?' the Eggman called out.

'The competition, that's what! Forgot clean all about it. Tonight is the final heat. Miss Northern Counties Ballroom Queen.'

On the instant all the girls in the room, including Roxy, pricked up their ears.

'What about *us*?' they cried. 'Why aren't *we* in for it? Yes, why aren't we, tell us that?'

'Ladies, please, *please*,' appealed Laird with outstretched hands.

One of the bolder ones, a right little firecracker called Teresa something or other, promptly hitched up her pelmet of a skirt – mind you, it hadn't all that far to travel – calling out, 'What's wrong with these legs then, mister?'

'And how about mine?' cut in the irrepressible, not to be outdone Roxy, adding her own contribution with a flash of triangular, taut silk while the Eggman sat transfixed as though a glimpse of Heaven had miraculously favoured him.

'No, no, no,' persisted Laird, 'it's a formality, nothing more. The judges came to their decision a week ago. A quick line-up of the finalists, the winner gets her crown and, bingo! Look, tell you what, girls, you're all invited to my place afterwards. What do you say?'

For the life of me I couldn't understand just why he was being so accommodating all of a sudden. In his position I think I would have turfed that whole yelling crew back downstairs where they belonged. Then, again, maybe not, who's to know? Anyway, after he'd disappeared, we all crowded to the glass to watch the fun below while the Eggman stayed wedged in his chair still not shifting his hot gaze from Roxy's spectacular lower half. I noticed how she seemed to have taken over the other girls like their big, bad, bold sister, all those giggling, little mascaraed harem play-mates letting her chivvy them around. And the moment the contestants filed on to the stage below to a muffled drum roll, Jack Laird mouthing his inaudible introduction because of the glass in between, she launched into a caustic running commentary.

'Get a load of the heifer in the striped number. And how about Miss Chubby Cheeks, second from the end? What must she look like in a swimsuit? And please, *please* take a dekko at Olive Oyl. Where in the name of all that's holy did they dig her up from? The City Cemetery? Tell you one thing, girls, if that lot down there haven't been dropping their drawers to get this far, then I'm Doris Day.'

Despite all my earlier reservations I was beginning to warm to Miss Roxy McKevitt. Something about her, something reminding me of Deirdre Hoy, I suppose, all that raw, rude bounce, must have got to me and even if she had landed me with a pet name that made me sound like a German spy there was no harm in it, no real harm in her, I decided. Anyway, to be honest, I quite enjoyed the attention and being ordered about, refuelling glasses for all her delightful baby sisters, and even though the Eggman was squatting there all the while like some malevolent mound of blubber.

Down below on the platform Laird was now placing a crown on the sleek, marcelled head of Miss Northern Counties Ballroom Queen. The skinny one with the goo-goo eyes had landed it, much to Roxy's disgust, but it was only play-acting, we all could see that, even Gerry, who seemed to be finding it hard to keep a straight face.

'Girls, you'll never guess what I'm going to tell you, but that one used to work alongside me in Gallaher's. Honest, I'm nearly positive. Even then she thought she was the girl in the big picture. Had to wear gloves on the conveyor in case she caught something. Look at her smiling there like she's Natalie Wood instead of Dolores Muldoon from Divis Street. Here, Hugo, don't be such a mingy wee shite with the whiskey. You'd think it was his own private stock instead of nice Mr Laird's. By the way, girls, what do you think of our Hugo, eh, in his lovely tailored suit and wee candy-striped, pink shirt? Wouldn't mind taking him home with me myself. You know what they say, short in the height department, but not elsewhere where it counts. Ach, look at him blush, would you.'

In the middle of it all I glanced across at the Eggman. He

was regarding me with a look at odds with the mood of good-humoured banter that reigned now in that upstairs room with its modern furniture and soft lighting and photographs of the proprietor in his heyday, all dazzling white teeth and dark, dago hair, a veritable youthful Tyrone Power in white tie and tails.

And then the man himself came through the door with the beauty queen in tow, still wearing her gold tiara and red velvet cloak over bare, skinny, freckled shoulders. We could hear the faint strains of the national anthem in the far background and, looking down on the confusion and milling crowd below, seemingly at a loss, as always, as to what to do with themselves now that the dance was at an end, and so quickly, too – *why always so quickly?* – with the band packing up their instruments, I felt a sort of pity for them, all that anticlimax and then their melancholy, little homeward journeys into the night outside with the dark, invisible sea breaking on the rocks on the distant side of the car park. Here, where we were, was light and noise and high spirits with plenty more promised in the wee small hours ahead.

Two of the girls had fallen asleep where they lay on a settee together, heads touching like a couple of sweet, lost babes in the wood. A drunken discussion began as to whether we should wake them or not, but it was decided – God alone knows why – it would be a pity not to leave them as they were curled up like that with their shoes kicked off and their delicate little pink soles showing.

'Last one out switches off the lights!' merrily called out Laird, leading us all in a drunken conga line down the stairs, across the bare, slippery expanse of the ballroom floor, then into the darkness of the car park where more tipsy argument and toing and froing continued to take place. But, finally, Gerry took up his stance by the open doors of Laird's big white car and in a shrieking rush the brunettes piled into it as if trying to break the world record for cramming as many

302

virgins as possible into the back of a Daimler Mark II. They were all singing as they drove off, leaving Roxy and me hanging around waiting for the Eggman.

'Like a drink, wee man?'

She was shivering and produced a near full half-bottle of Scotch she must have managed to snaffle upstairs. Silently we drank in turn and I tasted her lipstick on its chill neck.

'What's keeping that big ugly galoot, anyway?'

'Oh, he never rushes himself. Goes at his own sweet pace.'

'Like an elephant, you mean?'

'Never forgets either.'

I don't know why I said it, but she squeezed me close to her. What with the whiskey on top of the vodka, her perfume and proximity, I was beginning to get a semi-respectable hard on. I prayed she wouldn't notice or brush against it accidentally. But then another part of me – the one a lot lower down with far less restraint or conscience – insisted, *what the hell?*

'Tell you what,' she breathed boozily in my ear, 'why don't me and you clear off on our own, just the two of us.'

'Take the motor and leave him, you mean?'

'You drive, don't you?'

'Oh, sure, sure.'

'Well, how about it then? Dump the Eggman. Wouldn't that be some laugh?'

Up to that point I had been feeling pretty confident in a pleasantly woozy sort of way, but hearing her refer to him by his nickname suddenly, out of the blue like that, for some reason I got this relapse, you might say, a fit of nervous dread of the consequences of even talking about him in such a manner. It made me glance over my shoulder and, sure enough, didn't I see his shambling bulk emerge from the shadows back at the dance hall, turning his great blond head about from side to side in that short-sighted, almost albino way of his, looking for the car and me, of course, along with it.

'Speak of the devil,' Roxy said. 'And guess who he's got with him. Wouldn't you friggin' well just know it.'

It was Miss Northern Counties the ballroom queen herself, holding her crown on her head with one hand, high-heeled shoes in the other, Red Riding Hood cloak trailing behind in a flurry of velvet and white fur trim.

'Bet she got locked behind in the powder room, stupid cat. Suppose now I'll have to ride alongside her in the back instead of up front with you, sweetie pie.'

When he got to the car, with nothing more than a grunt the Eggman hauled himself into his usual place while we all continued to stand there.

'Where is everybody?' our barefoot beauty queen kept twittering. 'Where has everyone gone, I'd like to know? Mr Laird promised there'd be transport laid on. It's my big night, after all. It is, isn't it?'

Roxy took her by one skinny, freckled and now goose-pimpled arm. 'Don't be such a pain, Dolores,' she hissed. 'Get in the friggin' car, will you.' And she did, giving a sort of strangled, little girl sigh as if all the air had suddenly been let out of her.

'Where to?' I asked.

'Straight on. We're to meet up at the Bridge. Dino's,' replied the man at my side, and from his tone I could tell that his earlier, brief, skittish mood back at Marino's had run its course.

The suburban roads at this hour were deserted and we raced past darkened seaside villas and their expensive, well-kept gardens. Many of them had yucca-like palm tree things growing in them, plants you would never imagine indigenous to this part of the world at all. Their foliage appeared cut out of cardboard against the blue-black sky, a touch of the tropics, although outside the night air was anything but balmy. Behind me I could hear the ballroom queen shivering so I switched the heater on to high and after a moment heard her complain, 'But I don't live this way. Where are you taking me? Where are we going, anyway?'

'Oh, for the love of Christ, Dolores, would you give over. We're going to a party, that's what. In your honour.'

That seemed to mollify her for she said, 'Oh, really?' in that irritating juvenile's voice of hers. Then she said, 'Why do you keep on calling me Dolores like that? It isn't my name. It's Lana.'

'You don't say? Well, mine's Marilyn. OK?'

After that I heard the cap twist from a bottle followed by a gurgle and a sigh. Without having to look in the mirror I could just imagine the scene in that darkened back seat, sort of a silent cat fight developing with the participants drawing further and further apart from one another into their respective corners.

About twenty minutes later we started heading into town proper and when we reached the near side of the Bridge, ahead of us I saw the long line of cars parked outside our famous, all-night chippy where everybody stopped in the small hours after a heavy drinking session. Laird's big pale Daimler was drawn up on our side of the road and the Eggman directed me to drive right up to its bumper. I could see all the heads filling the rear window in front like the back of a school excursion bus, twisting round at our approach, and presently hands began to flutter and wave. I waved back.

'I don't know about the rest of you, but I could murder a fish supper,' announced Roxy.

I looked at the Eggman, but he stared straight ahead.

'OK,' I volunteered, making to get out of the car.

'Stay where you are,' commanded the Eggman, but before he could humiliate me much further in front of Roxy and

Miss Ballroom Queen, didn't I see Gerry making his way towards us with what looked like an armful of takeaways from Dino's.

The guy who owned the dump called himself Dino, although his real name was Albert McVeigh. In a matter of a year or two he would become a millionaire and could call himself anything he pleased, even drive a bigger, more expensive car than either of the two parked outside his place that night, but now was now and everybody liked to pull his leg about it, maybe even breaking into 'Volare', that hit of his dark-haired, Hollywood namesake, while he just went on serving and smiling back at them across the greasy, zinc counter of that shack of his under the arches, regardless of class, creed or colour, although I don't think anyone ever saw a dark face there, bar some poor, lost unfortunate off a banana boat in the docks.

'Mr Laird never keeps food in the house,' said Gerry, coming up and reaching a paper package of something aromatic and vinegary through the back window.

'I got some hamburgers for them that wants it as well.'

'You're a real dote, Gerry Keenan, so you are,' Roxy told him. 'Remind me to give you a great big hug and something extra special later on.'

He winked in at me then, his one, open eye suddenly huge and all-seeing through the thick, Health Service lens of his old-fashioned glasses. Minutes later he climbed into the big, purring white car in front again, pulling silently away and me following after in our own. In double convoy we drove through the dead city streets past the enormous blanched dial on the ever so slightly leaning Albert Clock, like some great moon face decorated with hands and plain numerals, while the smell of Dino's fast food filled the car.

'Care for a bit, Hugo?' Roxy offered, leaning forward into the light from the dash. She popped a piece of fried fish in my mouth. Delicious, it tasted, and from that point onward she proceeded to feed me titbits, all the more tempting for being served by her own fair hand. *Open up and say, ah, Hugo. Well, anything you say, nursie, and how about attending to this sudden swelling down here while you're at it?*

By one of those weird coincidences our Roxy actually worked in a hospital, something I got to discover later. The very thought of those downy arms below the puffed, short sleeves of a pale blue uniform, wristwatch pinned upside down over one magnificent breast, not forgetting, of course, the white stockings and shoes, exerted a tremendous thrill, I have to say. But long before any of that came about to torment me that night – next day, rather – for it was well past midnight by the hands of that great city timepiece, we nosed out into the dark countryside heading towards Jack Laird's place.

Ahead of us Gerry drove at a steady, almost sedate pace which suited me fine for, once I lost sight of that number plate in front, RUMBA 1, I felt certain I wouldn't have been able to find my way out of the maze of unmarked back roads that led to the Grey House, as it was called.

Somewhere off in the back of beyond a swinging, red lamp stopped us and, heart in mouth, I saw the police patrol up ahead. One of them came strolling up to the passenger side of the car in front, not the driver's, I noticed, and after a word or two there, approached the Eggman's rolled-down window.

'Good evening, and is that your good self, Lyle?' the bobby enquired ever so affably, while keeping the beam of his torch fixed on the ground with much the same consideration. 'A wee bit of a hooley over at Mr Laird's place, so I hear? Sure, you never know, we might just call in ourselves later. Anyway, enjoy your evening now, and drive safely.' Then as he stood back, we drove on past him and his little detail, all wrapped up in their dark, heavy greatcoats against the damp Antrim air.

'And Sieg Heil to you too, Fritz,' muttered Roxy under her breath, first indication to me she might well be a Catholic. One thing for certain, however, neither of the pair of us would have been accorded the same treatment as our two hosts if we had happened to be caught on our lonesome out here. That's where Roxy McKevitt and I would always be equals in the eyes of the law, and I quite relished the idea of that, kind of a bond, you might say, just like the one with Rocky, realising at long last, I suppose, where my true place might lie. Not in the Eggman's world, but maybe a lot closer to theirs.

The Grey House had been built by an architect about thirty years earlier right on the shores of Lough Neagh as a sort of modernist folly, flat roof, acres of metal-framed glazing, overlooking the dun-coloured, tideless waters. There he dwelt in unbroken isolation staring out across to the far side, as foreign to his city eyes as Tangiers or the Ligurian coast, while drinking himself to death. Whether it was the sheer loneliness, or impending bankruptcy that accelerated the process, no one will ever know, but after it had been on the market for more than a year Jack Laird bought the house for himself as his weekend pleasure retreat. The rest of the time it remained shuttered and silent, the haunt of water fowl who scratched nests in the lawn, while dock and thistle sprouted the length of the drive. I knew about it – we all did in the country areas – that glaring, pale object set down like something cubic and alien from another planetary system. Of course it never struck me I would ever be invited inside.

I remember we ground our way over some sort of cattle-grid affair, then bumped up the long, straight, disastrously potholed gravel drive. The moon had come out and was laying a trembling track across the water right to the house itself.

'So, are we here, folks?' Roxy asked, sounding that wee bit pissed.

No one answered her for it was obvious we were, even to her, I suppose, for, 'Welcome to Bel Air,' she said next, which I thought pretty perceptive, for maybe it was more than a touch Hollywoodish, in a film-set, over the top way.

We sat in the cars with the engines running, for it was chilly beyond the misted glass, until Gerry had gone inside, drawn back the shutters, lit fires, turned the heating back on up to full. At least I imagined that was what he was about as lights started coming on one by one until the entire place was illuminated like a gigantic, thirties slab of icing-cake set down there in the wilds like that. I wondered what all those backward farming folk on the far side of the Lough would think seeing a beacon burst into sudden life in that way, hear dance music drifting across the black waters towards them, for the moment we trooped inside the party took off all over again, without preliminary or awkwardness, at the twist of a button, turn of a switch. The drinks commenced to flow, the brunettes were feverishly mambo-ing together to Perez Prado on the big hi-fi, while, glass in hand, I allowed my gaze to browse freely over the wonders of Jack Laird's country hideaway.

From what I could see, the taste, the style, of the previous owner remained intact. Leather and chrome, smoked glass, blond wood, Swedish wall-hangings. What pictures there were seemed to be all nudes, not of women, which I would have appreciated, but of boys around my own age, staring back shamelessly from their rectangles of canvas. Going up the stairs I had a shock on the landing, feeling positive I recognised the face and figure, even if he was buck naked, of one of the sitters, sprawled on an unmade bed with what looked like a flower in his hand, bare as the day he was born. It was one of the young hooligans I had encountered that day at Glenrowan, I felt convinced of it, the lad with fair hair and spotty skin, although the artist, whoever he was, had given him a flawless, Palmolive complexion. I gazed into the mocking eyes and they grinned back, just as they had done that afternoon when I sat in the Eggman's car and their owner had leant on a garden rake demanding a cigarette. A face like that I would never forget, the face of one who had seen it all, old before his time in the ways of the world, and it came to me — men, also — like the one who had commissioned his portrait.

I was still feeling shaken by the coincidence — but, then, again, was it that? — when behind me on the stairs someone made the remark, 'You could get six months for what you're thinking.' It was Roxy and she was eyeing me in a strange kind of way.

'Oh, no, no,' I protested, 'you've got it wrong. I know who he is.'

'Wee pal of yours?'

Again I vehemently denied it, only getting deeper into the mess I had created for myself.

But then, taking pity on me, she clasped my hand in hers, saying, 'Relax, don't have a heart attack, I know you're not that sort. Mind you, just maybe your man downstairs might be.'

'Laird?' I said.

'Why not? AC/DC, even. But who cares? I vastly prefer him to your other friend sitting out in the kitchen any day.'

'He's not my *friend*!' Before I knew what was happening the words had come boiling out as if they had been simmering inside and, indeed, possibly they had.

'Your boss, then?'

'He's not that either!'

She gave me another of her sideways looks. 'Come upstairs and cool off.'

There was a gallery affair at the top of the stairs spanning the

310

entire width of the house and overlooking the big room below and we stood there together close, drinks in hand, smoking and leaning on its long, polished prow of a rail. In a cleared space in the middle of the floor Jack Laird was dancing with one of the brunettes, who performed as if already destined for the ballroom circuit. Hips swaying, arms waving, legs stiffly strutting, faces fixed in matching, supercilious masks, they closed, retreated, then grappled for the briefest of moments yet again to the beat of the cha–cha–cha. The music seemed to be ever-expanding to fill the entire house with its thudding, Latin rhythms.

'What's happened to his hair?' I whispered, suddenly noticing something unusual about that dark, oiled cap bobbing below like a ball in surf.

She gave a gasp, then a giggle. 'Blimey, you're right. It's a rug. Don't you just love it? A syrup.'

I looked at her. 'Syrup?'

'Syrup of figs? Wig? Get it?'

Then, 'Come along with me, blue eyes,' she commanded and for a heady moment I thought she might have one of the bedrooms in mind after all. But, alas, not my lucky night, for instead she steered me through a darkened glass door on to a sort of roof terrace with that great, ever so slightly stagnant expanse of still water spreading off to infinity below us.

'Isn't this tremendous?' breathed Roxy, holding me close for warmth. 'Isn't it? Like the South of France?'

'You're right,' I agreed, getting up the courage to return some pressure of my own. 'Here, take my jacket,' I offered, for I could feel her shivering. Stripping off my lightweight, barathea number with the shot silk lining, I draped it about her bare shoulders just the way Cary Grant might have done with Grace Kelly; all that was needed to pull off the scene for me to light two fags in my mouth at the same time. Which, of course, I didn't do, thinking I might fumble the operation, ending up looking like some complete dick.

311

'Tell me one thing,' Roxy enquired presently, 'just what are you doing with that big, fat gangster back there in the kitchen anyway? Someone nice like you. Gives me the creeps he does, the way he keeps looking at people.'

'Like something he can buy and sell, you mean?' There was a pause. So I had come out with it after all, the unspeakable. Somewhere out in the dark part of the water I could hear a solitary wild fowl quacking in fright.

'So, tell me, then, has he bought *you*, Hugo?'

It was a very curious moment that, for all of a sudden, feeling myself tremendously grown up, maybe almost as experienced as herself, I heard myself tell her, 'Part of me. Yeah, you could say that. A bit of me.'

'But the big question is, what part?' And as she said it the moment seemed to pass and once more I was back to being that hick again, shivering himself now, in shirt-sleeves and thin, summer-weight trousers.

'Never you mind, honeybun,' she murmured tightening her hold. 'I only want the part he hasn't paid for. At least, I hope so. Let's go back downstairs, you and me, and show 'em a thing or two. I bet you're one terrific mover in your own wee way.'

And we did dance, and pretty niftily at that, I considered, while the ballroom king himself looked on, for by now he was taking a breather on one of the big, plump, tan, hide sofas with a bunch of the babes crawling all over him as he lounged there, long, elegant stick-legs stuck way out in front, the toupee heading even further adrift, like a glossy bird's nest dislodged by a storm of some kind. *For Christ's sake*, I kept thinking to myself, *why doesn't he just take it off and be done with it*, as Roxy and I shook and shimmied together, sweat sliding in a delicious, damp trickle down the furrows of our backs, for I could feel Roxy's under my touch matching my own. And then, lo and behold, he did, which seemed to excite his fan club even more as they fought to caress his strangely tanned and glossily toned bare scalp. 'Like a baby's bottom,' one of them was heard to remark, with a kind of slurred reverence in her voice.

Gerry, meanwhile, kept everyone well oiled, dispensing the most complicated and occasionally exotic concoctions with tremendous aplomb. Ice, lemon, lime, olives, cherries, even, seemed not to present a problem. Indeed. '*No problem!*' came to be a yelled catch-phrase as the hours slid by, as if we were all ascending in some great, communal elevator of mood to a plateau of higher enjoyment, the climb going on and on and on. That's how I saw it, anyhow, but in reality it was more like a peak, or pinnacle, for at around three, things seemed to start sliding down the other side. It was then the party began to change, with other people, strangers, arriving, the headlights of their cars raking across the blackness of the great windows, followed by the crunching of feet on gravel, much laughter, then prolonged ringing on the doorbell. One of the girls – it was the beauty queen, actually – still wearing her cloak and tiara, kept staggering up to answer it, a fixed, welcoming smile on her face as if she had appointed herself unofficial hostess for the evening.

'Do come in,' I kept hearing her say as she stood swaying in the doorway with her smudged lipstick and one narrow shoulder-strap, half on, half off. For some time I had been watching closely to spot if and when that little left tit of hers would slip out and make an appearance, not in any real, lustful way for, holding my hand beside me, as I saw it, was the most alluring woman in the room, but because I had entered my I-spy mode, taking in everything and everybody with this beady little eye as if it might be called upon to recreate the scene in fine detail as evidence later.

By this juncture Roxy and I had climbed once more to our private lookout on the balcony. Looking down, we surveyed the scene below as the newcomers kept arriving, noting how they managed to get sucked into the mood of the occasion with barely a pause or curious glance around them. But then maybe they'd been well primed before they arrived. Hanging up there behind the slender, polished, pine bars of our private eyrie, it felt like we were a couple of kids peering down on the adults at play, apart and conspiratorial, in a smug kind of a way.

'What do you think?' murmured Roxy. 'Do you know any of this new crowd?'

'No,' I told her, 'but somehow they do look kind of familiar.'

'You think there's anyone famous? Someone maybe we should recognise?'

I knew exactly what she meant but, to be truthful, I didn't much care. From where we were standing they looked pretty much alike, foreshortened, drinking and socialising, dancing now, as well, for most of these latecomers seemed to be male, getting to work on Dossor's obliging little harem straight off the reel.

At some stage Roxy went off to powder her nose. That was the expression she actually used and it still came as a shock, even though it had struck me that early diagnosis of mine had been way off the mark. Anyway, while she was away, I went down to get us a couple of refills and events became a trifle blurred as if a bout of altitude sickness had started working in reverse. I know I ended up in the kitchen, probably looking for more ice, for Gerry seemed to have disappeared.

The Eggman was there, as Roxy had said he was, with the inevitable card game in progress. It was a four-hander and the table already had a pile of paper money at its centre the height of a modest molehill. I was over at the refrigerator rooting about without much success and feeling distinctly groggy by this time. Another vodka and Coke was not such a brilliant idea, but the quest for ice had taken on a kind of stubborn, grail-like quality, as so often happens after a load of alcohol.

'Hugo! There you are!'

The man who'd spoken my name was one of the strangers playing stud poker. He was grinning at me, someone about the Eggman's age, maybe a little younger, and like his two companions tie-less, in shirt-sleeves. I hadn't seen any of them being greeted by the ballroom queen earlier. Then I remembered the back door and decided they must have come that way. There was something faintly disturbing in that, I felt, as was the atmosphere in that bare, harshly lit room, as if the rest of us back there where the music was thumping away in Brazilian three-four time were the real gatecrashers and not this lot with their worldly and distinctly killjoy attitudes.

'You know I'm real sorry we missed one another that day you and J.J. called by our wee place. Promised faithfully he'd introduce us properly the next time he dropped in, but then, that's our dear J.J. for you. Rather, *was*,' the speaker continued, with a quick sideways glance in the Eggman's direction. 'Wayward as the wind, that one. But you really should have made yourself known, for it's not as if our paths were never meant to cross. Right, Lyle? Lyle and me, we go back, oh, a long, long way. No secrets from one another. Isn't that so, big man?'

'Perfectly true, Gus. Now are you going to talk shite all night or play cards?' replied the Eggman, as elegantly as ever.

For my part, I felt even more disorientated than I had been before. Just who the hell was this balding character with glasses and an excess of chumminess, anyway, who seemed to know all about me, while I had barely a clue as to who or what he was. He kept smiling over his specs at me in this distinctly unsettling manner while the others, seemingly ignoring my presence, concentrated on their hands.

'Well, Lyle, I'm waiting, so I am. If J.J. wouldn't do the

needful, why don't you go ahead and introduce me to the lad here.'

With a sigh the Eggman said, 'Hugo, meet Gus Gilmore. Gus, meet Hugo. Now the pair of you can go off into the sunset together. OK? Satisfied?'

The man on his right gave a wink and grinned over at the player opposite, who in turn shook his head resignedly as if he had been down this particular road many, many times before.

I made a move towards the door.

'Where are you off to, young Hugo?' said the Eggman, not raising his eyes from his cards. 'Gus here only wants to be friendly. Isn't that so, Gus?' More grins and knowing looks.

Still in my dreamlike state, I heard myself reply, 'I have to go to the toilet,' as if it was a declaration of immense importance, although why I simply didn't head for the door like any normal person without explanation or excusing myself, I will never know.

'No need to be so polite, son,' said the grinning one, slapping a card down with brutal relish. 'Sprinkle the rose bushes outside like the rest of us.'

'Yeah, don't be so fucking high-falutin', young Hugo,' the Eggman rumbled. 'You were brought up with a bucket in the backyard just like the rest of us.'

And suddenly it felt like they were all having a go at me and I hadn't sufficient stamina left to defend myself, and just as suddenly I was bursting as well, which seemed unaccountable, for I had only pleaded distress as an excuse to get away from them, especially creepy four-eyes, the one called Gus. So I opened the back door. Outside, where it was cold as Christmas, a line of pink no thicker than a thread had appeared, separating the Lough and the darker line of land in the far, far distance. Shivering, I stood there watching it stretch as though to breaking point as all the drink I had been pouring into me most of the night proceeded to stream straight out again. There were no rose bushes, no flowerbeds to deaden the sound, so I shuffled prissily forward to the water's edge, arcing my trajectory to merge with all that other abundance of H_2O out there. A solitary pleasure. Which it always is, in my opinion, especially after a bout of the booze.

But then behind me I heard the door open, briefly throwing a rectangle of light across the flags to where I stood, dick in hand. Presently someone came right up alongside and out of the corner of an eye I could see it was the Gus character.

'They're all non-smokers back there, would you believe,' he said, which I knew was a lie. 'Care for one yourself? When your hands are free, of course.'

He gave a sort of giggle at that, which had the immediate effect of turning off the waterworks for me.

'So, young Hugo, what's all this I hear about you being the little ladies' man? That you've something they all seem mighty partial to – as if we didn't know what that might be, eh? Just like J.J., as I recall. Wouldn't that same rascal be having himself a ball if he were with us right now? Wouldn't he just? I tell you, Hugo, the nights we've had here in the past, J.J., Lyle, big Jack, letting it all hang out, as they say. I could tell some tales, show you Polaroids – although that's hush–hush, you understand – that'd stunt your young growth for you. Sorry if that sounded like I was trying to be funny. I wasn't, I wasn't, I do assure you.

'Tell me truthfully now, tell me I'm not wrong in thinking you'd be up for a bit of fun yourself if the occasion presented itself. Which looks more than likely, the way things are shaping up inside. This wee birdie tells me there's someone here tonight you're pretty pally with who also wouldn't be afraid to oblige. A certain blonde lassie – am I right? Who'd be more than happy to do a turn, as they say. The pair of you? Maybe even more than that, depending on how hot

317

things get. I guarantee there'd be no shortage of volunteers, Hugo. Not with someone as dishy as your good self. Now, what would you say, Hugo, if you and I. . .'

And that's when, finally, I broke away – not before time, I hear you say – diving for an escape route off to the right of the terrace, leaving him in mid-flow, all that stuff pouring out of him and gathering pace like a run of crap down a toilet. I was shaking, yet felt a strong desire to go back and turf him in the Lough, closing his foul mouth for good. One push would take care of it. Maybe even with a bit of preliminary play-acting on my part, hand stretched out as though in compliance, followed by a jerk, then a shove. All over in a flash. Splash. Goodbye, Gus, or Gussie, or whatever the fuck your name happens to be.

The fantasy held up all the way around the side of the house to where I'd first felt gravel underfoot.

Ours had been the only two cars then; now I counted five, six, maybe more, parked in the moonlight. The Eggman's Cadillac hadn't been boxed in, which was what I was anxious to determine, for by this stage I knew what I had to do, the decision as clearly defined in my head as the outline of the car keys in my trouser pocket. I could hear the dance music pounding still, punctuated by high shrieks and catcalls, and for a moment I stood there among the silent,, cooling cars listening intently, trying to distinguish one voice from all those others. Once I heard it, I told myself, it would mean I could make a move without hindrance of guilt or con-science. But the harder I strained, the more any hint of it evaded me. So then I knew I had to go back in again.

But despite all those tough guy fantasies of mine I still didn't have the nerve for the way I'd just come, not knowing which was worse, the sex maniac on the terrace, or the Eggman himself, especially him, in the light of what I had in mind. Ringing the doorbell appeared the only alternative.

But, then, what if no one heard because of the racket going on? To my shame I half hoped that might be the case.

But someone did answer it, one of Jack Laird's little darlings who instantly threw her arms about my neck as if I was someone fresh, a potential heart-throb she hadn't met before. I have to say my resolve weakened that tiny fraction, for she was a pretty wee thing, although by this stage her eyes were rolling in her head, and there was a sort of dumb desperation in the way she clung on to me. Over her hot, bare shoulder – she was about my height, too, another good excuse for having second thoughts – I kept looking for the one who was the reason for me coming back for more punishment.

All over the room couples were locked together like Siamese twins, some still going through the motions, the pretence, of dancing, others curled up in chairs, on sofas, on the stairs, a favourite necking spot I'd often noticed at parties. Neither Laird nor Miss Northern Counties I could see anywhere, but someone had taken and hung his toupee like a redskin trophy over a marble bust in the corner. Don't ask me why, for it's still a deep puzzle, but after I'd manoeuvred the babe to a vacant space on one of the settees, gently unloading her there like a sweet-smelling, deliciously pliable sack of something, I took hold of the glossy scalp off its perch and carried it upstairs with me. It felt dry and scaly on the outside and rubbery within, like a scrap of carpet shag-pile. Some static there, as well, I couldn't help remarking.

There must have been about a dozen bedrooms at least, as well as bathrooms up there, like in a small hotel, and methodically I began trying the door handles of every one. Most were dark and obviously occupied, but in one – it looked like the master bedroom – the lights were on. Sprawled out together on the enormous bed like something from a movie set – I think it may even have been a four-poster – lay Jack Laird and the Ballroom Queen. Before I closed the door in a hurry I saw he was stark naked save for her tiara on his bald head, like one of those Roman emperors, gold-plated tin instead of a wreath, or chaplet, or whatever it's called. Her lower half was covered by her cloak and both were out for the count, dead to the world. I couldn't help wondering whether they'd actually had a chance to do it or not, or had passed out in unison before the big moment arrived. I have to say he looked remarkably fit for someone his age, in the buff like that, with an all-over tan which struck me as the very height of sybaritism and the mark of someone seriously rich at the particular period we're speaking of here.

At the end of the corridor was what I took to be a locked bathroom door and when I knocked, for I had run out of places to try by this time, a voice called out, 'Bugger off!' a voice I recognised, the one I had been anxious to hear all along despite its tone.

'Open up, it's me,' I whispered to the lock.

The handle turned. I went in. Roxy was sitting on the toilet – the lid down, I hasten to add – smoking a cigarette. 'I'd about given up on you,' she said, mood and accent still frosty. 'Thought you'd dumped me for one of our bimbos. Where the hell were you?'

'Don't ask,' I told her. 'Let's get out of here.'

She puffed on her cigarette one last time before twisting it out in the wash-hand basin.

'Have you seen what's happening here? It's a regular knocking-shop. The place is crawling with heavy breathers and sex maniacs. I had to lock this door. I must say, Hugo Dinsmore, you certainly have some very strange friends. All right, all right, they're not your friends, you've already told me. Now, can we go? Please? I take it you do have transport.'

I assured her I had and just saying the words felt the first real stab of terror at what I had it in my head to do.

Making our way back down again we threaded our way past the canoodlers on the stairs, then the others, still entwined and oblivious to everything, including the two of us inching past. The music was far slower now, lethargic, even. Most of Laird's guests looked half-asleep on their feet by this stage, while, of course, he himself had long since beaten them to it upstairs.

With Roxy's hand in mine, I towed her across to the front door, then into the night air where she shivered and gave a sigh, which I took to be one of relief.

Then, 'What's that you've got there?' she said.

'A souvenir,' I told her, and seeing what it was she gave one of her hoarse, sexy laughs.

'Christ! Does he know?'

'Not a clue,' I assured her and on a sudden whim I pulled down the aerial on the Daimler letting it spring back with that artificial hairpiece hanging on its tip.

'Now you've gone and done it,' Roxy said as we stood admiring my handiwork by the light of the moon. One of those furry, Mod, Vespa trophies, it looked like, dangling there. An expensive, one-off, racoon tail. 'No going back now, eh? Is that the way you want it?'

And hearing her put it into words seemed somehow to make the whole thing so much more inevitable, simple, too, as if there could be no other outcome save the pair of us climbing into the Eggman's big car and driving away from the Grey House together like that. I know it may be hard to swallow, but I think I genuinely felt I was on some sort of rescue mission getting her out of that place away from people like the Gus character and the Eggman and his pals, but also delivering me from something as well. That, I wasn't quite sure of – what exactly it was, I mean – but I had this feeling it would only come to me slowly, drip by drip, at its own pace, until whatever it was eventually took on its own recognisable shape and form.

But while I was waiting for that to come about I would just drive. It all seemed so easy in that moment, being close together staring straight ahead at the pale road unreeling under us. She appeared content just sitting there, legs curled up, not talking, while I concentrated on controlling the Cadillac. My reactions, I realised, were not as finely tuned as I would have liked. The big, pink brute itself seemed much more sullen and unresponsive than usual. I caught myself leaning closer and closer to the glass, once or twice narrowly missing clipping the nearside hedge, but Roxy didn't seem to notice any of it. However, there did come a time when I knew I couldn't keep it from her any longer – not how badly I was driving – but, more damaging to the ego, that I, we, were lost. Of course I kept going, but eventually I heard her ask, 'Where are we? This doesn't look right. Does it?'

And I had to give in to that, for the road we were on was getting narrower, twisting, too, in a curious, almost arbitrary fashion, as if it was rarely used by anything on four wheels, especially ones shod with rubber of our own fat, white-walled, imported variety. I could hear the brambles scratching the paintwork, and the sump, too, was taking more and more punishment, scraping over bumps and ridges and God knows what else.

'We're bound to get off this soon,' I kept telling her, but we didn't, for suddenly we were in a farmyard, the house ahead of us dead and dark in our raking headlights.

'Fuck!' I called out, as dogs began barking and an upstairs window flared into life.

Roxy started laughing then and continued doing so as I wrestled with the wheel, backing over a wheelbarrow, it sounded like, someone had left conveniently lying there. 'Oh, Hugo, Hugo,' she kept crying, 'we sure are in the manure now all right,' a droll reference I imagine to the state of the yard, but I was in no mood to appreciate such humour right then. By the time I managed to get us out of that hayseed's property the shirt was sticking to my back and I was still shaking despite all my efforts to hide it.

'Oh, Hugo, Hugo,' I heard her say again, but in gentler, more affectionate tones now, 'if you could just see your face.'

'All very well,' I told her, 'but these old country fuckers keep a loaded shotgun under the bed.'

'And you should know, for you're a country boy yourself. You are, aren't you, Hugo?'

But then she said, 'I like you just the way you are,' and leaning across laid a hand on my thigh – sadly, not as high up as I would have liked – and I felt her lips on my cheek.

After that events took an upward turn. I suppose I'm easily pleased in that respect, but sooner than expected we did hit a main road and spotted a signpost pointing citywards. Ahead the orange glow in the sky deepened like a second artificial dawn and there was no need for further directions as I aimed the car at its hot heart. Suddenly I was feeling at ease as if I'd come through some mighty ordeal and this was that blessed release at the other end of it.

'Tell me something, why did you come away with us tonight like that? From Marino's, I mean.'

'Like all those other wee tarts, you mean?'

'No, no, no, I didn't say that,' I protested.

'But you meant it just the same.'

'What I meant was,' I persisted, trying to start afresh, 'what about that guy you were with?'

'What about him?'

'Well,' I said, 'somehow I got the impression he was your boyfriend.'

'Was. Past tense. I was about to dump him.' She laughed. 'Don't look so serious, you didn't even know him. And, anyway, I wouldn't have got to meet you, now, would I, wee Hugo First? You don't know an awful lot about women, do you?'

I felt like saying, *and don't care to, thank you very much,* but that would have been one great whopper of a lie.

We were rolling past the first sleeping terraces now and I had this sudden, tremendously sad feeling that something was slipping from my grasp for ever, some opportunity missed because of my raw inexperience the moment we left the dark intimacy of the countryside, which was my territory, after all, I told myself, my home ground, not hers.

'Maybe you could teach me,' I said, looking straight ahead, moments later sensing a hand come across to rest a second time that evening on my thigh. But I could tell by its butterfly touch it could never mean what I wanted it to mean.

'Another time, another place,' I heard her murmur, and then she lit a fresh fag and, reaching across, put it in my mouth as I drove.

And the moment she did so the strangest thing happened, for suddenly I saw her in a completely different light, and I don't mean the reflected glow from the dash, or the brief flash from the street lamps, either. Quite suddenly, with those words and that gesture, Roxy McKevitt was no longer this sexy, unattainable goddess in tight rayon and jersey silk, with her casque of candyfloss hair, but someone pretty much like myself, even if a few years older, still in thrall to the same movies and their corny old one-liners as I was.

Descending to the city we skirted a solitary milk-float humming silently along in the middle of the road, its driver hunched in his door-less cab. So sunk in his preoccupations he barely noticed our passing, the only being, as far as he was concerned, still abroad and awake in the whole wide world of corpse-like sleepers behind drawn curtains. The sight of him like that brought it home with a pang just how long the night had been with all its strange events and reversals, and now it was almost a new day again, pearl-grey and cold.

'Take the next turning to your left, would you,' directed Roxy in a quiet voice, yet I still gave a little jump, so deep in my own thoughts had I been, just like that driver, I supposed, we had sailed past in his Dobson's Dairies electric chariot back near the Forum cinema. 'Third street on the right is mine.'

The red brick row was like most of the others I'd trawled with Rocky once upon a time and, recalling what she'd said about knowing him, I reckoned the area was one I'd probably driven into before. I tried to catch a name, I don't know why, but it evaded me. Halfway along its length Roxy told me to pull over and I coasted to the kerb.

'Well, big guy,' she said, 'looks like the end of the line.' Another old movie chestnut, but I really didn't mind so much any more. Who needed originality at five-o'clock in the morning anyway?

I thought she might have got out straight away but she didn't, lighting a last cigarette instead.

'You're not going back there, are you? Won't you get in trouble?'

'Trouble? What's trouble?'

'Big man,' she said with a laugh. 'But what *are* you going to do?'

I didn't answer that one.

Then she said, 'I'd invite you in, but what would my da say if I brought back this wee Prod with me, even if he is a dote.'

And it was an odd feeling, sitting there like that, two strangers in a car in a strange street. Up ahead a cat came loping out of an entry mouth and stopped rigid, its eyes blazing, staring at us. Then it merged into the shadows again. A black cat.

'Anyone ever told you you look a bit like James Dean?'

No one ever had, as far as I could remember, but before the idea took too much of a hold on me I returned what I supposed was meant to be a compliment. 'And you like Angie Dickinson?'

Then she climbed out of the Eggman's car and I watched her walk away without a backward look.

I sat there until she got to one of the terraced houses. Then, turning in her stockinged feet, looking quite small all of a sudden, not so statuesque or unrefined, she waved, before sliding her key in the lock.

I never saw her again, not even in court when my case came up, which left me puzzled, for it did create quite a stir at the time. I've got the clippings to prove it.

FOURTEEN

I don't know exactly what I was expecting to find when I turned up at Larkhill that same morning early. Something a little more animate than usual, I suppose, but then why should it have changed just because of how I felt? Then, again, maybe it had while I was away, maybe some amazingly dramatic upheavals had affected the folk sleeping inside, unlike the actual old dump itself. Sitting there in the Cadillac on that familiar, cobbled yard, crazily I kept waiting for lights to come on, voices – real and radio – to ring out, nuttiest of all, youngsters to erupt into the open, though where I got that from I'll never know, all because I happened to be there bursting with a tale to tell, yet knowing full well it was something I could never divulge to any of them. I felt packed with it like a turkey at Christmas. *Up to here*, I kept telling myself, *up to here*, fingering an imaginary line where my collar lay.

How long I sat there I don't know, a half-hour, maybe, but then a light did come on in one of the lower windows and I rolled my own down trying to catch hold of a sound to go with it. I felt convinced I heard someone coughing, that first, robust clearing of the tubes of the day and then, even more certain, who it belonged to. But I have to say I had absolutely no idea how I would react when Junior came through that front door. Somewhere inside, I suppose, I must have had this notion that he might be the one to rescue me. I kept listening for the sound of his tread on the hall floor flags, Junior never being the one for a muted approach. Already the beginnings of a warm rush for him and his rough ways was growing inside. I remembered we had parted on terms closer than we had ever been.

I heard the latch rise and the door open and a wheel appeared, not of the expected delivery-bike, but bigger, fatter than that, and then Junior himself came into view pushing a motorcycle of all things. He had on a war-surplus airman's helmet with hanging flaps and the rest of him seemed to be clad in secondhand leather as well. It made him look like some kind of agricultural Hell's Angel. On seeing the car he stopped dead, standing rooted there holding the heavy two-wheeler by its rubber grips. I got out of the car and we faced one another as though across some mighty, unbridgeable divide, two strangers in a setting where one of us no longer belonged, even though, at the time, driving back from the city in the grey dawn it had seemed like the only place to be, the only place left for me. But the look on his face told me, no.

'Everybody says you're Lyle Ritchie's bum-boy,' he said without preamble, pulling the bike back on its short stumps of legs. A Triumph, I noticed. Looking new, too.

'Not any more,' I told him, as he came towards me in his creaking, leather armour like a ship at sea, quite ridiculous looking, really.

'That's his motor, isn't it?'

'Not any more.' Same reply as before, like a refrain I had to keep repeating, like someone in a movie might say 'No comment,' or 'I take the Fifth Amendment.'

'You mean he gave it to you?'

I stared at him, feeling confused. What exactly had I meant that second time, anyway?

'Looks like she's had the arse tore out of her,' he said, walking around the Eldorado and peering closely at it in the dull morning light. 'Tail-light totally fucked, far headlight ditto, back bumper hanging off, scratched to buggery all down one side, big rip in the hood. Just where the hell has it been? Some sort of demolition derby?'

For the first time it struck home just how far gone I must have been driving back from the Grey House over those country roads like that. Like in a tank instead of someone's car, the Eggman's car, the Eggman's big, formally beautiful, pink, film star's, American car. I suppose I should have been shit-scared at the sudden realisation, the recognition of all that damage, but I wasn't. Junior's opinion seemed infinitely more important, even though he seemed as unimpressed with me as he'd ever been.

'Tell you one thing, sonny Jim, it's not staying here. No way.'

Which, oddly enough, had not occurred to me, simply to run it into one of the big outhouses and just leave it there to gather potato dust alongside the piles of King Edwards in the dark. But what about *me*? Where would *I* find sanctuary? Some cave or cellar, perhaps? Or how about a coffin, like young Master Dracula. And for no other reason than that, I suppose, into my head popped a memory of that wooden drawer I used to bed down in when first I came to Larkhill all those years ago. I could feel it, I could smell it in that moment, and other recollections came flooding back as well.

'Remember the marks we used to make on the scullery wall? The lines? Still there, are they?'

He stood back and looked at me as if I'd gone mental, which, in a way, I imagine I had, at least in his view of the world anyway. 'What marks? What fucking lines?'

'Never mind,' I said, 'never mind, forget it. So, how have

329

things been with you anyway, then? Still at McCabe's?' I knew I was starting to gabble but didn't seem to be able to do a lot about it. 'You were going to get hitched last time I saw you, I remember.'

'Married?' he said. 'Who to?'

But before I heard myself reply, *that old huer from Castle Street, that's who,* mercifully I dried up and we continued staring at each other in silence across that stretch of sweating cobbles like two strangers who had just happened to bump into one another in some yard in the middle of County Antrim somewhere.

'Don't be here when I get back. Leave us out of it,' he said. 'Clean up your own mess. Is that clear?'

But of course it wasn't, how could it be, and I had this terrible urge to detain him, just long enough for him to hear my side of things, for surely there had to be something left of what we shared once upon a time, a memory, some common fragment of experience, good or bad, didn't matter which.

'Look, I'll drive you to work,' I said, ignoring the gleaming new Triumph roadster sitting propped there on its stand like that, a pair of Rockfist Rogan goggles draped about its big, domed headlamp.

'Don't talk shite,' he said. 'Nobody needs you and your flashy car. Some of us have a hard day's work to go to. We can't all be spivs and gangsters. You've let us down, that's what you've done.'

In another and very different world I might have considered that a bit rich coming from someone like Junior Dinsmore, but my desperation overruled any such thought.

'How about some dough, then?' I pleaded. 'Something to pay you all back for taking me in the way you did. I always wanted to help out if I could, honest, but I couldn't. You know that.' And it was true. But hearing it come out that way made it sound phoney as hell.

'Look, let me show you,' I persevered, hauling open the

330

car door, then the glove compartment on the inside. He watched as I came out with this big bunch of notes in my hand, fivers, even tenners, and for an instant his eyes sharpened.

'Take it,' I told him, waving it about like so much worthless scrap paper, which to me it was right then. 'Buy whatever you like. Go on, take it, take it. I don't want it. I don't need it.' And then I said, 'No one'll ever know, honest,' and it was that final cry of desperation that made him back away from me as if I carried something infectious. It was in his face, in his eyes, and I watched as he walked back to the motorbike and pulled it off its stand. He began wheeling it away as I stood there alongside the Eggman's big car with the money still balled in my fist – his, the Eggman's too – despite my lavish display of extravagance a minute earlier.

When he reached the ruined pillars he kick-started the machine into life and with a shock the realisation hit me he was being considerate of the sleepers back in the house, something of a turn about for my rowdy relative. He drove off then, hesitatingly, I noted, which made me also think he must still be in the newfangled phase with his new toy. So there I was left with all that loot in my hand. Staring down at it I kept thinking of what Junior had said about it, about me, as well, and then I took a last look at Larkhill itself, at this hour, dead as the House of Usher and twice as depressing. There was no point in hanging around. I had outstayed my welcome, to use a corny phrase, and perhaps it had been that way for a long time.

Climbing back in the Caddy again like some weary wanderer destined to keep on travelling for ever, I reversed and bumped out of the yard the way I'd come, knowing I would never be back this way ever again. End of story. Rather – close of last chapter but one in this little tale of mine. In a kind of doped daze I idled out on to the road, simply letting the car take me wherever it cared to end up, now that, once more, I was adrift with no destination in mind. In the far distance I could see Junior *putt-putting* along like some canny, old pensioner, so I picked up pace until I was about fifty yards on his tail and following. He neither altered speed nor turned his head once and we stayed like that, him in front like some stiff-backed outrider to my royal progress, all the way as far as the Five Road Ends where he took the left fork towards the town, while I brought the Cadillac to a stop right there in the middle of that scoured turning-circle where all routes converged before making off towards their various, mysterious destinations. Maybe this was to be where my tether came to an end after all, right here at the heart of this lonely spot, leaving the car abandoned like some great, big, pink, foreign object for people to skirt around and marvel at as if it had simply run out of juice just like its driver.

Now, as I sat there toying with this notion, off to my left I detected an early morning plume of smoke ascending from a chimney and for the first time that morning the geography of the area, which once upon a time had been in my head so precise, so sharp, revealed itself all over again in fine detail like the coloured markings on a schoolroom map. If I closed my eyes, which I did, crazily enough, I could trace the outline and boundary of every field and hedge, bush and tree, every hill, valley and stream, wall and dwelling, as far as imagination could carry me before that interior map started to blur then fray at the edges.

The smoke came from a particular house – well, hardly a house, more like *half* of one – encircled by a collar of beech. I remembered it lay off one of the roads facing me where I now sat waiting as if a plug had been pulled out, for something seemed to be draining away. I felt it. But before the tank drained completely, in that house of the rising smoke, it came to me, lived someone I needed to confront one last time. Oddly enough, on my rambles, I had never got closer than the mouth of the lane itself. So it was a first – last, too, I suppose – the moment I turned the car in off the road and drove it up the track with those thorny hedges closing in on either side of me the deeper I went. More like a green, growing tunnel than a byway for human use, it carried winding on and on until finally coming to a full stop out in a patch of rough, broken ground, all mossy humps and grassy hollows, where once there must have been other buildings connected with the main ruin itself. Its broken windows were stuffed with rags, the door hung crookedly on one hinge, and the air of neglect and decrepitude was even more excessive than I had always imagined it to be. Like something out of a horror picture, and seeing it now in reality, in daylight, I half expected Lon Chaney's face to appear at one of the upper windows not already plugged with scraps of ancient cast-offs.

Inside was someone who had also stalked my young dreams once upon a time, someone I wanted to share just a little of that himself, so I sat outside his house and kept my thumb on the car horn, on and on, just to make sure he knew I knew he was in there and afraid to come out to face his wee Hugo one last time. The word would soon get out that the Eggman's car had been last seen at Sinbad Scully's place and that would be revenge enough when questions started getting asked, as I knew they would.

For a good couple of minutes I kept the barrage going before turning the car around, then driving back the way I'd come, dogs barking everywhere by now, the entire country-side quivering, as I imagined it, with the reverberations. Sort of a farewell, symphonic signature, you might say, hanging in the air. Hugo Dinsmore Was Here spelled out on an American klaxon long after he'd gone. Inside my upholstered tank I felt armour-plated and kept swerving from side to side, hitting hedges and bumps. I turned the radio on to some early morning, foreign station, singing along in Dutch, or it could have been German, with what I took to be a surprising aptitude for a language I didn't know but could still learn. Why not? Nothing was impossible.

It was exactly eight-thirty by the clock on the dashboard and the world was taking on a different complexion. I no longer had it all to myself, smoke from other breakfast fires was spiralling up now as well. As I drove my thoughts slowed to the revolution of the wheels as the Eldorado rumbled over the country roads, unstoppable, with a will of its own. Starting to think about it in that way, it struck me how big a part it had played in my life up to now, controlling, dominating, this great, rolling beast, with me sitting perched inside on an old, leaking, leather cushion like a baby in a high-chair. Or a precocious midget. The cruel image, the very *word*, hit hard, for the thing about my height, which at one time had been like a raw wound, had somehow dwindled to something barely significant, a trifle, like thinning hair or jug ears. Now it returned in all its old ferocity and in that moment I saw myself, me and the car both, as cruelly lit as in a bad photograph.

All along I suppose I did have some sort of hazy escape plan in mind, but for the very first time now it came to me I had to rid myself of the car if I was serious about making the break with the man who owned it, and me, too, up until a few hours ago. Yet something extra was needed, something more final than simply abandoning it on a road somewhere with me climbing out and just walking away, something memorable, an image people would remember and maybe talk about whenever my name happened to come up. I have to say I became quite excited thinking of it in that way, and when inspiration finally did arrive I pressed my foot on the accelerator and the car fairly flew towards its fate. My own would have to wait just that little bit longer.

334

Not far from Larkhill, for I was coming full circle back to old haunts, I slowed down, looking out for a part of the map still in my head. I told myself I would know it when I saw it, but landscapes change, just as people do, and I had this sudden dread the place might no longer be as I remembered it, altered in some brutal manner, hedges rooted up, a road built, for there was a mania just then for the laying down of fresh tarmac. Maybe someone had built a new house, a barn, an obliterating wall to frustrate my intentions. But then the moment I saw the old pylon again I felt relieved, for how could something like that be made to do a vanishing act, all that bolted angle iron and leagues of cable looping off to blue infinity? Crawling now, I peered out, searching for my old way in through the fields. Just about here there should be a gate, but there wasn't, and beyond that, where was that field dotted with whins where rabbits scampered, and now kale and cabbages grew in neat drills?

I stopped the car and lit a cigarette. The pylon looked smaller, diminished, and I wondered if it would keep on shrinking with the years in a sort of inverse equation the longer I stayed away, ending up like one of those souvenirs I had seen of the Eiffel Tower. But there it still stood, almost but not quite as I remembered it, straddling its patch of rough grass in the shadow of all that humming, metal Meccano, and which once I'd claimed for my own private domain, hardly bigger than someone's kitchen floor. I had it in mind to climb it one last time, you see, taking a final, farewell look over the place and places I used to know. Sentimentality didn't enter into it, for I felt glad to be seeing the back of it. So I finished the cigarette and threw the butt out of the window and after that events seemed to take over as if they couldn't have happened any other way.

At least that's how I described it later to those three paper-pushers facing me across a table at the remand place, two men and a female, which, as I've discovered, is invariably the

335

ratio on such occasions, the softer, more intuitive, female presence considered an essential, although Karen Bunting, as she was known, turned out to be a right bitch, scribbling down everything I said as though building up a case for a speedy conviction. *Why, why, but, why?* On at me like a mechanical talking doll, with that tight, woolly, blonde perm of hers and blue button eyes behind rimless specs. Oh, and I forgot – English, as well. And her two male colleagues seemed in awe of her because of it and the accent. They, at least, didn't need to be told the reason for me wanting to make the actual ascent. It may well have been the sort of thing they might have got up to themselves at some point in their younger, wilder lives – if there'd ever been such a thing. But, then, again, I suppose not.

However, the part about driving straight through a hedge, then across a cultivated field leaving a trail of damaged crops behind did appear to stump them, I have to say. To tell the truth, I didn't much feel like confessing I just couldn't be bothered getting out of the car by that stage, so put the boot down. With great satisfaction I remember watching the wave of harm spilling out like a torn, green tide in my wake. As for what I did to the car, everyone else but me seemed outraged by the mere thought of it, even three people sitting in a room who had never ever set eyes on the brute, not even after I was done with it. It was a moment of gratification to me in all that followed, knowing I had been right about it all along, what it meant, standing, as it did, for everything I needed to escape from that morning I drove it up hard against the base of one of our own electricity pylons, which in court I even discovered had an actual name. Zero Four O Two, according to the evidence, East Antrim Division. That, too, became a good moment, making me feel a little like Sir Edmund Hillary with my very own mini-Everest, even though I never got round to tying a flag, let alone a hanky, to its peak to mark my achievement.

Far above the sprawled countryside, I felt the breeze tighten my cheeks as I clung to all that rough cast-iron, feeling shocked, I have to say, at just how much rust there seemed to be at this altitude where no one but me could see or point it out. The gleaming, porcelain insulators hummed and sang as I kept turning my head, until I persuaded myself I could make out the sea away off to the east where dawn had broken earlier. For as long as I could bear it I hung on, gulping everything in, every field and copse, hill and hollow, every blob of water gleaming like mercury in the sunlight and then, looking down, I saw the car squatting below, no bigger than a Dinky toy, and it came to me simply to leave it there like that would be unfinished business, for I knew I would keep on picturing it in my head long after I had walked away from it for good. Something extra was needed, something with a drum-roll attached, something to make people ponder, *why, why, oh, why*, like Karen Bunting, some image to burn, then smoulder, long after Hugo Dinsmore had moved on.

Writing all this down I have to blush a little, trying to justify, even explain something irrational, vindictive, too, I suppose, to an awful lot of people, that happened away there all that time ago out in the wilds like that. Yet I've had plenty of practice since I've been here. The world I now find myself in seems full of Karen Buntings all anxious to know why, before finally turning the key on me. Personally I feel the question is irrelevant, but as long as it makes them happy, then I'll gladly go on providing them with what they want to hear, although I get the impression they think they know more than enough about me already.

But when it came to my day in court – more a morning, really – all that stuff about being orphaned at an early age, never really having a proper, settled, home background, or strong adult influence – *I swear to you, Junior, I never told them any of that, those paper-pushers* – none of it counted for a hill of

337

beans but the bare facts of the case on the charge sheet in front of His Honour Judge Justice Alexander Dunwoody.

But getting back to *my* version. When I reached the ground again, arms and legs trembling, I stood studying the Cadillac one last time – *goodbye, old Caddy, goodbye, Eggman* – before unscrewing the petrol cap. Pulling off my tie, I fed one square end into the open pipe, having nothing better I could think of to take its place. When it had soaked sufficiently – although there was no real, no proper, way of telling that – I drew it back out again, so that I had a freshly dampened wick of sorts trailing from the tank. It happened to be a favourite, navy, knitted number, but any regrets on the vanity front had long since departed. Not even the sudden feel and terrifying stink of Esso on my hands had the power to distract me.

For a time I looked at that limp, dripping tail, for I did wonder just how fast I would have to move once it started its work. The only occasion I'd ever seen anything like what I had in mind had been on a cinema screen after some getaway sequence. Feeling in my pockets for a match without success, I went instead to the cigar-lighter plugged in the dashboard, and leaning into the front of the car pushed it in, that bright little lipstick case, then waited for its tip to turn a glowing red. As I've said, I'd gone over every detail, or so I thought, on the climb down, so I did have a twist of paper ready to carry to the rear of the Cadillac, and so I lit it – it was a page from the tick man's notebook – holding it to that dark, dripping fuse which not so long before had been around my neck.

Momentarily a pretty, blue flame flowered, then raced up its length, a lot faster than I'd bargained for, and I flung myself into the rank grass, scrambling further and further back. From what I took to be a safe distance I watched and waited, but nothing seemed to be happening save a trickle of pale smoke pouring from the open mouth of the tank. So much for all those Hollywood spectaculars, I thought to myself, then a second later there came this *whoosh* like a giant softly breaking wind and the trunk and rear end of the Eldorado erupted in one roaring mass of orange and magenta. I could feel the heat on my face as the fire licked the bodywork, the canvas hood the first to go in a shower of sparks. There was an acrid smell which stung the nostrils and I kept moving back, back from the heat, all the while expecting further explosions to break out, but for some reason they never came, the fire raging in an almost controlled way until its ferocity faltered, then began to subside, like the car itself, as the tyres caught and burned down to the rims.

I stood there for I don't know how long and it would be a lie to say enjoying the sight, for after the initial explosion I felt a bit let down, to tell the truth, drained, I suppose, being the correct word. Eventually when there was nothing left but this smoking shell, a skeleton of metal and wire surrounded by an almost perfect, scorched circle in the grass, it was time to go. Just where had not been part of the plan, so I walked the way I'd come, following the wheel tracks through the cabbages, and when I reached the road, at the spin of an imaginary coin, chose tails, turning left towards the town for nothing better to do.

FIFTEEN

Now I'd dearly love to say my case was in all the papers, but then why should it be, except, of course, for the name of the man whose property I was accused of ravaging. Not much remains of my little moment of printed fame, save a paragraph or two in the local *Observer* alongside those other gleanings from the Assizes of assault, drunk behaviour in a public place, animal cruelty and minor motoring offences. Mine, of course, was very major indeed, according to the stipendiary magistrate, trailing a catalogue of subsidiary crimes which came as a great surprise. When first I heard his name read out it meant nothing to me, but when I saw him sitting up there behind that high, polished, mahogany pulpit, bifocals perched on that radish of a nose, I received the first shock of several that day. We looked at one another, but if there was the slightest hint of recognition in those bloodshot eyes then I certainly didn't see it.

Throughout the hearing I kept staring at him from my box, for, yes, they had given me the full treatment, bible, oath, wigs, robes, the whole judicial shebang. Sitting there, I felt conscious only my head and shoulders must be visible above the rail of my panelled crib and kept wondering what those present might think seeing me like a half-in, or was it half-out jack-in-the-box, no one having thought fit to provide a cushion. As well as that the clothes I was wearing were the ones I'd been arrested in, no tie, of course, so when people started getting up and making statements about me without shame or restraint of any kind as if they'd known me intimately, I was still too preoccupied with what sort of image I projected to react or take in what they were saying properly.

But as I've since discovered from some of my newfound comrades inside it invariably comes as something of a shock to hear what others say in evidence against you. First reactions being – who are these characters? Then, why are they telling these lies? Followed by, who paid them? So I sat there listening to it all but, as I've said, only half paying attention while everyone else in the courtroom appeared to be taking it far more professionally. Then again, others have told me the exact opposite, that they themselves were the only ones giving their case the attention it deserved, while all those pen-pushers rustling their briefs in the cockpit below were only thinking of their fees, their dinners, or that next round of golf with their dentist, or the man selling them a new Rover.

Never had I felt so alone, standing on my own two feet, literally, so, for early on I was told to rise and remain like that, humiliatingly, while witnesses were called on to testify as to what an irredeemably evil character I was. No one appeared for me. No Roxy, no Rocky, not even the Hoy sisters. I kept racking my brains trying to think of other names of those who might put in a good word for the poor defendant. Of course I may have got it all wrong, but just why was there no one there defending *him*? Perhaps the idea was, what he'd done was so indefensible anyway, why bother?

Standing to attention, gripping the rim of my half sentry-box, I searched the faces I could see. The most important, the most critical, in every sense of that word, I should have thought, turned out not to be present, not even in the gallery where a couple of old biddies in hats huddled together staring down at me as if I was a mass murderer. By the end of the trial, and with the weight of so-called evidence brought to bear against me, I might as well have been. The one person everyone kept referring to throughout as though he were the greatest philanthropist and all-round saint since Albert Schweitzer and Andrew Carnegie, hadn't made an appearance. But, then, shouldn't I have known he wouldn't turn up? Why break the habit of a lifetime of getting cronies to lie on your behalf and do your shady work for you.

Part of me felt relieved at not having those cold blue eyes browse over me, but then another part rebelled as the travesty continued to unfold, making me feel cheated at not having him there to hear in fine detail just exactly how I was supposed to have paid him back. Instead I listened as Jack Laird, in pale, Irish linen, the same creamy shade as his Daimler – which, as he stressed, could so easily have ended up the same way as the plaintiff's own 1957 pride and joy – painted a portrait of me in shades of unrelieved black. He told the court I was a person who bore a grudge, then went on to describe me as someone who seemed to bitterly resent what others, particularly those like himself and Lyle Ritchie, had worked so hard for. I had this envious, covetous disposition and destructive streak, so he said, which his good friend and business associate had tried to ignore, hoping the example and comforts of a decent and loving home life might soften in time and eventually eradicate. All this from someone I had met only the once.

But things became even more surreal when a couple, a man and his wife, supposedly, neither of whom had I seen in my entire life, took the stand to swear separately they'd

342

overheard me tell some girl at a party at the previous witness's house that 'the greatest thrill in life for me would be to watch as many big joints as this one go up in smoke' as there happened to be matches in the box I had in my pocket at the time. So, not only was I accused of being some kind of pocket arsonist, but one with anarchist, commie leanings into the bargain.

I stared back at them. Perhaps the woman was vaguely familiar, although she certainly wasn't one of the ballroom babes from Marino's. Curiously enough that cheered me up, I don't know why, and in my head I began indulging this scenario in which all of those brunette princesses kept telling the Eggman no, no, a thousand times no, they never would lie or blacken someone's character, not even if he paid them, not even if Jack Laird himself hand-picked them personally for next year's finals of the Northern Counties Ballroom championships. I was happily adding further embellishments – Roxy herself had now joined the fan club, Rocky, as well – and just as Junior's honest face was about to make an appearance, Judge Alexander Dunwoody rapped the table in front of him with his little Masonic pinky ring to bring the proceedings to a conclusion.

'An open and shut case, I think you have to agree,' began his summing up, 'with barely a solitary redeeming or mitigating shred of contradictory evidence to soften the verdict. But, just to recap, here are the salient facts of the case, and pretty grim and sordid hearing they make, too. Some time at the beginning of the month of November of this year the defendant Hugo Dinsmore did embark on a premeditated and carefully planned campaign of reprisal against the plaintiff and his property. I say reprisal, but for what? For what motive? As you've heard from several impeccable sources, not only was he taken in, fed, clothed and groomed by Mr Ritchie for future advancement in his own business, but he was also treated like one of his very own family, which as you also must know happens to be one of the most respected and well thought of in our farming community, and, may I say, so very different from the deprived background the defendant came from originally.

'But we are not here today to tease out the whys and wherefores of this young man's motives. That must be left to others more qualified in a psychiatric capacity, although I want to stress here and now, and most emphatically at that, throughout his campaign of wanton destruction the person you see before you was at all times responsible and in complete control of his actions. For, surely, they must speak for themselves, in all their calculated, malicious intent, namely that on the night of the ninth of November last he did take the plaintiff's valuable, imported, American automobile and drove it in a reckless and deliberately vindictive fashion, finally setting it alight in an attempt to conceal his crime.

'Luckily the police were able to identify it from its charred New Hampshire number plates, practically all that remained of a once priceless and cherished possession. Its owner, Mr Lyle Ritchie, has been excused by the court from appearing here today, being still far too upset by the loss of his much-loved motor car. But if I may be allowed to speak personally and briefly on his behalf, while the fate of his beautiful, early model Cadillac Eldorado weighs heavily on him, the treachery of someone he once treated like a blood-relation is just as painful for him to bear. Not only was his trust and property destroyed, but a substantial amount of money belonging to him, too, was stolen at the same time, and still not recovered. Despite his plea for clemency, in the light of the extreme seriousness of the offences and the obvious lack of remorse on the part of the defendant, I have no recourse but to impose the maximum sentence laid down in the statute book.'

*

I listened to all of this with a sort of almost dreamy detachment as if hearing an account of someone else's criminal history, not my own, this cross between Baby Face Nelson and the young John Dillinger, and not the Hugo Dinsmore who had torched a car. On a similarly baffling note, could this character across from me in curly wig and robes really be the same old piss-pot whose party piece was pulling on that same clump of yellowing fleece at his weekend get-togethers, then parading around ballock naked save for an enormous pair of Bugs Bunny boxer shorts? I felt confused, to say the least. Not even the sentence of five years had the power to shake me out of my daze. It was only much later when I was staring at a bare, peeling wall liberally etched with initials like some scabrous visitors' book, with higher up a barred window the size of something in a scullery or an outside toilet, that I started to shake myself out of it and began asking myself all those questions I supposed I should have asked before. Like – why me, basically? And why employ such an awesome, legal sledgehammer to crush a peanut like Wee Hugo Dinsmore? Just what had I done to the Eggman? Was it simply the car and the money? Or could it be something else?

But regarding the dough, let me set the record straight. Maybe at the time I did nurse some vague idea of plundering the glove compartment and skeltering South – or even East, like J.J., across the water – and for a little while, maybe, I did even indulge the fantasy that people might just swallow the theory that I'd burned up with the Cadillac as well, leaving only a pile of unrecognisable bone and ash, with the exception of the remains of a collar-stud. What really happened was I remembered too late about the cash being still in there and not in my inside pocket when I set light to the tie. But try telling that to a jury. Who would believe the stupidity of it? Much wiser to stick to the baby-faced arsonist line, for already, you see, I'm rewriting my own headlines, the ones I'd been cheated out of, particularly in a place like this where everyone embellishes their c.v. anyway.

It may seem an odd thing to say, but in a curious way I feel lucky to have ended up here. I do. After the first month, which as everyone will tell you is make or break time, I seem to have settled in a lot better than I could ever have expected. Maybe I'm being an optimist here, but if I'd been just a year younger I might have fallen into Gus Gilmore's tender clutches in Glenrowan along with those other doomed delinquents. The law saved me from that fate, even though on every other count it rubber-stamped me as expertly as if I'd been a blank sheet of paper.

A friend on the same wing – for I've made quite a few of those since I've been here, including a couple of murderers, mild-mannered as curates, the pair of them – always sings the same little ditty before the lights snap off. It's his signature tune, you might say, what distinguishes him from everyone else, which is something we all give a lot of thought to here. '*When the roll is called up yonder, I doubt if I'll be there,*' he croons softly, over and over and over, sending us off to sleep and ushering in our disturbed dreams. And he's probably right. None of us, I imagine, will be eligible when it comes to that particular sort of salvation. Still, I do have my own plans for when I get out – who knows, earlier than expected by all accounts, because of something called 'good behaviour' – so there'll be a lot of things to enjoy before the celestial Big Bang arrives.

Rejoice, Hugo, I tell myself, rejoice, for your apprenticeship is over. Now it's time for the next and much more worthwhile part of your career to get under way.